# WHEN STONE WINGS FLY

A Smoky Mountains Novel

Karen Barnett

KREGEL PUBLICATIONS

*When Stone Wings Fly: A Smoky Mountains Novel*


Published by Kregel Publications, a division of Kregel Inc., 2450 Oak Industrial Dr. NE, Grand Rapids, MI 49505. www.kregel.com.



**Library of Congress Cataloging-in-Publication Data**
Names: Barnett, Karen, 1969- author.
Title: When stone wings fly : a Smoky Mountains novel / Karen Barnett.
Description: Grand Rapids, MI : Kregel Publications, [2022] | Series: A Smoky Mountains novel
Identifiers: LCCN 2021063004 (print) | LCCN 2021063005 (ebook) | ISBN 9780825447174 (paperback) | ISBN 9780825477645 (epub) | ISBN 9780825469176 (kindle edition)
Classification: LCC PS3602.A77584 W45 2022 (print) | LCC PS3602.A77584 (ebook) | DDC 813/.6--dc23
LC record available at https://lccn.loc.gov/2021063004
LC ebook record available at https://lccn.loc.gov/2021063005

ISBN 978-0-8254-4717-4, print
ISBN 978-0-8254-7764-5, epub
ISBN 978-0-8254-6917-6, Kindle

Printed in the United States of America
22 23 24 25 26 27 28 29 30 31 / 5 4 3 2

"The quest of the endearing characters in this poignant family drama captivated me from the first page. I loved stepping into the history and beauty of the Great Smoky Mountains and Karen Barnett's expert weaving together of the past and present threads. Pure joy to read!"

—Melanie Dobson, award-winning author of *The Winter Rose* and *Catching the Wind*

"Barnett's tale set in the Great Smoky Mountains flows as smooth as wildwood honey. The two timelines are stitched together like alternating blocks of a quilt passed down through the decades, keeping family connected and rooted. I love a good Appalachian tale and Barnett's hits all the right notes from the familiar dialect to the natural beauty of the mountains. I felt utterly at home."

—Sarah Loudin Thomas, award-winning author of *The Right Kind of Fool*

"Once again, Karen Barnett paints America's historical landscape with deft skill and steady hand. Her deep-seated love for the Smoky Mountains etches each page like a poem. Pitch-perfect research and incomparable heart paint every corner of the brilliantly colored canvas of *When Stone Wings Fly*. Readers, get ready: your newest split-time fiction experience rests in the hands of a master."

—Rachel McMillan, author of *The Mozart Code*

"I loved getting to know Karen Barnett's characters in *When Stone Wings Fly*. I was right there with them, flipping through the pages as fast as I could to see what happened next. Compelling writing, gripping action, and fascinating Great Smoky Mountains National Park history make for a heartfelt story you won't want to miss."

—Ann H. Gabhart, best-selling author of *Along a Storied Trail*

"As a former park ranger, Karen Barnett knows the landscape of mountains, rivers, forests, and trails—and the inner workings of the National Park Service, both historical and present-day. Both leap to life in the pages of this time-slip novel set in the Great Smoky Mountains National Park where, faced with irrevocable change, one woman struggles to preserve what's left of her family and her mountain home, while another seeks to piece together a mysterious family history shattered long ago. Forging our dreams while holding them in open hands is a dichotomy poignantly explored by the engaging characters in this heart-tugging and surprisingly suspenseful tale."

—Lori Benton, Christy Award–winning author of *Burning Sky* and other historical novels

"*When Stone Wings Fly* brings to light a little known time period in history when the glory of National Parks usurped on the ownership of private lands. But more than that, this is a heartrending story of belonging, a place to call home, and what family truly is in spite of grievous errors and the turbulence of life. I was entranced in this tale of the Smoky Mountains, devouring it to the last page, and pondering its message long after the book was closed. As a dual-time author and reader, I can truly say that Karen Barnett has provided a story equally captivating in both time periods, and the ties of ancestry continue to show how intricately woven the past is to our present. This will be a cherished story on my bookshelves for years to come."

—Jaime Jo Wright, author of *The Souls of Lost Lake* and Christy Award–winning novel *The House on Foster Hill*

# WHEN STONE WINGS FLY

To the people of the Great Smoky Mountains–
all who went before
and all those yet to come.

# PROLOGUE

Great Smoky Mountains National Park
March 1942

THESE MOUNTAINS HID countless secrets—what was one more?

Benton rolled the tiny stone bird between his dirt-stained fingers, studying it in the last vestiges of sunlight coming over the ridgeline. *Her ridge.* Benton would never have claim to the mountain, no matter how many years he'd toiled making a life for himself here. He glanced up at the river rocks forming the cabin's tall chimney. He'd mended it just two months ago. How long until the forest reclaimed that as well?

He slipped the small figurine into his shirt pocket as the screech of an owl cut through the evening stillness. Jamming the shovel into the hard-packed dirt, he ripped a chunk of the earth free. Disturbance was the lifeblood of the forest. Even though Rosie's family had walked this land for generations, in truth the woods were constantly reinventing themselves. Dying and coming alive with every breath, every leaf, every new sunrise.

But if he worked at it hard enough, one thing might stay.

Sweat trickled down his back as he deepened the hole, opening a scar in the black soil. Tossing the shovel aside, he nestled the stone into the ground like a babe in its bassinet. No matter what happened to the cabin—to the land—this little piece of Rosie's heart would stay.

Turning away, he gazed around the small clearing. His daughter stood by the coop, using a twig to tap a playful rhythm on the metal wire. He wiped his dirty palms on his trousers before reaching for her hand. "Come on, McCauley. It's time to go."

She stared at him, her big brown eyes so much like Rosie's that his throat nearly closed. "Where are we going, Pa?"

He clasped her fingers in his, unable to answer. Thankfully, she fell into step beside him without asking a second time. Maybe someday he could find the words to explain to his daughter how the gunshot that had stolen her mother's life had taken their home as well.

Or maybe he never would.

# 1

Nashville, Tennessee
Present Day

FOUR YEARS OF college and she was back to juggling plates? This was not how she pictured her life at twenty-seven. Kieran swung a purse over her shoulder and made for the diner's rear door. "Can you use me on the breakfast shift, Ash? I need some hours."

Her friend, the owner and manager, hefted a stack of plates into a bin. "You practically live over at SeniorCo. Don't they pay you for all your work there?"

*When the funding allows.* "They'll sort it out, but for now—"

"Of course. We can give you a few hours tomorrow, but I've got some new girls coming in for the lunch rush."

Her husband, Nick, lifted a basket of shrimp from the fryer and gave it a quick shake. "Heading out already? Got a hot date or something?"

"You bet. With a handsome hero. Navy SEAL." Kieran edged past the prep tables, careful not to bump the salad fixings on her way out.

"Haven't you finished reading that military novel yet?" Ash wrinkled her nose. "You know I'm next in line. I've been done with book one for a week. How long are you going to make me wait?"

Nick grinned as he scooped the fried shrimp onto a serving platter. "I should have guessed. You don't strike me as the type to hang out with sailors. Now, army? Those are the heroes."

"We all know *you* are, at least." Kieran patted his arm as she passed.

Nick had done two tours in Afghanistan, and Ashleigh had been relieved when he'd finally left active duty. Opening the Gray Gull had been the culmination of a lifelong dream. All seafood, all the time. It didn't matter that the closest beach was a seven-hour drive from Nashville.

Ash clucked her tongue. "SEAL, Green Beret—does it matter? As long as he's got muscles and a sweet smile." She winked at her husband.

Kieran hid a laugh as she waved to her friends and ducked out into the fresh night air, away from the lingering odor of fish and fries. As long as said hero was safely ensconced in the pages of a novel, she was happy. That was how she liked her men—imaginary. Those were the fellows you could trust.

Parking her ancient Volvo outside of Sycamore Terrace Senior Living, Kieran took a moment to gather herself. Would Gran be awake this late? She checked her phone to find five messages from desperate families who'd searched SeniorCo's website for information on emergency housing, finances, and Medicaid. She'd be up late tonight reading through their questions and helping to find placements for their loved ones. If only there were enough affordable options for everyone. The problem tugged at her heart. No one's mother, father, or grandparent deserved to be on the street. A community that didn't care for the most fragile among them had no right to be called a community.

But first, her own gran needed her.

Kieran retrieved her knitting bag off of a heaping laundry basket in her back seat and tucked it under her arm. The half-finished sweater was a disaster, as always, but Granny Mac would save it.

She locked the car and hurried inside the squat brick building, barely pausing to wave at the night nurse and scoop up a visitor's badge from the front desk.

Gran dozed in her chair, the throw blanket on her lap a swirl of orange, purple, pink, and blue, like the darkening sky outside the window of her small apartment.

Kieran studied the tiny woman, so peaceful in sleep, such a

powerhouse when awake. Kieran brushed her arm. "Gran? Can I help you get into bed?"

Granny Mac's eyes fluttered. "What? No. I wasn't sleeping." Her fingers clutched the throw. "I was knitting. See? Almost done." Her brows pulled tight as she rumpled the afghan. "I must have dropped my needles. Where did they get to? I don't want to lose any stitches."

She'd probably owned the blanket for decades, but Kieran knew better than to point it out. "Don't worry, Gran. We'll find them." Pulling a stool close, Kieran sat next to her and patted her hand. "I'm happy to see you."

Gran's brown eyes clouded. "I'm sorry, dear, but I don't . . ."

"It's Kieran. Michael's daughter." Saying her father's name always left a bad taste in her mouth. He was nothing but the flimsy thread linking her to this wonderful woman, and his choices had left Kieran as lost as a dropped stitch.

"Mike's—" Her lip quivered. "Of course you are. You look so much like my mother. Have I told you about her?"

"Some." Kieran reached for the half-full coffee cup sitting on the end table. "Would you like me to pop this in the microwave?"

Gran frowned, her pinched face reminding Kieran of a cotton shirt that had been crumpled at the bottom of a drawer for too long. "No, ghastly stuff. There's some blackberry tea on the counter. I love that blend. It tastes like the mountains—"

"—especially if you add honey." Kieran finished the words as she headed for the tiny kitchen. They'd need to move Gran to the memory-care wing soon. She really shouldn't have access to a stove.

"How's work, sweetie?" Gran leaned back in the chair. "What is it you do again?"

Kieran smiled. "Oh, a little of this, a little of that." She'd tried explaining her life to her grandmother before, but it never stuck.

"So long as it keeps a roof over your head." Gran dug into the seat cushion beside her, apparently still looking for the knitting needles.

*If only.* Kieran found the tea-bags and retrieved the honey from the cupboard. Few things brought Granny Mac joy like the sweet tastes of her mountain home, though how her grandmother could identify the difference between Appalachian honey and store-bought made little sense to Kieran.

After filling their cups, Kieran returned to the chairs and settled in, exhaustion dragging at every muscle. She needed sleep, but she hungered for this connection even more than a little shut-eye. Gran's stories helped fill the holes left from Kieran's fractured childhood.

"You look so much like my mother, dear." Gran repeated the words as she took a sip of the tea. "Have I told you about her?"

Kieran rested her head against the upholstered seat, fighting to keep her eyes open. What was once more? "Tell me."

"I used to love listening to her and Papa talking late into the night on our front porch. Sometimes I was already tucked into bed up in the loft, and I'd fall asleep to that gentle sound. Then I'd awaken to her singing as she cooked breakfast. Papa said she was like a bird, always a song on her lips."

"This was in the Smokies?"

Gran nodded, a faint smile touching her face. "She had a little stone bird she kept in her apron pocket too. I think it had belonged to her Cherokee great-grandmother. She used to let me hold it." She stared down at her own knobby knuckles, as if seeing them for the first time. "Wish I still had it. I could pass it on to you."

"What happened to it?" It wasn't unusual for items to go missing when someone went into a care facility. It was one of the issues she dealt with in senior services.

A frown darkened Gran's face. "Where did those needles go? I've got to get this blanket finished."

Kieran reached for her bag. Sometimes it was better to let the memories scatter like autumn leaves, falling wherever the wind took them. Demanding answers only made Gran anxious. "I brought the sweater

I'm working on. I hoped you could help me. It's a bit of a mess." She pulled the misshapen object from her bag. Together they'd knitted and reknitted it several times. It was less about finishing a project and more about providing Gran an anchor while they talked.

Gran drew it into her lap. "You're pulling the stitches too tight again. Relax your hands while you're knitting—don't strangle the needles. The joy happens in the open spaces between the loops. Otherwise you'll get a solid wall of fabric instead of a supple, cozy piece." She demonstrated a few stitches. "A well-made sweater is like wearing a hug from someone you love, not a piece of armor to protect you from the world."

The words wove through Kieran's heart. "You make it sound so lovely, Gran."

"It had ought to be lovely, darling." She lifted the blanket from her knees and held it out, the folds opening to cascade down to her feet. "I made this'n for my mother." Her brows drew together. "Wait. That's not right. No, I made it *about* my mother."

"What do you mean?" Kieran set down her own knitting to touch the soft wool throw, the years causing the yarn to pill. Blue and violet blended into pink and orange.

"It was the view as the sun climbed up over the ridge and spilled into the holler each morning." She drew a shuddering breath. "Of course it already belonged to the park at that point."

"But you still lived there?"

"The government made Ma sign a paper saying she could live there until she died." Her eyes filled, tears coming more easily these days. "We thought we'd have more time." She dug a handkerchief from the pocket of her flowered housecoat. "Everyone thinks they've got all the time in the world, but that's not how it works. The world takes you when it will—when God wills. He knows best."

Kieran stilled, the thought creeping over her like a shadow. She'd only found Gran a few years ago, finally pulling together a semblance of family from the broken shards of her own childhood. If God wanted her grandmother, He'd have to get through Kieran first. "What happened to her?"

"They'd only get the land if she died. It's what they wanted all along." Gran glanced toward the window, as if the answers lay outside in the fading evening light.

"What are you saying?" Kieran tucked the blanket around Gran's knees. "It isn't as if the government killed her, right?"

"Her stone bird's still on the ridge. Rosie's Ridge, Pa called it." She pulled in a quick sob, covering her mouth and rocking in the seat. "I wish I had it. I could give it to you. You've been so good to me."

"Gran." Kieran grabbed her hands and planted a quick kiss on her fingers. "You don't need to give me anything. It's been wonderful just to have you in my life these past few years. You're the family I never had."

"The land, the ridge. It's still there, right?" Her wide eyes sought Kieran's.

"Of course it is. It's part of Great Smoky Mountains National Park now. Protected for all time. Rosie's Ridge is safe."

Gran struggled to rise. "You ought to go get it. It belongs to you."

"The ridge? No—Gran, it doesn't." Kieran jumped to her feet, the perpetually half-finished sweater tumbling to the floor as she steadied her grandmother. *Don't argue with dementia.* Wasn't that what she told her clients' families? "Let's get you to bed. It's late. We can talk about it tomorrow."

"Kieran, loosen up those stitches. You hold everything too tight. Tension's no good."

Tension never helped, especially with memory issues. The joy happened in the open spaces, as Gran said. "I will. I promise."

As they walked toward the bed, Gran took Kieran's arm. "'If a bird wants to fly free, first it has to release the branch.' That's what my ma used to say. You can't do that if you squeeze too tight."

After she settled her grandmother into bed, Kieran used the cramped bathroom to change her clothes and wash away as much of the *parfum de* fried fish as she could manage. Back in the car, she plugged her phone in to charge as she drove across town, looking for a good place to park for the night. Maybe she could sneak in a few minutes of reading before falling asleep in the passenger seat.

It had been four days since she'd been evicted from her apartment. Kieran knew every loophole available to secure housing for at-risk seniors, but finding an affordable one-bedroom in Nashville if you weren't on Social Security? Completely out of reach.

# 2

## Great Smoky Mountains, Tennessee
## March 1932

FALLING THROUGH THE kitchen roof was not on Rosie McCauley's list for today. Instead, she shuffled her rear closer to the edge, taking care not to put all her weight in any one spot. Gripping two rusty nails between her lips, she wedged the wooden shingle back into its place. She hoped driving a nail through the weather-beaten slat wouldn't cause the thing to crumble. With how life had been treating them lately, she wouldn't be surprised if the whole cabin collapsed in a heap.

Lorna found the oaken shake in the yard after last night's blow—right next to a fallen tulip poplar. The trunk had missed the old cabin by about twenty feet. If it had hit the house, a mere shingle would be the least of their worries.

Rosie hummed the notes of a hymn as she lifted her head, watching her sister hang bedsheets on the line to dry in the early spring sunshine. She'd spent most of her life keeping an eye on Lorna, as if that were the only reason the good Lord had put her here on the earth. Even though Lorna was grown, she'd always need looking after. God had put her together a little differently than most folks.

Rosie returned her attention to the roof. Moss caked in the cracks made the morning's chore a slippery adventure. How much longer before the mountains reclaimed what their father had built so many years ago? Rosie would add a new roof to the list of things she'd do when her ship came in, or if John D. Rockefeller stopped by with an extra million dollars.

After sinking the two nails, she sat back and surveyed her work. The sun's rays had warmed the wet surface till steam rose around her, like God redeeming the earth after the deluge. Wasn't that just like life? Rain fell, then out came the sun to kiss it all anew.

Beads of water still clung to the leaves on the nearby dogwoods, the light sparkling through each droplet. Her mama's mountain rose in the distance, the forest clinging to its crumbling slopes in much the same way Rosie held fast to this house—with deep roots. "God in heaven, it's beautiful. Thank You. And thanks for keeping watch over all my kin up there with You. I'm sure hoping You can spare a thought for us folk down here."

A familiar loneliness crashed through her. Resting her head against her knees, Rosie breathed in the damp scents of the forest, letting the chittering melodies of the birds soothe her spirit. The music of the mountains, her pa would say.

Crunching in the underbrush caught her attention, and she straightened to look. They didn't see bears round these parts much anymore, but you couldn't be too careful.

*Worse.* A stranger hiked through the woods with a pair of field glasses clamped in one hand, a roll of paper in the other. He didn't walk like a local, following the well-worn game trails, but instead pushed straight up the hill above her cabin. A revenuer? Her stomach clenched. Her pa's grave had hardly grown over, and the agents were already skulking around again?

They'd never find a still on her property. Not after what happened.

"Halloo!"

Rosie startled, one foot giving way on the slick rooftop. Someone must have walked up the road that ran along the far edge of her clearing. She peeked over the ridgepole toward the front of the house. The screen door slammed below, vibrating the boards under Rosie's bare feet. Lorna must have run for the house. She used to love trading howdies with folks in the holler, but no more.

Beau Tipton trudged up the dirt path, his hands jammed in his pockets. "Rosie-girl, you home?"

"Yeah, Beau, up here." She took a few careful steps. "Just fixing a loose plank." Rosie cast one last glance at the other fellow—the stranger on the ridge. Thank goodness Lorna hadn't spotted him, or she'd be fighting nightmares for days. Beau was familiar enough, but a revenuer? Hopefully, she'd get over these nervous spells soon and be back to her normal self.

Rosie scrambled down the wooden ladder, the seat of Pa's old work trousers damp from where she'd been woolgathering on the roof for the past ten minutes. She brushed them off with dirt-stained palms. "I ain't seen you or Maudie in a few days."

Beau pulled off his cap. "Been cleaning up our place. That storm was a real frog-strangler. One side of my cabin's caked in mud, and the water's all across the floor. Maudie's fit to be tied. I'll have to shore the place up. Don't want to get washed clean off the mountain, if you know what I mean."

"I'm sorry to hear that. At least you got a beautiful spot up there."

"Not a bad one right here. And a little more river bottom to work with. Not that it's going to do either of us good for much longer." He dug into his pocket. "I picked up your mail on my way through the holler. 'Fraid it's a mighty official-looking envelope. Folks been getting 'em up and down the road, and they ain't none too happy 'bout it neither. We ain't got one up at our place yet, but I reckon it's about the park."

"Park." She spit the word back, the taste of it as bitter as dandelion greens. "They've been going on about that for years now. What's changed?"

"Ever since Tennessee started talking 'bout condemning property, folks are as nervous as a long-tailed cat in a room full of rocking chairs. They're saying if you don't take the government deal, you get nothing."

Rosie lifted her gaze to the ridge, remembering her pa's stories of meeting her ma at a singing and following her home like a stray mutt. He might have built the house, but he always said it was Mama's mountain. *There's no way it'll ever be the government's.* "I told that state man, the only way he'd get me offen my ma's land was in a pine box." She was tempted to take the letter inside and toss it in the cookstove. Instead, she slid a thumbnail under the envelope's lip.

Beau rubbed a fist across his gray-and-brown whiskers. Apparently he was going to wait for her to read it.

She unfolded the crisp white sheet. The words "Tennessee Great Smoky Mountains National Park Commission" marched across the top edge. Rosie skimmed the brief letter, her heart sinking to her stomach.

"What's it say?" Beau edged closer to peer over her shoulder.

She lowered the letter to her side. "It says they're going to take me up on that deal."

• • •

Benton Fuller pushed through the laurel thicket, the whine of mosquitoes driving him to distraction. The hollows were thick with them this time of year, and apparently fresh blood was especially alluring. He smacked one off his neck. At least he had the comfort of knowing Dr. Hayden was facing even worse in the tropics. Benton's colleague had left on an Amazonian expedition ten days ago, taking half of Cornell's ornithology department and several deep-pocketed donors. Was it wrong to wish the man a few malaria-laden mosquitoes? Benton swatted away the professional envy like one more pesky bloodsucker.

Several weeks in the Smokies ought to ease his foul mood. Hayden could have the noisy toucans and macaws—Benton was more than happy with the birds of Tennessee and North Carolina. They might lack the same glamour, but they made up for it with mystery and secrets. He wanted to learn them all.

He pushed through to a clearing near the top of the ridge, offering a view of the mist-draped hills stretching into the distance. Benton stopped to catch his breath. A subtle fragrance hung in the air, the blend of trees and wildflowers far more pleasing than any concoction devised by a perfumer.

The government had finally listened to the public's cries to set aside this area as a national park. The west had Yosemite, Yellowstone, and the Grand Canyon, and now the Great Smoky Mountains would take their place among America's most treasured and protected lands, once the states of Tennessee and North Carolina finished purchasing the property.

Benton leaned against a hickory tree, the hardwood's strength speaking to the ageless endurance of these mountains. The land bore scars from those who had seen her assets stripped clean, but now that would change. In time the Smokies range would reclaim its former beauty. He could see it when he closed his eyes. The deer, the birds, the bears would all return in great numbers. But best of all? His owls.

A shrill call drew his attention, the sound echoing through the forest. He studied the treetops as the familiar *chirup-chirup-chirup* resounded. He'd expected to see Kentucky warblers but had yet to lay eyes on one for his census. The small songbird typically kept itself hidden in the dense foliage along the river bottoms. He needed a firm sighting before recording it in the official document.

He moved back down the slope toward the creek, careful not to shake the brush. Stopping, he raised the field glasses to his eyes and scanned the shadows for the flash of the warbler's yellow feathers. The call continued to ring through the woods.

The bird finally bounced into view as it flitted along the forest floor, picking at the leaf litter. Benton lowered the binoculars and reached for his notebook. It wasn't a rare Amazonian parrot, but the sighting still delivered a jolt of satisfaction. Another species could officially be listed in the new national park.

As he scribbled, the warbler's call shifted to a sharp *chip*. Seconds later, another. Benton lifted his head. He'd been here for several minutes already—why was it sending up the alarm now? A second warbler echoed the warning somewhere in the distance.

As if in reply, a lower-toned trill cut through the day, the notes descending like the soft whinny of a horse. Benton held his breath. *Screech owl.* He'd been hoping for this moment since he'd set out from New York but hadn't anticipated it midday. His colleagues had bickered as to whether any actually existed in the Smokies, though it seemed like prime habitat.

He shoved the book under his arm, turning to gaze around the treetops. He'd dreamed of finding a nesting pair early in spring so he could follow them through an entire life cycle. Ideally it would have been closer to where he was staying at Elkmont's Wonderland Club Hotel, but he knew better than to look a gift owl in the beak . . . or whatever.

Benton mimicked the call, hoping to catch sight of the tiny owl and follow it to its tree cavity. After two more tries, he received a tremulous response. He cocked his head to track the call through the trees. Jamming the notebook into his pocket, Benton shouldered his canvas pack.

Most folks thought of the forest as a quiet place, and in comparison with the city, he supposed it was true. But it was also alive with activity—leaves rustled on the wind, squirrels scampered through the limbs, water dripped from leaf edges and trickled from springs, and bird life created interesting melodies. The Smokies were a symphony of sounds and smells. The idea of returning to the classroom and Cornell's stuffy library was something he wouldn't dare consider at this moment. It seemed ludicrous that a love for birds and nature should lead to someone being locked away in academia.

A fluttering to his right stopped him in his tracks. The small owl rested on a limb about twenty feet up in a shagbark hickory. The bird roused its reddish-brown feathers and shook like a wet dog before stopping to preen them into place. If it hadn't been for the motion, he'd never have seen it. He mimicked the call again, a gentle trill from deep in his throat.

The owl turned its head left and right, as if trying to locate the interloper before responding in kind.

Lowering himself to one knee, Benton lifted the binoculars and studied his feathered subject. "Come on—show me your home."

Instead, the owl remained stationary for ten minutes and then closed its eyes.

Sometimes one had to endure long stretches of boredom to earn those fleeting moments of enchantment. Lowering the field glasses, he reached into his pack for the paper-wrapped sandwich he'd stashed earlier. He wasn't going anywhere soon, that much was obvious.

From this vantage point, he had a good view into the hollow. He traced a column of smoke to a run-down cabin just this side of the creek. The mountain people seemed to eke out the barest existence from their small farms. This family must be one of the few still fighting condemnation.

The familiar low trill made him look up. A second owl swooped over to join its mate. Ducking inside a hole in the decaying trunk, it disappeared from view.

"Got you." He reached for his notebook and scribbled information as fast as he could. He might be in the park to conduct a census of the overall bird population, but screech owls were his passion. If he could get enough info to send to the Audubon Society, they might fund future studies.

The owls and their nest were perfectly hidden in the tree cavity, safe from larger owls and anything else that might harm them.

*Hidden*. Benton glanced up at the nearby trees. A blind would be ideal for studying this pair. He could observe them whenever he wished, and they wouldn't be disturbed by his presence.

A branch snapped in a nearby thicket, and the warbler uttered its sharp *chip-chip-chip* again. Benton straightened. The owls might be safe from predators, but he was not.

The dark barrel of a shotgun slid into sight from the dense brush. "What're you looking for?" A voice growled from the cover of the laurels.

Benton's thoughts scattered like so many sparrows. "I . . . I don't . . ." He lifted his hands. "Birds, mostly. I'm not looking for trouble."

"You government?"

"I'm a professor of ornithology from Cornell University. So no." Benton considered the voice. It didn't sound like a grown man's. A boy perhaps? "I'm performing a bird survey for the new park. They want a record of how many different species are living in the mountains here."

"You ain't in the park." The shrubs quaked, and a young woman stepped into the open, her grip on the shotgun secure. She cut an odd figure, dressed in a man's plaid shirt and denim trousers. Underneath a beaten hat, a dark braid hung over one shoulder and reached nearly to her waist.

Benton retreated a few paces to keep a comfortable distance between himself and the business end of her firearm. "Begging your pardon, miss, but my map says it is—unless I somehow wandered off course."

"You're on McCauley land, and over yonder"—she gestured with the gun—"is Samson property. They're just as likely to shoot you as say hello. Iffen you're out looking for stills, I don't cotton to such business on my land."

"I'm simply looking for birds. Here, I can prove it to you." He lowered his pack to the ground.

The action caused her to step back and tighten her grip on the shotgun.

"I only want to show you my census." Benton unbuckled the straps and opened the bag, letting several books and charts slip onto the ground. "You've got some wonderful specimens in your woods here. I just located a nesting pair of Eastern screech owls." He opened his Audubon guide and pointed at the illustration.

"I've seen 'em. They come through every summer." Her brown eyes softened. "Never did understand why they called them 'screech.' They've got lovely calls. Now barn owls? Their screech could shave a year off your life."

He couldn't resist the grin spreading across his face. "You appreciate birds?"

"Don't most folks? They add a little color and music to God's world, don't they?"

"I think so—to our world, anyway." He'd never been much for God talk. Still, the knot of tension in his shoulders eased. "But I have a particular interest in owls. I'm hoping to do a study on screech owls while I'm here working on the bird census. I'd love to spend some time watching this pair, if you don't mind me on your property."

"Hootenanny?"

He closed the guide, suddenly feeling more lost than ever. "Beg pardon?"

"The owls—Hoot and Annie. That's who you're watching?" Her brown eyes held an air of mischief.

He smiled. "You've named them?"

"I name a lot of the critters hereabouts. My sister and I have done that since we was little." Her gaze locked on his book. "Why are they counting the birds?"

"The government wants to better understand the land they've purchased. Find out what's here and what's not."

"Purchased?" An unladylike snort escaped her. "They're *stealing* is more like it. Families been living here for generations, and the government thinks throwing a few dollars at us will send us packing? Where are we supposed to go?"

He'd heard the complaint before. Whereas the western parks had been carved largely from public land, this new venture was being cobbled together from bits of private land. Schoolchildren from North Carolina and Tennessee had been donating their pennies for years, and now that Rockefeller was matching their funds, things were moving quickly. "I know it's been difficult for the local communities, but this park is going to be beautiful. It will benefit so many people."

"You want to walk over to my family's graveyard and tell that to my Cherokee great-grandmother? Because she'd understand that sorta talk better than anyone."

Benton scooped the books into his bag. He wasn't here to debate with the locals. "I'm sorry about the trespassing, but I truly thought this parcel had already been obtained. Is that Jakes Creek down there?"

Her eyes narrowed. "It is."

He reached for the map and unrolled it, studying the contour lines that delineated the various ridges and hollows. "I was told everything from the Little Brier Branch to the top of Rocky Ridge had been purchased already. Perhaps your husband—"

"You're wrong." She shook her head, sending the braid swinging. "I ain't signed nothing."

Surely this young woman couldn't be the owner. He folded the map over. "You're going to be completely surrounded by park land soon. I do hope you're not alone out here."

That had been the wrong thing to say. Her face darkened, her hands tightening on the gun. The barrel rose slightly to point at his shoes. "I ain't alone."

He tucked the map under his arm. "Look, we started badly. I never even introduced myself. My name is Benton Fuller. And I'd really like to have the opportunity to study your owls. This will be part of the park eventually, after all, Miss—"

"McCauley. Rosie McCauley." Her brown-eyed glare had returned. "And you'd best get off my land."

• • •

The man's words haunted her for days. *"This will be part of the park eventually, after all."* She'd heard the same thought expressed by many people, but for some reason this birdwatcher's offhand comment had sunk right to her core. He was so matter-of-fact, like he was just talking about a change in the weather.

Rosie sank onto the ladder-back chair as the last of her energy drained out of her. She pulled the crisp white paper out of its envelope and studied it. Over the past weeks, three different neighbors had stopped by to say goodbye—families who had lived in the holler for generations. At this rate, she and Lorna might soon be the only ones left.

*"I do hope you're not alone out here."*

She let her head fall forward into her hands, lacing her fingers over her eyes. Once again the roof had leaked overnight, leaving her feather tick soaked. First thing this morning, she'd dragged it out to a sunny patch to dry, then had spent the early hours weeding the garden and tending the bees. Now she faced the unwelcome task of climbing back onto the roof. She didn't have money for new shingles and certainly not enough to pay anyone to do the work. To top it off, she'd found one of their two hogs dead in the woods, the meat long spoiled. If she couldn't track down the other one before butchering time, there'd be precious little bacon and lard this year. Letting them forage meant she didn't have to feed the animals from their minimal corn supplies, but it also put them at risk. Could she afford to keep the second one penned up all year? Could she afford not to?

Worst of all, would she have to choose between the roof and food for the table?

She unfolded the paper, spreading it flat and smoothing the creases.

The state land agent had come by at least four times in the past year to wave money at Rosie and make threats if she didn't take the deal. The idea rattled around her mind like a raccoon stuck in a box trap. Leave their home—the cabin Pa had built for Mama so many years ago?

*Pa, what would you do?*

Their neighbors, the Allens, had moved to Sevierville to live with their kin, but she and Lorna were alone in the world. She'd not felt it so keenly since they'd laid Pa to rest in the family cemetery six years ago. With the money the government was offering, they could buy a small house in town—but then what? Other girls dreamed of marrying and getting out of the mountains, but she couldn't put her mind to living anywhere else. And Lorna would never understand.

She ran a finger over the last line. This was the first time they'd offered a deal she'd even dare consider—a lifetime lease. They'd only peddled such offers to a handful of the older folks, ones who were nigh on to the grave anyhow. Had Lorna's hardship triggered this?

According to the letter, if she sold the deed to them, she and Lorna could stay right through Rosie's lifetime. She'd pay a dollar a year for the right to live on their land. For that, they'd pay her three thousand dollars up front. Three *thousand*. It was a heap more cash money than she'd ever dreamed of. It would pay for the roof and buy supplies for years. They didn't need much.

But the homestead would no longer be hers.

Lorna's shriek jerked Rosie to her feet. Her sister burst through the door and flew past, aiming for the loft ladder.

Rosie grabbed for her elbow but missed. "What's wrong? What's happened?"

Lorna's attention darted back to the doorway, mouth slack. She shook her head violently, lifting both hands to dig into her hair. A moment later she launched herself up the ladder like a bear cub clambering into a tree.

Rosie hurried out to the porch. Her sister didn't like guests, but this was a bigger fit than she'd thrown for anyone else. Was it that stranger from the other day?

Her breath caught when she spotted the Samson brothers coming up the road. Just what she needed. Resisting the urge to grab her gun from the pegs, she hopped off the edge of the porch and headed to meet them.

Will Samson weren't so bad, but his brother Horace could be a handful—and then some. Both of them had courted Rosie at one point or another, but Horace was the only one who'd tried strong-arming her into the woods after a barn dance. He'd reeked of shine that night, but he wasn't much better stone-cold sober. Her pa had always warned her to stay clear of them. She'd trusted his judgment after that.

And yet they were still neighbors.

"Afternoon there, Rosie." Will tipped his slouchy hat toward her, his other arm tucked tight against his chest. He'd injured his hand in a logging accident a few years before, and it hadn't been much good to him since.

"Will. Horace." She came to a stop at the edge of her clearing. She didn't aim to invite them in to visit a spell, not with how Lorna was acting.

Horace pulled off his cap and ran stubby fingers through his brown hair. "Beau Tipton said you got one of them letters. Curious what you're planning to do."

"I ain't made a decision yet. We could use the money, but I don't like the idea overmuch."

Will nodded. "We're staying, if that helps you any. We got work on the road crew, and they'll let us stay put for now."

Horace jammed a hand into his pocket. "In case you was worried about us deserting you."

The thought hadn't crossed her mind, but probably best to keep that to herself. "Glad to know we'll still have neighbors. Lots of folks are hightailing it out of here. The cash payments are mighty tempting." She folded her arms. "I'm needing a new roof and some other repairs. Our place took quite a beating in that last blow."

Will gestured toward her cabin. "We could help with that."

"That's mighty nice of you, but—"

"In fact . . ." Horace cut in. "We got a business proposition we wanted to discuss."

Will shot his brother a sideways glance. "Not that one has to do with the other."

"Iffen we work out a deal, she'd have the money she needed." He folded his arms.

Rosie couldn't imagine what he was talking about. "What sort of proposition was you fixin' to offer?"

Horace spat tobacco juice at the ground behind him. "Your branch. We want to use it. The water's cold and sweet—the best in the holler. By the time it gets down to our place, it's slow and muddy."

"We could have a nice little 'shine operation." Will's blue eyes caught hers. "We could pay you outright or split the profits, whichever you prefer."

Rosie's throat tightened. "You know how my pa died. How can you even ask such a thing?"

"It'd be good money." Horace jutted his chin forward. "Fix that roof and put a little aside."

Will lowered his voice, his tone gentle. "Your pa's death were an accident, Rosie. We'd be careful."

"And he wasn't? Is that what you're saying?" She heard the hypocrisy in her words, but she couldn't stop them. *If only Pa hadn't been so desperate.*

"Of course I ain't. But you don't have to worry. We'll set it far back in the woods—there'd be no risk to you or Lorna. You wouldn't even know it was there."

"I would know. And when the revenuers show up, they'd know. I saw a stranger in my woods a few days ago. I don't want to have to jump every time I see someone."

"There's no reasoning with McCauleys." Horace glared at her. "Never has been. Pa says the only reason the government's offering you the lease deal is on account of your feebleminded sister. Otherwise, you'd have to take the money and get, just like the rest of the holler."

"Horace . . ." His brother growled a warning.

Rosie curled her fists. "Don't you dare—"

"She was up at our place again last week." Horace's eyes flashed. "Stole a quilt off our line. She tell you that?"

*Stole?* A pit opened in Rosie's stomach. Lorna always brought in treasures from the woods, but she'd never taken anything that belonged to someone else.

"Now, we don't know that for sure." Will's face drew down.

His brother's nostrils flared. "I seen her. And she ain't supposed to be on our land nohow."

"Lorna doesn't mean no harm." Rosie found her voice. "She likes to visit your goats."

"Pa says he's going to the sheriff and get her committed."

To think she'd once found Horace handsome as the day was long. "Get off my land, and take your shady schemes with you." She turned and headed for the house.

His derisive snort sounded like a hog a-rooting. "Gladly."

"Rosie." Will followed her into the yard. "Horace's just jawing you. Don't listen to him."

She whirled on him. "Get her committed? Of all the fool things to say." Her shrill tone likely carried to where Horace was walking away. She hoped it did.

"Pa's just sore the park offered you a lifetime lease and not us. It's a right plum deal, 'specially since you ain't got no husband or kids." A shy smile crossed his face. "Not for my lack of trying." He tucked his weakened arm against his chest. "Rosie, you had oughta take it afore they change their mind. If they kick you and Lorna off the land, where're you gonna go? How would she make it out in the world?"

The thought sent a chill through her. Folks hereabouts weren't always kind to Lorna, but at least they were used to her odd ways.

"If you see the quilt returned, I'll talk to my Pa—make sure he don't cause trouble for y'all. But it was one my late mama stitched, so it's important."

"Iffen she has it"—she swallowed against the tightness in her throat—"I'll make certain she returns it to you."

He shook his head, eyes downcast. "Maybe you'd best bring it alone."

"All right."

"And, Rosie . . ." He released a long breath, splaying his fingers against his shirtfront. "Let me help with the roof. Please. Or we can have a working, if you'd rather."

His gentle tone melted something inside her. "I . . . I'll think about it."

He touched the brim of his hat in farewell and followed the path his brother had taken a few minutes earlier. The trail they'd oft walked together back in their courtin' days.

She went inside and climbed the ladder to the loft. "Lorna? They're gone now."

Lorna sat on the bed with her face buried in her hands. She peeked out over her interlaced fingers, a question hovering in her eyes.

"Will said . . ." A heaviness settled in Rosie's stomach as she glanced around the room. *Please don't be right.* "He said a quilt was missing. Do you know anything about it?"

Lorna stayed motionless.

Ignoring the tightening in her chest, Rosie set her jaw and walked to the trunk her sister kept near the window. Bending down, she unhooked the latch and opened the lid. A ragged yellow quilt lay wadded in the corner, wedged between Lorna's old doll and a few books that had belonged to their mother. Rosie drew it out, the fabric soft from age and too many washings. "Oh, Lorna."

Her sister jumped to her feet and grabbed a corner of the cloth, yanking it from Rosie's hands. She shoved it back into the box and slammed the lid.

"It don't belong to you." The thought of carrying the quilt to the Samsons' made her sick to her stomach, but there was nothing else to be done.

Her sister screeched, pushing Rosie away.

Rosie lost her balance, her tailbone smacking hard against the rag rug. She gaped at Lorna who'd thrown herself across the trunk's lid, sobbing. Her sister had never raised a hand to her, not once in all their years together. She was as gentle as a summer breeze. "What's gotten into you? What's happened?"

Managing Lorna had always been a challenge, but the past few months she'd been restless, like her nerves was all to pieces. Would she continue to worsen until Rosie could no longer keep her safe? What then?

Lorna gulped through her tears, her chest heaving with her rapid breaths.

Rosie had spent her life reading her sister's face, and this was an expression she'd only seen once before—when Lorna had found their pa after the still exploded.

Placing her hands over her sister's a-trembling ones, Rosie pulled her close. The quilt could wait. "You're safe, Lorna. You'll always be safe here."

After finally crying herself out, Lorna let Rosie tuck her into bed. She cuddled her rag doll and drifted off for a nap, like a six-year-old somehow trapped in a woman's body.

Rosie sat on the edge of the bed and watched her sister sleep. If only Lorna could tell her what was wrong and why she had stolen the quilt in the first place, maybe then Rosie could explain it to the Samsons. Then Eb Samson might rethink his plan to talk to the sheriff.

Sheriff Jones had been to their cabin only once before, the day Pa had died. This huge man who weren't afeared to go toe-to-toe with brawlers had shrunk away from Lorna like she'd been one of those lepers in the old-time Bible stories. Would he haul Lorna off to an institution just on Eb Samson's say-so? The idea curdled Rosie's stomach like a crock of buttermilk left in the hot sun.

Maybe selling off the land and heading to town would give the pair of them a fresh start.

The moment the thought crossed her mind, she dismissed it. Reality pressed down on Rosie, crushing every bit of air from her lungs. Lorna couldn't abide change. The only hope for her sister would be to keep things exactly as they were for as long as she could manage it—Samsons or no Samsons.

Rosie tiptoed over to the trunk and removed the quilt. She ran a hand over its worn seams, tracing the simple design. After clambering down the ladder, she laid the folded coverlet on the table. The government paper still sat where she'd left it.

There was only one way to prevent change in their little world.

Taking a fountain pen from the basket, Rosie sat down in the ladder-back chair. A lump settled in her throat as she unscrewed the pen's cap. *For Lorna.*

Rosie McCauley signed her name.

# 3

## Nashville
## Present Day

KIERAN SIGNED HER name to the stack of papers before pushing them to the side of her desk and repositioning her outdated keyboard. The one problem with helping people navigate social services was dealing with endless government forms. It was mind-numbing work, but easier for her than for eighty-year-old clients. Some of them struggled just to hold a pen.

SeniorCo's low-walled cubicles didn't offer much privacy, but on an early spring day like this, Kieran loved how they allowed sunshine from the front windows in to brighten the mood.

Fern Michaels scowled as she sat in the chair opposite Kieran's desk. "I've lived in that apartment for ten years now. When they first started talking about remodeling the place, I had no idea I'd be tossed out on the street like a stray cat. Is this how they'd treat their mothers?" Kieran's client thumped her hot-pink cane against the floor. "I don't s'pose they got mothers. If they did, they'd know better. They must have been raised by wolves."

Wolves made pretty good moms, according to a video Kieran had watched on her phone last night, but there was no sense arguing Fern's analogy. Especially since she agreed with the sentiment. "What about your daughter? Could you stay with her for a time?"

"She lives in Wisconsin, and I can't abide the cold. I've lived in

Nashville my whole life, and now I'm being priced out? We used to walk down to the Ryman Theater to watch the Opry stars come and go. Did I tell you about the time I kissed Little Jimmy Dickens?" Fern's smile transformed to a frown faster than she changed subjects. "Tennessee is my home. I was born here. I intend to die here. You understand, don't you, Kieran?"

Did she? Kieran tapped a few keys, scouring apartment listings for Fern—as if she hadn't spent hours last night searching on her own behalf. "I grew up in Pennsylvania, but I'm not sure I'd call it home." More of a muddled array of houses and part-time families. She'd been the youngest, the oldest, the only—but never the one who belonged.

Fern leaned forward, hooking her cane over the lip of the desk. "I thought your granny's people were from the Smokies. Wasn't she one of the folks put out of her home?"

"Mmm, yes. But my parents moved before I was born. I've only recently reconnected with her." Kieran kept her eyes locked on the computer screen. "I haven't even been to the Smokies yet."

"Oh, child. No wonder you're so untethered."

Kieran swallowed. Was it that obvious?

"These losses get passed down, you know. It's like a hole deep inside. How is your grandmother?"

"Oh look—here's a possibility." Kieran clicked on a listing and turned the monitor toward Fern, hoping this would sidetrack the woman's probing. Kieran's heart already bled with every tiny pinprick of this job. If she pulled open the curtains on her life, she'd lose her last line of defense.

The woman put on a pair of lime-green readers and scooted forward. "Where is it?"

"Piney Oaks."

Fern snorted. "Old people. Why does everyone want to lock us away together?" She drummed her fingernails on the desk but studied the pictures. "Doesn't look half bad." Her voice faded, a faint tremble evident in her words. "Is that the price?"

Kieran glanced at the fine print and rubbed three fingers over the tension settling in above her eyebrows. How much further could Fern's Social Security stretch? "I can talk to them. We'll work something out."

"It's not too far. Can I bring my cat?"

"I'll ask. Why don't we go take a look?"

The walking stick thunked against the tile floor. "You've got it, girlie. Then I'm treating you to lunch. It's the least I can do."

"You don't need to do that, Mrs. Michaels." Kieran pulled a sweater off the back of her chair. "I'm happy to help."

"Nonsense. In Tennessee, we repay a kindness with a kindness. It's how it's done."

Kieran couldn't resist giving the little lady a quick hug. She might not know what home felt like, but she hoped it was something like this.

• • •

Great Smoky Mountains National Park

Zach blinked as he stepped out of the woods and into the brilliance of the meadow at Andrews Bald. Early spring wildflowers mixed with hummocks of grass, even though patches of snow and ice still remained. He shifted his pack, his stiff shoulder reminding him of the tumble he'd taken last week on the slick rocks around Alum Cave. Days like this he found himself envying the rangers who spent their work hours in the field while he wasted away in a cramped office.

His friend Miguel came up beside him and whistled. "See, I told you the view here is even better than Clingmans Dome. Can't believe you hadn't made it up here yet."

The hillside dropped away to the south, revealing ridgeline upon ridgeline in the distance. The fresh spring vegetation at his feet stood in sharp contrast with the dark forested highlands beyond, where the deep green melded into blue and gray the farther he looked. Even prettier were the wispy veils of cloud clinging to the treetops. "You'd think it went on forever. The first settlers must have thought so."

"Living in the past, as always." His friend slid a stainless-steel water bottle from his pack and guzzled the contents. "Can't you just appreciate the beauty for what it is?"

"I'm paid to live in the past, or have you forgotten? You can focus on the science. I'll piece together the human story."

"What's to know? Good people stepped in and made it a park. Now look." Miguel spread his arms toward the vista. "It would have been a crime for all this gorgeous scenery to have been lost."

There was so much more to the Smokies than Miguel's quick explanation. Everyone left a mark on the landscape. Zach had spent the past year, since taking the curator position, learning the area's history and cataloging the various cultural resources identified within the boundaries of the national park. He could stay here a lifetime and not see it all.

"Since you sit in an office forty hours a week, I'm surprised you weren't the one having trouble keeping up."

"I'm a runner, remember?" In truth it was sheer excitement that drove him down every trail. During his years at Arizona State University, he'd spent summers in the Sonoran Desert and his winters in the library. He'd never envisioned himself surrounded by miles and miles of dense forest teeming with deer and bear. "You're fortunate that you get to work in the backcountry. I need to arrange for more hours in the field."

"You want to know how I spent my week? Tramping around checking wild hog traps in the pouring rain. The outdoor life isn't all flowers and waterfalls. I can't believe you talked me into hiking on my day off. I should be in Gatlinburg eating real food and picking up girls."

"In that order?"

His friend shot him a glance. "A man's got priorities."

"Well, I appreciate you showing me this trail. How about I grill some steaks when we get back to make it up to you?" Zach's stomach rumbled at the thought. Charbroiled meat sounded heavenly right now.

Miguel sighed. "Doesn't help with the girls. Got any of those around?"

"Not any I'd dare introduce to you." The last girl who'd broken Zach's heart still lived in Arizona. There was nothing like a thousand miles to help the healing process. He searched his pack for a protein bar. "But I've got plenty of real food at my cabin—potatoes, steak, garlic bread—and I'm not too bad with the barbecue."

"Rented the shack yet? Can I crash overnight?"

"There's no running water, and I'm still working on the roof. But if you don't mind sleeping rough, sure. Or you could stay on my couch."

"I've seen your couch. I'll take the cabin. At least it's got a mattress. I've been sleeping on the ground for a week. My bivy sack has seen better days." Miguel adjusted his ball cap. "So, steak?"

"If you want it. Of course, if you prefer to go clubbing in Gatlinburg, you're on your own. It's not my scene." *Anymore.*

The wildlife tech breathed out a long sigh. "Not really mine either. It's just something that creeps up on you after too much time alone in the woods. Tell you what—I'll race you to the truck, and the loser cleans the grill."

Zach gave the viewpoint one more admiring glance as Miguel headed off. His friend's comments about barhopping had released a cascade of unpleasant memories. Archaeology students might spend their daylight hours at dusty dig sites, but their nights were a different story. And ASU offered plenty of opportunities for trouble. He swiped a hand over his face. He never should have let things with Jordan get so complicated and inside out.

But it wouldn't happen again. Now he played by the rules.

• • •

Karen Barnett

## Nashville

Kieran leaned over the front seat of her car and dropped her damp towel and toiletry bag on top of the overflowing laundry basket. Even though SeniorCo had missed payroll this month, somehow her YMCA benefits remained current. The thirty minutes she'd spent on the treadmill should disguise the fact that she'd really just come for the showers.

*Transitionally homeless.* She could still hear her health and human development professor lecturing about the stages and categories of homelessness. Chronic, episodic, transitional, hidden. When Kieran had scribbled those terms in her notebook, she'd pictured meth addicts and grizzled old men with paper-wrapped bottles. Even with all of her trips through foster homes, she'd never thought of herself as homeless. But hadn't that been the fact all along? Was this really so different?

Pushing fingers through her wet hair, Kieran drew in a deep breath and blew it out between her lips. She closed her eyes and recited some of the positive points in her column—Granny Mac, Ash and Nick, a car that ran, library card, and warm weather. Back in Pennsylvania, it could be snowing. *Thank you, Nashville, for soft, sweet rain.*

The apartment she'd picked out for Fern had been perfect. "Move-in ready," as the paper had said. The facility had negotiated a fair lease agreement. No weird smells or undecipherable stains, and it even had a skylight in the bedroom. Fern and her calico cat would be able to hear the rain pattering on the glass from the coziness of her bed.

Kieran stared out the windshield, the droplets blurring her view of the deserted parking lot. She reached for the fake-fur blanket she kept tucked in the foot space of the passenger seat, spreading it over herself and letting the fuzziness tickle her chin. The Christmas gift from Nick and Ashleigh wrapped her in their kindness every time she curled up with it. They would be horrified if they knew she'd been evicted, but she couldn't bear to tell them. It was only temporary, after all.

In her mind, she pictured an overstuffed chair pulled up near a gas fireplace. Where had that been? *The Sandersons'*. Then there was the Millers' window seat, which made for the perfect reading nook. Mrs. Guthrie's back yard had a tire swing. If she thought hard enough, she could cobble together an image of a happy home from the fractured pieces of her life. And that picture gave her hope. Like postcard souvenirs from a long trip, she'd occasionally glance through the cherry-picked moments and leave the rest buried.

But lately in her car—alone in the darkness—less pleasant memories tiptoed in, unwanted. Maybe that was the real danger in living outside four walls.

With a sigh, Kieran tossed the blanket aside. She should check on Gran and stop at the laundromat before turning in for the night. Gran had been anxious the past few days, pulling up additional flashes from her childhood in the mountains. Did pain run in her family, or was everyone pockmarked in some way by their past? There must be people out there whose childhoods contained nothing but Saturday morning cartoons, Scout campouts, and family dinners.

Granny Mac had endured more than her share of heartache, starting with the death of her mother. An abusive marriage, the loss of one son in the Gulf War, the other incarcerated for life. It was the fact that she'd returned to using her maiden name, Fuller, that had caused child services to lose track of her in the first place—a paper trail gone cold. But Kieran could hardly blame her for wanting to leave that season of her life behind.

Kieran was still brushing the raindrops off her coat in the lobby of Gran's building when Ivy, the night nurse, waved to her. "There you are. I tried to call your apartment, but they said the line was disconnected."

"You have my cell number and my work number."

"I don't like upsetting folks at work unless it's an emergency. I figured you'd show up tonight."

Not an emergency. Good. "Did something happen?"

"Miss Mac has been a little out of sorts today. She's been wandering the halls, saying she lost her bird—whatever that means." Ivy patted Kieran's arm, a comforting gesture Kieran had seen her use time and again with many residents. "I keep walking her back to her room and telling her you'll be by later. I'm glad you didn't make a liar out of me."

*That bird again?* "Next time, call my cell. You can reach me anytime. I . . . I canceled my landline."

The nurse clucked her tongue. "So many folks getting rid of those these days. No one wants to be tied down, I guess. You two have a nice visit, now."

"We will, thank you. And, Ivy? Thank you for looking out for Granny Mac."

Ivy grinned. "My pleasure, sweetie. My pleasure."

# 4

## Great Smoky Mountains National Park
## 1932

Rosie hung back in the laurels and studied the Samson place. The contrast betwixt it and her own cabin weighed on her. While the weathered hand-hewn logs of her house looked like they'd sprouted straight out of the forest, they also seemed as if they might fade back in at any moment. The Samson's plank-board home was painted white and looked clean as a pin, with fresh shingles on top. If she didn't know the Samsons had lived there for two generations, she'd think it was built yesterday. They even had a white picket fence instead of split rail like everyone else.

The place still had Mrs. Samson's citified ways about it, even though she'd been in the grave two years now and her menfolk were as backwoods as they came. Eb Samson had hired young Widder Martin to keep house for him and the boys. The quiet woman cooked and cleaned all day, then scurried barefoot back to her father's home at the far end of the holler. Her man had been killed in the same lumber accident that had left Will with a feeble arm. To hear her tell it, she thought Will or Horace might marry her so she could stay on for keeps.

If Rosie had married one of the brothers, she might be living in that fine house—but probably as little more than a kitchen slave. The thought sent a quiver through her middle. Better to live in a shack and be her own woman, no matter how lonely.

The house looked as silent as a stone. Maybe no one was home. She smoothed the folded quilt over her arm, admiring the redbud blossoms sprigged across the yellow cotton chintz. Mrs. Samson had a fine hand at the needle, that much was certain. Even though the fabric was worn thin with years of scrubbing, you could still see the beauty in the stitching. It made sense that Horace and Will were attached to the keepsake. What puzzled her was why Lorna had seen fit to steal it. She'd never been a thief and didn't even seem to much care for objects of finery. What had possessed her to snatch it off the line and hide it in her trunk?

After five minutes of skulking in the bushes, Rosie gathered her wits and strode across the gravel road.

Her courage lasted all the way to the gate. The thought of throwing herself on the Samsons' mercy made a sheen of sweat break out under her collar. She cast one last glance up at the imposing house before draping the quilt over the fence pickets. It was a coward's move, but if the shoe fit . . .

Hurrying away, she unfastened the tiny cloth-covered buttons on her collar. She had chores to do, and Maudie was coming tomorrow to help her with the canning, so there weren't time to smooth over this little misunderstanding.

"Hello?" A man's voice trailed her down the path.

Her skin went cold, then hot. She ought to have stayed and begged the Samsons' forgiveness. Now she looked right foolish. Rosie spun, scrambling for excuses.

Instead of Will or Horace, a well-dressed man with a knapsack walked toward her, his long stride carrying him closer at an alarming pace. Recognition trickled through her—the slick-faced fellow from the woods. At his height and with his shoulders hunched from the weight he was toting, the man looked a bit like one of those long-legged herons she'd seen stalking frogs in the creek.

"Miss McCauley, wasn't it?" His clipped tones couldn't be more different than the Samson brothers'.

The tension in her ribs eased, freeing her to speak. "Yes. I'm sorry, sir. I don't rightly remember your name."

"Benton Fuller." He grinned. "We didn't meet under the best of circumstances, so I'm not surprised you don't remember."

"I didn't forget how you were traipsing about my land like it belonged to you, and I set you straight."

He paused, his expression faltering. "I'm sorry that's the impression I left you with. I'd really like another chance."

She waited, content to let him stew in her silence. Even though he was slight and not overly muscled like most of the men in these parts, he possessed a strong jaw—and those dark lashes framing his sky-blue eyes? She tore her gaze away. "What did you have in mind?"

"I would like to show you something, if I may. In your woods. If you agree to my proposition, I'll make it worth your while."

Rosie's skin crawled. *In the woods. Proposition?* "I'm not certain what sort of flimflam you're trying to pull, but I don't care to go nowheres with you."

Mr. Fuller's mouth opened slowly as understanding dawned. "N-no, that's not what I meant. Forgive me. I'm usually much better at stringing together words. It's the screech owls. I want to show you where they're nesting."

"You want to show me owls? I've seen plenty."

"I'd like you to see the location in reference to your cabin. Then maybe I can convince you to let me stay and study the birds. I could compensate you for any inconvenience, of course. Would you accompany me? It will only take a few minutes. Please."

Now that she'd signed the paper, did Rosie still have the ability to chase him from her land? She needed to look into the particulars. "My sister is—" She swallowed. "She's poorly. And I don't want her troubled." Even so, his words about compensation buzzed in her ears. She'd never considered that a five-inch owl could have any value outside of being interesting to look at. "What do you mean about making it worth our while?"

He ran a hand across his shirtfront. "I think we can get down to the brass tacks after you see what I'm proposing. First, let me show you the nesting ground. I think you'll agree that I won't be any disturbance to your farm."

She glanced down at her one store-bought visitin' dress. "I ain't exactly fixed for rambling about in the woods."

"I don't mind waiting." The man followed her through the gate and into the yard.

"All right, then." She turned and faced him, lifting a hand. "You don't have to come up to the house. I'll change and be back out faster than a raccoon with a hound on its tail." The last thing she needed was to set Lorna off again. She'd had enough upset for one day. For a month, even.

"I'll be waiting."

She'd spent every minute in the past few weeks fighting to keep the place running smoothly. The idea of a ramble in the woods set her heart humming, even if it meant being in the company of a stranger. Since the mountains were being taken over by the government, she'd best get used to seeing newcomers about. She pushed a hand up into her braid, fussing with a few strands that had come loose. She'd need to get Lorna accustomed to the idea as well.

Rosie walked around the house to the back and stopped on the edge of the clearing, studying the cabin with its porch leaning askew, all *sigogglin'*, as folks would say. It might not be fancy like Samsons', but it was home.

Lorna sat in one of the porch rockers, winding the new yarn Maudie had brought by yesterday. She glanced up, hair tangled and eyes red. Scowling, she crushed the woolen ball in her fingers.

The sight tugged at Rosie's conscience. So much went past Lorna's understanding, but waking up and finding the quilt gone? Of course it would put her out of sorts.

Rosie halted on the bottom step. "I'm sorry. You know that quilt weren't yours."

Lorna swiped a hand across her nose, her lower lip quivering. She shook her head and pounded her fists on her knees twice. Her stringy, sleep-mussed hair fell across her face.

"I had to return it—there was no doin' otherwise." Rosie took a deep breath to stop herself from explaining further. It wouldn't do any good to try to drag her reasons through the weeds and thistles. Her sister would calm down and forget in time. Lorna's head might not be quite right, but she made up for it with a kind, childlike heart. Her temper tantrums were loud and short, like a summer squall.

The rotted step creaked once as Rosie put her weight on it and crossed to stand in front of her sister. "Look, I'm going to change clothes, then climb the ridge a ways. I'll be home by supper." She studied her sister's face. "You want to come with?" She'd explain Mr. Fuller's presence somehow. One thing at a time.

Lorna shook her head and scrunched her lips into a wrinkled pout.

"All right, then." Ignoring the sour look, Rosie forced a lightness into her voice. "We don't have any more pie, but maybe we can have bread and honey for dessert. Would you like that?"

Her sister nodded. She lowered her eyes, tucking her chin to her chest.

Rosie crouched in front of the rocker, placing her hands on Lorna's knees. "Stay here until I get home. Do *not* go to the Samsons' place." She waited for the second nod. "You know I love you, right?"

Lorna didn't look up, but she patted her chest in answer—a tradition they'd started as girls.

Rosie placed her hand over her heart. A dull pain still lodged there, but Lorna probably felt it too. They only had each other, so even when the fights ended quickly, the hurts sank deep.

• • •

The sun beat down on Benton's head and neck, and he adjusted his fedora against the glare. Over the past weeks, he'd grown accustomed to the forest's shadows. He studied the McCauley cabin, a solid log structure with a wood shake roof. A massive rosebush clung to the lovely river rock chimney, extending nearly to the attic window. Laden with pink blooms, it would probably cast loose petals across the front yard whenever the breeze stirred.

Miss McCauley said he needn't come in, but surely she wouldn't mind him walking around to the shady side to wait. He followed the worn path around the house.

A young heavyset woman sat on the porch, scowling at some sort of handiwork. Miss McCauley had mentioned an invalid sister, hadn't she? By the description, he'd expected her to be bedridden. He backed several steps, rethinking his choice.

The woman glanced up, her mouth slackening as her jaw dropped. She jumped to her feet, the rocker sliding back and banging against the wall.

"Um, hello! I didn't mean to disturb you. I was waiting on Miss McCauley—the other Miss McCauley. I'm Benton Fuller." Benton raised his hands. "Should I go?"

She covered her face with shaking hands, like a child playing peekaboo.

Benton didn't know how to interpret her actions. He hooked his thumbs under the straps of his pack. "It's a lovely place you have here. That rose bush out front is stunning." He studied the back yard. Several small animal pens and dilapidated structures took up most of the clearing. A flock of speckled hens scratched and pecked in the dirt. "Nice birds. Are they good layers?"

The woman spread her fingers as if to look Benton's way. Evidently he'd said something right. She lowered one hand.

"I'm partial to wild birds myself." Benton pushed on, risking a step her direction. "I study them. But chickens have a . . . a magic of their own."

The woman nodded. She gestured toward the hens, then at a songbird flitting in the shrub by the far window. She patted her chest several times.

Perhaps she was without speech? "You like birds too?" He glanced toward the screen to see if Miss McCauley was coming to his rescue. No luck. "I found an owl feather this morning. Maybe you'd enjoy seeing it?"

Her eyes lit. She moved forward, coming to the corner of the porch and hopping down to the dirt rather than taking the step.

Benton pulled his knapsack open and retrieved a manila envelope he used to collect specimens. He drew out the long feather. "It's from a barred owl. Maybe you've seen them around here? It's a large owl with a round head, no ear tufts."

The woman nodded again, sweeping a forearm above her head in a circular motion.

"Round head—right." He handed her the feather. "It's a beautiful bird. Quite striking."

"Ah-ah-ahhhh," she intoned. She lifted a finger and pointed to her eyes, then gestured to some black buttons lining the front of her dress.

"Um, I don't—"

"Bah." She pointed to the buttons and then curled her finger and thumb around her eye, peering at him from the circle.

"Yes!" Understanding swept through him. "That's correct. They have black eyes, not yellow like some other owls. Dark, very solemn."

A grin spread across her face, and she waved the feather.

She might not have speech, but she had plenty to say. "I'm glad you like it. I have a turkey feather here too. I'm sure you've seen those before." He pulled the turkey tail feather from the envelope. They weren't rare, but the pattern was striking.

She reached for it and ran her fingers over the bands of color at the tip.

"The toms use those brightly colored feathers to woo the hens. You've seen them puff up and fan their tails, right?" He tucked his hands to his chest so his elbows bowed out like turkey wings before walking a slow circle.

His antics must have pleased her, because she chortled in response, her free arm flapping at her side.

He laughed along with her, reaching into his envelope for another feather as the door opened.

Miss McCauley appeared on the doorstep, a pretty flush springing to her cheeks. "What in tarnation?"

Benton shoved the envelope into his knapsack. "I'm sorry, Miss McCauley. I didn't mean to overstep."

She stared at her sister, her mouth dropping open. "Lorna? What are you doing?"

Her sister waved the two feathers, one clamped in each fist, and turned slowly in place.

Benton cleared his throat. "I was just demonstrating—"

"The turkey trot?" Miss McCauley's befuddled expression transformed into a smile.

Why did a woman's smile never fail to make his heart jump? "Well, it certainly wasn't a foxtrot."

She watched her sister for a long moment, then shook her head. "Mr. Fuller, you surprise me. My sister don't oft take to strangers, particularly menfolk. She's . . . she's . . ."

"I grew up with a cousin who was similarly afflicted. I know the language."

Her gaze fixed on him. "Most folks think she ain't got language."

"Most don't believe birds do either." He gestured toward the woods. "Shall we go find out?"

"You talk at birds too?" Rosie hopped to the ground, also avoiding the step. "Now that'll really be something." She glanced to her sister. "Lorna, you'll be wanting to give Mr. Fuller his feathers back now."

Lorna pulled them to her chest and frowned.

"She can keep them, if she likes. I have more." It was worth the sacrifice to see these ladies smile.

• ● •

Rosie watched Mr. Fuller push through the brush, noting how careful he was not to send branches swinging toward her. Twice he'd offered a hand to help her over a steep patch, but both times she waved him off. She was as surefooted as a deer, certainly more so than this fellow.

"This is one of my favorite spots. I used to climb up here when I was a little girl." Back when she had the time for meandering.

"You're fortunate to live in such beautiful country. I spent a few summers at my grandfather's farm in North Carolina, but wasted every school year locked up in the city, pining away for the forest and the fresh air."

"My pa would turn in his grave to know what I've done with his land."

Mr. Fuller halted, turning to study her. "What do you mean?"

"He was fierce proud of this place. Of wresting it from the woods and making it produce a living." She braced a hand on a nearby oak to stay upright on the steep slope. "He's been dead just over five years, and I've gone and lost it to the government. They intend to stand by and let it go to seed." She glanced back toward the cabin, now looking small in the distance. "It's a crime. A waste."

"You mustn't think that. You're protecting the land and all that dwells upon it. The trees, the birds—even you and your sister." He paused. "I take it the park commission is allowing you to stay?"

"You make it sound like they's doing us a favor."

He opened his mouth, then closed it again, as if thinking better of it. Maybe he had more horse sense than she'd given him credit for.

"The new rules say we won't be farming, except for a small garden plot. We can't trap, hunt, cut timber—what's left, I ask you? The money they're doling out will help us to shore up the cabin and put some aside for the future. But what then? A body still has to eat." She lifted her hands toward the trees. "Scenery won't put food on the table."

"No, I suppose not."

She sighed. Why burden this man with her troubles? "Standing here won't change it none. Weren't you going to show me the owls?"

"Of course." He gestured ahead. "We're heading for that tree over there."

"You know, if you're spending time in these hills, you had ought to pick up the language. We'd say it's over *yonder*."

He smiled. "I'll work on that."

She took the lead, digging her bare toes into the soft soil as she climbed the last steep section. Placing a hand on the trunk, she glanced upward toward its spreading branches. "This one? They live here?"

He stepped up beside her. "This is where I want to build my blind."

"A blind? Like for hunting?"

"In a matter of speaking." He turned and pointed toward an old snag about twenty paces away. "The owls are nesting in a tree cavity *yonder*, as you'd say. But I need a place to observe them without being a distraction." He pulled the binoculars from his neck and passed them to her.

She lifted them to her eyes and spent some time scanning the forest. "I can't see them, anywhere. Are you sure they're there?" His hand cupped under her elbow and adjusted the angle. The hairs on her arms prickled at the sudden touch, but she managed to maintain her stance.

"You can see the nest cavity about twenty feet up. Follow the trunk line and you'll spot it. They're likely resting now, in the heat of the day. I'd hoped the male would be out sunning himself, but no such luck."

"How many of them branches up?"

Even with the field glasses pressed to her face, she could feel him moving close behind her.

"You're looking a bit too high." His arm brushed past her shoulder and took hold of her wrist, lowering the trajectory. "About there. Do you see the moss-covered limb?"

She held still as a stone, her thoughts jostling against each other at the pressure of his touch. "You mean the broken one, hanging all slaunchways?"

He remained stooped behind her but released his grip. "Yes. Now, just above that."

"Oh!" Her gaze settled on a small hole, and she drew in a quick breath. "I think . . . That wee thing?"

"Yes. They're small owls, remember. Anything too big and they'd have to fight off larger birds."

The warmth of his body vanished as he stepped clear. She fought the sudden urge to follow him, like a dance partner. It had been ages since she'd found herself in the shelter of a man's arm. A shiver raced 'cross her skin. She lowered the glasses for a moment to make sure her feet was on solid ground, not casting about on some fool daydream.

Mr. Fuller gazed up at the tree, not twitching a muscle, right blind to the fact that he'd basically wrapped his arms around her. Worse, she'd nigh swooned in response, like a character in the potboiler weeklies her friends used to giggle about at school.

Apparently she didn't have the same effect on him. She lifted the device and focused on the hole. Best she remember why she was there. Just above the crevice was an interesting pattern in the cracked bark.

"I don't think they're coming out, if that's what you're waiting for." His voice was gentle. "They probably won't be active for a few hours yet."

"I saw a face."

He stepped close again. "In the hole?"

"About three branches higher." She spun and thrust the binoculars against his chest a little harder than she intended. "Look at the bark."

He pressed the field glasses to his face.

"Do you see it? It looks like an old granny woman."

"Your grandmother looked like an owl?" His lips curved up below the binoculars.

"It's not an owl I was seeing. It's the bark above the hole—a face in the bark. Do you spy it?"

He chuckled. "I rather think it spied me."

"Leave it to one of the oldest trees on the ridge to be watching over us all. Maybe she's already keeping an eye on Hoot and Annie." A sudden shyness swept over her. She needed to get some distance from this man before she lost all her good sense. "That means you can go home to your wife and kin and leave them to theirs."

"I'm not married." His focus settled on her, a sudden intensity in his blue eyes.

"You're not?" The crack in her voice sent a flood of heat to her cheeks. This was not good. She pressed a hand to her chest.

"I'm afraid not. And I'm here to study the birdlife of the Smokies. I'm not leaving that easily."

"But you need my permission to build your blind—right?"

"I'd like your permission, yes. It would be pretty uncomfortable sitting out here at night knowing you've got that shotgun pointing my way."

Rosie paced off the distance to the hickory tree he'd pointed out as the possible location for his hidey spot. Gathering her thoughts, she placed a hand on its trunk and glanced back to the old snag. "I suppose if the granny tree don't mind, neither do I. 'Specially seeing as how Lorna took a shine to you right off."

A grin spread across his face as he walked toward her. "Thank you. You can't know how much I appreciate it, Miss McCauley."

"Iffen you're going to spy on my land, you'd best start calling me Rosie."

• • •

Rosie let herself into the house, still relaxed from her walk. It had been nice to get out into the woods and put the worries of the farm and Lorna behind her for a few minutes. Sure, they'd talked about the government's sorry plan, but at least it weren't nipping at her heels. The man was so ignorant about their situation, it had only seemed right to lay it out for him. She'd never imagined someone to be so goggle-eyed over a simple owl. No wonder he weren't married.

The house was still as the air before a storm. Lorna must be out checking on her hens.

All this talk of birds had put her in mind of something she hadn't seen in a while. Pulling a chair over to the wooden shelves, Rosie retrieved the wooden crate of Ma's keepsakes and carried it over to the table. Her folks was seldom far from her thoughts, but holding special pieces of their lives often made them seem uncomfortably close. Almost like Pa would come busting through the door and demand to know why she'd moved the precious object from its place of safety and honor.

She mightn't need her father's permission, but Rosie still glanced about before untying the moth-eaten string securing the lid in place. On top were several folded pages—the pictures she remembered. Mama had liked to draw as a girl, and the yellowed paper held several sketches of birds and flowers. Rosie ran her finger over a fine drawing of a chickadee, nest fixins clamped in its tiny beak. Maybe she should find someplace to hang it up.

She set the drawings on the table and rifled through the other items. Rosie pulled out some quilt blocks and embroidered samplers, buttons, outdated hatpins, an ivory comb—but nothing that set off any recollections. Hadn't she ought to feel more of a connection to the woman who'd borne her?

Papa always said he could sense her in every tree, every rock of the ridge that towered over their cabin, and at one point Rosie thought she could too. She'd climb the forested slopes just to be close to her. But in time, the memories had faded. She'd been up there just now, and she'd not had one passing thought about her mother.

She scooped everything back into the box, determined to banish the useless junk back to the shelf. As she lifted it, something heavy slid along the bottom and thudded to the corner. Rosie frowned and dug through the trifles again. Wrapping her fingers around the heavy object, she drew it out.

A small stone bird nestled in the palm of her hand, gazing up toward her with tiny carved eyes. Rosie's breath stalled, as if the world had come to a standstill. This figure used to grace the mantelshelf next to Pa's pipe, but she hadn't laid eyes on it in years. She ran a thumb across its smooth surface, the stone warming in her grip. Rosie's great-grandmother had carried the carving with her from the Cherokee lands when her family fled into the mountains.

The quiet of the cabin finally dragged her attention away from her quest. Where was Lorna? Hadn't she returned from caring for the chickens yet?

Rosie tucked the bird in her pocket and clambered halfway up the ladder, poking her head into the loft. It was empty, as she'd suspected. Hurrying back down, she crossed the floor, walked out onto the porch, and hollered her sister's name. The heavy afternoon air seemed to absorb the sound.

Supper weren't started, the hens cackled in the coop, the kindling hadn't been brought in for the cookstove—so many chores to do afore bedtime, and she'd have to waste time tracking her sister all over creation. Maybe she'd just gone over to Beau and Maudie's. Normally Rosie didn't worry too much about Lorna's wanderings, but after what had happened with the Samsons, she didn't want to risk a second incident.

She squeezed the stone bird in her pocket and trotted down the path toward the road, only to spy Lorna coming from the opposite direction, shuffling along with her hair blowing loose behind her.

"I thought I told you to stay put. Where have you been? Tell me you didn't go to the Samsons' place."

Her sister folded both arms over her chest, pulling her elbows tight against her midsection. Her face was flushed from exertion, but her bulky sweater remained buttoned to the neck.

Rosie's stomach tightened as she noticed the tears pooling in Lorna's eyes. "What's wrong? What are you—" She followed her sister's gaze down toward her chest. "What have you got?"

Lorna twisted away. "Naaaaah!" The tears spilled over. She crushed her arms against her middle, bending nearly in half to shield whatever she'd hidden inside her sweater.

Hadn't they just gone through this with the quilt in her bedroom? Lorna had never been so contrary before, but now everything seemed a battle. It was as if this grown woman had suddenly entered her terrible twos.

"Come now, Lorna." Rosie forced her voice down and gentled her movements. "You must be warm in that thing. Let me help."

Lorna sniffled, releasing one arm to push a dirty sleeve across her face. After a few minutes, she relaxed and let Rosie unbutton the sweater.

Scraps of loose fabric tumbled to the dirt road. "What's this?" Rosie bent down to scoop up the strips. The cotton fabric felt soft to the touch, its edges torn and frayed. She turned over a piece in her hands, the redbud blossoms setting her heart to pounding.

Her sister backed two steps, her chin wobbling.

"Oh, Lorna. You didn't." Rosie swallowed hard. "This is from the Samsons' quilt, ain't it?" She crouched, grabbing up every scrap and clutching it to her own chest, as if that could somehow meld it back into a whole. "Did you find it like this, or did you tear it?" She met her sister's blank stare. Forcing herself to slow down, Rosie stood. *Yes or no questions.* "Was it like this when you found it?"

Lorna tucked her lower lip betwixt her teeth and made her cheeks puff in and out. It was a game she played when she was nervous.

Horace would be livid. His mama's quilt. There was no repairing the damage. The most anyone could do would be to restitch it into something new, but that wouldn't replace the item her sister had destroyed. A thorn buried itself in Rosie's chest. If Mr. Samson had railed about Lorna before, this would only throw fuel on the fire.

She grabbed Lorna's hand. "Come on. Let's get home so I can think." She pulled her sister behind her a few steps, before Lorna set her brakes.

"Naaaah. Na nuh-uh." Lorna stomped a foot in the dust.

"You can't stay out here. Once the Samsons discover what you've done . . ." She couldn't bear to finish the sentence.

Her sister backed farther before turning and hightailing it into the woods.

Rosie blew out a frustrated breath. Maybe it was for the best. If Lorna made herself scarce for a few hours, it'd give everyone time to simmer down.

# 5

## Nashville
Present Day

Kieran wiped her hands on her apron before delivering four plates to the waiting customers, the heady smell of bacon and coffee seeping into every pore of her skin. If only she could absorb the caffeine rush in the same fashion.

The older man tapped his coffee cup. "I'm still waiting on some cream, when you get a chance"

"Of course. I'll be back in a jiffy." Kieran headed for the kitchen. *Jiffy*. She really needed to spend more time with people her own age. Between SeniorCo, the diner, and the retirement home, she was even starting to talk like a senior citizen.

Warm air rushed over her as she entered the kitchen.

"How's it looking out there?" Nick glanced up from where he and Ash were shoulder to shoulder at the grill. "Is it slowing down at all?"

She resisted the urge to wipe a hand across her brow. "I think we're on the downhill side. You've got a four-top just seated, but they're all having the special, plus one order of shrimp and grits. So I think that might be it for a while."

"I just put on some more grits." Ash reached for a clean spoon. "I'm glad you could fill in this morning. Two servers were no-shows."

"I'm happy to do it." She could use all the hours the pair could throw at her now that SeniorCo was late with paychecks. "Need me to stay through lunch?" She tucked a handful of creamer cups into her apron pocket.

"James and Connor will be here any minute. I don't want to keep you all day." Ashleigh plated two more specials and slid them across the counter. "Hey, your phone's been vibrating over there on the shelf. You should probably check it."

"I will. Just let me deliver these." Kieran rushed the plates out to table two, dropped off the promised creamer, and let the new table know someone would be right with them. Back in the kitchen, she snatched up her phone. Five messages from Sycamore Terrace? Her chest tightened. She pushed the Voicemail button with trembling fingers.

Laura Bradford, the facility director, apparently hadn't bothered to wait for the beep ". . . And the staff is searching the property. But as you know, that wing is not a secure unit. Residents are allowed to walk the halls and courtyard freely, but we don't lock the doors and prevent them from leaving to run errands. It's time we discussed—"

Kieran ducked into the storeroom. Fumbling to dial the facility, she pressed the phone to her ear.

The director didn't bother to say hello. "I've been trying to reach you."

"Did you find her?"

Laura's voice faltered. "No, but the police have been notified—"

"The police?" She grabbed on to a shelf for support.

"She's been gone several hours, I'm afraid. I felt it best." She paused. "Kieran, we've spoken before about moving your grandmother to a memory-care unit. This is exactly what I feared might happen. For now let's focus on finding her and ensuring she's safe. Do you know any places she might go?"

"She doesn't know that neighborhood very well. But I'm on my way to help search."

Ending the call, she sagged against the shelving unit. Where would Gran go? Was she still thinking about the store? The library? Or was she heading home to the Smokies, like she'd threatened? It seemed unlikely that anyone would pick up a confused, hitchhiking old lady.

Ash met her at the door with her things. "I couldn't help overhearing. Nick's grabbing his keys."

Kieran straightened, tears blurring her eyes. "I can't ask you to—"

"We're your friends, and he's got a sixth sense for this sort of thing. James is already serving your tables. Go find Granny Mac. Let me know what happens."

Nick appeared behind her. "I used to locate hostages in enemy strongholds. I think I can find one little old gal wandering the streets of Nashville."

She didn't deserve friends like these. Clutching her keys, she pushed out the door and hurried toward the parking lot. "Oh, wait. My car is full of . . ." She stopped at the curb. "I-I was going to the laundromat later." The thought of Nick and Ash knowing she'd lost her apartment seemed like one more failure than she could manage today.

"Is your washer broken again? You should have called." He walked over to the small car and peered in the windows. His brows drew down. "This is a little more than laundry. Are you moving? You're not bugging out without telling us, are you?"

"No, nothing like that. Just cleaning out a few things." Kieran twisted the strap on her purse as she looked at the overstuffed vehicle with fresh eyes. She looked like a hoarder. You could hardly see in the rear window.

"We'll take my truck."

Twenty minutes later, Kieran clutched the edge of the seat in Nick's Tahoe. They'd stopped at the assisted living center and talked with the police, but it seemed obvious that no one had done even a cursory search of the neighborhood yet.

"She's on foot, so she won't get far." Nick kept one hand clamped on the steering wheel, the other elbow resting on the window frame.

He'd said that four times at least, but the bigger the circles they made, the more Kieran felt sick to her stomach. What if Gran had called a taxi? Or taken a ride with a stranger? She might be in one of the hundreds of little cafés or shops, and they'd never know it. "I shouldn't have involved you in this. You have a business to run."

He shot her a wounded glance. "You know what your problem is, Kieran?"

"Just one?" She clung to the truck's armrest as she leaned forward to peer down an alley.

"You keep folks at arm's length. You won't ask for help. In fact, you won't even gracefully accept help when it's offered."

"That's three problems."

"Ashleigh and I would do anything for you, because we think of you as family. And you've spent countless hours helping us at the diner. Why do you do that?"

She shifted on the massive seat. "It's your guys' dream."

"Well, it's *my* dream." He chuckled, guiding the truck around another right turn, keeping to a methodical pattern. "But you see a need, and you fill it. Just like your work at SeniorCo. How much are they paying you?"

*Nothing at the moment.* "It's pretty minimal. But my seniors, they need me. No one should be living out on the streets in their seventies and eighties."

"No one should be out on the street in their twenties either." His gaze didn't budge from the windshield, but his tone was clear.

"I'm fine. I'm just . . . between situations, is all."

"So let me understand. You help others. You also take care of your grandmother, pretty much single-handedly." His fingers tightened on the steering wheel. "The Bible says, 'Bear one another's burdens.' It doesn't say, 'Take care of everyone else and never ask for anything yourself.'"

"I'm a doer. I'm self-sufficient." Even as the halfhearted words slipped out of her mouth, Kieran knew she was fighting a losing battle.

Nick made another turn, heading into a sketchy neighborhood. "Self-sufficiency is nothing but pride on steroids. And trust me, I know. Pride's my number one stumbling block. Thankfully, I've got Ash."

Hearing the loving tone enter this soldier's voice when he spoke her friend's name warmed Kieran all the way through. "She keeps you humble?"

"Someone's got to." He shot a glance at Kieran. "And she's going to be angrier than a mound of fire ants when she finds out you've been living in your car and haven't told her. How long's that been going on?"

Kieran leaned against the window. "A few weeks. Five or six."

"*Six weeks?*" He scrubbed a hand over his mouth, as if to stop the flow of words. "When we get done here, I'm picking up your stuff. We've got a spare room with your name on it."

She turned her eyes toward the run-down playground on their right even as she fought against tears. The peeling paint on the climbing structure spoke to the income level of the neighborhood. Trouble was, she couldn't afford a studio apartment here, even working as hard as she did. How did families make it?

A woman sat huddled on a park bench in the far corner, staring at the empty swings. The familiar orange beret tipped sideways on the gray head sent Kieran's hand reaching for the door handle. "Stop, Nick. Stop!"

He hit the brakes, the vehicle bouncing with the sudden halt. "What?"

Kieran threw the door open and slid the distance to the pavement below. Sprinting across the sidewalk, she darted into the park. "Granny Mac?"

Gran turned her head, a blank expression on her face. "Can I help you, dear one? Are you lost?"

Sinking down beside her grandmother, she reached for her hand. Gran's fingers were cold to the touch. "Gran, what are you doing here?"

Nick had evidently found a place to park the truck, because he came up behind them, standing a fair distance away so as not to intrude.

Gran pulled off the crocheted hat. "I was looking for someone. But then I couldn't remember why, so I kept walking until I figured it out." She placed her other hand on top of Kieran's. "My ma's stone bird, I recollected where Pa left it. He buried it beside our cabin, right up next to the chimney, with a big flat stone on top." She sighed. "I reckoned I'd go back and get it when he weren't looking, but he took us away that same day."

"Gran, that was a long time ago."

"I had ought to get it afore it's too late. Mama said it taught her to fly free. I never knowed what she meant." Gran's soft mountain accent deepened whenever she stepped into her memories.

A raindrop splashed on the bench between them, and Kieran glanced up at the clouds. "My friend has his truck here. Let us give you a ride home."

Gran tightened her grip. "Yes, home."

She probably meant the Smokies again, but Kieran took advantage of the sudden compliance. She helped Granny Mac to her feet. "And no more wandering off on your own. You scared me to death. And Laura Bradford at the center too."

"Psh, Laura. I told her I needed to go home, but would she listen? Course not." Gran shuffled next to Kieran. "She don't know her knee from her elbow, that woman."

Nick approached, reaching a hand to her grandmother. "Mrs. Fuller, it's good to finally meet you. I'm—"

"Robert, when did you get home?" She bypassed his offered hand and latched straight on to his elbow, her smile stretching wider than Kieran had ever seen it. "Shame on you for not telephoning from the airfield. I would have come to get you."

Kieran's emotions went into a tailspin. Robert had died in the Gulf

War. *The good son.* She caught Nick's gaze over the top of Gran's head. "My uncle."

Nick put his arm around Gran and led her to the truck. "Well, we're all heading home now, aren't we? I think we might even get there before this storm completely breaks loose."

• • •

Zach clamped the pencil between his teeth, rubbing a hand against his stiff neck muscles and breathing in the intoxicating scent of fresh-cut lumber. He'd woken up with a crick in his neck, either from his worn-out pillow or from spending yesterday stuck at his desk. He wasn't going to let it stop him from getting in a couple of hours of work on the remodel before lunch.

He made the two necessary cuts and shut off the table saw. As the whine slowed to a stop, he could finally hear his phone blasting out his favorite playlist as it sat balanced on the windowsill.

"Seriously, dude. You need to warn a guy before you start that thing up at the crack of dawn." Miguel stood in the doorway, clad in sweatpants and a stained tee, his dark hair askew.

"Crack of dawn?" Zach snatched up his phone and lowered the volume. "It's ten thirty. I'm sorry, but I thought you were out on the trail already." His friend had made a habit of crashing on the lumpy mattress in Zach's rental cottage when he was off duty. Or what would be a rental someday. Right now it was little more than an outbuilding with serious dry-rot issues.

"I'm heading out at three and spending the night at one of the Appalachian Trail camps. There was talk of a rogue bear, so a buddy and I are making sure everything's square before they start letting campers back in."

Zach reached for the two-by-fours he'd cut. "That makes you, what—the bait?"

"Better than some hapless through-hiker. At least we know what we're in for."

Zach cradled the boards against his chest, appreciating the weight of it in his hands. Something about cut wood just felt . . . real. "Did you want me to knock off a while so you can get more sleep?"

Miguel ran a hand through his shaggy bed head. "Nah, I needed to get moving anyway. You mind if I grab a shower over at your place?"

"Door's open."

"I'm going to regret when you actually finish this shack and I have to find my own housing."

"I'll be glad of the income." Zach reached for a box of nails.

"About that—"

"I'm not charging you. No heat? No running water? I'd be the worst kind of slumlord."

"There are probably people who would pay for a view like this, even without the amenities." Miguel shuffled over to the window.

Zach had bought the property based on the view and the proximity to the park. Even though the roof leaked and the wiring was suspect—even in the main house—it was worth every penny to wake up to that view each morning. And once he got the rental up to code, it would help cover the mortgage payments. But first he had to build that bathroom. And finish about two hundred other little things. He reached for his water bottle. "And someday they will. But for now it's yours."

"Well, you're on your own for a few nights. I won't be back until Wednesday at the earliest. If you—you know—wanted to have a girl over or something."

Zach choked on his mouthful of water but managed to get it down. "Not likely. But thanks for the heads-up."

# 6

## Great Smoky Mountains National Park
## 1932

Rosie spread the torn shreds of fabric across her kitchen table, her stomach churning. What would she tell the Samsons? If Eb Samson thought Lorna needed to be locked away before, what must he be thinking now? She fell into the chair and stared at the tiny buds dancing across the fabric. Obviously this quilt meant something to Lorna. But what?

"Rosie-girl? You home?" A holler came from outside the yard.

She rose to her feet and peered out the front window. Will. *Thank goodness it's not Horace.* She walked to the open door. "Come on in."

The man ducked through the low doorway, pulling his hat from his head and pressing it to his chest. His hair was flattened down, sticking to the perspiration on his brow. The grim expression testified to the trouble brewing at their place.

She waved him to the table. "Sit a spell. I'll put the kettle on. I think I might be guessing why you come by."

He cast a dark look at the torn quilt blocks. "I 'spect you do." Pulling out a chair, he plopped down and spread his dusty boots out in front of him. "I'd hoped I was wrong."

Rosie filled the pot, her thoughts capering about like chipmunks. She settled the water on the cookstove and added a log to the fire. It was a hot day already, but tea sounded more soothing and neighborly than spring water about now. If it got too warm, they could escape to the porch rockers. She took the seat across from Will, afraid to lift her eyes to his face. Instead, she reached for one of the scraps, rolling it between her fingers. "I don't know what happened. I asked Lorna, but—"

"But she can't tell you nothing."

She glanced up, the heavy emotion in his voice catching her by surprise. "No. Can you?"

"Me?" His pale eyes were almost luminescent in the dim light of the kitchen. "She never caused us no trouble afore. Comes to pet the goats all the time, and I sort of like having her round. But Pa and Horace . . ." He pressed his lips together. "They run her off."

"She never meant no harm—you must know that." Rosie glanced at the scraps on the table. At least, she hadn't before this.

"The girl's gentle as a piglet." He swept his good hand over his mouth and nose. "A mite slow, perhaps. But that never bothered me none."

Rosie managed to relax a pinch. Will had more understanding in his little finger than the rest of his kin lumped together. "God made her different, is all. Leastways, that's what my Pa always said. Do you've any idea why Lorna's set such a fixation on this quilt?"

"I think that's my fault. You won't tell Horace or my pa?" His brows gathered inward, and a long moment passed in silence. "Our nanny goat had them two li'l kids last month. I let Lorna haul them around, wrapped up in it. It was foolish of me, knowing how my Pa is. Horace caught her with it and scairt the living tar outta her. It's causing all sorts of grief now, ain't it?"

"Seems to be." If only she'd made up some biscuits or something, she'd have a peace offering for the Samsons. "Look, maybe I can fix it. Stitch it back together or something. I'm not real handy with a needle, but—"

"Rosie." Will sat forward. "You're mistook 'bout this. It weren't Lorna who tore the quilt."

She stopped, her mind scrambling to catch up. "What?"

"Horace spotted her lift it from the fence. When she wouldn't hand it over, he got all high tempered and knocked her down afore I could stop him. He took a hunting knife to the quilt, right in front of her, saying it would stop her from coming round. I didn't realize she had come back for the pieces."

"But I thought he loved the quilt." Rosie poured out the tea, a fluttering rising up in her chest.

"I guess he hates Lorna more. Or how she is, rather."

"He and your pa, they was talking . . ." She paused, trying to still the tremor in her voice. "They was talking about having Lorna put away. I can't let that happen."

He reached across the table and touched her hand. "I don't want that neither. Mebbe you could keep her at home 'stead of letting her wander about? Leastways, for a time."

"Do I lock the doors? Or build a corral like we did for the hog? Maybe hobble her like an errant mule?"

"No, but—" Will sat back and blew out a frustrated breath. "But betwixt you and me and the fence post, if we don't work out something, I can't guarantee what Pa's gonna do next time he catches her up at our place."

A shadow on the porch caught their attention, and Rosie jumped to her feet.

Lorna appeared in the open doorway. When her eyes locked on their neighbor, the color drained from her face. She scrambled backward off the porch and out into the yard, squealing the whole way.

Rosie pushed through the screen so hard it slammed closed behind her like a shotgun blast. "Lorna, come back!"

She was too late. Her sister was gone from sight, her voice trailing off through the trees.

Will came out to stand next to Rosie. "I'm sorry. She never used to be so afeared of me. We was friends."

Rosie slid her hand into her apron pocket and closed her fingers around the stone bird, rubbing her thumb across its worn-smooth curves. There seemed to be a heap load of *used tos* with Lorna these days. "I'd best go after her."

"I'd lend a hand, but I reckon you'd be better off without me."

The man's wry smile pulled at her heart. At one time she'd thought Will Samson might be the answer to all of life's problems. He'd proved her wrong long ago with his moonshining and drinkin' and all, but at least he was a decent friend.

• • •

Benton sat with his back propped against the hickory snag, head tipped to feel the filtered sun on his cheeks. With his eyes closed, he sorted through the birdsongs infusing the forest with sound. Mixed with the gentle rustling of the foliage and the distant trickle from the creek, these mountains were better than any concert hall.

The undergrowth crunched down by the stream. Benton hooked his glasses over his ears and sat up.

Rosie's sister came barreling through the woods, like the devil was on her heels. Her breaths came ragged, as if she'd already run off the worst of her terror. Had something happened at the cabin?

Benton pushed to his feet, using the trunk for support. "Miss McCauley?"

She stumbled to a halt, her eyes locking on to him. Retreating a few steps, the incline of the hill caused her to trip. She went down hard and rolled twice.

He rushed forward to assist, but she pulled away from his grip, her eyes and mouth wide. "Nah-nah-nah . . ."

"Whoa, I'm not going to hurt you." He held up his hands, palms outward. "Is everything all right at home? Your sister?"

Lorna pulled up to her knees and curved forward over them, like a supplicant at prayer. Her voice careened skyward, transforming into a whimpering caterwaul.

The sound drove up the hairs on the back of his neck. He dropped beside her, his hands pressing against the dirt. "Shh, it's all right. No one will hurt you." As her sobs slowed, he reached for his pack, looking for something to distract her. "Remember the feathers? Do you want to see them again?" Benton drew out the manila envelope. He'd been collecting them for some time, adding interesting ones as he came across them. None were particularly rare specimens, just ones that caught his fancy.

Lorna pulled both legs beneath her and used the hem of her dress to wipe her face before reaching for the packet.

"Wait—" He pulled it back. "One at a time. Open your hands."

She followed his instructions without a peep, cupping her palms together and holding them out like a child asking for a scrap of bread. So she understood basic directions. Whatever her issues, Lorna wasn't completely without intelligence.

"First, is your sister all right? Is she well?"

The woman nodded, pushing her hands forward.

Benton's pulse slowed a bit. Drawing a small feather from the envelope, he laid it in her trembling palm. "This is one of the downy feathers. They trap warm air and keep the bird from getting cold."

She pulled her hand in to rub her opposite elbow, like one did when chilled.

"Yes. It keeps them warm. Are you warm enough?"

Lorna nodded, though he could see goose bumps rippling down her arms.

He dug in the pouch and took out a striped contour feather. "These are the outside feathers. They overlap like the shingles on your roof." He passed it to her. "That's how birds can stay out in the rain and not get soaked."

She lifted it to her face. Running a finger down the shaft, the barbs pulled apart giving the feather a jagged-toothed appearance. She whimpered and pushed it back toward Benton.

"Don't worry. Let me show you." He ran the feather between his finger and thumb. "They weave together like so. See? The birds can fix them with their beaks."

Lorna explored the repaired barbs, tugging gently at the vane to pull them apart a second time and repair them herself.

Studying her, he couldn't help but notice the similarities between Lorna and her sister. The family resemblance was uncanny, but that was as far as it went. Rosie was quick-witted and pragmatic, but a flash of . . . *something* . . . blazed in Lorna's brown eyes as she fumbled with the items he'd handed her. Interest? Fascination?

People were so quick to cast off individuals like his cousin and Lorna because they didn't live up to certain expectations. If only they took the time to truly see them for what lay inside. Precious sparks of life. That was it. It was *life* that shone in her gaze.

Lorna fumbled in the pocket of her apron and drew out some cloth scraps. With a frown, she thrust them toward him.

He took the pieces. "What is this?"

She gestured toward the feather, sliding her fingers along the barbs, then pointed at the torn cloth. "Bah-bah-bah," she chanted.

He glanced at the pieces, the frayed edges indeed reminding him of the feathers. "Um, no. I don't think—"

She swung her hand and knocked the scraps from his grip. Tears spilled down over her cheeks. "Nya-aaah."

A woman's voice called Lorna's name from a distance, the sound carrying through the trees like birdsong.

Lorna pulled her arms about herself and tucked her head. A soft moaning escaped her lips as she rocked in place.

"Is it your sister?" Rising, he glanced downhill to see if he could spot Rosie. He reached for the envelope and pulled out a fistful of feathers. "Lorna, here—look at all of these. I'm going to walk down the hill for a minute, but I'll be back. Will you keep these safe for me?"

She opened one eye, her moans fading.

"That's right. You stay here. Will you do that?"

She nodded, even as fresh tears streamed down her reddened cheeks. Lorna pulled the odd pile of plumage into her lap, the browns and grays melding with the blue of her dress.

He might have only moments before Rosie called out again and sent Lorna back into hysterics. He trotted down the trail. A fat drop of rain splatted on the edge of his hat, followed by another. He glanced up at the darkening sky. They were going to get soaked, that was certain.

Rosie appeared out of a laurel thicket just as he rounded the bend. "Benton?" Her face lit. "I didn't know you were still here."

"Are you looking for your sister? She's over there." He gestured with one arm. "She seemed upset, so I've been sitting with her."

"Yes, one of our neighbors . . . We've had some trouble. It's been a difficult day, I'm afraid."

As they walked up the hill together, rain plopped about them, bouncing off the leaves and soaking the ground. Benton pushed through the damp brush, backtracking to where he had left Lorna. She sat with her back against the tree. The woman's eyes were screwed shut with such intensity, wrinkles splayed out on either side of her face and up her brow. She gripped a single feather in her fingers, drawing circles on her cheek with the soft end.

Rosie sighed and touched Benton's arm, as if issuing a request.

He stood a good distance away as Rosie kneeled in front of her sister. Her shoulders curved forward, speaking in hushed tones he couldn't decipher.

Lorna's expression softened. Dropping the feather to her lap, she tapped her chest several times with her fingertips.

Rosie replicated the gesture and helped Lorna to her feet. "Mr. Fuller, thank you for your kindness." She lifted a hand to shield her face from the increasing raindrops. "Would you join us for supper?"

"I planned to head to the Wonderland Club in Elkmont. That's where I'm staying. It's a bit of a walk."

One corner of her mouth quirked up. "Why don't you come with us, at least until this storm passes." She glanced at her sister. "Lorna does seem to like you."

At least he'd won one of them over. "I'm honored. Thank you. I'll grab my things and be right behind you."

"Bah-bah." Lorna waved the envelope of feathers, a smile lighting her face.

Benton chuckled. "You've got that for me, do you? Thank you, Lorna." He should have realized she wouldn't give up the feathers that easily.

• • •

The rain had slowed to a gentle patter by the time Rosie balanced the empty bucket on her hip, watching the pig gobble the kitchen scraps mixed with some corn. There hadn't been much left from supper since she'd already thinned the stew with some water and added a couple mealy potatoes to make it stretch for the three of them. But Benton's enthusiastic response to the food had warmed her right through.

Benton and Lorna sat on the porch, enjoying the quiet evening, but Rosie had grabbed on to the idea of chores to secure a moment to herself. Having a guest was a rare pleasure, but it also set her nerves a-jumpin'. She didn't know how to act around the man. He didn't seem put off by their simple fare or their home, but she couldn't help seeing every speck of dirt and loose board in the cabin.

Rosie glanced over her shoulder to make sure neither was watching her before she grabbed the wooden fence post and gave it a shake, checking its stability. Losing their winter meat supply was not an option. At least the bees were producing nicely.

She rubbed a hand over her arm to rid herself of the unease their guest stirred deep inside her. What mattered was keeping Lorna safe, not impressing some man who'd never lifted a hammer or butchered a pig. There might be money in the bank now, but Rosie had every intention of making it last. She'd withdrawn enough to purchase some basic roof supplies, but the rest would be for emergencies. She'd find some other way to provide.

Something other than what the Samsons proposed. Stills on her land? *Never again.*

"Rosie?" Benton's voice sounded behind her. "Can I lend you a hand?"

"That's right kind of you, but I think I got it." The idea made her smile. What would he know about hogs?

He folded his arms across his chest. "I really ought to be going since the rain has let up. I do appreciate your hospitality."

She hung the bucket's handle over the fence post and glanced up to where dusk crept across the ridge, swathing the forest in near darkness. "It's too late for you to make it back to the Wonderland Club. You'll be tripping over your feet."

"I agree. I thought I'd watch the owls for a bit until it got too dark to see. Then I'll bed down until morning."

"You shouldn't have to sleep rough." It weren't neighborly to send a body off into the night without someplace to rest his head. But where could she put him? The indecision only lasted a heartbeat. "You'll stay with us for tonight."

He met her eyes for a long moment before glancing down at his shoes. "I've imposed enough, don't you think? You let me traipse over your land, brought me home for supper, and allowed me to wait out the rain."

"Horsefeathers. You don't know us mountain folk well if you think I'd let you saunter off like that. We take pride in our hospitality, remember?"

"It seems like you take pride in a lot of things."

The man's teasing smile sent a quiver through her. She folded her arms, pressing them hard against her ribs. Why were her hands trembling? Pa always said she was tough as a pine knot. "Then you understand it'd vex me iffen you refuse. I can share the loft with Lorna. We used to do it as girls, anyhow."

Benton shifted his weight between his feet. "I don't think it'd be proper, Rosie. People might talk."

"Folks are going to jaw no matter. It's what they do. I've never paid that no nevermind."

"I tell you what." He rubbed his chin. "I'll spend tonight with the owls. But I won't turn down a hot breakfast in the morning if you're cooking. That stew was remarkable. Much better than the food at the hotel."

She managed to choke down a laugh. Wonderland Club's chef would have been shocked at her use of sprouted potatoes. The garden best start producing soon. "All right, then. Eggs and hotcakes. And homegrown honey." She glanced down at the pig. "The bacon'll have to wait till Brownie here packs on a few more pounds."

"Sounds delicious." He grinned. "The thought of that honey will keep me warm all night long."

• • •

Benton rolled over, water squelching from his blanket. He'd obviously tossed off the oilcloth at some point during the night, likely before it started raining again. By the time he'd realized his error, he was wet through. Another shiver coursed through him. It might be spring, but yesterday's rainstorm had rinsed the air of the day's heat. With dry clothes, it might have been fine. Sopping wet and half-frozen, he spent the wee hours regretting his refusal of the McCauley sisters' hospitality. He could have slept in the chicken coop and been more comfortable than this.

He scooted into a sitting position and retrieved his eyeglasses, rubbing the lenses against his damp shirttail. Dawn was breaking over the distant ridge, but the hollow below was still wrapped in darkness. How early was too early to show up for breakfast? The fact that he couldn't even see the cabin in the morning gloom suggested he had a while to wait.

He struggled to his feet, kicking free of the damp bedroll. A good hike would stoke his inner furnace. Jumping up and down, he flapped his arms like a fledgling testing its wings. He gathered the sodden blanket and gave it a good shake before spreading it over a bush to drip dry. Sunrise from the ridgetop might make the uncomfortable night worthwhile.

By the time he made it to the viewpoint, early morning light spilled over the world, the colors spreading through the treetops like a kicked-over bucket of paint. These were the moments he lived for. The long months stuck in the classroom faded whenever he stood on this hallowed ground. Here one could feel alive, like the first person to ever draw a breath of mountain air.

Trouble was, he wasn't alone. A sour-faced man stepped out from behind the trees, a rifle braced over a forearm. His hat hung low over his eyes. "Who're you?"

Benton locked his knees rather than step back. "Name's Benton Fuller. You?"

The fellow cleared his throat and spit at the ground near Benton's feet. He swiped a wrist over his chin to catch any loose spittle. "Revenuer?"

These mountain folks were quick to assume the worst about strangers. Did that suggest guilt or just a general distrust of government?

"No." Benton instinctively pulled his hands from his jacket pockets in case he needed to defend himself. Not that they'd be of much use against a gun. "I'm a scientist. I'm doing a bird study for the park service."

The mountain man's lip curled. "You ain't wasting no time, are you? The ink's hardly dry on the parchment and you're fixing to lay claim to what the government's taken."

"I'm here to do a job. I don't mean to cause any trouble." Benton unbuttoned his coat, the brisk walk having worked up enough heat to make him sweat. "And your name is?"

"Samson." The man gestured with his head back toward the hollow. "Horace Samson. Live over yonder."

"I thought this was Rosie McCauley's land."

Mr. Samson growled low, like a wolf. "You know Rosie?"

The hairs lifted on Benton's arms. The man's rifle remained pointed at his chest. If he answered wrong, his body could end up lost in these woods forever and no one would be the wiser. "Miss McCauley has granted me permission to survey her land for birdlife."

"That so?" A single eyebrow crooked upward. "Don't sound like her. She don't like *furriners* about."

"I'm sure she appreciates you looking out for her and her sister. Are you a neighbor?"

Samson ignored the question and used the barrel to gesture down the hill. "What's say we pay the woman a visit and see if she vouches for this tale of yourn. I'm guessing she don't know you from Adam's house cat." The scowl left little room for negotiation.

"She's expecting me this morning anyhow." A risky assertion, but he threw it out there regardless.

A strangled sound came from the man's throat, somewhere between a laugh and a huff of disbelief. He jerked his head toward the path, black stringy hair flopping across his shoulder.

Benton started off down the hill, Samson staying several feet behind, as if he might catch some exotic disease from this outsider. The men walked in silence even as the morning birdsong continued unhindered. It seemed the feathered company couldn't be bothered with the fact that Benton was being death-marched down the ridge at gunpoint. Dr. Hayden had bragged about brushes with spear-bearing Amazonian natives, but was this really so different?

Before entering the McCauley yard, Benton swiped a hand through his hair and resettled his fedora. His rough night and equally harrowing morning couldn't have done much for his appearance, and the last thing he wished was to drag in here looking like an apprehended fugitive.

"Arright, stop right there, G-man. Hey, Rosie, you home?" he bellowed across the clearing.

Benton sighed. Whatever happened to politely knocking on a door? Little wonder they called these places "hollers."

The screen creaked open, and Rosie appeared, cupping a hand over her brow to see out into the bright morning sun. "Horace?" When her gaze settled on Benton, her eyes widened. "What's all this?"

Benton managed to push a smile to his face. "I'm here for breakfast. Didn't expect an armed escort, though."

She scowled. "Horace, put that down this instant. Mr. Fuller is my guest."

Samson tucked the rifle up against his shoulder like a minuteman. "When did you get friendly with the government, Rosie? You've been one of the loudest voices against the park. Now you're cozying up to the enemy since you signed that lease?"

"I'd rather have a government birdwatcher on my land than a moonshiner any day." She grabbed a handful of her apron and straightened her spine. "I thank you for looking out for us, for me and for *Lorna*." The emphasis on her sister's name was unmistakable. "But as you can see, we'uns are just fine."

"I'd best be going, then. Got to check the traplines."

"It was a pleasure to make your acquaintance, Mr. Samson." Benton tipped his hat, not bothering to keep the sarcasm from his voice.

Rosie watched as the meddling neighbor slouched out of the yard. "Checking traplines on *my* land, most like." She turned to Benton, the lines around her eyes softening. "Good morning, Mr. Fuller. I trust you slept well."

The tenderness in her voice melted him like candle wax. "I wish I could say I had."

"I couldn't help worrying after you. You ought to have stayed."

"I'll never argue with you again. I have paid for my folly." He followed her up onto the porch and through the door. The kitchen was empty. "Is your sister out doing chores?"

"We did those hours ago." She removed a stout mug from a nearby shelf and grabbed the percolator off the cookstove. "Once she heard Horace's voice, Lorna hightailed it up the ladder into the loft." She tipped her head toward the corner, where the ladder disappeared into a hole in the ceiling. "She's afeared of most menfolk lately."

"But not of me?"

"Can't say as I understand, but that seems to be the case." Rosie tipped the steaming liquid into the cup.

Benton walked over to the ladder and peered up. "Lorna?" He waited for an answer that never came. "I hope she's all right."

"She's fine. Once she calms down, she'll appear, like nothing happened."

He returned to the table, pulled out a chair, and sat across from her. "But you said she hasn't always been like this?"

Rosie filled a plate and passed it to Benton. "She used to like visitin'. She'd practically fly down the road to meet folks as they walked past, grinning like a possum the whole way. So many things are a guessing game with her. I've known her all my life, but she still finds ways to surprise me."

He breathed in the heady fragrance of fried eggs and hotcakes. "Meeting Mr. Samson up on the ridgeline was enough of a surprise for me today."

"Horace Samson's akin to sandpaper—useful at times, but definitely rough around the edges. Even so, he and his brother are good workers. They wrested their rough patch of ground into a showpiece farm, put in long hours with some of the logging operations, and now are helping with the roadbuilding." She shot a glance toward the window. "And they've been known to run various other *businesses* on the side."

He couldn't mistake the sudden shift in her tone. "Like what?"

"Anything that could make money. The rule round here is, as long as it ain't hurting no one, it's fair game."

The creaking of the ladder put a halt to their conversation. Lorna lowered her bare feet to the floor and sniffed the air like a greedy pup.

"Good morning, my friend." He shifted in his seat so he could see her better. "Are you hungry?"

Rosie hopped up to fill another plate. "It plumb amazes me that she doesn't mind you being here. Treats you almost like a member of the family."

It had been ages since he'd been part of a family. Sitting here over the breakfast table swept him back to the lazy summers with his grandparents. His prestigious education had opened doors for him that he'd never thought possible, and yet now all he longed for was those simpler times. And belonging.

Rosie flitted about the room like a goldfinch. He'd never met anyone quite like her before. His heart quickened at the thought, but just as rapidly he grabbed it back. He was here to study, not to get overly sentimental about the mountain folk.

They were on opposite sides of a battle that was raging for control of these hills, and there was little question that the government would win.

And for the first time since he'd become involved in the project, that fact made him sad.

# 7

## Great Smoky Mountains National Park
## Present Day

Zach pried off the crumbling sheetrock, hoping no toxic mold lurked behind the surface. The deeper he got into the project, the more he understood why the former owners had boarded up the place.

The circa 1960s wallpaper had come down with some steam and elbow grease, only to expose water damage hidden beneath. While patching the roof last fall, he'd discovered an entire colony of little brown bats in the rafters. Miguel had helped him safely evict the tiny winged creatures, but the mess left behind? A nightmare.

He dug the pry bar behind a stud and gave it a mighty heave, the wood shrieking as it gave way. The good thing about demolition was that you could work out your aggressions and not worry about breaking anything. Back in high school, he'd spent a couple of summers working for his contractor uncle, and demo had been his specialty. Want to keep a sixteen-year-old boy out of trouble? Hand him a wrecking bar and lock him in a bathroom.

His uncle had expected Zach to get his contractor's license one day, but by the time he'd hit college, Zach's passions had veered to history and archaeology. It had been tough to explain to Uncle Karl why he was trading his reciprocating saw and sledgehammer for an unpaid intern position on an archaeological dig. The man lived for building homes and tearing them down—not just in his professional life but in his personal one too. He'd demolished every relationship with his own hands, including his marriage. The memory turned in Zach's stomach alongside the day-old takeout he'd scarfed down for breakfast. After all the mentoring his uncle had lavished on him, the life lessons had been the hardest to swallow.

*When I build a home with someone, it will last.*

Two hours later, freshly showered and dressed in his park service uniform, Zach pulled into the Collections Preservation Center just outside the park's Townsend entrance. He had a slew of paperwork to process today, and he still needed to finish the latest reports on the remaining Elkmont structures.

He pushed open the glass doors, relishing how the rush of chilled air chased away the day's stickiness. In twenty minutes he'd be shivering, but for right now it felt awesome. The archive housed a massive collection of artifacts, photographs, and paperwork regarding the park's history. Except for the temperature—a constant 65 degrees and 30 percent humidity for optimal preservation—digging through the acid-free storage boxes reminded him of his days in the Mojave with pick and brush.

Zach dropped into the rolling chair and opened the laptop. A lingering odor of mildew and dust wafted over from a stack of decomposing cardboard boxes taking up valuable real estate in the far corner of his office. If he managed to get through all this work, maybe he could finally tackle cataloging the family papers and black-and-white photos donated by the Ownby estate. It would be nice to tick something off his ever-expanding list.

A soft knock sounded at the open door. "Hey, Zach. I just sent you a list of contacts regarding the new display at Oconaluftee. Mike wants you to do a fact-check before they finalize the text for the new signage." Marley, his intern, took a few hesitant steps into his office. "I told Sean you could get that back to them by tomorrow. Plus he wants to talk to you about the Native American pipe a visitor brought by and find out if there are any legal issues he should be aware of."

So much for the boxes. "I can do that."

She leaned one hand on his desk and tipped her head, letting her red curls cascade over one shoulder. "Any plans for the weekend?"

Sure, he had a hot date with a pry bar. He clicked open his email to retrieve the message she'd sent. "I'm remodeling, so I've got plenty of work."

"That doesn't sound like much fun."

He could almost feel her gaze. The intern had been hinting her interest for several weeks running, but so far he'd blocked every advance. Even if he wasn't her direct supervisor, he'd sworn off casual dating for a time. It wasn't worth the risk. "It depends on your idea of fun, I suppose."

"Do you need some help maybe? I'm sure you could teach me a few things about tools and stuff. I'm a quick study."

"Hmm." If he ignored her request, would it go away? He pointed to the screen. "This list is no good. Tell Sean I need to know exactly which era he thinks the pipe is from. I'm not going to call every Native American historian and try to authenticate the piece without some more information. And I'll need better pictures of the item. Or he could run it down to the museum in Cherokee and ask them for assistance."

Marley leveled a sigh strong enough to create a breeze as she headed for the door. A sliver of guilt pierced him. She didn't deserve his cool dismissal, but he didn't dare give her reason to hope. It might be time for an awkward conversation about boundaries. Or maybe he could introduce her to Miguel.

Had the air conditioner actually shut off in the past few minutes? He unzipped the vest and pulled it off. Reading through Sean's email again, he mulled over the questions. "Marley?"

She was at the threshold in an instant, almost as if she'd been waiting. "Yes, Zach-a-ry?"

The saccharine in her voice sent claws scraping down his spine. "Forget what I said before." He reached for his keys. "I'm going to head over and see Sean in person."

Her brows lifted. "To Oconaluftee? You'll be gone half the day."

Exactly. "I'll pick up the artifact from 'Luftee and run it to the museum in Cherokee. I've got a contact there who could probably identify it on the spot. If Sean's got time, he can come along."

"*I've* got time." Her lips parted. "And I'd love to see the museum."

"I need you working on the backlog of photo filing." He stood, patting his pocket to check for his phone. "But it's well worth a visit. You were looking for something to do over the weekend, weren't you?"

He closed the laptop and pushed in his chair. A long drive through the park topped off with a trip to see the historian at Cherokee sounded like the perfect way to spend a sunny Friday. Much better than ducking overzealous interns. He cast one last regretful glance at the Ownby boxes. They'd endured fifty years in someone's attic—they could surely withstand a few more days here.

That was one good thing about studying history. It didn't have deadlines.

• • •

Kieran flew through the door of the retirement home, her handbag slapping against her leg. Three calls in one week—that had to be a record. Her stomach churned. The administrator had added Gran to a waiting list for a room in the locked memory-care unit, but it might take time. She'd called other facilities, but the situation was the same all over, and it would be best to keep Gran in somewhat familiar surroundings.

Ivy met her in the hall. "Kieran, I'm so glad you're here. The visiting nurse gave Mac a sedative, but she is still overwrought. I hope you can keep her calm." She glanced toward the office. "You know I love Mac, but I can't spend any extra time with her. I've got other residents and—"

"I *know*." Kieran cringed at the snap in her voice. She touched the woman's wrist. "I'm sorry. I do appreciate what you're doing for my gran. I'll try to figure out what's wrong. Thank you—for everything. You're a gem."

Ivy nodded, but the shadows around her eyes told a deeper story. Something needed to change.

Kieran stood outside Granny Mac's room and took some long, slow breaths. She needed to radiate calm. Thankfully, a few solid nights' sleep in Ash's guest room had helped. Yesterday they'd sat on the sofa leafing through a glossy book of photos of Great Smoky Mountains National Park that Ash had picked out at the library for her. Such a beautiful place, it was little wonder that Gran missed it.

Tapping on the door, Kieran let herself into Granny Mac's room. Gran lay curled on the bed, turned toward the window.

"Gran?" She set her purse on a chair and tiptoed over. Maybe the medication had done its job.

Granny Mac stared toward the closed blinds as afternoon light filtered through the cracks.

"Hey, Gran." Kieran pulled a chair close. "I hear you're having a rough day." When her words drew no response, she scooted closer. "Can I make you some tea? Turn on the radio maybe?" She'd taken to streaming old-timey gospel music on her phone during their visits. Gran didn't understand the technology, so they just referred to it as "radio time."

Finally, Gran moved. Lifting a shaking finger, she gestured to the curtains. "Open those, would you? And the window? I like hearing the birds, but these people here keep shutting everything out."

"Sure." Kieran hopped up, glad for something to do. She drew back the heavy drapes. "I think they were hoping you'd take a little rest."

Almost in response, a chickadee fluttered to the window ledge. A clear acrylic feeder was affixed to the glass with suction cups. "Oh, that's nice. Has it always been there, and I didn't notice?" Kieran searched for a way to open the window, but they were all sealed tight. Probably for the best.

"One of the gardeners put it there."

"They must know how much you love seeing the birds."

Granny Mac struggled up to a seated position. "My mother's pocket bird . . . I want to give it to my granddaughter. She's going to need it."

Kieran turned from the window. "I don't need anything, Gran. I'm just happy to have you and your stories."

"No. You don't understand." Her voice rose, and she thumped her arm against the bedding. "Get the bird. Kieran needs it."

The rising tone in her voice sent a shiver through Kieran. "I *am* Kieran, Gran. And I'm fine. I'm good."

Lifting knobby fingers, Gran covered her face and wept. "I failed her. And her father."

Kieran scooted closer, laying a hand on her grandmother's leg. "Look, Kieran is in a good place right now. She's got great friends. Do you remember meeting Nick the other day?"

"I must give it to her afore I go. I've been praying for God to bring it back to me. He'll do that, won't He?"

This visit was going the wrong direction. Gran had been calm when Kieran arrived, but now her anxieties circled like vultures in search of a meal. Kieran straightened the sheet. "Okay, okay. We'll find it." How easy the lies had become, first to her friends and now to her grandmother. But what else could she do? "Everything will be all right. I'll find your mama's bird."

"And you'll get it to Kieran?" Gran's eyelids were looking heavy. Either she'd worn herself out with the emotional storm or the sedative was taking effect.

"I . . . I will. Whatever you want." Tears sprang to Kieran's eyes, her throat closing with emotion.

Granny Mac seemed to settle at that, as if handing the problem off had lessened her burden.

Kieran sank into the chair. She needed to talk to Gran's doctor in the morning. He'd voiced some concerns that her medications might be worsening the dementia. It was always a balancing act between keeping her body healthy and her mind intact. She wished they could find the right mix to give Gran more good days than bad.

If only Kieran actually could find this thing Gran longed for. Wouldn't it be incredible to walk in here and set that bird in Granny Mac's hand?

The book she and Ash had been reading said there were remnants of old cabins scattered around the national park. It seemed likely the park would have records of the people who'd owned the land previously. If she could locate her family's property, maybe she really could find the old heirloom. The idea sent a chill across her skin.

She looked over at her grandmother, sleeping on her side with fingers curled into a fist near her chin. Gran was losing touch with the real world piece by painful piece. Giving her back this memory from her childhood might provide an anchor to keep her in the present.

She'd counseled families that memory boxes and keepsakes helped some dementia patients reconnect with those around them. A man in the memory-care unit carried around an old baseball glove, and evidently the smell and feel of the old leather transported him home to happier days.

Gran's memento might do the same.

If Kieran left early in the morning, she could be at Great Smoky Mountains National Park by lunchtime.

She leaned over and touched Gran's arm through the sheet. "I'd move heaven and earth for you, Granny Mac. Whatever will bring you peace."

# 8

## Great Smoky Mountains National Park
## 1932

ROSIE FASTENED THE long braid into a bun at the nape of her neck, studying her reflection in the small mirror. A lot of the younger women in these parts sported shoulder-length bobs, while others pinned longer styles in a soft chignon complete with loops and curls. She glanced down at the framed portrait of her grandmother. Mee Maw's stiff countenance had been earned from witnessing a lifetime of sorrow. What was Rosie's excuse? She was only five and twenty.

Reaching up, she teased a few locks free and attempted to pin it into soft waves. The resulting mess looked like she'd gotten caught in a summer storm. She turned her head and checked her profile. After the storm, she must have tripped and tumbled down a hill.

*So ridiculous.* How did women get anything done?

This was all Benton Fuller's fault. He'd taken to visiting regular and had sat at their table for at least a half dozen meals. His ready smile and laugh had brought a new sense of joy to Lorna's life. Probably Rosie's too, to be honest.

Rosie rubbed a mosquito bite on the back of her neck as she pondered this revelation. Trouble was, she didn't know how to deal with these unfamiliar feelings any better than she did her own mane. Having a man at the table, in her home—in her heart, even—she was at a complete loss.

*Lord, is this Your doin'?*

If the Almighty were looking to grace her with a husband, seems he'd pick a sturdy farmer or logger. He certainly wouldn't pick a bookish man from the city who cared more for feathered things. And as much as Benton loved her mountains, he didn't call them home.

Whatever the good Lord was doing, she had to admit it was nice having this fellow around, even if it was only for a season. In the meantime, she needed to keep these romantic thoughts hog-tied.

The rattling of an engine drew her attention, and she dropped the brush on the dressing table before scurrying to the window. Automobiles were common enough in town, but they rarely made their way up her washboard road—not since the logging camp shut down a few years ago, anyway.

A green Ford pulled up next to the fence, and Benton climbed out from behind the wheel.

Her heart leapt, no matter the scolding she'd given it less than five minutes before. Pulling off her kitchen apron, she ran a hand across her dress before heading to the door and stepping outside. "Where you been hiding this contraption?"

Benton was already unfastening a large box from the rear bumper. "How did you think I got to the far side of the park to work on the bird survey?"

She came down to join him, admiring the car's jaunty appearance. "I only ever saw you hoofing it through the woods, so I never really thought about it."

Benton smiled. "You've done something different—your hair?"

She smoothed it with her palm, wishing she hadn't run out quite so quick-like. "What've you got there?"

He swept off his fedora. "I've been thinking of how often you and Lorna have been feeding me, and it gave me an idea."

Charity. The thought draped over her and stuck, like those spiderwebs that caught her unawares. She'd ought to have expected this turn.

She took a handful of her skirt and twisted it, worrying the material. "What sort of idea?"

"Let's take these inside, and then you'll have to hear me out. I know you're going to say no right off, but I want you to consider on it carefully."

"You'll tell me now afore I allow a single morsel into my home." She tried to keep her voice firm, but she still took the box from his hands, the fragrance of brown sugar tickling her nose. "Iffen I'm going to say no, then I don't want to haul it all back."

Benton already had the last two crates balanced in his arms. They must have been heavy, by the way his muscles strained against his rolled-up shirtsleeves. He leaned against the car, juggling the load against his chest. "The government is paying for my room and board while I'm here, but as I see it, I'm not really getting my money's worth."

"What you mean?" She darted a glance at the contents, her eyes locking on a tin of coffee.

"I'm rarely at the hotel in time for meals. Sure, they pack a dinner pail for me, but I need more sustenance than that to get through a day in the field. You've already proved to be a far superior cook."

Tinned coffee was a luxury she hadn't seen for some time, except at church gatherings. "Lorna and I are happy to have you. You don't have to bring your own victuals."

He shrugged. "The government is paying for the food. But if you don't want it—"

"Let's not be hasty. Might as well bring it in. Since you're here and all."

His smile sent a rush of pleasure through her, even though it meant he'd won this round. "I wasn't sure what you'd be needing or wanting, so I just got a smattering of supplies for now. Cornmeal, molasses, and the like. If you have specifics, you can write me out a list."

She balanced the lighter box on one arm and dug through it with her free hand. Packets of crackers, pickles, cheese, and brown sugar lay beside the coffee. Should she reserve this food for their guest, or could she pilfer a bit for her and Lorna?

"I hope you don't mind," Benton continued as he followed her inside, "but I picked up some hard candies. I've got a bit of a sweet tooth, and I thought Lorna might too."

"Don't let her hear you say that. She'll be searching your pockets every time she sees you."

He lowered his packages to the table. "So I was thinking, when I'm in the area, I'd like to eat meals with you. But if I'm not here, you and Lorna feel free to prepare the food for yourselves."

"And then you'd return to the Wonderland Club to sleep? That seems like a heap of trouble. You said they pay your room and board—might as well room here too." The words slipped from her lips before she'd had much time to consider on them. *Lord, do I really want him under my roof?* Trouble was, she did.

His brows pulled together. "I couldn't, Rosie. Where would you even put me? You don't have the space."

"Families in these parts wedge twelve kids in a cabin this size—smaller, even. I'd be content staying up in the loft with Lorna. There's a good feather tick in the bedroom."

"I won't put you out of your bed." He shook his head. "Cooking for me is already asking a lot."

A shout from outside caused Rosie to drop the tin she was holding, sending it crashing to the floor.

Lorna came dashing into the house, surging straight past the two of them. She was scrambling up the ladder by the time Rosie made it to the front door.

Horace Samson's chest was heaving as he strode up the path, a belt coiled in one fist. He stopped short of the step. "I thought I tol' you to keep that girl off our land. I found her out there with the goats again."

Rosie pushed through the door and stood on the porch, unable to tear her eyes from the leather strap. Had he used that on her sister?

"She don't mean nothing by it, Horace. She's harmless. You know that."

"They've got places for half-wit trash like her." He swept a hand over his bristly chin, as if to wipe the disgusting words from his mouth.

Benton came to stand behind her. "Watch your tone, Samson. You've got no right—"

"Stay out of this, furriner. It's you ain't got no rights here." Horace yanked off his hat, his sharp eyes fixing on Benton.

Rosie wished she'd grabbed the shotgun off the top of the doorframe. She didn't want to point it at a neighbor, but having it in her hand might make her worth listening to. "I don't want trouble, Horace. I'm sorry Lorna's been bothering your goats. She's taken a fancy to that spotted nanny and thinks of it as her own. I'm having trouble convincing her it ain't, especially since Will was so kind as to let her come care for it so often."

"Well, I might've just knocked that notion out of her addled brain for her."

"You . . . what?" Rosie's knees weakened for a moment before the fire rushed in to fill her chest. "You wouldn't dare touch my sister."

Benton pushed past her, stepping down to stand even with Horace. "I should call the law on you. Beating women is for cowards."

Horace laughed, the harsh sound echoing through the yard. "Try it. The sheriff will cart that imbecile off to the state hospital where she belongs." He hefted the belt over his shoulder. "Unless you would rather settle it with fists like a real man."

At that Rosie scrambled backward and retrieved the gun. "Get off my property." She leveled it at him, her arms shaking. "And don't come round here no more."

Horace aimed a sneer at Benton. "If you're thinking of laying claim to Rosie here, you'd best learn to fight your own battles."

Benton crossed his arms. "Looks like she's got enough fight for the both of us."

Rosie's hands were growing damp. "Git, Horace. I won't warn you again."

"You used to be partial to your own kind, Rosie."

Benton moved to her side. "Miss McCauley and her sister have been gracious enough to let me board with them. So I'll be here to keep an eye on things."

Horace's brows shot up. "Is that how it is, now?" His eyes flicked from Benton to her. "Well, you've made your bed now, ain't you, Rosie?" He snapped the belt one last time before skulking down the road.

Rosie grabbed the porch post for support, its weathered roughness reassuring under her fingers. She needed to go to Lorna, but she also wanted to confirm that Horace skedaddled back into the woods. "So you're taking me up on that hospitality now, are you?"

Benton turned, his gaze unflinching. "I am. But not in the house. I remember seeing a small barn out back."

If she weren't feeling so flustered, she might have laughed. "That shed's nothing but an old goat shelter. You don't want to bunk there. It's hardly fit for beasts, much less someone like you."

"I've done research in the jungles of Borneo. I think I'll manage. It's got a roof and a floor—am I right?"

"Of a sort, I reckon."

"Then I'll be fine." He made himself at home in one of the porch rockers and gazed out at the road as if expecting Horace to double back.

This fella was fixin' to trade the comfort of Wonderland Club Hotel for a goat pen just to keep Lorna safe. The realization spilled through her like long sweetening over hotcakes. Benton might not be the strapping farmer or logger she'd asked the good Lord for, but he was a right good man—perhaps better'n she deserved. She studied his intense blue eyes for a moment longer than she should afore heading inside.

Not having him under the same roof was probably for the best. Especially if her heart were all-fired determined to venture into dangerous territory.

• • •

Benton braced himself with one arm around the tree trunk and used the other to hold the next board in place. "It's not too shabby, if I say so myself."

"Just a few more licks." Beau Tipton hammered the final nails into the platform. He balanced on one knee, long whiskers hiding the front of his shirt. "It ain't fancy, but it's high and dry. Leastways when it's not raining."

Benton squatted on the far end, trying not to think of the ground twenty feet below. "I certainly never expected this blind to support two people. It's far more than I could have hoped for." He reached a hand out to the man. "I'm in your debt."

Tipton grinned, clasping his palm and nearly breaking Benton's fingers. "I've built a few hunting blinds, and even helped a feller build a keep-watch post for his still back in the day. Some folks do little more than nail a chair to the trunk, but in my mind, it's good to have room to spread out jes' in case you pack a stiff moonshine and need a lie-down. But the last thing you want is to roll off and find yourself laid out afore your burying time."

Benton gripped a branch to steady himself. The tree swayed gently, a sensation that would take some getting used to.

The clear view of the owl's abode drew his attention. He wouldn't even need his field glasses to watch the pair as they fed their owlets, as long as they did it before the forest was completely swathed in darkness. Benton couldn't wait to spend an evening up here. It was probably best to let the pair acclimate to the new structure in their neighborhood first. Besides, he'd planned to drive over and survey the Roaring Fork area and see how many species he could add to the growing bird list. As much as he'd like to spend every minute studying his favorite specimens, he needed to focus on the job he'd been hired to do.

As Tipton made his way down the makeshift ladder they had

constructed from sections of tree limbs, Benton glanced toward Rosie's cabin near the base of the hollow. There was something comforting about seeing the little curl of smoke wending up from the chimney. It was quickly becoming his home away from home.

He'd set up a cot in the rustic shelter and even fastened some boards together to make a makeshift desk and shelves to get his belongings up off the dirt floor. It wasn't the Wonderland Club Hotel, but it was a welcome respite.

"You got company, Fuller!" Tipton glanced up the tree trunk, his foot on the lowest rung. "Miss Rosie is coming, probably to make sure we ain't loafing around."

"Beau!" Rosie's voice rang out. "Don't go telling tales. I'm just bringing goodies."

Benton shifted around to hang his head over the edge, watching Rosie climb the last little bit of the hill to reach their tree. "You should come see this, Rosie. It's like sitting on a cloud."

Tipton chuckled. "Don't think clouds are made of hardwood. Still, it's a nice perch."

She looked up toward Benton. "May I?"

"Did you mention food?"

"I did." She turned to his helper. "What about you, Beau? Butterscotch bars? Coffee?" She held up a vacuum bottle.

"No coffee for me. Maudie's brew ate a hole in my gut years ago. But I won't turn down something sweet if you got plenty there in your poke." He took the paper bag and pulled out a crumbly treat. "I've got to get on home to feed the stock. Be dark in a few."

"I can come give you a hand with the food." Benton moved toward the ladder.

"No need." She swung the bottle's leather strap over one shoulder and tucked the bag into the bib of her overalls. "It's been a while since I climbed a tree, but I think I remember."

"If any woman could manage, it's you."

In a few minutes she was clambering up beside him and brushing flakes of tree bark from her hands. "You fellows have been busy. Is it all finished?" She pulled the bottle free and passed it to him.

He unscrewed the cap, breathing in the rich fragrance. "I think so. I might try to add some camouflage around the front so I'm not just perched out here for everyone to see."

"The owls must think you're a funny-looking bird."

*And you're the prettiest one they've ever seen.* He retrieved the tin cups she'd stashed in the paper bag. "I don't think I've ever eaten in a tree before."

"Lorna weren't too happy to see me wrapping it up, though she'd already sneaked a few of those licorice drops from the cupboard. I can't believe you bought her more candy."

"I wanted to get some bacon to go with your hearty breakfasts. The pig keeps giving me a dirty look whenever I go to the goat shed. I think it knows its destiny."

She leaned against the trunk, her shoulder bumping his arm. "Everyone has a role here in the mountains. Hers is to provide Christmas dinner, sausages, and salt pork."

He poured the coffee out into a tin cup. "So what's my role, then?"

"I'm still piecing that out."

As he passed the drink to her, the brush of her fingers against his sent an uncomfortable longing through him. If they stayed up here cozy like this for long, he wouldn't be able to resist kissing her. And then where would he be? *Probably flat on my face in the leaf litter, twenty feet down.*

"Oh, look, there they are." Her voice remained soft, but she grabbed his sleeve, sloshing coffee across his leg.

Benton grimaced. "What?" He glanced toward the tree cavity opposite. One of the screech owls was peering out of the opening, its round yellow eyes staring directly toward them. "Be still."

Rosie kept her hand locked on his wrist, unmoving.

Warmth spread up his arm even as the dark stain cooled on his pant leg. After a few minutes, the owl stepped out of the opening and flittered to a nearby branch. It clacked its beak a few times in warning, studying them from a distance.

Benton did his best to concentrate on the bird rather than his companion, but it was a challenge. "That's Annie," he whispered.

She scooted closer to him, her leg resting against his. "How can you tell?"

"She's the larger of the two. Female owls are bigger." Owls did a lot of head bobbing and winking in their elaborate courtship, but he doubted such antics would work on Rosie. He settled for sliding his hand over to capture hers.

Her smile softened, and she squeezed his palm rather than pulling free. "Where's Hoot?"

If he rolled off this platform right now, he might just float. Benton glanced toward the nest just as the male's head appeared in the gap. "There."

"Do they have eggs?"

"They have big fluffy babies now, nearly ready to fledge. If I return early enough next year, maybe we can observe the whole breeding season."

She swung her head toward him, dark eyes round and solemn. "Next year?" The words were so soft, he wasn't even certain he'd heard them correctly.

He laid his other hand on her forearm, running his fingertips along the soft skin of her wrist. If he pressed down, would he feel her pulse racing like his own? "If you'll have me."

The tightening grip on his palm felt like an answer. "They stay together, then, these owls?"

"They do. For life."

With that, Rosie's head tipped down and rested on his shoulder.

Benton eased back against the trunk, letting it support them both.

# 9

## Great Smoky Mountains National Park
## Present Day

ZACH RUBBED HIS forehead, trying to push out the headache that had gathered since leaving the Oconaluftee Visitor Center about an hour ago. He'd picked up Sean's mystery artifact and driven it south to the Museum of the Cherokee Indian only to learn the pipe was a clever fake. The museum director pointed him to the original artist, who seemed amused that anyone had mistaken it for authentic. He'd created the soapstone pipe in the ancient style but never attempted to pawn it off as real. As sometimes happens, once it left his studio, the piece took on a life of its own.

Maybe this day wouldn't turn out to be a complete waste. They needed artisans capable of creating replicas for the park museums, since displaying actual artifacts presented an unacceptable risk. The fact that the pipe had fooled both Sean and Zach was impressive. And embarrassing.

Passing the Elkmont cutoff, Zach glanced down at the speedometer and eased his foot off the gas. He wanted nothing more than to crawl into bed, but driving fast on park roads after dark was a recipe for disaster. And a law enforcement ranger pulling him over—while driving a government rig, no less—would set him up for months of ribbing.

A shadow bounded into the circle of his headlights, and Zach slammed his foot against the brake, sliding into the far lane just as a black bear lumbered across the pavement and into the darkened trees on the far side.

Heart pounding, Zach managed to steer back into his lane before anyone came his direction. Just off the road, he noticed a small car in the old Millsap pullout, a glow flickering inside the darkened windows. Engine trouble maybe? There weren't any trailheads nearby, so the lot on the Little River should be empty.

Zach drummed fingers against the steering wheel. Normally, he'd call it in and let one of the rangers deal with it, but he was nearly stopped anyway. Pulling up beside the car, he grabbed a flashlight from his glove box and stepped out of the truck.

A woman slept in the vehicle's passenger seat, her head tipped against the window and a blanket wrapped around her shoulders. A clip-on LED cast a glare across the pages of a novel sitting open on her lap.

*Illegal camper. Great.* Zach tapped on the glass.

The figure in the seat shifted, causing the reading light to bobble. The window rolled down and the woman's face appeared—eyes wide and hair standing on end.

Zach took a step back, praying she wasn't some sort of drug addict preparing to knife him. At least the gold badge on his chest made him look like a law enforcement officer, even if he wasn't carrying a firearm. The fact that LEOs and historians wore the same uniform wasn't lost on him. "I'm sorry to disturb you. But you can't camp here."

She rubbed her eyes. "I'm not actually camping. I just stopped to read a few chapters." She lifted the book and waved it. "It's not good to drive drowsy, remember? I thought this would help me wake up a little until I could get to a campground."

Likely story. "Which campground? You're only about a half mile from Elkmont."

She bit her lip, glancing down at her lap. "I can't remember the name."

"Let me call them and make sure there are openings."

"O-okay." Her voice trembled. She wadded the blanket into a ball and tossed it into the rear seat.

The sight tugged at Zach. She certainly didn't look like a drug user, just someone who'd had a long day. He leaned into the truck and grabbed the radio.

She stepped out, dropping the book onto the seat. "Look, it's late. I'm not hurting anyone by parking here for a few hours of sleep, am I? Couldn't we—"

Park dispatch answered quickly, and he turned away to focus on the call. "Can you do me a favor and check if there are any openings at Elkmont or anything nearby?" When he glanced back at the woman, she frowned, her lip protruding like a five-year-old's.

"What's your name?"

"Kieran Lucas."

He finished the call and signed off. "All right. Elkmont is full, but if you turn around and head west, the campground at Cades Cove has sites available."

Lines formed in her brow. "I just came from there. I drove all the way from Nashville, then spent the day exploring. That's why I'm so—"

"Your other option is to head out of the park and find a hotel, but you can't stay on the side of the road. It's against the rules. Otherwise we'd have people parking all over the place."

She balled her fists. "I'm just one person, one car. It's late."

A wave of annoyance shot through him. This was the perfect end to an already irritating day. "Make your choice."

Ms. Lucas's eyes narrowed. "*Thank you*, Ranger." She headed around her vehicle and climbed into the driver's seat.

The engine sputtered a few times before catching, just long enough for Zach to worry he wouldn't be rid of her anytime soon. The car signaled and pulled away, heading toward Cades Cove.

"And that is why I don't work in visitor services." Zach returned to his truck and reached into his bag for the Tylenol he should have taken an hour ago, chasing the pills down with a swig from his water bottle. Leaning his head back, he relaxed for a moment. If he hadn't been battling a killer headache, he might fall asleep here too. Wouldn't that be a story to tell?

He shook off the weariness and started the truck. Ten minutes later he spotted the same vehicle parked farther down the road. Pressing on the brake, he groaned. "You've got to be kidding me." This woman was trying his patience, and he had little to spare tonight. He should just call it in and get it over with. If she chose to flaunt the rules, it wasn't his responsibility to protect her from the repercussions.

As his hand closed around the radio, the image of her tired face played through his mind. Maybe she really was too sleepy to drive to Cades Cove, over an hour away on the dark road. Was he putting her in danger by insisting she follow the letter of the law? He turned the truck around and rolled up beside Ms. Lucas's car.

She pulled a sour face. "Look, it's late—"

He put up a hand to stop her words. "If you're that tired, I'll drive you to the campground. Grab your tent and stuff. I don't want you to die in an accident and have that hanging over my head."

"I'm not getting in a truck with a stranger."

He ran his thumbnail along the steering wheel, trying to maintain some composure. "Then I'll follow you. But you're *not* staying here."

She covered her face with her palm, but not before he noticed the tears filling her eyes.

*No, don't cry. Please don't cry.* A sudden tightness tugged at his chest muscles. "I'm trying to help. Honest."

"I can't pay for the campsite. If I do, I won't have enough for gas."

"It's only twenty-five . . ." Zach paused, thinking better of his words. A twenty-five-dollar campsite might have been an extravagance at one point in his life too. "Okay, but I can't let you stay here. I've only got ten in my wallet, or I'd pay it myself."

"I couldn't take your money." Her voice cracked. "I'll go find a Walmart somewhere. They sometimes let people park overnight."

He scrubbed a hand across his face. "Staying alone in your car doesn't sound safe."

"I've done it before."

That truth settled uncomfortably on his shoulders. "Look, I've got a little guest cabin at my place. If you're not picky and you want it for the night, it's yours." *Just don't tell my boss.*

The sound of the idling engines barely obscured the chirping of the night insects. She sniffled and glanced up, finally meeting his gaze. "I can't ask you to do that."

"You didn't ask. I'm wiped out, and you look about the same. If I call this in, I have to stay here and keep an eye on you until they arrive. By crashing at my place, you'll save me a lot of trouble." He turned his head, trying not to notice how her damp cheeks glistened in the low light. "The cabin is barely even habitable. No heat, no running water. But it's got to be better than your car. I'm really not doing you any favors—you're doing me one."

"And you're not some kind of serial killer, right?"

"I'm too tired to step on a spider, so I'm certainly not going to bother you."

Finally, the faintest smile touched her lips. "In that case, yes, I accept."

"Good. Thank you. Now let's get out of here."

As he pulled back onto the road with Ms. Lucas's headlights following behind, it dawned on him that he'd thanked *her* instead of the other way around. *The story of my life.*

• • •

Kieran blinked her eyes open, the scent of fresh-cut lumber jarring her senses. Sitting up, she flung aside the nylon sleeping bag and pressed both hands into the small of her back to stretch. This cabin, with nothing but a thin mattress tossed in the corner, would probably get less than one star in an online review, but it was cozy, nonetheless.

The park ranger had gone above and beyond by letting her crash here. Now that she saw it in the daylight, she couldn't help comparing the cottage to those adorable tiny houses she liked to drool over on YouTube. The stack of building materials in the corner suggested the owner had renovation plans.

She'd been so worn out and miserable last night, she must have dropped off within minutes of pulling the covers over herself. It was little wonder. After getting up at the crack of dawn and driving four hours to the park, Kieran had spent the rest of the day exploring the cabins and cemeteries preserved in Cades Cove and poring over the museum exhibits about the early settlers. By evening, she'd realized that finding Gran's childhood home in the park's five-hundred-thousand-plus acres of mountains and valleys was going to be a monumental task. Or worse—an impossible one.

A knock on the door sent her scrambling, and her stomach clenched. She hadn't anticipated an early morning visitor. What if the man had decided she owed him something in return for his kindness? She ran fingers through her hair before opening the door. The ranger stood on the doorstep, a mug in one hand and a plate loaded with waffles, eggs, and fruit balanced on his arm.

She swung the door wide, her suspicions giving way to disbelief. "Whoa—I didn't realize this was a bed and breakfast."

He walked in, setting the food on the folding table. "Between the mess and the dumpster-worthy mattress, I thought cooking breakfast was the least I could do."

"I was happy to have a roof and a place to close my eyes without feeling like someone was going to come knocking on my window." This man was tough to figure out. Last night he'd refused to cut her an inch, and today he was cooking waffles?

He picked up one of the power tools cluttering the floor and carried it over to the corner, dropping wood shavings over his jeans and T-shirt. What had happened to the park-service green? This was the same guy, right?

She studied him. "I realized after you left last night that I never got your name."

"Sorry. It's Zach. Zach Jensen." He brushed his palms on his pant legs before sticking one hand out to her.

"Kieran Lucas." Only he already knew that. She shook his hand, aware of how she must look in her baggy sweatpants and stained tank top. "Do you often pick up strays on the side of the road?"

"No, never." He laughed. "But as I saw it, I couldn't just leave you out there."

"Why not?" She crouched down and pulled a clean hoodie from her bag, quickly yanking it over her head.

"It's not how I do things." He gestured toward the plate. "You should eat while the food still has memory of being warm. I've got to head in to work, so I'll be pulling out of here in about twenty minutes or so."

"Then you'll want me packed and gone." She reached for her sleeping bag, sending her novel sliding across the wood floor. "I didn't realize you were leaving so early. I should have known."

"Take your time. There's a shower in the main house—you're welcome to it. I'll set out some towels."

The bag dropped to her feet. "That's very trusting."

"I don't really have much to steal, and frankly, you don't look the type." He shrugged. "Are you heading into the park today? Hiking, maybe?"

She picked up the plate, glancing around for a place to sit. There wasn't any, unless you counted the mattress. "No hiking, probably. I'm here doing research. Family genealogy and such." Researching a family tree probably sounded more respectable than tracking down a family heirloom lost in the woods.

"Really? I work at the Collections Preservation Center. We might be able to help."

Her breath caught. "Are you serious? I figured you for a bear wrangler or something."

"Only in my spare time." He folded his arms, a light dancing in his blue eyes. "No, I'm a total history geek. I call in the professionals for wildlife problems."

"You're one surprise after another." She set the plate down. "Yes, I'd love your help with my project. I'm looking for information on my great-grandparents. They lived here in the park somewhere. But I don't know much more than that."

"Why don't you come to my office around ten?" He jutted a thumb toward the main house. "I'll leave my card on the kitchen table. The center's here in Townsend, so it only takes a few minutes to get there."

A short while later she caught a glimpse of him dashing for his truck, dressed in the neatly pressed uniform. As soon as he cleared the drive, she slipped her feet into a pair of flip-flops, grabbed her overnight bag, and headed for the house. She couldn't believe he'd just leave the door ajar for her like that. Where she grew up, you'd have your place cleaned out in five minutes. This guy was something else.

Nick would have been proud of her last night. Not only had she accepted help, but she'd done so with minimal protesting. After all, if she was murdered in the process, she could at least blame him.

Zach Jensen's house was simple and sparse, but the rag rug in the hall and the antique chair by the front window suggested someone who appreciated things that last. A Bible sat open on the table, several verses underlined with pencil and notes written in the margins. At one time, she might have been put off by a guy who was into that sort of thing, but she'd spent enough time with Ash and Nick to realize she could use a little more Scripture in her life.

She bent to read a marked verse. "Trust in the Lord with all your heart; do not depend on your own understanding. Seek his will in all you do, and he will show you which path to take." She scanned across to the note he'd scribbled in the margin. *Trust God = straight paths.*

A ranger equating trust with pathfinding. That seemed fitting. She preferred charting her own course.

Kieran paused to study the photos displayed on the refrigerator. A teenage Zach appeared in the midst of a huge, smiley family, of which he looked to be the youngest. In the center were the most beautiful mom and dad anyone could ask for, complete with laugh lines and soft, huggable shoulders. Kieran's throat tightened, and she forced her eyes away. She'd spent enough of her life wishing for other people's parents.

She'd realized at a young age that without family, she was a nobody. Thankfully, Granny Mac had changed everything for her. And that was why Kieran would do anything she could for her grandmother—while she still had the time.

Anything.

# 10

Great Smoky Mountains National Park
1932

Rosie laid two more plates of cornbread on the table set up in the yard as a chorus of hammers beat out a chaotic rhythm. Ladies chattered here and there as they arranged the food, sharing the gossip and news of the day. The fact that she had a strange man living in the goat shed for the past month had fueled speculations, but thankfully enough time had passed that she was no longer the primary source of scandal. She needed to thank Maudie Tipton for squelching the worst of the talk. Everyone trusted the holler's granny woman, so her word was considered nigh on close to the preacher's for being gospel truth.

The roofing materials had been delivered last week, the yellow boards and freshly riven oak shingles looking newer and prettier than anything Rosie had ever lit eyes on before. It was a crying shame she'd come to trading her land for such necessities. Pa would have gone out and split his own, but such skills were becoming a thing of the past, and they were clearly out of reach for Rosie.

The neighborhood men and boys were making quick work of laying the shingles and hammering them into place. The job that would have taken her weeks was being completed in a few short hours. She'd gone to her share of workings, but this was the first time she'd been the one blessed.

Maudie added a plate of fried pies to the table. "The place is looking mighty fine, Rosie. Some of the fellas are working on your fence and outbuildings too, since there's so many folks turned out."

"I can't believe it. Pa would have been as pleased as a pig in mud."

"We don't have many chances to get together no more, not since the park come." The older woman heaved a sigh. "So few folks left on this side of the holler."

Tildy came over to join them, her freckled cheeks flushed red from the sun. "We saw the Coopers off just last week."

"I never thought Jeremiah and Millie would pack up and git." An ache burrowed into Rosie's chest. What would she and Lorna do when everyone had gone?

Tildy moved one of the platters to make more room. "We're fixin' to leave next month. Pa decided 'twas better to squeeze a few dollars from the government than to lose the place outright. All the fight seeped out of him since the Olivers lost in court." She shook her head, curls framing her round face. "It's a crime."

"But you're going off and getting hitched." Maudie bumped her arm.

"I know, but I just can't picture my folks living in town. Me and Jamie are heading to Michigan. His kin have a place on Lake Superior. Sounds mighty cold to me."

"I'll miss you." Rosie slid her hand through her friend's elbow. "You'd best write to me."

As Maudie scooped up a squalling infant and headed for the porch, Tildy leaned closer to Rosie. "Talk is, you got a man buzzing around you. A city fellow? He here?"

Rosie swallowed the protests rising in her throat. She *was* falling for Benton, and fast. "He's away just now, and I wouldn't say he's buzzing exactly. He's bunking here for a time while working for the park. It's been good having a man about the place. And Lorna seems to like him."

Tildy squeezed her arm. "Question is, do *you* like him?"

"Just 'cause you're getting married don't mean we all got to." She shooed a wasp away from Mabel Sue's sorghum pie. If she could only chase off her own fool notions as easy.

She hadn't seen Benton in over a week, as he was off surveying some wild corner of the park, and it bothered her how much it rankled. She hadn't realized talking with him had become such a bright spot in her days. Who'd have thought an outsider could worm his way into their lives so?

Tildy followed her, draping a red-checked cloth over the food to keep it safe until the noontime meal break. "No matter. I hear he's fixing to leave soon anyhow."

"He—what?" The word tumbled out afore she could gather herself.

Tildy giggled. "I knew you was fibbin' me. I can see it in your face. I've visited you three times since April, and you never said pea turkey 'bout this Fuller fellow."

"It's not like we was courting."

"I'm not sure you'd know if a man was courting you. You're the workingest woman I ever knew, always slaving from can't see to can't see." Tildy brushed a curl away from her eyes. "Where is Lorna anyhow?"

"She got scairt and took off, soon as menfolk started arriving."

"What's gotten into our girl? She used to be as friendly as all get-out."

"She seems to have calmed down a tetch since Mr. Fuller come. I think having him around has done her a heap of good." She stopped and lifted her eyes to study her friend. "So what's this about him leaving?"

"He told Beau Tipton he had to get back to his other job."

Rosie hadn't thought much about the man's outside ties of late. The thought of it swirled in her like the stewed turnips bubbling in the cook pot. She might be little more than a source of entertainment for the fellow. For all she knew, he could have a girl in New York.

Tildy bumped her arm with a plump elbow. "If he goes, you still got Will Samson trailing you like a hound dog. He's been after you since we was children."

"I—no." She cast a glance toward the cabin where Will stood tying another load of shingles to haul up to the roof. "Not for years now."

Her friend rolled her eyes. "Talk is, he still walks that path to see you often enough."

"I ain't seen him here in over a month now. Not since Horace came after Lorna with a strap."

Tildy frowned. "That's not what I heard. Charlotte Martin, who cleans house for the Samsons, said so. Or at least, he's off sparkin' *some* girl—she thought it was you."

"It's not me. But I'm right happy for him."

"I wonder why he's keeping it such a secret? Seems like Charlotte would know. She's finally landed Horace—you heard that?"

"Truly?" Rosie tried to picture the two together. Charlotte's first husband had been gentle and sweet. Then there was Horace.

"Maudie says she's 'flying over a field and settlin' on a cowpie.' But Charlotte's long been set on living in that house. She couldn't turn Will's head, and the old man is just too . . ." Her nose wrinkled. "Well, you know. I guess she figured Horace was her last hope."

Rosie slid her hand into her pocket, the habit of rubbing her thumb over the tiny bird becoming ingrained. "I'll pray it goes well for them."

When Tildy got called away, Rosie lifted a hand to shade her brow and watched the men working atop her cabin. It would be such a blessing not to have to put buckets around the loft to hold water from all the leaks. Her lean-to bedroom had become nearly unlivable.

She couldn't resist glancing up the ridge to where Benton's little platform sat hidden in the trees. She'd climbed the ladder a couple of evenings this week, sitting there by herself and watching the fledgling owls stretching their wings and hopping about on nearby branches in the last light of day. They'd likely take flight afore much longer. Then they'd leave the nest for good.

"The roof's looking fine." Benton's voice sounded beside her.

She jumped, as if her thoughts had somehow conjured the man. "I figured you weren't coming back until tomorrow."

"I thought I might lend a hand. Doesn't look like they need it, though. And to be honest"—he shrugged—"I'm not sure what help I'd be."

"You're welcome, regardless." She pressed her hands in her pockets to make sure they didn't reach for his arm. To do so in this crowd would spark all the rumors anew.

"I thought it might be good for Lorna too—seeing a friendly face." He took off his hat and ran a hand through his hair, standing it all on end like porcupine quills.

"I don't know where she's gotten to." Rosie frowned. "I knewed this would be hard on her, to have all these men about. But we really did need the help to get that roof on."

He leveled his gaze at her. "I wish I could be more of a hand to you and Lorna, to better earn my keep."

"The extra money has been welcome, but jes' having you about has been nice." The thought of him leaving settled in the dead center of her chest. "I don't think you know the light you've brought to our lives—to Lorna's and to mine."

A smile spread over his face, small at first, then widening. "And you've been to mine as well." Benton reached for her hands, showing none of her hesitation. "I don't understand it completely, but you've changed something in me, Rosie."

She stepped back, pulling her arms to her sides. The words were sweet, but she'd have the truth out of him. "And yet you're leaving us."

His gaze faltered. "You heard."

"You might could have warned me. It'll be sore-painful for Lorna."

"Just Lorna?" He didn't lift his chin to look at her.

Folks were watching. This weren't the time to go to pieces.

He stepped closer and softened his tone. "Can we talk more later? Maybe this evening after everyone has gone? I have an idea that might please you. I hope it will, anyway."

She nodded, even though there weren't nothing he could say to make her happy right now. Not if he was planning to stretch his wings and skedaddle, just like the fledgling owls.

• • •

Benton handed the last two saws to Beau Tipton as they cleaned up after the work party. Everyone else had moved to the tables spread across the yard, laughter and chatter brightening the place more than Benton had ever seen it before. "I'm sorry I couldn't be of more assistance."

"You done plenty helping me put these tools right to sorts. It's been a long day, but it's good to see the old place looking so fine." Tipton cast his gaze up over the cabin. "I knowed Rosie's pa well—one of the first folks we met after moving here from Cades Cove. He'd have hated to see it coming down around his girls' ears. We ought to've been here afore it got so broken down. Don't speak well for our community." He shook his head. "Ain't what it used to be."

"You'd never see a work party like this in New York. You'd have to hire a crew, not just pass the word among neighbors."

The man folded arms across his bib overalls. "Used to be, you could just raise your voice and holler. Folks all around would come running. Now we're all busy sorting out who's staying and who's a-going. I'm mighty worried about these girls staying on after folks leave. Not sure how Rosie's going to hold it all together."

The thought had dogged Benton too. He didn't like the idea of leaving next week, knowing the closest neighbor had it out for Lorna. And yet his life was in Ithaca, not here. The telegram he'd received from the department chair had hit him like a bucket of cold water.

Dr. Grant Hayden was dead.

He pushed the grim news away. Tonight wasn't the time. "But you're not moving, are you?"

Beau pulled a bandana from his pocket and used it to mop his brow. "Me and Maudie will stay on awhile. The superintendent of the new park says there might be some odd jobs here soon, building campgrounds and such. I'd hate to see 'em bring in furriners to do it considering we got scores of out-of-work men right here."

Benton resisted the urge to point out that he was also a stranger to this community. Best not to state the obvious. Beau was one of the few men who'd even speak to him as it was. "So everyone heads home after supper?"

The corner of Beau's mouth hitched up. "You really ain't from these parts, are you? Work, then eat. Pray, then play."

"Pray? You're having a church meeting?"

"Not a meeting, since the circuit preacher is over in Cosby right now. But we'll have a singing, and maybe a few will say some words."

"And after?"

"The Bibles get put away, the jugs come out, and the fiddles start a-wailing. Iffen you're lucky, you might catch a dance with Rosie or one of the other girls. I've heard a few of the women whispering about you, so I hope you're fast on your feet."

Dread ratcheted along Benton's spine. He could manage a waltz and a few of the other steps expected in the university ballroom, but not the clogging style of dance he'd seen practiced here in the Smokies. It might be good to make himself scarce. Perhaps he could hide out on his birding blind. No one would think to look for him in the treetops. "I think I can handle the singing, but I've got two left feet when it comes to dancing."

"That's good to hear. I think of few of the single fellers was worrying." The bigger man chuckled. "But get a few swigs of the mountain dew down your gullet and you'll be dancing like everyone else."

A slug of moonshine would only assure his destruction. Someone had forced a taste on him back at Wonderland Club, and he'd felt it burn from his tongue clear to his stomach. Either he didn't have the constitution for the stuff, or these mountain folk built up tolerance to it over a lifetime. Perhaps over generations.

"Looks like they're starting." Beau put down the last of the tools as voices lifted in the distance. "We'd best get over there, or folks'll start thinking you're a heathen, and you got enough tongues a-wagging as is."

Benton followed his new friend over to the group gathered in the yard. A few of the elders sat in chairs carried from Rosie's cabin, but most of the others were resting on benches made from sawhorses or on quilts spread over the ground. They'd lit a small bonfire and arranged the seats in a circle around the musicians. "Blessed Assurance" rose into the evening sky, followed by a toe-tapping version of "Just Over in the Gloryland."

The people hereabouts sang without the typical reserve he remembered in the church of his youth. Was that peculiar to this mountain culture, or was it just that they were outside in the fresh air and not confined in a musty old chapel? Children ran about, the tiniest one toddling from one bench to another before getting scooped up by an old lady in a rocker.

Benton hovered in the back, unsure whether to sit or stand, sing or stay silent. He edged around the perimeter of the group, as much an outsider here as when he was birdwatching. An observer, never a participant.

He didn't see Rosie until he moved to the far side of the circle. She sat on a red quilt with a couple of other young women, her smile obvious even as her mouth opened in song. Below the hem of her cotton dress, her bare legs and dusty toes were crossed in front of her. Would a woman in Ithaca ever dare be seen without hosiery and shoes? He couldn't imagine any of the faculty members' wives displaying themselves so, and yet Rosie looked every bit as natural as a white-tailed deer bedded down in a grassy meadow. She was truly in her element here among friends and neighbors. Her eyes found his across the circle, and her expression wobbled a bit before she lifted a hand to wave him over.

He couldn't resist the invitation. Benton slipped between the groups and took a seat near her.

She leaned close, a soft tang of honeysuckle teasing him. "I thought maybe you'd sneaked off to be with your feathered friends."

"I didn't wish to be rude to my hostess." Every fiber of his being wanted to take her hand, but dozens of eyes were probably fixed on him right now. "I might still, when the dancing begins."

"Coward," she whispered and patted his arm.

The bold touch gave him confidence, and he scooted closer. "I'm just protecting you from embarrassment. If these folks see my stumbling attempts at dancing, it will bring shame on your lovely gathering. But if you need me, you know where I'll be."

"Will I?" She turned her gaze back to the fiddler. "Or will you be halfway to New York?"

The subtle jab hit home. He pulled his gaze from her lovely face, trying to push down the demands his heart was making upon him. He'd spent his entire career languishing in Hayden's shadow. Benton had never wished the man harm, but he'd longed for the same opportunities. Now fate had thrown it at his feet. Everything he'd ever wanted was waiting for him in Ithaca.

*Almost everything.*

The fiddler and banjo player launched into a new song, and the crowd clapped along. Rosie hopped up to her feet and reached for his arm. "You'll like this one. Joe—the fiddler—he learnt it from a cousin back in Missouri who knows the fella who wrote it."

With her help, he clambered to his feet, momentarily wishing he could kick off his own shoes. Listening as everyone around him joined in the unfamiliar tune, Benton thrust his hands into his pockets and rocked on his heels. Even through the wide collection of voices, he only heard Rosie's. Her eyes shone as she sang the words to "I'll Fly Away."

The song pulled at him in an unfamiliar way, the sensation unsettling. These folks proclaiming their joy and freedom from earthly bonds were the same people quick to pull a shotgun on a stranger—and sometimes a neighbor too. He struggled to make sense of the contradiction.

A minute later Lorna jostled him, wedging herself between them. Apparently after spending the day in the woods, the music had drawn her out of hiding.

Rosie stretched an arm around her sister's waist. "There you are. I'm so glad you joined us." She glanced across at Benton and smiled.

His heart lifted, maybe even flying a bit like the song suggested. Perhaps there was something to be said for this hymn-singing business after all. If the music could draw Lorna's wounded soul homeward, maybe it could work on him too.

• • •

From his lofty perch, Benton caught glimpses of the bonfire in the distance, the sounds of music and laughter floating up through the night air. The owls must be rethinking this rather noisy neighborhood. The male had flown off earlier, presumably to hunt for the night. The female and fledglings were nowhere to be seen. Rosie had told him the young ones had been standing on branches near the nest during his absence, so maybe they'd taken flight by now. It'd be a real shame if he'd missed it. Unfortunately, his survey took precedence over personal research.

He'd stayed for part of the festivities. Lorna's idea of dancing included grabbing onto his hands and spinning like a wooden top until they couldn't breathe for all the laughing. Rosie's friend Tildy, old Hazel McKinnon, Maudie Tipton, and a few of the other ladies had managed to drag him out for some actual dances by refusing to take no for an answer. Overall, he hadn't embarrassed himself too badly.

Evidently Rosie hadn't been impressed, though, because she'd stayed far from him during the dancing. There were plenty of other partners clamoring for her attention.

He'd never felt more the outsider, and retreating only confirmed the fact. As much as he loved Rosie's world, he'd never be a part of it. Benton lifted his eyes, leaning back against the trunk to stare at the night sky. Much of it was obscured by the tree canopy, but in between the branches he caught glimpses of star-studded loveliness and the glow of a full moon. Out of reach, just like everything else in his life.

Soon he'd head back to Ithaca. He pulled off his spectacles and scrubbed a palm over his face, pushing away the jumble of feelings that had overtaken him in recent weeks. He'd come to the Smokies to study birds, to prove himself an explorer like his colleague, and to unwind from a busy year. He hadn't expected to find love.

The thought of leaving Rosie behind stirred up an ache deep in his chest. If only he could stick a paperweight on the calendar pages long enough to figure out what his blasted heart was doing to him.

But the university president was insisting on his immediate return. Someone needed to get the department in shape before the fall term began, and apparently it fell to Benton. He folded his arms as he watched the tree cavity opposite him. Birdwatching did offer a man time to think. Too much time.

He blew out a long breath. A few months ago he'd have been delighted with the turn of events. Not with Hayden's death, mind you, but with finally being recognized for his work and his passion for native birdlife. He'd long toiled for status and prestige in his field, only to be eclipsed by the ornithologists who caught the fancy of donors with their exotic, tropical discoveries.

But accepting the honor meant leaving this place—leaving Rosie—behind. Maybe not forever, but for long enough. Next time he returned, it would probably be with research grants and a team of students eager to obtain specimens and skins for the growing ornithology collection at

Cornell's Museum for Vertebrates and the new museum the park hoped to build at Sugarlands. Things wouldn't be the same.

One of the owls fluttered to a landing on a branch near Benton's head, its pointed ear tufts conspicuous in the moonlight. Benton held still, determined not to frighten the creature and lose the opportunity for close observation.

The owl fixed its piercing yellow-eyed gaze on him, a mouse gripped in its talons. A moment passed before it released the branch and sailed over to the nest cavity, the female popping her head out to greet him.

Benton put his glasses back on, his hands trembling, and watched as the couple shared the meal. Hoot and Annie—as Rosie referred to them—would never be skinned and mounted, nor any of their progeny. If he returned for specimens, he'd assure they were obtained from another area of the park. It wasn't proper to get attached to one's subjects, but the deed was done.

A twig snapped nearby, and Benton leaned to the side to catch a glimpse of the trail below. Rosie's face appeared warm in the lantern light. Could she even see him?

She doused the light and reached for the ladder rungs.

Benton tried to keep himself in check, but he was pretty certain a dopey smile had overtaken his face. "I'm surprised to see you. A hostess shouldn't abandon her own party."

She landed her posterior on the rough boards. "Only for a few minutes. Lorna's gone off to bed, though, so I don't have to worry after her." She scooted close to his side, as had become their habit of late. "How are Hoot and Annie and the kids?"

"Hoot brought his mate a mouse, but I think he's taken off again. I haven't seen the others. I think the fledglings may have flown."

"How quickly they grow up and leave us." She sighed, nudging his arm. "Won't be long afore you're flying off too."

"I don't want to think about it." Like he'd been doing anything but.

He slid his arm around her waist, as he'd longed to do all evening. "Not tonight."

"I wish you could stay."

The words tugged at him. If only she knew how tortured he'd been. "I have to go back."

"I know." Her hair smelled of woodsmoke from the bonfire. She didn't often wear it loose like this, but he relished how it draped over his own shoulder as she rested her head. "You said you wanted to talk about something. I ain't got much time."

Benton turned so he could face her, determined not to waste this opportunity to say his piece. If there was even a chance of her agreeing, it was worth the risk.

The moonlight filtered its way through the tree limbs and glistened across her hair and cheeks in a way that made his thoughts slow. He touched her jaw, brushing his thumb along the feather-soft skin of her cheek and then her lower lip. If only he could somehow capture this moment, he would live in it until the end of time.

Every planned word scattered from his mind, so instead he leaned forward and kissed her.

Her soft intake of breath gave him pause, but after a moment she pressed her lips back to his, sending a wave of desire through him. The touch of her fingers on his chest was more than he could handle. He pulled her closer, nearly onto his lap, wrapping both arms around her.

"No, wait." Her hand landed hard against his chest, fingers splayed.

With a monumental effort, he drew back. The sight of her brows drawn low over troubled eyes made his stomach clench. "What's wrong?"

"Say it." She curled her fingers inward, leaving her fist resting against his ribs.

"Say what?"

"Whatever you were planning to tell me, jes' spit it out. Because if I find you're kissing me to say goodbye or to soften some bit of hard news, I . . . I'll . . ." Rosie shook her head, squeezing her eyes shut. "I'll push you backward off this here platform."

"It's not like that." He gripped both her arms, fighting the urge to crush her against him. "Or at least not intentionally. I wish everything could stay as it is right now. This moment."

She moved her palm to his face. "Me too."

"One more—please. For courage." He waited for her to nod before kissing her again, gently this time. Then he released her, and she scooted a little distance from him. All the better for rational thought. He'd been very lacking in that department lately. Benton took a deep breath and threw out the crazy idea that had been hounding him all evening. "Come with me, Rosie. Come to New York."

Her mouth opened for a second before she managed a half laugh. "You're joking me. You know I can't. My sister—"

"We'll bring her with us." He captured her hands again. "I have a place in Ithaca. There are doctors and teachers there. Maybe they could help her open up some. Learn to speak even."

She slid away, her head shaking. "No. I won't uproot her just because you are feeling protective of us."

"I'm not being protective. I'm being selfish." Benton bit back a stream of arguments. Quibbling about words would get him nowhere. "I want to marry you, Rosie. I want you to be my wife. I love you."

"Your . . . your . . ." Her mouth fell open—the lips he'd been kissing just a minute before and had every intention of doing so again.

"My wife. Please say you'll marry me."

She let go of his hand, reaching over to grasp the trunk. "I don't know what to say."

"Do you love me?"

"I do, but—"

"Then marry me." The space she'd put between them felt like a canyon, and it was deepening by the second.

"No. I can't. Now stop this nonsense and start hearin' me—please."

She pressed a fist to her lips. "Benton, I do love you. Marrying you would be a . . . a dream. But you must know that I can't."

The words knifed through him. "Why?"

"This is my home—mine and Lorna's. It's my land."

"It's *government* land."

The jerk of her head upward sent a sickening sensation through him. He might as well have slapped her. "I'm sorry. That was . . ." He reached out but stopped just short of touching her. "Rosie, it wouldn't be forever. We could summer here, like I did at my grandparents' place, growing up. We can work out something with the lease. I'll make sure we don't lose access to the cabin." He blathered on, hoping he could stem the tears now sliding down her face. "You've never seen a city as beautiful as Ithaca at Christmastime. You'll love it."

She curled her arms inward toward her chest. "It's not that I won't live anywhere else, Benton. I *cain't* live elsewhere. This place is in my blood, my bones. I won't leave here, not ever."

"My work is in New York. What do you expect me to do?"

Rosie drew the little stone bird from her pocket and laid it on her lap, running a thumb over its surface. He'd seen her fiddle with the keepsake before. Did it offer some sort of peace he couldn't provide?

Without lifting her eyes, she whispered in a husky tone, "You could stay here. Iffen you stayed, we could be wed."

He closed his eyes and lowered his forehead until it touched hers. "I'm no one here. An outsider."

"I'd be an outsider there." Her breath was warm against his cheek.

"It's not the same. You'd make friends, fit in, with enough time." He slid his hand over hers, the stone warm between their clasped palms.

"And you will here." She looked up at him through her damp eyelashes. "In time."

"I won't. The people here, they're set in their ways. I'll always be the G-man, the newcomer. Unwelcome."

She squeezed his hand. “I came around, didn’t I? And Lorna. Beau and Maudie?”

He sat back as his thoughts jumbled. “A wife is supposed to follow her husband.”

“This land belonged to my ma’s kin. When they wed, my pa came to live here and built the cabin. He always said the cabin was his but the land was my ma’s.” She lifted the Cherokee carving, holding it in her flat palm. “And in the tradition of my great-grandmother’s people, the man joins his wife’s clan.” She bit her lip. “I reckon your way ain’t the *only* way.”

“But I live in the real world, Rosie.” He hated the bitterness creeping into his voice. “I’m up for department chair at the university. I’ve waited a lifetime for such an opportunity, and I’m supposed to throw it all away for . . .” He gestured to the bonfire down below. “For a shack in the mountains?”

She jammed the bird into her pocket. “Of course not. That would be plumb crazy.” She scooted to the end of the platform and onto the ladder, descending a few steps. She stopped with just her face showing above the edge of the platform, her eyes trained on her hands. “You might be a professor at some fancy college, but you’re dumber than a sack of rocks, Benton Fuller.”

# 11

## Great Smoky Mountains National Park
## Present Day

KIERAN SAT IN the chair across from Zach's desk. She'd pictured a woodsy ranger station, complete with log walls and a stuffed bobcat mounted under glass, but this modern building couldn't be more different. The window behind him looked out onto the parking lot, and a large poster print of a log cabin hung on the wall.

"Right." Zach tapped a few keys on his computer. "I hope you didn't have any trouble with the hot water. It's been a little unpredictable lately."

"I thought I was in heaven, trust me."

She earned a half smile for that. His chair squeaked as he leaned back, his lanky frame not really looking at home behind a desk. "So you mentioned your great-grandparents. They lived in this area?"

"That's what my Granny Mac tells me. She's shared memories of living in a cabin in the woods and said that the land was taken over by the park."

"Do you know what part of the park?"

"That's what I'm trying to figure out. I don't have much to go on." She bounced her knee. "My gran is . . . she's suffering from dementia." Putting the malevolent name on Granny Mac's situation always felt like dropping a stone into a deep pool. The ripples moved out from somewhere near Kieran's stomach all the way to her fingertips. "She's fixated on her childhood, and the memories seem disturbing. I'd like to understand a little more about her experiences."

"She lived in the cabin too? Long enough to remember it?" He folded his arms. "Most of the property was bought up early, in the late twenties and early thirties. How old is your grandmother?"

"I think she's around eighty-five."

He shook his head. "So born around 1937 maybe? Since the park was established in 1934, that doesn't really add up. Are you sure the property was in the park? Maybe she actually grew up in one of the nearby towns?"

"The land was seized by the park service. That's one thing she's been quite adamant about."

His jaw appeared to tighten at the word "seized." It was probably good that she didn't mention Gran's theory about the government being responsible for her mother's death. After all, that might be her illness speaking.

Zach picked up a pen and tapped it on the table, like the rhythm could help him untangle the story. "There were some areas on the North Carolina side of the park that were added later." He unfolded a map and spread it in front of her. Pointing at the southern boundary, he ran the pen tip over a large lake. "The Fontana Dam was built right after the attack on Pearl Harbor to supply electricity to the Aluminum Company of America. Communities around Hazel Creek were inundated, and the land along the north shore of Fontana Lake became part of the park."

Kieran scooted forward in her seat and studied the map. "North Carolina, though? Because she's always said she's from Tennessee. Are you sure there weren't people living in Tennessee who were displaced by the park—within her lifetime?"

He stood up and crossed to a nearby filing cabinet. "There were a few families still living in the Tennessee section even after the creation of the park, plus some vacation cabins in the Elkmont area." Zach slid open a drawer and thumbed through some files. "One thing that makes this park unique is that it was the first national park to be created out of entirely private land. Most of the earlier parks were carved out of publicly owned land—a much simpler scenario than displacing entire communities and farms."

"That must have been hard on the families."

"Most of that land was purchased outright by the two states and then donated to the federal government. It was a big project." He slid a file out of the drawer and carried it to the desk. "But some families fought the process, as you would imagine. Even though it was the Great Depression, they didn't always want to trade their family farms for a check from the government."

"I can imagine. It's such a beautiful place."

He nodded. "In order to speed things up, the government condemned some properties and offered lifetime leases to others. With the leases, owners would sign over the deeds in exchange for the assurance that they could live out their days on their land."

Kieran's heart jumped. "She said they had to leave because her mother died. Do you think my great-grandparents had one of those leases?"

"What was the family's name? Is it the same as yours?"

"No. It's Fuller." She held her breath as he sorted through the documents.

"With the exception of Cades Cove and Elkmont, there isn't a compiled list of lifetime leaseholders in the park. What was your great-grandfather's first name?"

"I . . . I don't know. I'm sorry."

He chuckled. "Don't apologize. I probably couldn't come up with mine either. My sister is the genealogist in the family. She keeps track of all that." He flipped through a few more pages. "Here's a Mr. George Fuller. He didn't have a lifetime lease, it looks more like a special-use permit, but often it worked out much the same. He and his wife lived over in the Cosby area, not far from the park boundary."

"Really? Does it say when or why they left?"

"I'm afraid not. But it's not listed beyond these records in 1947, so they left before then."

She threaded her fingers together to keep from flapping her hands in excitement. "Could I go see it? Is it accessible?"

Zach glanced up at her. "You want to see the property? I thought you just wanted information."

*Get the bird. Kieran needs it.* Kieran swallowed hard. "I thought maybe I could take some photos. It might ease my grandmother's mind. Help her see that her nightmares aren't real."

"The property's not far off the Appalachian Trail, but it would take a bit of bushwhacking to locate anything. Are you prepared for off-trail hiking? Familiar with orienteering using a compass and such?"

She lifted the phone from her lap. "I have GPS."

"That's not going to help you out here." He leaned back in the chair. "I'm not comfortable sending you wandering through the forest alone. If you got lost—or hurt—no one would know. Isn't there someone who could go with you?"

Her social circle was pretty limited. When did she have time? "I have a friend who's former military, so he's probably good at that bushwhacking stuff." Nick wouldn't be able to get away on such short notice, but at least she was telling the truth. "Could you draw me a map? How many paces from the trail, that sort of thing?"

"I'll sketch it out for you guys. And please let me know what you find. You've got me curious now."

She nodded, breathing deep to calm her frazzled nerves. "If I—we—do find the cabin, could I take a little souvenir for my gran? If I just found something lying around?"

The man's brows shot up. "It's against park regulations to remove anything from a historical site."

"It's not a historical site, not really. No one would miss a small stone from the fireplace or something." *Or a stone buried near the chimney.*

"I'm sorry." He pulled a trail guide from the drawer. "The Archaeological Resources Protection Act strictly prohibits disturbing historical or cultural sites on public land. But you can take photographs, like you said. Show those to your grandmother. Maybe make a little video or something for her."

Kieran nodded, twisting her fingers in her lap. "Sure. I'll do that. I just thought I'd ask."

"I'm glad you did. Plenty of folks just do what they want and don't think about the repercussions. Even small infractions can land you with thousands of dollars in fines, plus jail time. Now, when are you planning to go?" He began sketching a map.

"Um, soonish?" She couldn't afford to stay long. "Maybe tomorrow morning, bright and early?"

"You're welcome to use the cabin again. Assuming the moth-eaten mattress didn't scare you off."

Her heart melted. How could this man go from annoying to adorable in two seconds flat? "Are you serious?"

"Does it look like I have a line of renters?"

"You would if you advertised it. But I suppose most vacationers prefer a bit of running water."

"The cabin has running water—whenever it rains. Trust me, you don't want to experience that."

She laughed. "I want to pay for my keep, then. If you won't take cash, I could make dinner for you. I don't get to cook often enough." She should be able to scrape together enough for a few groceries. Her check from the diner had deposited early this morning. Ash must be worried about her.

"It's a date." His grin faltered. "Not a date . . . a d-deal. I don't date women I pick up on the side of the road."

"Or ones who sleep over?"

He covered his face with a hand. "Forget I said anything."

She swallowed a laugh. It was nice to watch someone else struggling with words for once.

• • •

Seeing Kieran's little car sitting there when he rolled into his driveway that evening made Zach smile, despite himself. He liked having people around, and it had been over a week since Miguel had dropped in. After growing up in a big, noisy family, eating alone always seemed more chore than pleasure. He ended up picking off things in the fridge and eating over the sink. That meant fewer dishes to wash, but he'd trade that all for clever conversation and a few laughs.

This woman seemed gifted at both. He'd been reduced to tongue-tied silence a couple of times already. It was a good thing she was a temporary guest, or he could see himself falling for this girl.

Taking home a stranger had been foolhardy, but it felt like something his mother might do. She was continually bringing folks into their house, and if anyone questioned her, she'd point to the verse in the Bible about entertaining angels. Maybe he'd look up that Scripture tomorrow morning during his prayer time.

He turned off the engine and sat in the car for a long moment, imagining what it would be like to come home from work to a wife and family instead of an empty house. When Zach's thoughts trailed back to Jordan, he shoved the door open and hopped out. No need to plow through painful memories.

The evening air held a chill. He should make sure Kieran took a couple of extra blankets to the cabin tonight. Or maybe he could talk her into sleeping on the couch. He ran a hand across the back of his neck. Whatever happened, he didn't want it to sound like he was making a move on her.

Zach opened the door, the mingled smells of bacon and grilled onions flooding over him. He dropped his messenger bag in the mudroom. "This place has never smelled so good. What on earth are you making?"

"Welcome home, Ranger Jensen." She smiled, a flush on her cheeks—from leaning over hot pans or from sunburn, he couldn't tell. "It's almost ready. I went hiking this afternoon, so I cut it close on time. Good thing this recipe is quick."

"Please, call me Zach. I'm not actually a ranger. I'm a curator." He hung up his hat. "And you must have shopped too. I didn't have any bacon in the fridge, or I would have fed it to you at breakfast." He hadn't thought to give her money for groceries.

"I just picked up a few things. Don't worry, I'm a bargain shopper." She swiped a wrist over her brow, pushing her hair to one side. "The bread needs another minute."

He leaned over the stove top, admiring the pasta dish she'd concocted. Florets of broccoli peeped out from under colorful spiral-shaped noodles, dotted with shreds of bacon and some dark-red bits—peppers? Tomatoes? He took a deep whiff, catching some garlic. "I think I could just stand here and smell it."

She shoved him gently on the shoulder. "You get cleaned up. We'll eat in ten minutes."

He grinned all the way to his room, racing to shed the uniform and change into jeans. Clean up? He worked in an office, not a construction site. Well, not today, anyway. Still, he washed his hands and splashed water over his face, running his hand over his chin. He'd shaved this morning, so there was no need to do so again. *Can't believe I'm even considering it.* Pulling a shirt over his head, he returned to the kitchen.

She'd already sliced the bread and added it to the table beside a bowl of salad big enough to feed a family of five. Plates, utensils, and mismatched glasses filled with ice water sat in front of the two chairs. Much better than eating over the sink.

"I couldn't find napkins, so paper towels will have to do." She set the pot of broccoli pasta on top of a folded dish towel, as if concerned about messing up his thrift-store table.

"Sorry. That's what I usually use. Do you mind if I bless the food?" He waited for her to sit down.

Her eyes flickered up to meet his gaze, then lowered quickly as she sat. "Um, no. Go ahead."

His hunger encouraged him to keep the prayer short. "Lord, we thank You for this food and for the hands that prepared it." He couldn't resist opening his eyes and glancing her way. She'd bowed her head but caught her lower lip in her teeth. Had he embarrassed her? "Bless it to the use of our bodies. Amen."

She took a sip from the water glass. "Thank you for letting me stay again. Somehow I doubt that's included in your job description."

"Clearly I'm getting the better end of this deal." He lifted the salad bowl and held it out to her. "You might actually be more comfortable in your car than in that drafty shack."

She smiled, taking the tongs and heaping her plate with the green stuff. "It will be amazing when you're done renovating. I love the idea of creating something homey out of that."

"I don't know how homey it will be. I've been perusing the vacation rental websites. I was thinking about built-in bunk beds. I could squeeze in at least four beds that way. Maybe six, depending on how I turn them."

Kieran glanced up, her brow furrowing. "Why cram them in?"

"Then a big family could stay together."

"I suppose that would be good. But no parents would want to sleep in bunk beds. You're going to end up with drunken frat parties."

That thought was less appealing. "What would you suggest?"

That touch of color reappeared on her cheeks. "It's not my space, but if it were . . . I'd make it rustic and cozy and advertise it as a couple's getaway. Lots of pillows, nice linens, or maybe flannel sheets in buffalo plaid. A good coffee maker." Her eyes took on a faraway look. "With that view, it could be a real draw, especially for people who don't like to camp." She took a bite, covering her mouth with the paper towel, as if she were afraid to chew in front of him. "Oh, and you should make sure the place is accessible—wide doorways, a roll-in shower with grab bars, that sort of thing. There aren't many good options for people with disabilities or for seniors who need a little extra help."

"That's a really good idea." With the exception of whatever "buffalo plaid" was, he could almost picture the place coming together as she described it. "Go on."

"If you really want big families, build an addition for a second bedroom or two. Allow the parents a little privacy. That could be your bunk room, if you're determined to have such a thing."

"I like your description of a couple's getaway. I can see where that might be appealing." Had she been picturing someone when she'd described the romantic escape? Tearing off a hunk of crusty bread, he studied her over the table, her brown ponytail draped across one shoulder. He hadn't noticed how attractive she was when he met her last night. "So . . . your army friend—is he coming to hike with you?"

"Um, about that . . ." She pushed the lettuce around her plate with her fork. "I'm afraid Nick can't get away, and I have to head home Wednesday for work. So it's back to just me." Kieran lifted her eyes, the brown color containing a flintlike spark. "But I can do it. I'll be careful. Nick knows where I'll be, and so do you." She cleared her throat. "I gave him your phone number—I hope you don't mind. The one on the business card."

His appetite faded. "You know you're not just going to step off the trail and bump into an old cabin. Most of them were razed. You might find a chimney, if you're lucky. There could be nothing at all. And your cell phone likely won't get any bars."

"I won't need it. I've got your map."

"It's a crude drawing at best. What if you get lost?"

She laughed and threw up her hands. "I don't know. I'll climb a tree. Yell for help."

He pointed his fork at her, a noodle hooked on the tines. "You're stubborn."

She narrowed her eyes. "And you're patronizing. It's not as if I'm trekking to the North Pole. I'm walking maybe a half mile from a known trail system. How much trouble can I get into?" She dug into the mound of salad on her plate.

Zach couldn't help running the scenarios through his head, but he didn't think it would help to voice them. If she or her boyfriend didn't take the danger seriously, why should he?

"And I don't need your permission. Do I?" She took a sip of water. "Is there a permit system or something I'm not aware of?"

She had him there. "Not unless you're going to camp, no."

"Then I declare this discussion over." She smiled. "I win."

He choked, the broccoli sticking in his throat. "You win? You win what?"

"I might be a bit competitive." Dabbing her lips with the paper towel, she shrugged. "Look, I'll be extra careful. I'll lay a trail of breadcrumbs, if that would make you feel better. I appreciate your concern. I really do."

Her softened stance helped him unwind. Why was he giving her such a hard time, anyway? It wasn't like she was his responsibility, just because he'd picked her up off the side of the road. He took the last bite from his plate, restraining himself from reaching for a third helping. A thought struck him. "I have some comp time due. I could take tomorrow off and go with you, if you'd like company."

She stood, picking up her empty plate and reaching for his.

"Hey, now." He put a hand on his dish, accidentally brushing her fingers. "You cooked. The least I can do is wash up." Obviously he'd overstepped with his rash suggestion. Now she was making a run for it.

She eyed him. "I was clearing space for dessert. You're welcome to the dishes."

"Dessert?" He pressed a fist against his stomach. "You should have warned me."

"It's only a store-bought strawberry-rhubarb pie and some ice cream."

She opened the refrigerator and crouched to retrieve something from the bottom shelf. "We could skip it, if you prefer."

"Let's not get crazy." He hopped up to grab clean plates.

"About tomorrow—"

A loud crash outside made them both jump. Zach slammed the cupboard shut and jogged to the window.

"Is that a prowler?" Kieran's voice shook.

He pressed his face to the dark glass, cupping hands around his eyes to block the light. A large shape moved around out there. He added motion-activated floodlights to his mental list for the hardware store. "I'm not sure." Ducking down the hall, he yanked open the back door.

A couple of black bear cubs tussled with each other, rolling away from a skillet sitting in the dirt. A larger bear ambled over and sniffed the pan before hunkering down on its haunches and scooping it up with massive paws, dipping its snout inside.

"Oh no." Kieran had come up behind him and peeked around his arm. "It's the bacon grease. I didn't want it stinking up the house, so I set the pan outside to cool."

"That's one way to get it clean." He went back and dug a large spoon and pot from the cupboard. "But leaving food out isn't a good idea in bear country. We don't want to encourage them to view people as a food source." Swinging the door open a crack, he banged on the pot.

The mama bear lifted her head and stared. With a huff, she led her cubs off into the woods, the handle of the skillet still clamped in her jaws.

"Will you ever see that again?" Kieran turned away from the scene. "Or do I owe you a frying pan?"

He closed and locked the door. "I'll look around for it tomorrow. Maybe she'll drop it nearby."

"About tomorrow—"

"Forget it." He lifted a hand to stop her flow of words. "I realize how presumptuous and *patronizing* it probably sounded, me offering to accompany you. You don't need my protection."

"It's not that—not exactly. Visiting my gran's old place . . ." She lowered her gaze. "It's more than simple genealogy for me. This journey is kind of personal."

"I understand." Zach studied her profile. Something about her expression tugged at him. He'd known her all of twenty-four hours, yet he had to fight the instinct to pull her in for a quick hug. "But at the risk of coming off as too controlling, can I ask a favor?"

She glanced up at him. "Anything."

"Call me when you get back in range."

• ● •

Kieran rolled over on the lumpy mattress, trying to wake up enough to push herself out of the cozy cocoon. She wanted to start out before daybreak so she could find Gran's cabin and be back on the road before it got late.

Zach had been kind to offer to join her. She'd grown up in the city, so the idea of traipsing alone into the dark woods felt like she was about to act out every horror-movie cliché she'd ever seen. Anything could be out there, like serial killers, rabid bears, snakes, or screeching owls. Even bats. Did bats live in the woods? As soon as Zach had made the suggestion, she'd had to bite her tongue not to jump at the offer.

Her small backpack not only contained important stuff like trail mix and a water bottle—it also held a folding shovel. No matter what he'd said about regulations, Gran needed her mom's stone bird.

Kieran twisted in the sleeping bag, tucking her knees up to her belly. *Thousands of dollars of fines, plus jail time.* Isn't that what he'd said?

A noise outside the dark window drew her attention. She jerked upright as footsteps thudded on the porch. That didn't sound like an animal. Had she locked the door? Did it even have a lock? This was what she got for going home with a stranger.

When the hinges creaked, Kieran scooted back against the wall and shrieked.

Light splashed into her eyes, blinding her to whatever lay beyond. She screamed a second time, the sound dissolving into a choking sob. She was going to be murdered before she even made it to the woods.

"Whoa—I'm sorry!" The beam of light wobbled, then lowered to illuminate a pair of dirty hiking boots. "I'm a friend of Zach's. I didn't realize he had company."

Kieran struggled for breath, her chest heaving. Somehow she'd rolled off the mattress and onto the floor. The novel she'd finished last night pressed into her hip. Scrambling to worm her way out of the bag, she pushed up to her knees before remembering that she'd slept in a T-shirt and underwear. She yanked the covers up to her ribs. "Who are you?"

"I'm Miguel—wildlife intern. I crash here sometimes. Are you okay?" He lifted the light so she could catch a glimpse of him. A gray hoodie obscured his head, but his face looked earnest.

Her breathing eased a notch. "You know Zach?"

"Yeah—oh, here he comes. You must have woken the whole neighborhood."

Zach probably *was* the whole neighborhood.

"Miguel!" The familiar voice called from the direction of the distant house. "Get over here."

The young man lifted his hand in front of him. "Sorry. I'll just pull the door shut behind me."

"You do that." Kieran was surprised at the snap in her voice. But then again, it was hard to be a morning person when a stranger waltzed into your bedroom.

After the door clicked shut, she freed her feet from the bag and reached for her things. No way was she going back to sleep now. After two nights with a roof over her head, she'd let her guard down. If she'd been tucked inside her Volvo, she'd have expected intruders.

Fifteen minutes later she was loading her car when Zach stepped out his door, shoving his arms into a jacket. "I'm so sorry. I had no idea Miguel was coming. I'd given him an open invitation, so it should have dawned on me."

"It's an unusual time to drop in on someone."

Zach ran a hand through his rumpled hair. "He keeps odd hours. I think the man is part raccoon." He pushed a paper bag toward her. "I wanted to give you this before you took off. It's breakfast to go, plus some leftovers from last night. It might do for lunch."

Her throat tightened. "You do know when someone is staying free of charge, you're not required to feed them."

"I know. But you've got a long day planned, and I wanted to give you a decent start. There's no coffee, but I put a bottle of sweet tea in there."

"Thanks." She took the bag and pulled it close to her chest. "I can't tell you how much I appreciate all you've done for me. I might have to fill out one of those employee comment cards. 'Zach is the best. Give him a big raise.'"

He chuckled. "Please don't. I don't want to explain to my boss why I took a visitor home with me. Miguel's already giving me grief about it."

"Then I suppose you'll have to make do with this." She grabbed his arm so she could rise up on her toes and plant a kiss on his cheek. The spontaneous move seemed to take them both off guard. Kieran stepped back, putting extra space between them. "Thanks again. I'd better get going. I'll . . ." *I'll call you.* Hadn't she said she would? Why did that now feel weird? "I'll let you know how my expedition turns out."

He gave her a quick nod. Jamming one hand into his coat pocket, Zach offered a half wave with the other before climbing the steps toward his door.

She couldn't jump in the car fast enough, still feeling the prickle of his unshaven cheek against her lips. It was a good thing he wasn't coming with her today. There was no way she could hide a blush for that many hours.

# 12

Sweat dampened Kieran's T-shirt, and she hadn't even taken a step yet. She clutched the hand-drawn map and stared at the signpost for the Low Gap Trail. Less than three miles to the junction with the Appalachian Trail. It was nothing. She studied the fog-draped forest and tried to push away every dark thought gathering in her head. *Do it for Gran.*

Checking the laces on her old running shoes, she forced herself forward. The directions said that the creek crossed the path in two miles, then to follow that upstream until she found a clearing. If she was lucky, the cabin would be there somewhere.

She walked the first half mile slowly, her head swiveling back and forth as she imagined every possible hazard. Zach thought she wasn't taking him seriously, but she'd watched enough true crime shows to realize that if she disappeared out here, her body might never be found. Best not to think about all the crawling insects moving around in the soil beneath her feet, waiting to attack. Kieran hooked her thumbs under her backpack's straps and trudged on.

Some people actually enjoyed this sort of outing. The fresh air and quiet was supposed to refresh her soul, wasn't it? Maybe she needed to give it a fair chance. Drawing in a deep breath, she allowed the earthy fragrance of damp trees and moss to wash over her and push some of her fears into the background.

A trickle of water crossed the path, but she was able to step over it without any problems. Kieran pulled the map from her jacket pocket and unfolded the lined sheet. Zach's pencil sketch looked like a treasure map, minus the yellowed paper and calligraphy. But he had drawn a big *X* at the end. The official trail was marked as a dashed line, the creek as a meandering solid one. Just past the creek, tiny dots showed the suggested traverse up to the cabin site. He'd even drawn a cute little map key, as if she couldn't figure out his meaning. His careful and methodical ways were sort of endearing, if a little over-the-top.

This tiny streamlet hardly qualified as a creek. She scanned the hillside. Was this it, or was there a larger stream ahead? She tucked the paper away. She likely hadn't come far enough yet. Maybe this one wasn't big enough to qualify for its own line on the map. It was more of a cute little baby creek.

She continued walking as the sun broke through the fog, illuminating the droplets of water hanging on the tips of nearby leaves and a spider's web draped across the trail. She'd already face-planted her way through several, so it was nice to duck this one. Was that the real reason people carried those graphite hiking poles? Spider defense?

The climb grew steeper the farther she hiked, and she didn't relish the thought of leaving the safety of the trail and bushwhacking her way through wildwoods. Rather than imagining tumbling into some hole filled with snakes, she forced herself to visualize stepping into a magical meadow of wildflowers, a rustic little cabin appearing out of the mist on the far side. *It could happen.*

The next creek looked much more promising. The cataract tumbled its way down the steep slope, bouncing over rocks and cobbles and drowning out the buzz of nearby insects. A wooden footbridge spanned the short width, allowing her to cross without muddying her shoes. She drew the map out again, its folds becoming soft and warm in her fingers. The bridge was marked on the map with tiny little brackets where it crossed the stream. Of course. Why hadn't she noticed that before? Maybe because Mr. Perfectionist hadn't put it in his list of menu options.

She pushed away her annoyance at herself for wasting so much time at the little rivulet earlier. Obviously, this was the correct choice. The realization sent a quiver through her stomach as she glanced up the hillside. This was much rockier and more vegetated than the last spot. She'd need to scramble with both hands and feet in a few places, from the looks of it.

It couldn't be helped. She'd refused Zach's offer, so there was no sense in turning back now. *Self-sufficiency is nothing but pride on steroids.* Isn't that what Nick had told her? Evidently, she had to learn her lessons the hard way. And repeatedly.

Sucking in a deep breath, Kieran glanced around before stepping off the trail. She hadn't seen a soul since she'd left the road earlier, but she really didn't relish explaining why she was traipsing off into the forest alone. *No one to hear you scream.* The line from a thousand horror movies slithered through her memory before she could brush it away. But it also meant no one would see her make a fool of herself.

She dug a toe into the soft forest duff and grabbed a nearby sapling to help hoist herself up the first muddy incline. After a short slip, she managed to plant her knee in the muck and then push to her feet.

And so it went for the next several hundred feet. Up, slip, smoosh, crawl, walk, scramble . . . She lost count of how many branches whipped her in the face and how many imagined spiderwebs she brushed from her eyes. Kieran focused on keeping the creek to her left as she ascended the rugged hill, but the thick vegetation kept pushing her farther from the water's edge. It made sense that the shrubs held tight to the creek bed, and it shouldn't matter as long as she could hear its sound. But it also meant that she was veering off the path Zach had set for her. How far did she need to go before finding the lovely flowered meadow?

Kieran paused, panting. Turning around, she sat her rear down on the muddy ground and glanced toward the path, just to check her location.

The trail had vanished.

Her hands went clammy. Kieran tried to push up to her feet for a better view, but her rubbery knees refused to cooperate, and she splatted down onto her pockets. "No, no, no . . ." She shouldn't have gone far enough to lose sight of her lifeline back to civilization. Her heart thudded double time. Brushing her dirt-stained hands on the front of her jeans, Kieran leaned forward and hung her head between her knees—an easy feat on this incline. Wasn't that what they said to do in novels if you were hyperventilating? Or was it breathe into a paper bag? Of course, if she stayed in this position long, she might just roll down the hill.

Giddy laughter bubbled up from her chest. Kieran rotated and pushed her way farther up the hill. Another hundred yards or so would make little difference if she were already lost, but stopping short would be admitting defeat.

Finally the hill leveled out and Kieran was able to stand, her legs shaking. The trail was still out of view, but up ahead she could see more light. Perhaps it was the clearing she was looking for? Whether Zach had mentioned a clearing or whether her mind had merely constructed that detail, she grabbed on to the hope and surged forward. Trotting the short distance, she glanced about for some evidence of human habitation. A cabin would be ideal, but at this point she'd take anything—a fence, a forgotten tool, an overgrown orchard.

Nothing.

Well, not exactly nothing. There did seem to be several large cow pies dotting the grass. Wait—cows in the woods? Kieran refused to let her mind dwell on what else might create piles of manure of unusual size. She walked the edges of the oblong-shaped clearing. Was it an old homesite or just a random open patch in the trees?

She'd already walked across the meadow about four times, but in one last-ditch effort, she traversed the field again, staring down at her feet, hoping to unearth some hint of Granny Mac's past. A coin, a plate—anything. She'd never recover the bird statue if she couldn't even find where the house used to be.

Ten steps in, the soil gave way under her left foot and her shoe dropped a good twelve inches into a wet hole. A jolt of pain shot up her calf, and she yelped, going down on the opposite knee. Pulling her foot free, Kieran rolled to her back and whimpered. What was she doing? There was nothing here but mud, brush, and trees . . .

And beautiful clouds. Her breath came in ragged gasps as she stared up at the sky, waiting for the throbbing in her ankle to ease. This truly was a lovely spot, even if Granny Mac's family cabin was nowhere to be found. She could picture Gran here as a little girl, skipping through the meadow and climbing trees in the woods—probably smart enough to avoid stepping in gopher holes, or whatever that had been. Kieran pushed up on her elbows in the dirt. A gorgeous place for a cabin, just like Gran had said.

She swiveled her head. Hadn't Gran spoken of a ridge? Her mother's mountain? Kieran sat up. There was more of a rise behind her, but she wouldn't call it a ridge. She was practically on top of the hill already. Exhaustion draped over her. As pretty as this spot was, it wasn't a real match to what Gran had described. She'd mentioned the creek and a hill that rose above the cabin, casting its shadow down on them.

Kieran tried to imagine the place through a child's eyes, but it was no use. No matter how small the kid, that hill wouldn't match Gran's memories.

She sighed and dug the map out of her pocket one last time, tracing the lines with her finger. She'd followed the course Zach had set out for her. This had to be exactly what the *X* showed.

But it wasn't the right site.

• • •

Kieran pulled into the parking lot at Ash and Nick's condo with a cloud over her head. The trip to learn more about her kin had been a waste, and perhaps she was a fool to think there was any value in tracking her roots. Maybe family was nothing but a construct of society like her sociology professor at Penn State had claimed. As a naive freshman, she'd argued the point with the man, but she'd had too little ammunition for the battle. With a dead mom and a father in prison, her experience of the family unit was limited to the scraps of normalcy given to her by foster parents. Maybe that was why she'd chosen psychology over sociology.

When an impromptu internet search had done what child services never could—tracking down Granny Mac—she'd grabbed on to the relationship with both hands. Most people moved to Nashville to be near country music. She wanted family. Real family. Now the threads of memory connecting her to Gran were unraveling, and the one item that might slow the process had eluded her grasp.

Trying to shake off the gloom, Kieran grabbed her backpack and wadded up the sleeping bag under her arm. Maybe SeniorCo would get their ducks in a row this week and issue those overdue paychecks. As much as she loved Ash and Nick, she didn't want to take up space in their apartment any longer than necessary.

Ash threw the door open before Kieran even reached the mat. "You're home! Tell me everything."

*Home.* Kieran let the heavy pack slide down her leg and thump on the floor before giving her friend a hug. "There's little to tell. The Smokies are gorgeous, but they're good at keeping secrets."

Minutes later, she and Ashleigh were sprawled on the sofa, swiping through the pictures on her phone. "That's the view from the cute little cabin I told you about."

"The hot park ranger's?" Ash beamed. "Did you get a picture of him?"

Kieran sat up. "I never said he was *hot*. I said he was a pain."

"You've never liked having anyone tell you what to do."

"Or what not to do. Especially when I wasn't hurting anyone." She turned the screen so she could relive the fantastic view from the cabin's porch. She should have gotten a photo of Zach. "But then, he did take me in and helped me research Gran's story."

"Sounds like a hot prospect to me." Ashleigh's wicked grin spread. "But he didn't find anything to corroborate Granny Mac's story about her mother being murdered?"

"I didn't mention that bit because it sounds so far-fetched. But he did say that some people were allowed to live in the park even after it was opened to the public." Kieran patted her bag. "I bought a couple of history books at the gift shop. One said that the last leaseholder died in the 1960s, so that lasted a long time. And some people were able to keep their vacation cabins up through the nineties."

Ashleigh took the phone and flipped through a few more shots. "Why didn't your great-grandfather stay there to raise Granny Mac after his wife's death? Too many bad memories?"

"Maybe." Kieran stretched and yawned. "I'll pay attention if Gran says anything else. She might give some more hints. But I don't think I'll be able to find anything that will help her."

"Maybe you'll find something to help *you*."

Four hours later she woke to find herself still on the sofa and the apartment dark, one of Gran's knitted afghans draped over her. She crept off to the spare room and climbed into bed. A few more hours of sleep and then she could check on Granny Mac, put in eight hours at SeniorCo, and head over for a shift at the diner.

Her whole body ached from the long day of hiking and driving. If only she could just close her eyes and imagine herself someplace quiet and peaceful, like Zach's little cabin in the woods. Maybe someday she could go spend a real vacation there. A romantic getaway for one—just her and a stack of novels. That sounded perfect.

• • •

Zach centered a nail on the two-by-four Miguel held in place for him.

His friend groaned. "Hurry up. This is getting heavy."

He'd never managed to sink one in a single strike, but he still made quick work of securing the board. "A few more of those and we'll have the bathroom framed in."

"As long as you don't get the bright idea to enlarge it again." Miguel walked over and stared at the designs, spread on a couple of sawhorses. "And it's a long way from framed in to plumbed in. Let me know when that happens, and we'll celebrate."

Kieran's suggestions regarding accessibility had hit home with Zach, and he'd completely revamped his plan for the bathroom and kitchen, ensuring adequate room for wheelchairs and walkers. The cabin would appeal to a larger clientele with just a few modest changes. He'd have to be sure to thank her for the insight. "The plumber comes tomorrow."

"Yeah, well, take your time. Once you're done, I'll be apartment hunting. Is your little friend making a return visit anytime soon? Next time I'll be sure to call."

Zach drove another nail into the support. "It was more of a one-time thing. I got a text from her. The place we'd marked out on the map was a no-go. I think I sent the poor woman on a snipe hunt."

"I get out to the Cosby section of the Trail sometimes. Are you sure they lived out that way?"

"Not at all. I just found a record of a Fuller having a cabin there."

"Fuller." Miguel's brow furrowed. "That was the family name? Was he park service?"

"I don't think so." Picking up the T-square, Zach marked off the next three cuts. "Why do you ask?"

"I read a paper about owls recently by a biologist named Fuller."

Zach's hand stilled on the saw handle. "This guy wouldn't still be publishing papers."

Miguel's lip quirked up. "It was written in the thirties. He was the first to identify many of the bird species in the park." He walked over to his backpack. "I've got a copy. We've been trying to evaluate how much the populations have changed. I remember seeing the name. Any chance he's your guy?"

Zach's heart jumped. Two days spent scouring the files, but it was an offhand comment from a wildlife tech that clued him in? Research could be that way sometimes. "Are you kidding me? If he was park service, I can track him through his service record." He paused, his mind spinning to the conversation with Kieran in his office. She'd said the park had evicted her relatives after someone had died. That was why his mind had gone to the lifetime leases. But if the great-grandfather worked for the park, maybe there was another reason they'd left.

Pulling the dog-eared sheets from the front sleeve of his pack, Miguel flipped it over and grinned. He jabbed a finger at the last page. "B. Fuller, 1934."

"No way." Zach took it from his hand and stared at the name. "Look who's becoming a historian."

"Does this mean your beautiful houseguest will make a return trip? Maybe you'll introduce me this time."

"I think you already made a bad first impression."

"She obviously made a good impression on you."

Zach unplugged the saw. "Can I hang on to this article for now? I'm going to go see if I can track the fellow down. I owe you one."

"Grill up some ribs tonight and we'll call it even."

Five minutes later Zach was poring over computer files looking for Fuller in the park's records. There was precious little to be found. If he'd worn the uniform, there should be mention of him. He located an abstract for Miguel's article, plus a handful of others that listed the man as author. But he couldn't find any employee records. In fact, Fuller's credentials were from Cornell, so in all likelihood he was just a visiting scientist. Zach's knee bounced a steady rhythm below the desk, a nervous habit he'd picked up as a teen.

Researching visitors' genealogy was not his job, but something about Kieran's story tugged at him. Or maybe it was just Kieran. Zach ran both hands over his face, in a vain attempt to push away the disconcerting sensation that Miguel might be right. He never figured himself for the type to be swayed by a pretty face, and yet he couldn't stop thinking about her wit and her lively brown eyes.

*The woman is taken.* He'd reminded himself of that many times in the past two weeks. He really should let this search go, for the sake of his own sanity. She hadn't even asked him to keep looking.

He pushed back from the desk. If he didn't get the grill fired up, they weren't going to eat before midnight.

But he didn't rise from the chair. *What if Fuller met a local girl and stayed?* Zach slid forward and tapped a few keys, bringing up the page of notes he'd written regarding Kieran's initial information request. He'd failed to get a maiden name for the great-grandmother.

He stared at the screen for five minutes before clicking into his email. This was a bad idea.

• • •

Kieran took a final swig of her latte and tossed the paper cup into the trash bin outside Granny Mac's building. It was getting progressively more difficult to drag herself through the doors and face the staff. Once a room opened in the memory-care wing, they'd be moving Gran to the more secure area. But for now, the CNAs were having to work twice as hard to keep her grandmother calm and safe. She dreaded the next phone call.

Kieran pushed through the doors and headed for the front counter.

The lobby was mostly empty, so she managed to get signed in without any fuss.

Her phone vibrated as she walked down the long hallway lined with watercolor paintings of old barns. The notifications showed an email from Zach, and she stopped midstep. She hadn't heard anything from the historian except the brief apology for leading her astray.

The subject line read, *Found B. Fuller.* Clicking the message open, she devoured the words. Cataloging birds for the National Park Service? Could this be her great-grandfather?

The fact that Zach was still pursuing this surprised her. She'd jumped right back into life and work, hardly having a moment to mull over her experience in the Great Smokies. Well, not exactly true. Her thoughts had lingered on Zach many times, as her rapid pulse now confirmed. *He's just helping with family research. It doesn't mean he's into you.*

At the bottom of the note, he asked for more details about her great-grandmother. A full name and date of birth might help track down the family land. Kieran returned the phone in her pocket and tapped on Gran's door. There had to be a way of getting that info without upsetting her. "Granny Mac? It's Kieran."

Gran looked up from her recliner, a bundle of yarn loose in her lap. "Hello, dear. Come on in." The television news blasted at full volume.

"You look good." Kieran dropped her bag on the table and walked over to claim the chair next to her grandmother. "What are you watching?"

Gran reached for the remote and turned down the racket. "Just bad news. That's all they ever talk about anymore. But a body can only take so many home makeover shows before all your brain cells turn to mush."

"I love the ones where they redo someone's house while they're on vacation."

Gran shook her head. "What's wrong with their old ones, that's what I say. We need to be thankful for what the good Lord's given us. There's something to be said for the old ways." She glanced down at the knitting project. "For things made by hand and for family heirlooms. Instead, it's out with the old and in with the new."

Probably not a good day to bring up her impending move to the memory-care unit. "What are you working on?"

She lifted the half-made project from her lap. "A baby blanket, but I can't recall whose baby it's for." She latched her gaze on Kieran. "Is it yours? You're not expecting, are you?"

Kieran laughed. "No, not me. There's not even a man in my life, remember?" She needed to strike the word "remember" from her vocabulary. It always sounded a little demeaning.

Gran rubbed a thumb over the fall-colored yarn. "I suppose there's always another baby coming along somewhere who will need warming. I only had the two, you know. But my mama had four, even though she died young. I was the last."

Kieran sat forward. "You've never mentioned siblings. Does that mean I have great-aunts and great-uncles?"

Her smile fell as she patted Kieran's knee. "Once upon a time, dear one. Now, are you Robert's daughter?"

"No, Michael's." The silken threads of family slid through Kieran's grasp once more. Without Gran's help, she'd never be able to weave it all together. Her throat tightened. "You must have been such a blessing to your parents."

"Papa would have wrapped me in cotton batting if Ma had let him. But she always reminded him fledglings needed to stretch their wings in order to learn to fly." A dark look shadowed her face. "Her great-grandmother had been a Cherokee woman of the bird clan. Did I ever tell you that?"

"Really? I didn't realize we had Native American heritage." Kieran tried to count the generations in her head. If it was true, that would make Kieran what—six generations removed?

"Ma had some wonderful stories. I think that bird stone she carried was a Cherokee carving."

Kieran thought about Zach's news. She hadn't told Gran about her trip or her search for information about her great-grandparents. "What about your father? Did he like birds too?"

"Oh yes. Papa could mimic nearly any birdsong you can imagine. I hear them sometimes when I'm sleeping, and I open my eyes, thinking he's in the room somewhere." A smile crossed Gran's lined face. "He was a university professor. We lived on the campus at Florida State University after we left Tennessee. I've told you that before."

She certainly had *not.* Kieran dropped her hand onto the armrest with a thud. Zach had been right. "Florida? I thought you'd lived in Tennessee your whole life."

"No. After Mama died, he took us south." Her nose wrinkled, and she shuddered. "I missed my mountains."

She'd learned more about Gran's history in this short conversation than she had in the two years she'd known the woman. Kieran drew her phone from her pocket and discreetly turned on the voice-recorder app. "How old were you when you moved to Florida?"

Gran retrieved the tissue she always kept hidden in her sleeve. "I lost everything when we left Tennessee. My mother, my home, my . . ." Tears filled her eyes. "I *hated* Florida. I think I made him pretty miserable." Her voice even sounded childlike in that moment. "He died a few years later in an automobile accident. I lived with some family friends after that. But never got back home."

Apparently Gran's childhood was as untethered as Kieran's. "How did a university professor end up living in the Smokies?"

Gran grew quiet, shifting in her seat and staring down at the knitting. "I'm knitting a baby blanket. Who's having a baby? Is it you, sweetheart?"

And just like that, lucidity evaporated. No matter how many classes Kieran had taken on aging, nothing prepared her for watching someone she loved lose and then find pieces of herself, only to misplace them again. "Not me, Gran. Not yet."

"Someday you will, dear. Someday." Gran wiped the tissue over the tip of her nose and sniffled. "My mother never gave up on babies. You ought not either. It ain't the McCauley way." She folded the blanket and tucked it into the sewing basket beside her chair.

McCauley was Gran's first name, though few called her that. Kieran leaned forward and touched her grandmother's hand to refocus her attention. "Is McCauley a family name?"

Gran gripped her cane and heaved herself upward to a wobbling stand. "I think I'm going to turn in. I'm bone weary."

Kieran jumped to assist her, but Granny Mac shook her off. "You can go, dear. We'll do tea next time. I think I'm clean out anyhow." She clucked her tongue as she made her way to the bathroom. "Bring that nice fellow too. He's a looker."

"Nick? I'll ask him." Kieran checked the time. Maybe she could stop at the grocery store on the way home and pick up Gran's tea, plus a few groceries for Ash and Nick. They weren't letting her pay rent—she should provide something.

Gran turned on the bathroom light and turned to face Kieran, one hand on the doorframe. "McCauley was my mother's family name. Rosie McCauley Fuller. If your father had told me about you afore you were born, I would have asked him to name you after your great-grandmother." She glanced toward the window, eyes cloudy. "She deserves to be remembered."

Kieran's heart rose in her chest. "I'll make sure she is, Gran."

# 13

Great Smoky Mountains National Park
October 1932

THE COOL AIR nipped at Rosie's cheeks as she followed Maudie through the woods to her favorite patch of persimmon trees. Gold and red leaves fluttered down around them, like the forest throwing one last shindig afore settling into a restful sleep. "I think it's going to be a cold winter. It's chilly already."

Maudie balanced a basket on one hip. "It's a mite airish, for sure. But we ain't done with the warm days yet. God's just reminding us to prepare for what's to come."

"Good persimmon weather."

"That's right. You know how's awful they taste when you bite into one afore it's had a freeze or two." She stopped at the scrubby tree, fruit dotting the ground around its base. She cast Rosie a grin. "Makes you all pucker-faced."

"I only made that mistake once." She wouldn't mind feeding a few of the early ones to Benton. After his ill-convenient proposal during the barn dance, he'd left the very next day—not even bothering to say goodbye. She'd spent the next few weeks comfortin' Lorna, all while her own heart was bleeding.

Maudie started gathering the orange fruit and laying them carefully in the basket. "Beau told me you was fixin' to deliver some of your honey and jams to the store in town. Maybe I can show you how to whip up some of my persimmon butter to go 'long with it." Maudie made the best fruit butter in all the holler. Every time she came visiting, she brought another jar.

"I'd like that, but this first batch is for a cake. Lorna's birthday is coming up."

"That might perk her up. She's been mighty down ever since Benton left." Maudie gave Rosie a pointed look. "Both y'all been pretty long-faced. You missing him too?"

"More than I would've 'spected." Rosie bent down to rescue some of the fallen fruit. "Got used to having him around."

"I think it's more than that."

Nothing got past Maudie. She'd been a granny woman for nigh on ten years now, delivering most of the babies in the holler. She also knew more about love and family than just about anyone.

"Perhaps so." As they filled their baskets, she shared the story of Benton's proposal and her refusal.

The older woman clucked her tongue. "Tough choice, lovin' folks."

"I couldn't leave my pa's land. He shoulda known that."

"Probably did, deep down." Maudie leaned against the trunk. "But sounds like he couldn't see a way outta his life neither, and that can make a body mighty desperate."

"Don't know why God would put such a fellow in my life anyhow. The only thing I ever asked was to stay on Pa's land. The Lord gives me a way around the whole park thing but then drops this in my lap?"

The older woman wiped her hands on her stained apron. "Maybe the good Lord's tryin' to tell you something, girl."

"What do you mean?"

"You ain't a tree, Rosie. God didn't root you in the ground here. He might just want you to fly."

Rosie bent down to pick up another persimmon, the stone bird in her pocket bouncing against her knee. "So you think I made the wrong choice? I should have walked away from everything my pa built and uprooted Lorna from all she knows?"

Maudie plucked a fruit from one of the low branches and smelled it. "You seen how Lorna holds on to her treasures with everything she's got. You and I know that it's nothing but a pretty little cone or beetle that'll crumble to dirt one day. But she closes them tight in her fist."

"She's constantly hauling stuff home like that."

"Well, we's all a bit like that. We hold on to the things we want—our dreams, our friends, our loved ones—with both hands." She cupped the persimmon in her palm, curving her fingers around it. "If I did that with this here fruit, it'll crush." She walked over to Rosie and reached for her hand, placing the fruit in her palm. "That's why we hold it lightly."

"I don't see how that's anything like this land—my home. I'm not crushing it. If anything, the government is doing that for me."

Maudie turned away and started around the far side of the tree, searching out the best ones for her persimmon butter. "You said Lorna's been holding on to a bunch of cloth scraps. Something from an old quilt, right?"

Every time Rosie spied the shreds of fabric, her stomach turned, remembering the altercations with the Samsons. "She's got a mess of them hidden in her trunk."

"What if God's got a beautiful quilt ready for her, made with the finest store-boughten cloth? She'll never see it iffen she ain't willing to let go of what she has now."

Rosie grabbed on to one of the tree branches. It was clear this conversation had little to do with Lorna. "Maudie, Benton's already skedaddled. I'm not sure what good it does to break this ground now."

"Didn't he say something about coming back to see those owls?"

Rosie ran her fingertips over the pocket bird. Benton returning felt less likely each passing day. "And if he does? Nothing's changed. What is it God wants me to do?"

Maudie walked to Rosie's side, setting her basket on the ground. She held cupped palms in front of her. "Go to the Lord with empty hands, Rosie, just waiting to be filled."

"But what if . . . God wants me to leave here? I just cain't."

"Then mebbe he'll show you how to open your fingers."

• • •

March 1933

Rosie batted a bee away from the gauzy material protecting her neck. The smoker had put most of the insects into a stupor, but a few stragglers had returned as she worked at settling in the new bee gums. She and Lorna had managed to put up enough jars of honey and jam last fall to stock the little store in town. She'd meant to keep the rest for themselves, but then hikers started stopping by the front gate hoping to sample and buy her wares. She wouldn't be caught shorthanded again this year.

Beau had hunted up several more bee trees for them, and if the gums continued to do well, she ought to double her production by the end of the summer. They'd be able to trade the honey for canned goods at the store. She blamed Benton for giving them a taste for the store-bought food. She hadn't even bothered raising hogs this year.

She placed the lid on the last gum, eager to get the garden weeded next. Springtime weeds were popping their heads up faster than green grass through a goose. Trouble was, stray thoughts popped up just as quick, especially since her talk with Maudie last fall. Maybe she'd have liked living in New York. It were tough to imagine, but at least she wouldn't have this pain from missing him so much.

Rosie carried the tools to the shed and grabbed the garden hoe, keeping her eyes away from the cot, now folded and stashed in the corner. If she didn't get on, she might just piddle the day away.

The sound of an engine in the distance set her heart to thumping.

Rosie ducked behind the shed, trying to quiet her nerves. It could be anyone. Peeking around the corner, she spotted the familiar green Ford wheeze to a stop.

A wash of heat raced across her skin. She hadn't expected to see Benton Fuller again, especially after he'd left without saying a word. He hadn't even sent a single letter. The fact that her heart now fluttered at the sight of his vehicle only vexed her more.

Seconds ticked past without the man making an appearance. What in tarnation was he waiting on—did he expect her to run out to welcome him? Throw her arms around him and weep happy tears? She wouldn't. Darting through the yard, she headed for the woods. If Benton wanted to see her, he was going to have to work for it.

Lorna popped out of the chicken coop, her eyes as round as pancakes. "Eh?" She cocked her elbow into a wing shape, flapped it, and then pointed toward the front.

"Yes, I think it's him. You can go say hello if you'd like. I'm going for a-saunter."

Lorna's brows drew together, but Rosie didn't explain herself. She'd cried countless tears in Benton's absence, growing more irked with herself by the day. How like a man to show up just as she started to get life figured out.

Her bare feet picked up speed, her braid slapping against her back like a wagon driver snapping a horse's reins. Rosie ducked through the budding laurels alongside the stream, slowing only to pick her way over the rocky bits. The trees swayed in the late-afternoon breeze, the tiny bursts of spring leaves doing little to block the hopeful blue sky beyond. Usually it was Lorna a-running. Maybe they was more alike than they was different.

The family cemetery lay off to her left, her kinfolks' stones marking their bodies' final spot of rest after their souls winged their way heavenward. Up ahead, she could keep climbing the ridge till she reached the top, but what then? Rail at God for allowing this man to stir her up so? Maudie said to ask Him to help open her hands, but she'd been too afeared that He might just do it.

She sidled off the path to the one place she'd found peace in recent months. Stopping at the tree, she grabbed the bottom rung of the ladder and clambered up into the branches. It was a right foolish place to go, but she'd returned again and again, as if punishing herself with the memories of his kisses. It was torture, but it was also a sweet reminder that she'd been loved.

Rosie lay down on the wooden platform, letting the breeze dry her damp cheeks and steady her nerves. Benton and Lorna were likely still at the house, wondering what had happened to her. Lorna couldn't tell him she'd run for the hills. Wiping her nose with her handkerchief, Rosie sat up, dangling her legs off the edge. A wisp of smoke rose from the cabin's chimney, but the yard remained empty. Perhaps he'd grown weary of waiting. She'd probably squandered her one chance to pitch a hissy fit. She ought to have told him he'd been a fool for leaving just 'cause she'd refused him. And how many times she'd thought about answering him different.

She took the bird from her pocket and nestled it in a crook of the tree's branches, like a sparrow choosing to settle in its nest rather than fly.

The memory of standing beside Benton singing "I'll Fly Away" tugged at her. It had been the same night he'd asked her to go to New York with him.

"*You ain't a tree, Rosie. God didn't root you in the ground here. He might just want you to fly.*" Maudie's words bubbled up like a sweet water spring.

God would ask her to fly away someday too. Was it wrong of her to want to stay? Rosie closed her eyes, picturing the jumbled row of gravestones shoved into the earth, each marking one of her people. Her grandparents. Ma. Pa. A couple of uncles. But Pa always said her ma weren't really in the ground—she was clog dancing with Jesus in heaven.

Whoever had penned that song had made it sound like a great joy to spread his wings and launch hisself into God's heavens. She'd been so quick to push away Benton's offer—would she do the same when the Lord came calling? What was the hold this place had on her? Rosie slid her palm along the tree's bark, wrapping her arm around the trunk and resting her head against its rough surface. She opened her hands. "What would You have me do, Lord?"

Leaves crunched below her, and Rosie leaned forward to catch a glimpse of whatever was making its way through the brush.

Benton walked the path, his head low.

Something stirred in her chest, as if the Lord had taken to whispering to her heart.

*If a bird wants to fly free, first it has to release the branch.*

Benton's hair had been neatly trimmed since she'd last seen him, his dark coat a little too clean for mountain life. She shifted as he grew closer, as if she could somehow reach across the distance. She cleared her throat. "I ain't got my gun this time, Benton, but iffen I did, you'd be in a heap of trouble."

"Rosie?" Cupping a hand over his eyes, Benton squinted toward the tree blind. "I'd gladly face your shotgun if it meant lighting eyes on you again."

She slid over to the ladder and climbed down. She'd run away earlier, but now—as if she'd gone plumb crazy—she hurried toward him. Several feet short, she caught herself and stopped. "You . . . you left. What brings you back?"

Benton's eyes were shadowed. "I couldn't bring myself to say goodbye. I never wanted to." He smoothed his shirtfront. "Rosie, I'm so sorry. I know it must have been difficult to explain to Lorna."

*And to me.* "She's tougher than she looks."

"I know." He pulled off his gold-rimmed glasses, passing them from hand to hand. "But it was cruel of me. I was hurting, and I didn't think I could face you."

"*You* were hurting?" A fire lit in her belly. "You gave me a nigh-on impossible choice and then punished me for not giving you the answer you desired."

"I wasn't trying to punish you." He tucked his spectacles into his shirt pocket and moved several steps closer. "My proposal was the act of a desperate man. I couldn't imagine a life without you, but I couldn't see a way through the mess I'd made."

"What sort of mess?"

"Falling in love with someone who could never fit into my life as it was. Asking you to go with me was like asking one of these mountain birds to be a canary. It wasn't fair, and I shouldn't have done that to you." He closed the distance betwixt them and reached for her shoulders.

His touch melted her resistance, and she stepped fully into his embrace, the sensation as intoxicating as she'd imagined moonshine to be. She didn't know if she could give it up again.

"Rosie," he whispered into her hair. "I put in my resignation."

"You . . . you what?" She jerked back so she could see his face.

"I quit my job. I've got little to offer you. I'm useless with a splitting maul or a shotgun." He shook his head. "I've never butchered a pig or even cut down a tree."

"Useless, are you?" She slid her hand up his back, marveling at the feeling of warmth under her cold hand.

"It sounds even worse now that I'm standing in front of you."

"It's sounding pretty apt to me." She studied his eyes, suddenly seeming as blue as the forget-me-nots in the family cemetery. "But why'd you haul off and quit?"

"I thought I wanted that position and all the prestige that went along with it. But when I was locked there in my little office, all I could think of was you. And Lorna." He lifted his head. "And this place."

"It gets into your bones."

"It does at that. But when I left you behind, I left my heart alongside you." He lifted his gaze, scanning the treetops like he'd always done before. "I told you I didn't belong here, because my work was elsewhere. But, in truth, my life is here . . . because *you* are here."

The hairs raised along her arms. "I'll always be here, Benton."

"And that's why I returned."

She struggled to take a deep breath. "For how long?"

"If you'll have me . . . I'll stay forever." A smile spread across his face. "You can put me back in the goat shed, if that's how you want it. It's what I deserve for leaving you high and dry like I did last summer."

"It gets mighty cold out there this time of year."

"A wise person once told me that in Cherokee culture, a man leaves his home and comes to live with his wife's clan after they are wed." He brushed a finger across her cheek. "If you'll accept me, Rosie, I'll spend my days striving to be worthy of you, and I'll make it my life mission to be sure that you and Lorna never have to leave this place."

• • •

May 1933

Benton ran a comb through his hair, trying not to think of the crowd of men gathering in Beau's outer room and the larger group of folk amassing at the Elkmont church. Rosie's friends and her community—even a few kinfolk from far away—were coming out to see them wed. News had spread like wildfire, and he'd grown accustomed to being referred to as Rosie's "city feller." They all looked at him in a strange combination of awe and condescension.

He hadn't invited anyone from his old life, because who would understand it? His university colleagues already thought he'd lost his mind. The president had said the pressure had gotten to Benton. But then, none of them had met Rosie. Her love had changed him, and he was only starting to understand his new self—how could he expect any of his old friends to recognize him?

Beau stuck his head in. "You done fussing? I want to introduce you to my brother from Cades Cove afore things get to rolling." The man wore a dress shirt and tie under his clean overalls, a suit jacket over the top.

Benton grinned at his friend. "You're a regular Dapper Dan today."

The man ran a hand across his jacket. "It's my marrying and burying suit. I'm glad we've got the happier occasion today." He crossed the small room and came to stand next to Benton, studying his appearance. "You'll do. Don't think our Rosie-girl will change her mind when she looks at you."

"I think some folks around these parts would be relieved if she sent me packing."

Beau laughed, his big voice booming through the cabin. "You took this holler by surprise, but you got to give it some time. Mountain folk are slow to warm up, but once they do, there's no more loyal a bunch. Fierce in our grudges . . . just as fierce in our steadfastness."

"Some will never accept me."

"Keep your grip on the people who matter." He clapped a hand on Benton's shoulder. "You make our Rosie-girl happy, and a lot of us have been praying for that for many a long years. Ever since her pappy passed and she took on not only the farm but her sister too. I hated thinking of them two girls up there alone. You're an answer to prayer, son. Don't you forget it."

"I appreciate it, Beau."

"The good Lord works in mysterious ways. It ain't my place to question God's plans." Beau hooked his thumbs under his overall straps. "Now we'd best git on to the church, better'n we? Wouldn't be seemly for the girls to arrive there first."

Benton grabbed his coat. "I'm right behind you."

An hour later they were still waiting outside the church, the congregation gathered and already "singing up a fog," as Maudie had said. Benton paced out front, his heart hammering in his chest. "Tell me she's coming."

Beau grinned. "Don't you worry. I seen plenty of brides cross the threshold of this here church, and they all show eventually. Rosie's been waiting for you plenty long. You can bide a spell."

Benton turned to the road, his spirits spiraling upward as he spotted the big farm wagon in the distance, pulled by a nicely matched pair of chestnut mares. The widow Martin—now Mrs. Samson—held the traces in her tight grip, but Benton had eyes only for his bride.

Rosie's thick dark hair was swept back and curled, tiny ringlets clinging around her face. She wore a new store-bought dress of robin's-egg blue, and she clutched a large bouquet of white flowers. But it was her alluring smile that made his heart leap. How did it always look like she held on to some joyful secret and it was just waiting for the right moment to bust out of her mouth?

She met his gaze as they pulled up to a stop. "Y'all are supposed to be waiting up front."

He came to meet her, lifting his arms to help her down. "We were, but I got a little uncomfortable with the jealous stares. It's like every man in the Smokies was gunning for me, hoping to take out the competition for your attentions."

"I won't have no other." She squeezed his hands.

Lorna jumped down from the back of the wagon, where she'd been riding with her legs swinging. She raced over to join the couple and reached for the circlet of flowers on her head.

"No, honey." Rosie intercepted her hands. "Leave it be." She turned to Benton. "She's been wanting to show you her wedding crown, I think."

Lorna beamed as she threw herself at Benton and hugged him hard.

He chuckled, wrapping his arms around his sister-to-be. "I don't want to muss your dress, but I'm glad to see you too. It's quite a day, isn't it?"

She looked him square in the eyes, something she rarely did. Lifting a hand, she placed it on the center of his chest and patted it twice. "Beh."

Rosie sucked in a quick breath. "What did you say?"

"Beh." Lorna grinned. She tapped Benton's chest again. "Beh. *Ben*."

The ground could have opened and swallowed him whole at that moment, and he'd have died happy. He glanced at his bride. "Did she just say—"

"Ben!" Lorna smacked his sternum harder this time, causing him to take an involuntary step back.

Rosie folded her hands together and pressed them to her lips, her eyes glazing with tears. "She did."

Lorna adjusted her flower crown and marched into the church, leaving them on the front step.

He shook his head. "That's about the best wedding gift I could imagine."

Rosie slipped her hand into his, the sweet fragrance of flowers drifting up to meet his nose. "I've got a few more in mind when we're done here. Assuming I get through this without fainting."

"Rosie McCauley—the strongest woman I know? Never."

She pressed a hand to her stomach. "I ain't near as strong as you think. I guess you'll find that out soon enough, iffen we're going to be man and wife."

"There's no 'iffen' about it." He took her elbows and gazed into her eyes. "You *are* going to be my wife, and I don't doubt your grit for a moment."

She lifted up on tiptoes and pressed a kiss to his lips once and then a second time. "I think I was supposed to save that for the end, but I never was good at waiting for dessert neither."

He pulled her close and kissed her soundly. "No more waiting. Nothing but dessert for the rest of your life."

"You promise?"

Maudie stuck her head out the door. "Okay, you two, everyone's wondering why the bride ain't in here yet. Unless you're planning to run off."

"We're coming." Benton turned to Rosie, taking a moment to cup his hand to her cheek. "Aren't we?"

The fire in her eyes warmed him all the way through. "Lead the way."

# 14

Nashville
Present Day

KIERAN SKIMMED THROUGH the history books she'd picked up at the park bookstore, scanning for the names McCauley and Fuller. Chances were, Zach would have far more luck in the archives, but she wanted to do her part. The accounts of families forced to give up their homes tugged at her heart. There were also several descriptions of the lifetime lease system, including the story of the five unmarried Walker sisters who stayed on until the final sister passed away in 1964.

Ash popped her head into the open doorway. "I just got in. I'm glad to see you. For a houseguest, you hardly spend any time here."

Kieran dropped the book onto the covers. "Granny Mac turned in early."

Her friend flopped onto the end of the mattress. "I might do the same. I'm wiped. Nick's still there, closing up with one of the new guys." Ash used a curled fist to block a yawn. "Ohhh, I shouldn't have laid down." She stared up at the glow-in-the-dark star stickers on the ceiling, her face softening. "I'd forgotten about those."

"I love them." Kieran switched off the bedside lamp, the ceiling coming alive with tiny stars and planets. She lay back beside her friend. "It feels like we're camping."

"Without the bugs, yeah. It was Nick's idea to put those up. He had some on his ceiling as a kid. He thought the baby would like looking up and . . ."

Kieran took Ash's hand and squeezed it. There were no words that could chase away the pain of that empty room. But maybe words weren't what was needed.

"Nick wants to try again," Ash whispered.

"What do you want?"

A lengthy silence followed. Ash rolled to her side. "I still ache from losing Liam. I want a baby, but getting pregnant again—it seems like we'd be forgetting. Replacing him, almost."

"You won't forget." Kieran thought about the blanket Granny Mac was making for a forgotten baby. "But you're going to be the best mom, Ash. You can't give up on that. Any child would be fortunate to have you and Nick as parents."

"I told him I'd pray about it."

"That's a good idea." Granny Mac would probably do the same in the face of a big decision. Even though Kieran believed in God—in sort of a distant, practical manner—prayer had rarely been her go-to. It was a practice that demanded patience and trust, neither of which she excelled in.

Kieran's phone buzzed, its screen flashing light into the dark room.

Ash grabbed the device and tossed it to Kieran. "It might be about your grandma."

Kieran had gotten to where she jumped every time the phone made any sound at all. Long gone were the days when she could ignore messages. "It's just a text." Seeing Zach's name made her sit up straight. Earlier this evening, she'd typed up everything Granny Mac had told her and dashed it off to him before she'd even left the parking lot at Sycamore Terrace. Evidently he'd wasted little time putting the information to work.

*Found it!*

• • •

Kieran tapped the end of the pen against her desk, trying to focus on the computer form. One of her clients had been squabbling with the Social Security Administration for years. First they'd denied his disability requests, then his retirement, and now his pharmacy assistance. It was almost like some low-level administrator held a personal grudge against the man. Why was his case always flagged?

A rush of muggy air flooded in as her supervisor, Jocelyn, elbowed her way past the glass door, juggling a tray of coffee cups. Her flushed cheeks and the damp circles under the arms of her silk blouse paid homage to the surprise heat wave that had descended on the city this week. Jocelyn typically looked like a television anchor, perfectly powdered and every hair in place. And she never delivered coffee.

Time seemed to slow as her boss stopped at the first desk in the row, bending down to talk to Gary, the floor manager.

Kieran drew her keyboard close and typed out a terse email to a contact at the SSA so she could get this case moved to the top of the heap. What she really needed was a wormhole through the red tape.

Jocelyn's mid-height heels made a gentle tap as she walked the two rows of cubicles, stopping at each to deliver a cup and then step in close for a quiet word.

Kieran's stomach churned. *She's delivering more than coffee.* The room grew progressively quieter.

Her cell phone vibrated on the desk, dancing its way over to the edge. Kieran scooped it up, intending to silence the call until "Sycamore Terrace Senior Living" flashed across the screen. "Crud." Jocelyn was still two desks away. Swiveling her chair back, she pressed the phone to her ear.

"Kieran, it's Ivy. Your grandmother is missing from her room again." Her voice was hushed.

"You're kidding me."

"The director is planning to call, but she's stalling and hoping to find Ms. Mac first. I didn't think it was right to wait."

Glancing toward the window, Kieran's throat tightened. "It's sweltering outside. Are you sure she's left the building?"

"We're turning the place upside down, hoping she's here. But if she's not—"

"I'll be right there." Glancing down the row, Kieran spotted Jocelyn en route. It was like staring at an oncoming train. Jumping up, she grabbed her purse. "Jocelyn, I've got to—"

"This will only take a minute." The cardboard tray squeaked as Jocelyn freed one of the cups and set it on the desk. The smile on her lined face didn't match her somber eyes.

*Guilt coffee. Bitter to the last drop.*

"I just wanted to let you know . . ." Jocelyn rolled her perfectly lined and glossed lips inward for a moment, then opened them with a slight popping sound. "We've sent the overdue paychecks in for direct deposit, so it should be at your bank now. I'm terribly sorry for the delay. I hope it didn't create too big of an inconvenience."

The breath Kieran had been holding rushed out as a wispy laugh. "I thought you were coming to deliver bad news. That's great, because I have to run out and—"

"There's more, I'm afraid." Her boss frowned. "Actually . . ." She paused, glancing around the room.

Gary stood, the beanpole of a man easily visible above the cubicle wall. An armload of books and papers were balanced against his chest. He added a stone pot of succulents to the top of the stack and headed for the door.

Jocelyn turned back to Kieran. "We're shutting down. Effective immediately."

• • •

The ambulance sitting in front of Sycamore Terrace sent Kieran's heart skidding about in her chest. She'd barely gotten parked before throwing the door open and launching herself out of the car. *It might not be for Gran. It's an assisted living center. They must get lots of calls.* She leaned against the car to grab a calming breath, but it was like drawing in a lungful of steam from the diner's dishwasher.

She shook her blouse free from where it had glued itself to her skin and headed for the front door. "Please, Lord. Please." She wasn't even sure what she was asking for at this point, but Gran said the Holy Spirit always knew, even when we didn't.

A cluster of uniformed paramedics blocked Kieran's view of the gurney as Laura, Ivy, and several other staff hovered nearby.

Kieran rushed over to join them. "Is it—"

Ivy grabbed her hand. "We found Ms. Mac in the courtyard. I'm not sure how long she'd been out there, but—"

"But she'll be fine." Laura's eyes flashed. "The paramedics are just a precaution because of the heat. Your grandmother's health is of the utmost importance. We want to be absolutely certain we're doing everything we can to make sure our residents are receiving the best care at all times." The rhetoric spilled from her mouth with practiced precision.

"Where was that care when my gran wandered outside alone?" Red-hot tears blurred Kieran's vision. "How come no one noticed she was out there on the hottest day of the year?"

Ivy touched her arm. "I'm praying for her, honey."

Kieran bolted toward the medical technicians. "Gran? Excuse me—that's my grandmother."

Gran lay on the gurney, the back inclined so her head was up. An oxygen mask covered her mouth and nose. She lifted a hand and grasped Kieran's.

"Is she all right?" Kieran choked out the words to the attendants.

A young woman with a pixie cut fastened straps around Gran's legs. "We're transporting your grandmother to Saint Thomas Midtown. Her temperature is dangerously high, and she's dehydrated. We'll know more once the doctors there get her stabilized."

"Can I come with you?"

"Of course."

Kieran's legs shook as she followed the crowd of medics out to the waiting van and climbed in. As soon as she sat down, she leaned forward and placed a hand on Granny Mac's arm. She didn't know if she was reassuring Gran or herself, but right now she needed the comfort that only physical contact could bring.

Gran reached a hand up to the mask and pushed it aside. "Ma?" Her voice rasped.

"You need to keep that on now, Mrs. Fuller." A second paramedic reached for the device, trying to reposition it.

"They're taking you to the hospital, Gran. It's going to be okay. I'll be there with you." Kieran slid her fingers down to grasp Gran's hand.

"I'm ready to fly . . ."

# 15

## Great Smoky Mountains National Park
Present Day

The tension of the past weeks melted off as Kieran took a deep breath of the mountain air. She watched a tiny bird dart through the tree branches above her head, and her heart rose with it, as if it could take wing as well. What a difference ten days made. From hospital room to forest trail, it had been a crazy path. The rich fragrance of the pines and decaying leaves was a major improvement over the antiseptic smell of the hospital.

All talk of "no beds available" in Sycamore Terrace's memory-care unit evaporated after Kieran's complaints triggered a visit from an investigator with the Tennessee Board of Health. *Don't cross someone who works in senior services. We know where the bodies are buried. Literally.*

While Gran was still at Saint Thomas's, the staff at the assisted living center made sure her belongings were moved and ready. They'd even hung the framed cross stitch of the mountains in its place over her bed, put her old dresser close to its usual spot, and suction-cupped the acrylic bird feeder to the window. Within a week, Gran was back to ordering around the staff and working on her baby blanket.

Now Kieran stood next to a burbling stream, admiring her still-needing-breaking-in hiking boots—a birthday gift from Ash.

Zach glanced up from rummaging through his pack. "I'm sorry this is taking so long. I know it's in here somewhere."

"Take your time. I'm just thrilled to be here and to have company for the hike." She couldn't resist studying him as he dug through his belongings. With a flannel shirt hanging loose over his snug T-shirt and a blue knit cap that matched his eyes, she couldn't decide if he looked like a lumberjack or a Smoky Mountains version of Chris Evans. Either way, she didn't mind the view.

"Here it is." Zach drew the map out of his pack and unfolded it. "I was worried there for a moment. We've already hiked thirty minutes. I'd hate to confess now that I didn't have the details for the homesite."

Kieran took a swig of water from her bottle. "If you'd seen the circles I walked in last time, you'd know I can be pretty forgiving."

"Having your great-grandmother's maiden name really opened some doors for us. It never dawned on me that the lease would be written out to a woman—not in that era."

She fell in beside him as they headed down the trail. "My family has never been normal. I guess that goes back a few generations."

"What is normal anyway?" He shrugged. "None of us look like *The Andy Griffith Show.* And he was a single dad, for that matter."

"I saw the photographs on your refrigerator. It looked like the Jensen family was pretty stable and content." She hoped her jealousy didn't show in her voice.

He turned and offered her a crooked smile. "My folks are probably the exception. But two of my sisters are divorced, and my favorite uncle's been married numerous times and cheated on each of his wives. I'm thankful he taught me building skills, but I'll look for relationship advice elsewhere."

"So who would you go to for dating advice? Your parents? Because that seems like it could be a little awkward." Awkward, but sweet.

"Not often, no. But when things got really bad once, I did." His smile faded, settling into a darker expression. "They've got a strong faith, so it helps guide what they say. It's nice to know I can trust them to point me in the right direction. Someday I'd like to have a marriage like theirs. In fact, I'm determined not to settle for anything less."

"That sounds like a lot of pressure on your future wife."

"Not at all." He glanced down at the map, running his finger along a creek drainage. "The weight is on me and the choices I make. I've screwed things up in the past because I wandered away from truths I believed in. Rules are there for a reason. You can't just ignore them."

"Rules? Seriously?" She couldn't hide the incredulous laugh. He was sounding more like a Dudley Do-Right all the time.

"I'll put it this way." He pointed at the trail. "If you veer off the path, it takes a lot of effort to get back to where you want to be. It's easier to not get off track in the first place. So I'm watching my step."

She wasn't sure if they were still talking about relationships or if he'd moved on to orienteering. Maybe in his book, they weren't all that different.

"What about you?" He lobbed the question back. "Who do you go to for advice? Or maybe you don't need it. It sounds like you're in a steady relationship."

"I—what?" Her thoughts scattered. "A steady relationship? What gives you that idea?"

Zach stopped in the middle of the path. "You said you were dating some army guy."

Kieran laughed, the image more than she could handle. "You're talking about Nick? He's my friend Ashleigh's husband. They own the diner where I work sometimes. He's a good friend, sure, but we never—*never*—dated." Her voice hitched upward as her throat tightened. Suddenly it felt important to make sure he understood. "No, I'm single. Very single. Longtime single." *Stop. Now.*

His brows flicked up. "Oh, I'm sorry. I misunderstood." He refocused on the map, staring at the lines as if they'd somehow become lost.

*This is why I stick to fictional boyfriends.* She fumbled with the tie on her hoodie. How had they gone from awkward to excruciating in such a short conversation? "Actually, Ash and Nick are the ones I'd go to for advice. If I needed any. Which I don't. Because . . ." She swallowed.

He glanced up, the smile returning to his eyes. "Because you're single."

"Yeah." Good thing they had cleared the air. Now they could crawl back to their pathetic single lives and forget they ever had this little talk.

He pointed at the bridge ahead of them. "This is the creek we want to follow. It looks like the homesite was just up from the creek bed to the west. They must have saved the narrow bottomland for farming."

She followed him into the forest, picking their way through the trees. "It's hard to imagine anyone farming this."

"Most of these trees have grown up since that time. The Smokies looked a lot different in her era. Probably not unlike Townsend, Gatlinburg, or Pigeon Forge."

"I drove through Pigeon Forge on the way here. It looks nothing like this. It's packed full of mini golf places and gift shops. Isn't that where Dollywood is?"

"Yeah, that's why I don't go that way too often. Some folks love that stuff, but I prefer peace and quiet."

They continued scrambling up the hillside for another mile. Kieran stopped and uncapped her water bottle again. "I don't want to sound impatient, but how much farther?"

"I think we should be nearly on top of it. Start looking for anything that seems out of place. Piled stones, ornamental plants, fence lines."

"Ornamental plants? Like daffodils?"

"Sure. Or orchard trees. Sometimes it can be tough to find these sites if there's not much left. The park service wanted the place to recover naturally, so unless it was a unique structure, they did little to protect them. Sometimes they even intentionally removed them. People came in and salvaged the beams for other projects." He pointed to a stump closer to the creek. "There's some signs of fire too. There's a chance the place burned to the ground."

They spent the next three hours climbing up and down the hill, scrambling over blown-down trees. No matter how focused their search, it appeared that the forest had reclaimed its rightful place.

"There's got to be something left." Kieran yanked off her backpack and flopped down on a fallen log.

"Remember, this is just one of three possible locations."

"Ugh. And you do this for a living?"

"Most of my job is cataloging artifacts and writing reports on the status of historic structures. I do this sort of thing for fun." He sat down next to her, propping his long legs out in front of him.

She tipped her head back, watching the branches sway in the breeze, a sliver of sky showing between the green leaves. "I don't mean to complain. This has been a lovely day, even if we don't find anything."

"It sure beats eight hours in the office."

"Unfortunately, I won't be in my office anytime soon. They just let me go."

His brows lifted. "Really? That's too bad. It sounded like important work."

"Important work doesn't always pay the bills." She sighed. "I hate to think of all the seniors who will suffer without us there to help with housing transitions and life planning. I worked with some great people. Who's going to help them now?"

"Will you be all right? When you were here before . . ." His face grew serious. "It seemed like you were already in financial straits."

She played with the lid on her water bottle. "You could say that. But I still have my diner job. And I've got a place to stay—for now."

"You're always welcome at my guest house. It's not much, but if you ever get in a bind, it's there."

This guy had to be the sweetest man in all of Tennessee. Here he was tramping around in the woods searching for something that probably no longer existed, listening to her whine about not finding it, and then he turning around and offering a roof over her head. She reached out and touched his wrist. "I appreciate that. I really do." His skin was warm under her fingers. She hadn't intended to touch him, but now that her hand was there, she wasn't in any hurry to pull it away.

"I tell you what. I think we're about done here. We can hike to the next two locations tomorrow. How about we head out and grab some dinner—my treat?" Zach stood, her hand dropping away as he did so.

She hopped up. "You've done too much for me already. How about I cook again?"

"As tempting as that is, it's my turn. And I want to take you out." He paused, turning to catch her eyes. "I mean, I want to eat out—if that's okay with you?"

She glanced down at her sweaty clothes. "Like this?"

"It's the Smokies. People are used to hikers. I know this great little hole-in-the-wall in Gatlinburg. You'll love it. They've got great food."

"I'm in." She turned and surveyed the patch of forest they'd searched. The rhododendron bushes were loaded with clumps of white blooms, nearly glowing in the rays of light filtering through the trees. "Well, this is a lovely spot. If my great-grandparents didn't live here, they missed out."

"There are hundreds more spots just like this one."

She groaned. "Don't say that. Please."

# 16

Great Smoky Mountains National Park
October 1934

Rosie wiped the lids with a damp rag, admiring the rows of jelly jars on the table. Dried apples, pear butter, green beans, beets, corn, and now jam, finished. The garden had produced well this year with Benton's help, and they would have preserves to last all winter. She pressed a hand against her spine, the spasm sending her reaching for the edge of the sink for strength.

Benton came in with another armload of wood and frowned at her. "It paining you again?"

"I been on my feet too long."

The wood clattered into the box. "Then sit down. You don't need to work so hard. It's not good for either of you."

She swiped a palm over her damp forehead. She was nearly as cooked as the jam. "What'll be good for us is eating this winter."

"We'll be fine. All of us." He took her arm and laid his hand in the small of her back, his fingers knowing right where to go.

Even after more'n a year of married life, it still surprised her how well he seemed to know her, almost like he could feel every twinge of this pregnancy—or maybe he could just read it on her face.

He led her out to the porch, the cool air a welcome diversion. They'd screened it in earlier this year, so she didn't even have to worry about the bugs. "Sit down and rest. I'll get you some cold water." Rather than moving, he stood there and frowned. "I don't like your color. You're as flushed as one of those pink-skinned apples. Should I fetch Maudie?"

"Stop your fussing. The kitchen was hot is all." She pressed her lips together as another twinge cut through her back muscles.

He dropped to a knee beside her, pulling her hands into his. "Let me hire someone to come in and help you. How about that young Miller girl whose father works for the park service?"

"No. I don't want anyone here but us." Her husband's tender care was going to turn her soft. Women had been having babies in these mountains since nigh on forever. She'd tried explaining that to him, but it fell on deaf ears. How quickly she'd gone from being the "strongest woman he knew" to a fainting flower in his eyes. All because of one tiny baby.

The babe moved, the thrill racing through her anew and flooding her eyes with tears. Maudie had told her expecting might could make her soppy, but she hadn't figured on crying at every fool thing. She blinked hard. If Benton saw her cry, he'd cart her to that fancy hospital all the way in Knoxville. And she weren't stepping foot off this property. "I'm fine, Benton. *We're* fine. I'll rest a spell. Maybe I'll even rock this little mite to sleep."

"Is he kicking?" He moved closer and laid a hand on her belly, a smile crossing his face for the first time all day.

"She's gonna be a clogger like her mee maw." She'd never seen a man so in love. Most menfolk round these parts seemed to take a woman's childbearing with a casual disinterest, at least in public. Benton was besotted.

They'd explained things to Lorna, and now her sister had begun hauling her dolls around again. If it was one thing Lorna loved, it was babies. She would be a wonderful auntie, as long as they were careful not to leave her unattended with the child—at least for a time. She was loving, but not always gentle.

He remained there on one knee, his hand pressed to her belly, lowering his eyes, as if in prayer. "He's a busy little man."

"*She'll* be a hard worker so long as you don't wrap me up in quilt batting." Rosie moved her hand to his head, running her fingers through Benton's hair. It was growing longish. "I'll be careful, but I'm not changing anything. I'm happy with things exactly as they are. You don't know how happy." She bit her lip hard, anything to keep the waterworks from starting up again.

"Aren't you the least bit afraid? We're so far from help here. And . . . and with how your mother died—"

"Maudie is a wonderful granny woman, and she's just a twenty-minute walk—less if you take the auto. This baby is going to be fine and strong, like her daddy. And then we're going to have at least six more."

He sat back on his heels. "Six? I'm getting gray hairs with this one. What am I going to look like by number six?"

"Every bit as handsome as the day I married you."

As he went to get the promised cup of water, exhaustion draped over her like a sheet. Closing her eyes, Rosie pushed the rocker into motion, the squeaking of its runners against the floorboards soothing. A few more minutes of this and she could doze off. She hadn't taken naps since she was a babe herself, but now most afternoons she found herself so weary she could barely keep her eyes open.

Benton's footsteps roused her, and she reached for the tin cup in his hand. He pressed a kiss to her head. "If you're sure you're all right, I'll go help Beau with that stump he's trying to pull. Then he's going to give me another shooting lesson. It shouldn't be long."

Her husband had changed so much in the past few months. Quick to lend a hand, always working hard. One would hardly know he hadn't been raised to this life. "Take them a jar of those preserves, would you?" It would give her a chance to rest without feeling his eyes on her. His constant worrying was as tiring as the pregnancy itself.

A couple hours later, she jerked awake. The baby fluttered in her belly, and she patted the mound before pushing up to her feet and stretching her sore muscles. She went back inside and smiled at the tidy scene.

Benton had already put away the jars and cleaned the big enamel cook pot. He was spoiling her, that much was certain.

The fall sunshine came through the colored leaves and bathed the kitchen in a lovely golden light. *Thank You, Lord. Thank You.* The words seemed to constantly be on the tip of her tongue these days. Rosie grabbed her shawl off the peg. A saunter through the leaves would give her the energy to get up some supper. Benton was right—she didn't need to work every minute. It was good to take some time to appreciate being alive and out in God's beautiful world. She'd fought hard for her right to stay on this land. It was proper to take time to enjoy it.

Her fingers traveled gentle circles over her belly, imagining the years ahead when she'd be holding a child's hand on afternoon rambles. She blinked away tears again as a rueful laugh bubbled up from her chest. She'd cried more in the past weeks than when either of her parents had died. But these were happy tears, signs of God's blessings overflowing like spring runoff.

A man's voice echoed through the yard, calling out a greeting.

Rosie stepped outside, lifting a hand to shade her eyes. They didn't get many neighbor folks coming by to trade howdies anymore.

A tremor rushed through her as she spotted Will heading for their gate with a goat in tow. She and Benton had attended his pa's burying last week, but they'd managed to slip away without speaking to either brother. The pain on Will's face at the graveside still haunted her. She knew he despised the difficult man, and yet grief could be a cruel taskmaster. It had a way of wrenching open long-padlocked doors in your heart even while it slammed others shut.

She hurried out to the fence, pulling the wrap around her shoulders. "What's this?"

He met her at the gate, luring the goat along with a wilting dogwood branch. "I want Lorna to have this nanny goat. It was her favorite." Will's attention fixed on Rosie's belly before darting away. His cheeks reddened above his whiskers.

She tightened the wrap, as if to somehow obscure the way her dress pulled at the seams. Hadn't Will noticed her condition at the burying? "We couldn't accept that, Will."

"The animal wouldn't even be alive if it weren't for her." He kept his eyes averted, likely afraid to look at her a second time. "It were the smaller of a runty set of twins, but when I went for the knife, Lorna pitched a fit—as mad as a mule chewing bumblebees."

"I can imagine."

"Yeah, well." The hint of a smile vanished from his lips, as quick as it appeared. "I bottle-fed the critter instead. Grew into a sturdy doe and real tame 'cause of all the handling."

"That were right nice of you. But—"

"I miss her, Rosie. I miss having Lorna about." Even as Will latched onto her gaze, his shoulders sagged under the heavy weight he was carrying. "I miss you too." He faltered and looked away again. "I know my pa made life hard for you and her, but he's gone now, and even Horace has mellowed some—"

A squeal from up the road drew their attention. Lorna bolted toward them, Benton following along behind. She dropped to her knees by the goat, rubbing her face on the doe's neck. "Meh-meh-meh."

The animal answered with a nudge and a soft bleat.

Rosie released a long breath. So much for turning away the gift.

Will grinned, staring down at her. "I brought her to you, Lorna."

Benton's shirt and trousers were caked with dirt. His gait stiffened as he approached the three of them. "Mr. Samson. I hope all is well at your place, considering."

Will dropped the lead rope and backed a few steps so Benton could pass through the gate. "Been pretty quiet."

"I just had a long chat with a park ranger over at Tipton's." The strain in Benton's voice was unmistakable. "Apparently they've seen evidence of poaching in the area."

Rosie tensed. "Lorna, take the goat over to the shed, will you?"

Lorna tugged the lead rope, and the animal happily followed her into the yard.

Their neighbor folded his arms, hiding the weakened one against his chest. "I wouldn't know nothing about no poaching."

Rosie took her husband's hand. "Will brought the goat Lorna helped him raise. Wasn't that neighborly?" It didn't seem right to hold grudgement against Will for what his brother and pa done, especially with his father so recently in the ground. She hoped Benton understood.

Benton met her eyes, his stance softening. "She does look happy." He turned back to Will. "Thank you. It's kind of you to think of her."

Rosie's heart lifted. Lorna had so few friends in the world. Maybe with Eb's passing, things would improve for her.

Will shoved his hat back, his brows lifting. "You're welcome." He glanced back at Rosie, his eyes lingering on her belly for a long moment. "It was good to see you, Rosie." He turned back to her husband and extended his good hand. "Congratulations. You're mighty blessed."

After a moment, Benton shook his hand. "Can't argue with that."

# 17

## Great Smoky Mountains National Park
## Present Day

Zach tightened his grip on the steering wheel, fighting to keep his eyes on the winding road. He'd kept tight reins on his heart, because even though he was desperately attracted to Kieran, he'd thought she was taken.

Only she wasn't.

He shouldn't pursue this. Switching from attraction to actual dating was like trying to cross a stream with no bridge or stepping-stones in sight. He'd been swept down that river before. Years had passed, and he was still processing the hurt from Jordan. He wasn't ready to go through that again.

Trouble was, his feelings weren't listening to his head. Currently they appeared to be dancing a conga line around his chest. *Lord, help me. I don't want to get in over my head.*

Kieran sat dozing in the passenger seat, curled slightly toward him and perfectly at ease.

Did she have any clue what she did to him? When she'd touched his arm earlier, he'd practically jumped out of his skin. A minute later, he was asking her out. He should have let her rest up for tomorrow's hike, but instead he was driving forty-five minutes to his favorite Cajun restaurant.

The fact that Kieran had nestled against the headrest and shut her eyes sent a wave of warmth through him. She didn't feel the need to fill the air with brilliant conversation. She trusted him enough to relax in his presence.

As they approached Gatlinburg, she stirred and opened her eyes. "Ohh," she groaned, arching her back and stretching. "I didn't mean to zonk out on you. You should have woken me." A lock of hair had escaped her ponytail and now hung loose. She slid the band off and shook her head, letting the glossy hair cascade over her shoulders.

He dragged his attention back to the road. "You had a long day. On top of all the hiking, you also drove from Nashville."

"That's no excuse for being a lousy copilot. So where are we going?"

"It's an oyster bar right downtown. Lots of crawdads and shrimp, but I remember seeing salads and such on the menu too. And there's always plenty to go around."

"Sounds perfect. I'm starving." She ran a hand across her sweatshirt. "They won't mind that my boots are muddy and I smell like a pig?"

"If you smelled, I think I'd have noticed by now."

After arriving in Gatlinburg, they spent the next hour and a half sitting at the table tucked against the front window overlooking the busy street. The conversation never lagged. Kieran entertained him with stories about the diner and some of her favorite clients at SeniorCo, and he volleyed back with tales from the office and his archaeology days—leaving out any mentions of ex-girlfriends.

He could have sat there all evening, listening to her laugh and watching her dark eyes gleam when she spoke. She had a way of leaning forward that made it seem like she was practically hanging on his words. Normally he was content to let others shine and carry the conversation, but she seemed to draw him out in a way few others ever had. *Comfortable.* She made him comfortable in his own skin.

By the time they finished, the sun hung low in the sky. They walked down the sidewalk toward the parking garage, their arms comfortably bumping as they strolled. He could almost imagine reaching over to take her hand.

"Hey, look, the skybridge." She pointed to a sign hanging over the street. "I saw an ad for that. It sounds incredible. Have you gone?"

"The suspension bridge with the glass bottom?" He shook his head. "Sounds like a tourist trap to me."

"Oh." Her face fell, like he'd pulled the wings off a butterfly. "I suppose you're probably right."

He didn't really want the evening to end. Reaching out, he snagged her elbow and turned her toward the place. "But it could be fun with the right person."

She rewarded him with a huge smile. Grabbing his hand, she launched toward the ticket booth, as if afraid he'd change his mind. Minutes later they were riding a ski lift up the nearby ridge, the hubbub of Gatlinburg falling quiet behind them. They hadn't traveled very far, but just being carried away from the busy street traffic made Zach's tension ease. And to be honest, having his leg pressed against Kieran's as the chair rocked beneath the wire wasn't too shabby either.

After they reached the top, they hopped off and wandered around the high vantage point. He had to admit that the view of the Smokies from this angle was nice, especially with the sun starting to sink low, framing every ridge in a swath of orange-hued light. Downtown Gatlinburg sat far below, nestled among the forested hills. They made their way past a series of fountains and over to the suspension bridge, a long walkway strung over a deep forested ravine. Zach had never been afraid of heights, but even he felt a little lightheaded looking at the span.

Kieran went first, easing herself out onto the wooden planks and gripping the cables as if they would provide some kind of actual safety. "This is crazy. I didn't think about how high in the air we'd be."

He chuckled, trailing a few steps behind. "That was the point, wasn't it?" He stepped aside as a noisy group of teenagers passed them, making the platform bounce under their feet.

She seemed to relax as they progressed along the swaying structure, but came to a standstill when they reached the glass-bottomed section. Pointing the toe of her hiking boot, she tapped the surface like she was testing the water of a swimming pool on a summer's day. "This was my idea, wasn't it?"

"Sure was." He stood still, not wanting to rush her. He could stand there for a good long time just watching her take in the view.

She straightened her shoulders and edged out onto the clear surface, sliding her feet rather than taking full steps.

He couldn't help laughing until he took his first step onto the glass. The sensation was brutal, his brain arguing against what felt like stepping into nothingness. He glanced up to see how far Kieran had gotten without him.

"It's not so easy, is it?" She reached a hand toward him, keeping the other locked on the metal cable that served as a handrail. "Come on."

Like he could resist that? He'd probably step into open air if she asked him. Moving forward, he kept his attention fixed on her. The setting sun lit the edges of her brown hair like kissing it with fire.

As he reached her, she leaned in to embrace him. "I can't believe this. It's amazing. Thank you."

"I'm glad you talked me into it." He pulled her close, almost unaware of the groups of tourists jostling past them. "Like I said—with the right person." The feel of her leaning against his side made every nerve ending come to life, his fingers aching to trace the curve of her hip.

It was too soon. A fragile bond had formed between them, but the wrong move could send everything stampeding in the wrong direction. He'd frighten her away—or worse, he'd fall in love too fast. Again.

When she smiled up at him, his thoughts stilled. *With the right person.* Maybe God was calling him to step out into the unknown.

The promise and hope mingling in her eyes drew him in until, before he realized what he was doing, he shed all sense of caution into the ravine below. He lowered his head even with hers and brushed his lips against her cheek and then her jaw, breathing in the warmth of her skin. As she reached up to touch his face, he bent close and kissed her lips. A charge rushed through him, like he'd grazed up against a low-voltage electrical wire but couldn't seem to step away. Or rather, he didn't want to.

She pushed up on her toes to return the kiss, burying her fingers in the hair at the nape of his neck. Her lips met his with a hunger that surprised and delighted—and terrified him.

He drew back a few inches to give himself a breath of air, hoping his brain would kick in. But even as he did so, he slid both arms around her waist and held her close, lowering his chin to the top of her head. The wind whipped at her hair, flicking it against his cheek. Not that he minded.

Kieran leaned against his chest. "Best. Day. Ever." She murmured the words into his shirt.

She'd get no argument from him.

• • •

The high of last night's date and its crazy-romantic kiss carried Kieran through much of the next day's hiking. She and Zach had followed several creeks and tromped through seemingly endless patches of forests so far. Bending down, she rubbed at a fresh scratch on her calf. Surely one of these sites had to be her great-grandparents' place. But after a full day of searching, they'd scoured both locations. At least he'd taken the opportunity to show her Meigs Falls and The Sinks on their way out this morning. She loved waterfalls, and Zach promised if she made another trip later this summer, he'd take her to see a few others.

Her ankle caught on a bramble, and she kicked her foot to free herself. Thorns raked down her calf, digging through her pant leg. Biting back some unkind words, Kieran crouched and disentangled the weed from the fabric with her fingers. "Better not be any poison ivy out here."

"I wouldn't count on that." Zach's voice drifted to her from some distance away.

She flung off the vine, tracing its source to a jumble of stones just a few feet away. No, not a jumble. Kieran walked closer. There were more—cleanly stacked and stretching in a line away from her. Her heart jumped.

"Zach?" She straightened, looking about. They'd taken to wandering farther apart, trying to cover more ground before losing daylight. "Zach!"

"Yeah?" His voice echoed from the area of the creek. A moment later, he appeared, coming toward her.

"Look at this." She bent down, laying a hand on top of the crumbling stonework. It wasn't mortared like a chimney, just stones stacked and fitting together. "What do you make of it?"

He walked around to the far side. "It's probably a fence line. You see ones like this around. But it's clearly man-made."

The weariness of the day faded as adrenaline rushed to fill its place. "This could be it?" She glanced up at the steep hillside rising beyond.

"Maybe." He shot her a don't-get-too-excited look.

They followed the crumbling segments of fence line over a small rise and into a clearing. Kieran walked out into the grassy patch, nearly a perfect square in the middle of the woods. "Tell me this isn't natural." She turned a slow circle, studying the opening. It wasn't her idea of a farm. Maybe a yard of some kind?

"Definitely not." Zach walked partway across the clearing and crouched to examine a stone jutting from the ground.

"What is it?" She hurried to join him, not sure what made that rock unique from the several others nearby.

He laid a hand on the pointed stone. "It's a grave marker. This is a cemetery."

Kieran froze, seeing the spot in a new light. "That's a little creepy. Way out here?"

"There are quite a few family graveyards scattered around the park. The park service has identified most of them and keeps tabs to make sure they're not disturbed."

"Is this one listed?"

"I won't know until we check the records."

She kneeled by one of the protruding stones, little more than a spike rising from the ground. "They weren't engraved? Or have they worn off over time?"

"Hard to say. Some families couldn't afford formal cemetery markers. But sometimes they've simply eroded away because not a hard enough stone was used."

Zach's words echoed somewhere in the depths of her soul, like falling down a deep, dark well. "These were people who lived real lives, and they're just lying out here forgotten? These could be *my* people." A lump formed in her throat. Before she'd found Granny Mac, Kieran had felt much like this. Forgotten. Alone. Unwanted.

"Some folks might see it that way. But I don't think peoples' spirits are trapped in the cemetery or wandering ghostlike about these woods. They're with God."

The stitch that had formed around her heart loosened a hair. It was what she believed too, or so she'd thought. She called herself a Christian. But it was hard to look around at these lonely, unnamed plots and not feel a sense of emptiness.

She stood, pulling her phone from her pocket. "I want to take some photos and see if we can figure out who these people were. Maybe we can connect the dots between them and my gran." There were enough holes in her history. She'd grown up thinking it was just her immediate family that was fractured. But from the sounds of Granny Mac's stories, the cracks went back multiple generations. Evidently her lineage was less of a family tree and more of a chopped up stack of firewood.

"Of course." He pulled a notebook from his pocket and sketched the layout of the ground and the general placement of the graves. "If we find out this is your ancestors' land, will you show those pictures to your grandmother?"

Kieran took a close-up of a marker. "I don't know. I don't see how it would bring her any comfort." Faint etchings on the stone caught her attention. She crouched to examine it, running a thumb along one groove. "Is this a name?" She squinted, trying to make the markings form "McCauley," but there weren't enough letters.

Zach opened the camera app on his phone and spent some time fiddling with the settings before pressing the shutter button.

Kieran looked over his shoulder. With the contrast boosted to the max, she could read the word engraved on the stone. "Baby."

# 18

Great Smoky Mountains National Park
December 14, 1934

LITTLE HENRY LIVED for ten days. It weren't near enough.

Staring down at the freshly turned earth, so dark against the frost-covered ground, numbness pussyfooted through her heart. It was December, nearly Christmas. Rosie should be at home knitting baby sweaters and singing lullabies, not standing here with empty arms. *Should, should, should.* Those words would haunt her the rest of her days. *God, you shoulda saved him.*

The preacher had left, and so had the families who had come to share their grief. Now she and Benton stood alone in the little family plot on the hill, a stacked rock wall marking the borders of the sacred space. She couldn't leave. Benton stood beside her, the sound of his ragged breathing a reminder that she weren't alone in her grief.

"I don't understand." She whispered the same words she'd been saying for three days.

Benton remained quiet. He'd given up trying to answer the questions she'd thrown at him and at the doctor who'd arrived too late to do anything. Turning, he pulled her in his arms, his coat rough against her raw cheek.

Rosie leaned against him, greedily taking his strength to keep her upright, but still peeking around his arm to the temporary board marking their son's place. Her son.

In those days leading up to Henry's arrival, it'd felt like the Almighty was pouring out all the joys on her she'd never thought she'd have. The more fearful Benton grew about the birth, the more certain she was that everything was going to be fine. After all, he was fretting enough for the both of them.

Henry had been perfect in every way. Every toe and fingernail. Every feather-soft hair on his head.

Ten days.

A sigh deeper than the grave escaped Benton's lips, and he kissed the top of her head. "Lorna will be waiting."

"I don't want to leave him. Not yet." She closed her eyes, burying her face in his sleeve, no longer able to look. "It's so cold up here." Sliding her hand into her pocket, she wrapped her fingers around the bird, like a shard of ice against her skin.

"Watch over Henry, Lord. And us."

# 19

## Nashville
## Present Day

KIERAN SAT BESIDE her gran's bed, thumbing through the photos of her last trip. She had taken several shots from the swinging bridge in Gatlinburg, and the mountains were brilliant in the setting sun. She laughed at the blurry shot of her boots on the glass section of the expanse. Her hands must have been shaking. But it was the three selfies she and Zach had taken together that made her heart flutter. She'd snapped them just after they'd kissed, her goofy smile and flushed cheeks giving her away.

And he looked completely relaxed. Figures.

She hadn't expected the evening to end that way. Sure, she'd already forked over her own heart, but Zach hadn't offered her any inkling that he felt the same. She'd certainly never imagined a historian would be a romantic. Kieran's thoughts wandered, her mind reliving the touch of his lips, the feel of his arms around her waist. It had only been three days, but she missed him already.

She shouldn't get carried away. It had been the perfect evening, but that didn't mean they had a future. In the final shot, his hand draped over her shoulder and he gazed at her instead of the camera. Sweet longing stirred in her chest. She wanted more than just a lingering kiss or a never-to-be-forgotten date. She wanted a lifetime of this.

That was a little much to ask from one perfect weekend, but a girl could dream.

She flicked forward, scanning through the pictures she'd taken at the cemetery. Graveyards typically gave her the creeps with their acres of stones all laid out in a perfect grid. This seemed different somehow—burying family members in a private plot instead of alongside lines of strangers. There was something sweet about it. Keeping your people close.

She'd gone on this search to help her grandmother, but maybe finding out how she connected to this place would be a good thing too. Would it bring her a sense of belonging?

Her fingers stilled on Zach's edited image of the gravestone. *Baby.* How could such a joyful word also evoke such misery? Kieran sighed. One only had to look at Ash to know the truth.

Granny Mac stirred in her sleep, her lips moving.

Kieran settled a hand on her grandmother's arm to soothe her. Nightmares weren't uncommon among dementia patients, but the lack of good sleep also cut into her lucidity, making everything spiral downward. Kieran ran her thumb over her grandmother's hand, noticing the brown spots decorating her skin. At one time this hand had held *her* mother's—Rosie McCauley Fuller. Was one of those forgotten stones Grandma Rosie's, alongside the buried baby and the others? It was odd to think about. Generations and places linked—hand to hand to hand.

Gran's face pinched. "Lor—na." She muttered. "Lorna."

Kieran leaned in. Was that a name? She held her breath, waiting for more. Minutes ticked by on the old clock, the audible clicking registering the passing time in a way digital clocks never did.

Gran's breathing grew labored, her feet twitching under the covers, as if she were running in place. "Auntie . . ." She cried out, gripping onto Kieran's hand.

Kieran jumped, the sudden pressure knocking her from her reverie. "It's okay, Gran. I'm here." She kept her fingers tight and added her other hand on top. "Shhh, you're safe. I'm with you."

A whimper, like a toddler's cry, escaped Gran's lips. "Lorna, where's

Ma? Was that a shotgun?" And then her arm relaxed, her breathing steadying into deep sleep.

Lowering her head, Kieran kept her hands wrapped around Granny Mac's. Gran's past seemed to be bleeding through into her present, carrying with it memories and people she'd never discussed. Kieran had heard stories of her father and uncle when they were boys, and of Kieran's grandfather—a hard, cruel man. Gran had been through a lot in her life, but she'd pushed through and found healing. Her faith had given her a deep well of forgiveness, far beyond what Kieran was able to understand. So why this? Why was she still haunted by her mother's passing and the loss of her family home?

Dementia was cruel, giving and taking at will. Kieran concentrated on the warmth of Gran's hand and the softness of her aged skin. This woman had given Kieran her heart's deepest desire—a place in the world and a family to call her own, small though it was. Even though there was no way she could repay that gift, she'd do anything to ease her grandmother's mind. But right now, it seemed the only way to bring Gran peace was to heal the wounds of her past.

• • •

Zach pressed a fist against his yawn, the chill of the office not doing a great job of keeping him awake. He and Kieran had been getting to know each other better through nightly phone calls and texts, and yesterday neither of them had wanted to hang up until well after midnight. Today he was paying the price. He scrolled through the microfiche, wishing they had the time and money to digitize all of this information. Microfilm had been the hot, high-tech storage device of the 1980s, but it paled in comparison to today's methods. Not to mention, it was really hard on tired eyes.

He reached for his coffee cup, remembered he'd already drained it, and set it back down. He'd come in early to put in a little extra research on her project. Now that they were dating, it didn't seem appropriate to spend work hours on what could be construed as a personal project. John, his boss, probably wouldn't care, but Zach did.

Comparing the GPS coordinates with the cemetery database, he'd finally connected a family name to the stones they'd found. Unfortunately, it wasn't McCauley or Fuller. Kieran would be crushed.

*Samson.* He scrawled the name on a pad, adding the birth and death dates of a few of the individuals. Some of them would have been contemporaries of Kieran's great-grandparents, so it was possible they knew each other. Maybe he could locate a descendant or two. There was an active historical society in the area, filled with hobby genealogists. Most of them had rabid appetites for solving puzzles and loved nothing more than connecting the dots on family trees. He'd already spoken to a few of them about Kieran's quest, but so far they had no leads. But perhaps they knew something about this family?

His three hits on the McCauley name had led him to this area near Jakes Creek, so it wasn't completely farfetched that the families were connected in some way. Marriages, friendships, distant kin—it seemed everyone was related in some fashion.

Zach picked up the phone. He'd learned over the years that the historical society's director wasn't much for email. When Zach had first arrived in the park, he'd resisted going to the group for data. Since the park service had hired him as a curator, it felt like they should be coming to him for help, not the other way around. But eventually he'd locked his pride in a drawer where it belonged and learned to rely on the volunteer group for leads whenever he hit a dead end.

After chatting with Bruce for several minutes, he got down to business. "I'm still tracking that McCauley family I told you about."

The fellow sighed. "I'm sorry I couldn't help more with that. I know there were McCauleys about, but I wasn't able to unearth any details."

"I think I may have something." Zach bounced the eraser end of his pencil on the tabletop. "Kieran Lucas and I went out to the three sites I told you about last time, and one of them turned up a cemetery."

"That could be useful. Any names?" Bruce's tone lifted, as if his interest had been piqued. Kieran might have been creeped out, but there was nothing a historian loved better than a graveyard. It rendered names and dates and sometimes even specified military service records.

"Nothing legible. But I tracked it to another family, and I wanted to see if maybe there was a link with the McCauleys or Fullers." Zach glanced down at his notes. "The name is Samson."

The man grew quiet. "Hold on—let me check something." The phone clunked down onto a hard surface. Did he not even have a cordless phone?

Zach glanced up at the books on the shelf perched above his desk. Standing, he grabbed one on Great Smoky graveyards.

The phone line rattled in his ear as Bruce returned. "Hey, Zach, I've got something for you. Do you have reel-to-reel capability?"

Chuckling, Zach rolled back his chair and stood. "In the storeroom somewhere, yeah. I'll have to get someone to remind me how it works."

"Bring the machine with you, I can set it up. I keep forgetting you're from the music-streaming generation. My grandson was just showing me that the other day. Remarkable."

"What have you got on tape?" If he took the time to drive over to the historical society during his lunch hour, it had better be worthwhile.

"I've got more than just birth and death records for the Samsons. I've got Horace Samson's voice."

• • •

Zach pulled to a stop outside Bruce's house in Sevierville and drew his phone from his pocket. It had vibrated three times during the short drive. Three texts from Kieran, a sight that made him smile. He hoped these tapes would be the link to finally nail down the location of her ancestors' homesite within the park. But he wasn't quite ready to get her hopes up yet.

He opened the messages.

*I might have another name from my gran: Lorna. An aunt maybe? You busy?*

*Lorna McCauley? Lorna Fuller? Call me when you get a break.*

Zach's thumb hovered over the Call button. No. Best to wait until he spoke to Bruce. Then he'd have something to tell her. He texted her that he had a meeting and would call soon. Jamming the phone into his pocket, he scooped up the heavy tape machine from the passenger seat and headed to the door.

Bruce let him in and waved him into his cluttered study. Books lay open on the large desk, and papers sprawled across two folding tables. "Sorry about the mess." He lifted a stack, glanced around, and finally added it to the top of a teetering pile on the desk, clearing a spot. "Set your player here. I'll find an extension cord."

Zach slid another few papers aside to make the spot large enough for the aging piece of equipment, then eyed the fraying cord Bruce dragged out of a cardboard box. This office had "fire hazard" written all over it. "I don't have much experience with these, even though we've got a ton of tapes in the archive. I'm surprised you don't have your own player."

"Oh, I do." Bruce glanced around. "Somewhere." He retrieved a gray file box and pulled out a metal reel. "We'll see if this one still works. If it does, I'll send my stash with you for the center. I know y'all have a special freezer to keep tape from degrading."

He looped the tape through the mechanism and wound it into a matching take-up reel on the opposite side, rolling the device with his palm until the tape grew taut and both wheels moved in sync. "Okay, let's see what we got." He pressed the Play button.

Zach drew up a chair and opened his notebook, balancing it on his knee rather than trying to find a spot at the desk.

After a minute of crackling, a woman spoke. "Voices of the Smokies, oral history recorded February 15, 1962. Mr. Horace Samson." The tape continued hissing through the machine.

Halting at first, but smoothing out into proper Southern-storytelling mode, Horace Samson's voice floated into the room like a phone call from the past. His intonation was clearly Appalachian, what Zach might have termed "hillbilly" before coming to work in the Smokies. He'd learned quickly the "h-word" was only to be used by locals, not outsiders like him.

"I was born on August 16, or nigh about then, 1907. My folks weren't big on celebrating birthdays, so all I got to go on is the mark in the family Bible, but my brother told me he saw our pa fill all those dates in later. So I'm not sure if he had the numbers correct or nothing. My brother Will was born a year later, but our Ma passed from the fever a few months after he was born, so we weren't a big family like some. Pa says there was a few babies afore us, but they didn't make it out of infancy. Not unusual for that time, as y'all know."

Samson continued, sharing tales of his childhood, the one-room school he attended with his brother, hunting dogs, the coming of the park service, and his later life in Sevierville. His stories skipped from childhood to adulthood and back without much of a break, making a timeline of the man's life an impossibility.

Zach ran a hand over his chin. Samson was leading them down an endless string of rabbit trails. Everyone who grew up in the Smokies seemed to have a plethora of tall tales and casual reminisces, but as interesting as they were, it didn't mean they'd lead him to the information he sought. He eyed the box of tapes lying on Bruce's desk. More oral histories? It was research gold, but it would take a long time to dig through it all.

Maybe it'd be a good job for Marley. He could set the intern up with headphones and have her transcribe the tapes for the archives while the machine made a digital copy. It would be a better use of resources, plus it would preserve these stories for the future.

Zach closed his notebook. "You know what, Bruce? I might just . . ."

Samson was midway through another boyhood tale when the name Zach been waiting for jumped out at him. "Wait—stop the tape. Roll it back."

Bruce wound the tape in reverse, creating gibberish through the speaker. He pressed Play a second time.

"We was always sneaking up the branch—the little one off Jakes Creek near the spring—close to where this gal Rosie McCauley lived. She and her sister liked to wade in their creek, looking for crawdads and salamanders and such. Her sister was feebleminded—you know—dumb as a brick. And I liked nothing better than to scare the living tar outta her. We'd play we was outlaws sneaking through the woods, then haul out and start screaming like we'd seen a haint. Lorna would run home cryin', but that Rosie, she up and busted me one in the chops that I didn't soon forget. Deserved it, I guess. But she grew up to be a real pretty thing. Shame how it all turned out for her, though."

And with that, Samson rolled into another story.

Bruce fixed eyes on Zach. "Mean something to you?"

This time Zach rewound the tape and set up his phone to record. "Yes, it does." He'd play it for Kieran tonight. The first mention of her great-grandmother, and it was how the little spitfire had stood up for herself against a bully. Why didn't that surprise him? And had the man mentioned that name Kieran had texted him—Lorna?

He pressed Play, and the reels launched themselves from reverse to forward with a jerk, snapping the tape in two.

Zach's stomach dropped. "Oh no."

Bruce chuckled. "No worries. It's probably getting old and brittle, like me. It can be fixed. I got some empty reels around here we can spin the rest onto." He opened a file drawer, digging through but coming up empty. "They must be hidden away with my player. You know what? I got a buddy who's really good at this sort of thing. I'll run it over to him and have him splice the tape and then record the whole thing on the computer for you. That way you don't have to deal with this stone-age technology. Let us relics handle that."

"You don't have to go to all that trouble. I could do it at the preservation center." Zach scribbled down what he could remember of the story, most importantly the specifics on the location of the McCauley girls' home. They'd been very close on that last hiking trip—they just hadn't followed it up toward the spring. They'd probably missed it by less than a mile.

"Nah, he gets a charge out of this kind of stuff. I think he'll want to hear them too. Once he's done, I'll drop them off at your office and you can tuck 'em away in that freezer."

"Thank you. This means the world to me. I want to hear the rest of what Samson's got to say. I'm sorry about the tape."

Bruce gripped Zach's hand as a smile found its familiar position on his face. "I like to see people your age taking an interest in the history of this place. So many stories, so little time, and we got to pass them on." He jerked a thumb to the other reels. "You want Joe to record those too?"

"Mind if I take them? I'll put one of my interns on it. She could use the busywork." Plus, it'd keep her out of his business.

"They're all yours." He grinned. "Let me know if you find anything good."

"I already have." Zach lifted his notebook and waved it.

# 20

## Great Smoky Mountains National Park
## April 1936

THE OWL TORE tiny shreds of meat off its prey, feeding it to each of the young in turn. Benton pressed the field glasses against his eyes in the diminishing light, wishing for the millionth time he'd chosen a diurnal bird to study. Catching the screech owl pair when there was enough light to actually see what they were doing was a growing challenge as his vision worsened. He needed new spectacles but didn't want to leave Rosie long enough to drive into town. Not now.

He glanced toward the cabin, the kerosene lamp she used on the porch flickering like a tiny beacon in the night. She'd wait up for him—she always did.

A second light glowed in the loft—Lorna getting ready for bed perhaps.

A well of unshared grief opened up in his gut, blurring his vision further. He swiped his shirtsleeve over his eyes. Four years into their marriage, and it was still just the three of them living in the little cabin. Rosie had boasted to him once that mountain families would fill a place like theirs with a dozen children and still count themselves blessed.

*But we haven't been.*

Henry had lived ten days. Their second child, Everett, for only seven.

Benton drew in a shuddering breath, dropping his head into his hands, the owls forgotten. *Blessed?* Why would God bring children into their lives only to tear them away?

The night after Everett's burial this past summer, Maudie had sat with Rosie on the porch long into the night. Benton still remembered the snippets of conversation drifting in the open window, mixed with the nighttime chorus of katydids.

"I know all about the streets of gold, Maudie." Rosie's voice had been so faint, like she just breathed the words.

"Oh, child." Maudie had clucked her tongue. "There's so much more. The Good Book, it says God will bring about a new heaven and a new earth. Imagine sweet springs of pure water, glistening mountaintops, trees that have never known the lick of an axe.

"The government, they thinks they can build that right here in the Smokies, but we know the truth. These mountains will whisper our stories long after we're gone. They're filled with the bones of our ancestors, and those who came afore us. But God's new heaven and earth? We'll be walking those sun-dappled paths with our beautiful babies."

Benton lifted his eyes as the mother owl dropped from her perch, swooping soundlessly through the woods in search of another meal for her nestlings. How many owlets had he watched them raise now? He noted the time in his logbook. That was one bright spot—the Audubon Society had published his paper on screech owls of the Great Smoky Mountains. It hadn't meant much income, but at least it justified the time he spent out here.

He glanced toward the house. The light was moving. Perhaps Rosie had gotten chilled and decided to move inside to wait. Darkness nearly swallowed them now.

The article could lead to job offers. He'd promised Rosie he'd never ask her to leave her home, but he couldn't help wondering if they lived somewhere with better doctors . . . maybe their boys would still be alive. Benton would take her to the moon if it meant he could give her a healthy child.

That *this one* would live.

Because discovering she was with child again had been almost more than either of them could bear.

• • •

Rosie sat in the rear of the church, listening to the voices raised in song. How beautiful and serene it all felt, like fresh cool water on her scorched soul. She couldn't bring herself to sing, because right now she was too afraid to draw a deep breath. It might pop the fragile bubble in which she'd hidden her soul.

Even though she was five months along, she refused to say she was "expecting." The word held too much hope, and her heart hadn't yet healed from losing the last two babies. She wouldn't allow herself to think of what lay ahead.

*God giveth and God taketh away. Blessed be the name of the Lord.*

The words were harsh for Scripture, but also strangely comforting. Like they was all finding their way on a trail that led them around in a great circle back to the Almighty's arms. Only, her sons had made tiny little circles, and hers were a much longer road. She'd always liked to ramble a bit, and she'd half expected her children to take after her in that regard. But no, they flitted back to heaven, not even caring to stay at their ma's side more than a fistful of days.

Benton reached over and took her hand, folding his larger one over hers, as if aware of her melancholy. The losses had torn at him too. His head hung forward a little, his shoulders no longer lifting as high.

She leaned against him, relishing the touch. Maybe this time.

Lorna fidgeted on Rosie's other side, her hands gripping and releasing the edge of the pew repeatedly.

She'd grown sullen and sour-faced in recent months, disappearing into the woods for long stretches, her dress grass stained like a wayward child instead of a woman of thirty-odd years. Benton said to give her space, and Rosie had tried, but it was hard not to worry after her. So much could happen when she was out in the woods alone. Every year they saw more bears returning to the mountains, as if rushing in to claim the land the people had abandoned. What if Lorna ran into one when she was out wandering? Would she know what to do?

After a few minutes, Lorna jumped from her seat and hurried down the aisle. She blasted her way through the doors like the devil trying to escape the fires of hell.

Benton jerked his head up, glancing at Rosie with lifted brows.

She patted his leg. "I'll check on her."

By the time Rosie made it outside, Lorna was around the far side of the church, retching into the grass, her hands clutching her stomach.

Coming up beside her, Rosie laid a hand on her shoulder, noticing the sweat that dampened the fabric. "You poor dear. I didn't know you weren't feeling well." She dug in her pocket for a handkerchief.

Lorna shook her head and pushed it away. "Nah." She swept an arm up over her face, the splotches on her round cheeks only emphasizing the pale skin and dark circles under her eyes.

"How long have you felt ill?"

Her sister turned and leaned against the wooden church, closing her eyes. She held up two fingers.

"Two days?" Rosie reached up and felt her forehead. Cool and clammy, not fevered.

"Day." Lorna nodded. "Two day." She'd been picking up words in the past couple of years, as if learning to say Benton's name had somehow triggered something deep in her head. It had been a joy to hear her master new words, though it was still hit-and-miss.

"Like this? Sick?" How could she not have noticed?

Her sister nodded, dragging her wrist across her lips. "Ham. Monday."

"Monday?" Rosie thought back to their ham supper. That had been six days ago, not two. "I think we'd ought to call the doctor. That's a long time of being sick." But Lorna couldn't have been under the weather the whole time. She'd been doing her chores yesterday and gone to the barn dance with Benton. Then again, she'd looked really pale yesterday morning.

Lorna reached a trembling hand out and touched Rosie's swollen midsection. "Baby?"

The jolt of pain through Rosie's chest was palpable. Lorna didn't understand the losses they'd suffered. There weren't always the right words to explain to her how the world worked—or how it didn't. Even though they hadn't talked to her about the pregnancy this time, Lorna wasn't unobservant. Tears sprang to Rosie's eyes. "Yes. Baby."

Lorna's brows pinched, and she pulled her arms tight against her rib cage like she was going to be sick again. "Baby."

Rosie shook her head, not ready to discuss the matter further. "We'll send for Doc when we get home. Do you want to sit in the auto until church is done? Or had I ought to get Benton now?"

"Ben." She sagged against the building.

He was already coming down the steps. "What's wrong?"

"She's feeling poorly." Rosie heard the hitch in her own voice. "Just a stomach upset, I think." There was no reason to think it was anything more, but she no longer trusted her judgment on these matters. Life had become too fragile. "I want to take her home and fetch the doctor."

He took her hand and threaded it through his arm. "Do you really think that's necessary? Maybe breakfast just didn't settle right. Or those two slices of pie at the dance last night."

"Two?" Rosie had been too tired for the dance, so Benton had taken Lorna for a short visit. She certainly wouldn't have eaten dessert if she wasn't feeling well.

"Let's get her home. These things blow through fast. You know that."

• • •

Doc came out of their bedroom, rubbing a hand through his graying whiskers. "I'm sorry, Mr. Fuller. You can't know how sorry."

Benton sank into the kitchen chair, unable to draw in a decent breath. "Boy or girl?"

The doctor paced to the window, staring out at the darkness. "Another boy."

The fire crackled in the hearth, breaking the silence in the quiet room. Benton's heart must have ceased beating as well, because if it were, he'd be feeling more pain. Not this quiet emptiness in the pit of his stomach. "And my wife?"

"I gave her a powder, so she's sleeping right now. Maudie is sitting with her." His voice deepened, for a moment sounding just like Benton's grandpa. "At least Mrs. Fuller didn't carry it to term this time. That's a small mercy, I reckon."

Mighty small. Benton closed his eyes for a moment.

The doctor continued to stand there facing the window, as if waiting for the weather to clear before riding off to give some other family dreadful news that would crush them into little pieces.

A chill washed over Benton. He stood, legs trembling. "There's more, isn't there?"

"A couple of things, I'm afraid." Doc cleared his throat and turned to face him. "And there's no way to candy-coat this pill."

His heart had chosen a poor time to start beating again. For once in his life, Benton wished he were a drinking man.

The doctor pulled an envelope from his pocket and laid it on the table. "I'm going to leave these powders here for Mrs. Fuller. It will help her rest, at least for the next few days. But, son . . ." He glanced up and matched Benton's gaze, unflinching. "I don't think you two should try to have more. There's a pattern to these babes not making it past a certain age. And I see no reason to think that's going to be different with another." He shook his head. "Do you hear what I'm saying?"

"Why?" Benton choked out the word.

"I did some studying after the first two, and I hoped I was wrong. But this seems to happen with some ladies. Their infants—those that are born alive—are feeble and die within days. Scientists think it's something in the mother's blood." He stepped closer, laying his hands on the table and leaning forward. "They don't survive."

"None of them?"

The doctor dropped his gaze. "For *some* mothers, it seems to only affect boy babies. But is it worth the risk?"

"We've had three boys in a row. Maybe the next would be a girl."

Doc spoke slowly, as if waiting for him to accept what he was saying. "We don't know if a girl would survive either."

He might as well have kicked Benton's legs out from under him. "She can't lose another child. It would kill her."

"Then we're in agreement."

Benton felt the world around him slow. How would he even begin to tell Rosie?

Maybe she already knew, somewhere in the depths of her soul. She often sensed things even before he could put them into words. If God had any mercy left in Him, this would be one of those times. Benton couldn't be the one to land the final blow.

He listened, waiting for the doctor to cross to the door, but the room fell silent. Would the man never leave?

Instead, Doc pulled out a chair and sat at the table. "I hate to bring this up, seeing as y'all got more than you can handle already."

Benton walked over to the stove and put the kettle on. That was what Rosie would do in this situation. It might not fix anything, but it was something to do.

"I need to talk to you about Lorna."

• • •

"Lorna is . . . what?" All the air seemed to have escaped from Rosie's lungs. The doctor and Maudie had kept her sleeping off and on for nearly a week. Now her head felt as if it were packed with cotton wool, unable to string thoughts together.

"Lorna is expecting." Benton sat on the edge of the bed, the shadows around his eyes deeper than she'd ever seen them. All this time she'd been drifting somewhere between sleep and wakefulness, had he rested once?

"That's plumb crazy. She can't be."

He lowered his eyes. "I don't know what to say. Other than it's the truth."

Rosie's mouth went dry, but she didn't dare reach for the glass next to the bed. Her hands were shaking too hard. "My sister can't—she's never even had a suitor. Lorna ain't capable of such a . . ." She covered her mouth. "She hardly *speaks* to men, except for you."

"I'm not saying she's been off courting. I suspect she may have been . . ." He glanced toward the ceiling, as if avoiding her gaze. "Maybe she was tampered with."

*But who would have . . .* Acid rose in the back of her throat. *Was she sweet-talked? Cajoled? Or was she forced?* Any of the scenarios made Rosie queasy to think on. "Benton, who would have done such a thing?" The question was so faint, she wasn't certain she'd spoken it aloud.

He shook his head, rubbing a hand over his mouth and chin. "I don't know."

The room fell silent, but Rosie's heart continued whispering questions and suspicions—each more dreadful than the last. Only Lorna had answers. "Have you spoken with her? Did she say anything?"

His eyes finally latched onto hers. "How am I supposed to do that? Lorna and I, we talk about birds, we talk about meals and chores, and you. We don't talk about . . ." He waved a hand toward Rosie and then back at himself. "We don't talk about things that happen between men and women. Do you?"

Rosie's heart thudded in her chest. "Not really, no. I mean, she knows some things, I'm guessing. She spends enough time around the animals, and this house ain't that big. But she's like a child, Benton. She's not interested in such."

"I think we may have been wrong to assume that. She's a grown woman, after all."

Her sister, a grown woman. And having a baby. A baby . . . which Rosie might never be able to bear. The thought refused to sink in. "Can she carry it? What did Doc say?"

"He said there was no reason to think she couldn't. Maudie agrees."

"Maudie knows?" Tears filled her eyes. "What will we do? Lorna can't raise a child."

"No." He took her hands and squeezed them. "But she's got us."

# 21

Great Smoky Mountains National Park
Present Day

Zach was seriously starting to love this section of the park around the Elkmont Campground. Not only was it close to where he first ran into a stubborn young woman determined to sleep in her car, but last night he'd witnessed her delight as he introduced her to the Smokies' synchronous fireflies. Fireflies were common enough, but Elkmont's were as unique as the woman who'd clutched his arm in the dark, watching nature's show with wide eyes. As the glimmers of light had spread through the trees, the males' shimmering patterns flickered in time with one another—an organically choreographed dance to sweet-talk the females of their species.

Sitting there hand in hand with Kieran, he couldn't have imagined anything more magical, almost like the night sky had settled into the forest to perform just for them. He could almost feel God smiling on them, like a father watching his children enjoy a rare gift.

This morning they'd hit the trail early once again. With any luck, today would be the day they finally located the family's homesite.

"We were already up this way, right? It's looking familiar." Kieran pushed through another laurel bush. "Or it's all starting to look the same. I'm not sure which."

"We're coming in from the opposite direction. It's a lot shorter from this angle." He laced his fingers through hers as they walked.

"So he really mentioned my great-grandmother by name? He said her whole name?"

"Yep, Rosie McCauley and her sister, Lorna." He glanced down at her, trying to get used to seeing her with her hair loose. The only other time she'd worn it this way was that night in Gatlinburg. "And Rosie evidently coldcocked the boy for teasing them."

"Go, Grandma Rosie. I think I'd have liked her."

"He sounded like a real piece of work. Also like he might have had a thing for your great-grandmother."

"I'm sure glad she didn't end up marrying that guy." She stopped, pulling him to a halt beside her. "You don't suppose Lorna did, do you? You said it wasn't uncommon for close neighbors to marry."

"Her name's not listed in his family tree."

"Good." She sighed. "I've got enough screwy people in my lineage."

"There's the creek. We turn off here and follow it upstream toward the ridge."

"I'm getting used to those sorts of directions finally. What is this, our fourth try? Well, your third. My fourth."

"Next thing you know, you'll be through-hiking the Appalachian Trail."

"Could be fun." She gave him a side glance. "With the right company. Tell you what—I'll hike part of that trail if you promise to visit Dollywood with me. Wait—what's that?" She scrambled up the hill, using her hands for balance on the crumbly soil.

Up ahead was the unmistakable sight of a squat, crumbling building. Too small to be a house, the hewn timbers had rotted through in places, and the roof was gone. "It looks like a springhouse." He circled the short walls, coming around to the opening in the front, where the door had probably hung. Water trickled out from underneath, feeding into a thick clump of vegetation. "Mountain refrigeration at its best."

"Smart." She turned to gaze around the woods. "Not much of a clearing, though. Do you think this is our site?"

"We've got to be right on top of it." He pulled the hand-drawn map from his pocket. He lifted his head, studying the ridgeline looming above. "Let's look around."

They split up, heading opposite directions. Ten minutes later, Kieran yelped.

Zach turned and sprinted toward her.

She stood frozen, staring at a lonely river rock chimney rising from a sprawling clump of brush.

He came up beside her and wrapped an arm around her trembling shoulders. "You ready to explore what's left of your great-grandparents' cabin?"

She nodded, apparently incapable of speech for the first time since he'd met her.

The chimney was in such perfect condition, it could have been built last week instead of sometime in the previous century. The rounded stones were nearly identical in shape, color, and size, the thick mortar holding each in place long after the cabin had crumbled to dust. Or ashes, from the looks of it.

Benton crouched, examining the bits of charred wood forming what would have been an outside wall. As Kieran ran her hands over the old fireplace, he walked the exterior. It was always strange to think of the hands that had built a cabin and the people who had made it into a home.

Kieran's eyes were glassy with tears. "I feel . . . I feel like I'm home. Is that weird? I mean, we're not even one hundred percent sure that this is the right one, are we?"

"We're pretty certain."

She touched the stones again. "Gran said her grandfather had built the house. That means"—she paused, as if thinking it through—"my great-great-grandfather put these here."

"And they're still standing strong."

She walked around to the back side, her eyes traveling up and down the towering structure. She shoved away the trailing canes of rosebushes growing along the bottom edge of the chimney, uncovering a large flagstone.

"Did you know that was there?"

"Granny Mac mentioned it. A flat stone at the base of the chimney, outside the cabin. It's still here too." She ran a hand along the stone, brushing away the loose dirt. "Zach, can I ask you something?"

"Of course." He took a knee beside her. "Anything."

"My gran told me . . ." She grasped the strings on her hoodie, wrapping them around her finger. "She said her mother had a small stone bird that she carried around in her pocket. Gran thought it might have been a memento from her Cherokee grandmother."

"There were some Cherokee in this area back in that time. They'd fled into the mountains when the government was enforcing the Removal Act in the 1830s." He stopped himself. "That's not what you were asking about, was it?" *Once a historian . . .*

She lowered her head, her dark hair falling forward over her shoulders. "Gran talks about this little bird all the time. Whenever she gets confused or upset or has a nightmare, she begs me to find it."

"What happened to it?

"Her father buried it." She patted the ground. "Right here." Her brown eyes latched onto him, the question unspoken but still hanging in the air.

"Kieran." His stomach rolled. Zach dragged his palms across his pant legs. Had this been her plan all along? "We can't—you know it's not allowed." The exact wording of the Archaeological Resources and Protection Act clamored in his brain, but somehow quoting legalese didn't seem appropriate. "This isn't your family's property anymore. It's a historical site on federal land. We can't disturb it."

Nodding, she pushed to her feet, refusing to meet his eyes.

"You wouldn't want other people digging here." His throat tightened as he struggled to explain. “The rules apply to everyone. Even descendants.”

“I thought as much. Who knows—it might not be there, anyway. Gran’s memories aren’t very reliable.”

And yet those memories had gotten them here. He shook his head. “I’m sorry.”

“It’s fine. Don’t worry about it.” Kieran patted the chimney. “I’m sure it’s not nearly as pretty as these, anyway. I’m happy just to be standing here. With you.” She offered him a hesitant smile.

His tension eased a fraction. “Let me get your picture.” He slid his phone from his pocket. It was a sad consolation prize, but she looked so gorgeous standing there, hair fanned out over her shoulders. He snapped several shots as she leaned against the chimney.

“Here, take one on mine too, for Gran and Ashleigh. Wait. You should be in it—we can do a selfie.”

“You won’t get much of the chimney that way. Let me take this one first. You’re standing on your gran’s special stone, after all.”

Her smile faltered, but she straightened and smoothed a hand over her shirt. “Okay, ready.”

They snapped several selfies, and he even managed to turn and plant a kiss on her cheek in the last one. The shared laughter helped disperse the awkwardness from earlier.

They spent the next hour walking the forest around the cabin, locating various other curious structures. In addition to the springhouse, it looked like there had been several outbuildings. The McCauleys had done well for themselves.

“There’s a path over here,” Kieran called out.

Zach hurried to join her. “Probably just a game trail. But we can check it out.” Winding up the steep hill, it seemed to be leading nowhere, until they stumbled on a small iron gate. He took her hand, suddenly suspicious of what lay ahead.

Together they walked into the family cemetery. Carefully arranged headstones stood as solemn reminders of days gone by, many etched with still-legible names and dates. Zach held his breath as Kieran walked through, mouthing each name as she passed. She paused near a short pillar standing beside three smaller markers. The image of a broken rosebud decorated its surface, just above the words "Budded on earth, to bloom in heaven."

He stood behind her and wrapped both arms around her for support.

She leaned against him as she read the names on the stones. "Henry Benton Fuller, 1933. Everett Malcom Fuller, 1934 . . ."

"Infant Boy Fuller, 1935." He read the third inscription, the words clinging to the inside of his throat.

She sighed. "They buried three babies in three years. Can you imagine? Ash and Nick lost a baby boy, and they're still struggling years later. Grandma Rosie buried three?"

"It wasn't unusual for the time, but that probably didn't make it any easier to bear." A familiar ache burned through his chest, but he shoved the unwanted memories away. This wasn't the time to let old hurts rise to the surface, especially when he wasn't ready to talk about them. He let his hands drop from Kieran's waist, and he took a few more steps. "Kieran? You'll want to see this one."

A simple limestone marker stood to one side, its edges softened by the passing of time. The top was etched with the design of a bird in flight.

Kieran took an audible breath, as if readying herself before reading aloud. "Rosie McCauley Fuller. Beloved wife, sister, and mother. Born 1908. Died 1942. Rooted on earth, now flies free."

• • •

The small space heater clicked off, the sound jarring Kieran from her near doze. The cabin was dark except for the flickering night-light she'd added in the kitchen. Since her last visit, Zach had replaced the old mattress on the floor with a queen bed and a delicious memory foam mattress, topped with nice sheets and a locally crafted quilt. Pity none of it helped her sleep.

She rolled over, lifting up on her elbow so she could see out the side window. It looked toward Zach's house in the distance, the porch light a welcome reminder. He was close.

Flopping onto her back, she stared into the darkness. Granny Mac's stories were true. All of them. When Kieran had brushed her fingers across that flagstone, she'd realized she was mere inches from Gran's treasured heirloom. All she needed to do was dig her fingers under the edges and pry it up.

She could picture it as Gran had described. Buried there, forgotten in the dirt, just like all those graves on the hillside. She couldn't help the lives that had gone before, but she could do this one thing for Gran.

Only . . . Zach.

She had felt his eyes on her in an instant, almost as if he could read her thoughts. She could still hear his cold, sober voice from that first day at his office. "*It's against park regulations to remove anything from a historical site.*" At the time, she'd shrugged it off. What the park ranger didn't know wouldn't hurt him.

But Zach wasn't some uniformed stranger any longer. And she'd taken a big risk telling him about the bird.

She pulled the feather-soft quilt up to her nose, her stomach turning. She had kissed the man—fallen for him—all the time knowing she was going to have to break his rules to accomplish her goal. And then this sweet, trusting guy had led her right to the spot.

If he'd been a hero from one of her novels, he'd have dug up that treasure like a modern-day Indiana Jones—saving Granny Mac and making Kieran fall madly in love with him.

But Zach wasn't just some invented character—he was flesh and blood with his own moral compass and personal hang-ups. Integrity wasn't just the uniform he wore—it was woven into his very being. He'd said as much on their first hike together when they talked about past relationships. And if he thought rules were important for dating, then those involving his job probably counted twice as much. He couldn't bend them for her. He wouldn't.

His faith guided his decisions, just as it did for Granny Mac and Ash. Kieran *believed* in God, but she was less certain about faith. It required trust. If she put complete confidence in God, it would mean walking out of here empty-handed.

Kieran turned to face the porch light again, scooting to sit upright on the edge of the bed and pondering the man inside the house across the way. She'd never felt like this for anyone before. She'd dated a little, but Zach made her feel like her heart was living outside her chest.

A snapshot of an old chimney wouldn't help Granny Mac. Her mountain home was nothing but a patch of forest littered with relics of the past. Kieran ran her hands through her hair, pulling it away from her face and mindlessly winding it into a knot behind her head.

Her mind kept returning to those three tiny gravestones set in a perfect line. *Budded on earth, to bloom in heaven.* Those weren't just strangers out there. They were Gran's brothers. Henry, Everett, and the poor unnamed babe—her great-uncles. Her kin. Her people. And her great-grandmother Rosie, who buried three children before giving birth to Granny Mac and then died tragically at only thirty-four.

The names rubbed at a raw place in Kieran's soul, the wound left behind by her own mother's untimely death. Her father's incarceration. Her years in foster care, never realizing she had one family member who still lived and breathed and walked the earth.

She closed her fingers on the pillow and drew it up against her chest. *They're my family.* Her one last link, Gran, was slipping away, lost to nightmares of her mother's murder.

*The government, they did it. They killed her. They wanted the land, and when she was in her grave, they took it.* Those were the only bitter words she'd ever heard her grandmother utter. She'd lived through wars, an abusive husband, a son lost in Afghanistan, another put away for life. But it was her mother's death that haunted her.

*At the hands of the park service.*

Kieran closed her eyes, turning away from the glimmer in the window. It made no sense. But if the lease was in her great-grandmother's name, the others would have no right to stay past her lifetime. *Could* someone in the government have pulled the trigger? Maybe even someone who wore the same uniform as Zach?

That gunshot still reverberated today—a slow-moving bullet ripping through Gran's life right into the fabric of her earliest memories.

Now the same government agency had the arrogance to forbid her from reclaiming the *one item* that could help Gran find peace. They owed her that much. Kieran tightened her fists, the tension radiating up her arms.

She wasn't trying to steal a priceless artifact from a museum or rob the antiquities of an Egyptian pyramid. The folks who made the rules didn't even know the bird existed. It was rock, buried in the dirt like so many others. No one would ever even realize it was gone.

And the folding shovel still sat at the bottom of her pack.

# 22

KIERAN TURNED THE mud-stained carving over and over in her hand, an ache settling in the back of her throat. She leaned against the driver's seat headrest and glanced toward the glass doors of the Collection Preservation Center. Ten minutes remained until her lunch date with Zach, but already it felt like ants crawled all over her skin. She should have canceled and headed home early. And yet the idea of coming up with some lame excuse made her stomach turn even more.

Grooves ran down the stone bird's sides, as if representing wings or feathers. Just above the carefully shaped head and beak, miniature pinprick eyes glared at her. The figure was simple in its beauty. Kieran closed her fingers over it and pulled it to her chest, the stone warm against her palm. The bird had touched countless lives over the generations, but its story wouldn't be complete until she placed it in Granny Mac's hand.

Her cell vibrated in the cup holder, and Kieran jumped. She jammed the carving into the front pocket of her backpack and reached for the phone. Ash's number lit up the screen as Kieran clicked Accept. "What's wrong? Is it Gran?"

"Hello to you too."

Kieran paused for a moment, gathering herself. "I'm sorry. It's good to hear your voice. I've got a ton of news to share. Pictures too. But I doubt that's why you're calling."

The long pause said volumes. Something *was* wrong. Ash cleared her throat. "First off, Granny Mac is fine—I want you to know that. Nick and I spent time with her last night, and she had plenty of stories to tell. I went back this morning, and she was advising one of the nurses on a knitting project."

"Oh good. That's great. I'll be heading home soon."

"One thing, though. We probably stayed a little too long last night, so she got tired and confused. She started talking about Lorna again. I know you were concerned last time she mentioned the name."

"We've figured out who Lorna was. She was Gran's aunt."

"I think there's more." Ash's voice faltered. "Granny Mac tried to leave. Nick had to catch her, and she got really upset with him."

Kieran glanced up. "Hang on a second, Ash. Zach's coming." She unlocked the doors and waved him over.

"You both might want to hear this," Ash said.

"I don't know." Kieran cleared the passenger seat, double-checking her backpack was firmly zipped before moving it to the rear seat. The last thing she needed was for that bird to tumble out. "I don't really want to burden him with more of my problems."

Zach climbed in, folding his long legs into the Volvo's cramped space.

"This is about Lorna and Rosie. I think it might help."

Kiran lowered her voice. "All right. I'm going to put you on speaker. Be good. Don't embarrass me." She pulled the phone from her ear and touched the icon.

"Hey, Zach, that's my best friend you're sitting beside, so you be good to her, ya hear?"

"That's my plan." He cast Kieran a smile.

"Ash . . ." Kieran covered her face.

"Just had to get that out of the way." On the line, they could hear water running, like she was washing dishes. "As I was saying, Granny Mac got mad at Nick for keeping her there in the room. She said we were keeping her prisoner."

A jab of pain hit Kieran in the chest. "I'm sorry. I'd hoped she wouldn't give you any trouble."

"Please don't apologize. She said—listen to this—she said she wouldn't be *committed* like her aunt Lorna."

Kieran straightened. "Committed? Like to an asylum?"

"I think that's what she meant, yes. She repeated it several times. Begged Nick not to leave her there like he'd left Lorna."

Her mind racing, Kieran thought back through Gran's life story. She turned to Zach. "That oral history you listened to said something was unusual about Lorna, right? She was slow—simple? Something like that?"

"I think his word was 'feebleminded.' It's not a term people use anymore."

"We discussed the history of mental institutions in one of my psych classes." Kieran wrapped her fingers around the steering wheel. "They were pretty gruesome places. I wonder if she was sent to Central State Mental Hospital in Nashville?"

"It could have been after they left Tennessee. Where did the family move?"

"Gran said her father was a university professor in Florida."

They finished the call with Ash and headed to a nearby coffee shop for lunch. When Zach tried to take her hand across the table, Kieran gave his fingers a quick squeeze-and-release. If her clammy palms didn't give her away, the dirt wedged under her nails might. Even with the tiny toothpick from her Swiss Army knife, she hadn't managed to get it all. Her fingers were mocking her.

He didn't seem to notice the brush-off. "There's a state mental hospital not far from my sister's place in Tallahassee. We could do some digging and see if Lorna's name turns up in their records."

"I shouldn't be surprised to find a link to mental hospitals in my family's past. In some ways it seemed more realistic than finding some Nobel Prize winner."

His brows drew together. “You haven’t really told me anything about your family, outside of Granny Mac. What about your folks? Siblings?”

A pit opened in the depths of her stomach. If she turned over one more rock in her family’s history, who knew what sort of snakes might crawl out from underneath. “I don’t really like to talk about my past.”

Their food arrived at that moment, giving Kieran the perfect distraction.

But Zach didn’t start eating. “Kieran, whatever it is, please know you can tell me. If something’s bothering you, I’d like to hear about it.”

*If only I could.* She stared down at the plate, the smell of the turkey sandwich and pickle suddenly nauseating. She wouldn’t get a single bite past the lump in her throat. He thought it was her family that upset her? No, it was the canvas backpack sitting at her feet.

Kieran opened the bag of chips just to have something to do. “There are so many places Lorna could have ended up. A private facility. A TB hospital.” She forced herself to look up at Zach. “Besides, we’ve already found the homesite. Maybe we don’t need to run this down.”

“It’s up to you, of course.” His blue eyes were luminescent in the light spilling in from the tall windows. “I didn’t mean to jump ahead.”

“You’re not. I was excited too, at first. But I think we should let Lorna rest in peace. Digging up her dirt, and that of the rest of my kin, it just doesn’t seem right somehow.” *Digging. Dirt. Are you trying to give yourself away?*

Zach smiled. “Then consider it closed.” A flicker of . . . something . . . raced through his expression. “So your search is over. Did you find the answers you were looking for?”

“We found the cabin, or what’s left of it, anyway. And now I know where my gran was born.”

He reached over and threaded his fingers through hers.

The warmth of his touch brought relief from the chill that had descended on her, and this time she didn’t pull away. Part of the joy had been finding the site with Zach, and he’d seemed almost as moved by the discovery as she was. "But finding the homesite was only one piece of the puzzle. I suppose there's no way we'll find out all the answers."

"To which questions exactly?"

"When I first approached you about this project, we didn't really know each other." She allowed herself to meet his gaze again. "You worked for the park service—the government."

"Yes, and I still do." His forehead furrowed. "Is that an issue?"

She tightened her grip on his fingers. "Gran said the government *seized* the land."

His mouth fell open slightly for a second, then he closed it, jaw firming. "The state of Tennessee paid her parents for the land. You saw the lease papers."

"I know. But Rosie still died young—mysteriously—and the family was put off the property." It still sounded like a crazy conspiracy theory. "I guess I'd like to know more details about what happened. It doesn't sound like she passed from an illness."

He sat back in his seat. "Kieran, your grandmother was very young at the time. I think her perception of the situation might not be very accurate."

She pulled her hand free. "She was correct in her descriptions of the cabin site."

"Because it was her home. We all imprint on our childhood home."

*Not all.* Kieran shook off the brusque comment. It wasn't the time to burden him with her story. "Look, I know it sounds crazy. But Gran was repeating what her father had told her. And he was an eyewitness. Even if her memory is a bit unreliable, she truly believes it."

"That the park took the land unjustly?" He sighed, reaching for his cup. "A lot of people around here feel that way."

"Not just that." She laid a hand on his wrist. "She believes that someone with the park pulled the trigger."

# 23

Zach leaned against the window frame, staring out toward the little cottage. He'd grown accustomed to thinking of it as Kieran's place, but it was time to work on the renovations again. Only trouble was, he didn't have the heart to face it tonight. He took a final gulp of room-temperature coffee from the mug in his hand.

Kieran had seemed strangely preoccupied at lunch today. She was eager to get home and see her grandmother, of course, but it still left Zach feeling lost. They'd grown close over the past weeks, searching down the old homesite. In just a few months, thoughts of her had become all-consuming—and that shook him to the core.

If she closed the book on her Great Smokies quest, did that make him another piece of her past? She'd dropped into his life like the flash of a firefly on a summer evening, and he really hoped she didn't disappear just as quickly. Zach sighed, turning to lay the cup in the kitchen sink. It wasn't like him to be so morose. Only the Lord knew his future.

The flash of headlights on his front window made him turn back around. Kieran would be home in Nashville by now, and he wasn't expecting guests. He made it to the front porch even before the car's engine died.

The door hinge on the old pickup squeaked as Bruce pushed it open and clambered out. "Hey, Zach. I got something for you." The director of the historical society leaned on his cane as he walked up the front steps. "Well, it's not with me, but I wanted to tell you where to find it."

Zach waved him inside. "What are we talking about?"

"The tape. My buddy repaired it and transferred the whole thing to a digital file." He held out a scrap of paper with a URL on it. Only Bruce would hand deliver a web address.

"And that's so urgent you drove right over?"

"I took the liberty of listening to the rest. I think you'll want to hear it. There were other references to the McCauley woman. That fellow seemed quite obsessed with her and the family. I marked down the time stamp I thought you'd most want to pay attention to. It's very peculiar."

Peculiar? "Well, grab a seat, then. Let me pull out my laptop."

The older man claimed a chair at the table and lowered himself into it with a grunt. "I was starting to think I'd heard all the crazy stories of these mountains. It tickles me that this one was sitting under my nose all this time."

Zach retrieved the computer from his bag and opened it. "Now I'm intrigued." He typed in the address and scrolled down to the file. Fast-forwarding until he reached the time stamp Bruce had specified, he listened as Horace Samson's drawl started up again.

"Me and my brother had been running stills in the woods since we was boys, you know. Plenty'a mountain folk did. Now when the park moved in, it got a little more discreet-like, but continued just the same. Our creek weren't the best for shine, too warm and silty by the time it got to us, but the spring that fed the McCauley's branch was cold and sweet. Rosie didn't like us using it, so we just kept it under wraps best we could. Now her husband—she married this *furriner* who was all cozy-like with the government. He got me hauled in once for poaching. He had the ear of the park superintendent, so made our life difficult. Rosie shoulda married my brother when she had the chance, but Samsons weren't good enough for the likes of her. Will was a fool for that girl, even after the wedding.

"It finally came to a head one night when that feller lit after us with a bunch of park rangers, trying to bust the still operation we had going. I was fit to be tied at that point, so I decided to meet 'em head-on.

"Y'all know what happened. Folks still talk 'bout it to this very day. My brother took a bullet. And that Rosie? We all knew the government been watching for a chance to get out of those lease deals, so one of them rangers just decided to take care of their li'l problem for good. Shot her dead."

A voice murmured in the background, as if the interviewer had asked a question. Zach reversed the recording three times but couldn't make out the words, even at full volume.

Samson's voice boomed. "Nah, they'll never admit to nothin'. Why would they?" He paused for a long minute, and the sound of spitting rang through the kitchen, preserved for people to hear decades later. "Iffen they want answers, look no further than that *moron*. She saw the whole thing—watched a ranger put that slug into her sister." A snort followed. "Not that no one's ever gonna put no stock by her babblin'."

A second unintelligible interruption set Zach on edge. If the interviewer had intended to ask questions, she should have worn a microphone.

A sour laugh rattled the speakers. "Sure, heard about that. Shoulda done it years afore. But the neighbors said they spied her few months back. Must have gotten out for good behavior. 'Twas a known fact in these hills she could be *reeeeal* good when she wanted—ready as a rabbit, if you know what I mean. Not that you could tell, lookin' at her. Fact is—"

The recording cut off abruptly. Zach restarted it and listened a second time before turning to Bruce. "What happened? Did the tape break again?"

The older man shrugged. "That's all that was on there. Joe said it was just tape hiss after that, so he trimmed it up. Thought maybe the interviewer pulled the plug." He leaned forward in his seat, the chair squeaking against the kitchen floor. "That'll just burn your biscuits, won't it? I don't know the story the feller's talking of, but whatever happened, sounds like he puts the blame squarely on the park rangers."

"The park service doesn't bump off people who get in their way.

There were plenty of other lifetime lease contracts, and most of the former landowners lived out their days in relative peace."

"But this lady *was* killed?"

Zach marked the URL and time stamps in his notebook, alongside the other things he'd learned about the Fullers. "Yes. And the woman's daughter claims it was by gunfire."

"Do they know who shot her?"

"She also believes the government was behind it." Zach sighed and closed the laptop.

Bruce pushed back his chair and stood. "Well, there you go—this corroborates her allegation. Maybe there's something to it. Life was different then, you know. I can do some digging in the local papers, see if anyone wrote up the story." He grabbed his keys and headed for the door.

Zach followed him. "I'd appreciate that. Knowing the National Park Service, there's got to be a report somewhere too. Give me a call if you find anything."

Watching the man's truck roll down the driveway, Zach picked up his cell and stared down at the most recent series of texts with Kieran. It might be best to do a little more digging before sharing this new information. Zach walked back to the table and sat in front of the computer. Passing along Samson's bizarre claims would be like pouring gasoline all over Kieran's grandmother's stories.

Hopefully, whatever he found next wouldn't be the match to light the fire.

• • •

Kieran held the bird figure under the stream of water in Gran's bathroom, using a fingernail brush to clean eighty years of dirt from the grooves. The reddish-brown surface was smooth, but she didn't know if that was typical for this type of stone or if it had merely been rubbed silky soft by passing through many hands. She ran her thumb along the wing, imagining what sort of tool the carver had used to etch the lines. The thought of an ancient Cherokee craftsman shaping this out of its original stone sent a flutter through her stomach.

She'd gone after it believing the item belonged to her grandmother, but as it lay in her palm, she was overwhelmed with the knowledge that it had come to her through history. Did something this old really belong to any of them?

Clearly it would do more good in Gran's possession than moldering away in the soil. She couldn't imagine why her great-grandfather had chosen to leave it behind. It wasn't likely to be some kind of cursed totem like you'd find in a gothic novel. Then again, her family's lot hadn't really improved with the burying of the sculpture, so it couldn't do any more harm to return it to their possession.

She stepped out of the small washroom, pausing to watch as her grandmother showed Ash how to tear out a row of stitches in her knitting project.

Ash frowned at Kieran. "I did it wrong—again."

"You'll get it, girl. Just keep trying." Gran handed the sweater back. "And soften your grip. Both you girls need to learn to hold things loosely."

Kieran moved closer to sit in the seat on the opposite side of Gran. "I have something for you."

Granny Mac's eyes brightened. "You didn't have to bring me anything, honey." She gestured to her room. "I don't have room for all the stuff I've already got."

"I know, but this is special." Kieran slid her thumb over the bird's curved head. Turning Gran's hand over, she laid the figure in her lined palm. "I found it, Gran. I found it for you."

Her eyes went wide, then brimmed with tears. "My mama's bird?" She pulled it close to her face. "How in the world—" Her attention flicked up to Kieran, her brown eyes huge behind the oversized glasses. "You went to the Smokies?"

Kieran let the tension she'd been holding in each muscle flood out of her. "I did."

Granny Mac lifted the bird to her lips and laid a kiss on its smooth surface, her hands trembling. "I can't believe it."

"It was right where you said it would be."

"I used to play there when I was a child. I'd stack pretty rocks on top of that slab—and feathers too—ones my auntie brought from her wanderings."

Her aunt. The one that had been committed. Kieran pushed the thought away.

Gran ran her fingertips across the etchings on its surface. "My father was the one who studied birds, but this belonged to my ma. It had been her mother's, and her mother's mother had been a full-blooded Cherokee, or so I was told." She stared at the object in her hand. "Such a proud history, our people."

Kieran wasn't sure if Gran referred to her Native American ancestors or to her own family's fight for the land, but beyond all that, she couldn't help but picture the rows of stones in that cemetery. Maybe pride was all they had to cling to in the end.

"I'm afraid there wasn't much left of the cabin where you were born, but the site is beautiful." Kieran pulled her phone from her pocket. "Do you want to see some pictures?"

"I don't think so, dear. But tell me what you saw. I want to see it through your words."

Kieran thought back over her long hikes with Zach, memories stirring in her heart. She hadn't called or texted him since getting home. Every time she pictured his face, she thought of the dirt clinging to her fingers.

He hadn't called either.

"There's a small clearing where the cabin used to be, but it's surrounded by large trees going down to the creek. Across the stream, there's a ridge that casts a shadow over the woods. I can't imagine it gets much sunshine there."

"Not down in the holler, no." A smile crossed Gran's face, though her focus seemed far away. "Just enough for our garden, but not like it is up top."

"We didn't climb up there, but I'd like to see it someday. I can imagine it has a wonderful view."

"Rosie's Ridge, that's what Pa called it. I don't know its rightful name. He always said that he'd come to live in the shadow of her mountain."

"Well, it's beautiful. I can see why she didn't want to leave it."

Gran lifted the stone, pressing it against her cheek. "She shouldn't have had to. But the park wanted us out, and they found a way to make it happen."

Kieran fell silent, not sure if she should redirect the conversation or just let Gran get the story out while she could.

Ash had stayed silent through the exchange, clicking her knitting needles. She glanced up at Kieran and lifted a brow.

Kieran took her teacup from the end table. "How did they 'make it happen,' Gran? I couldn't find anything about that in the records."

Granny Mac set the bird on the table. "Our family is proud, Kieran. But sometimes that pride gets in the way of living the life God has set out for you. Ma said once that Pa tried to get her to move from the Smokies, afore I was born. But she wouldn't hear of it." A tiny smile tugged at her lips. "He had to agree to come live in the Smokies iffen she was to wed him. Pa said she was the stubbornest woman he'd ever seen, but he loved her anyway."

Kieran reached for her phone and opened the voice recorder. "She wanted to stay in the mountains she loved. I can understand that."

"There was more to it than that." Gran folded her knobby fingers in front of her. "She was protecting my auntie. She knew what would happen if she took her away from the mountains."

"What was that?"

"Pa said he'd wanted to keep us safe—Ma, Lorna, and me. And that he'd failed Lorna long afore Mama died."

"Before?" Kieran took her grandmother's hand. "Ash told me your aunt ended up in a hospital. Was that here in Tennessee?"

Rocking in place for a long moment, Granny Mac took a shuddering breath and dug for the tissue she kept stashed up her sleeve. The words obviously cut deeply.

"I'm sorry, Gran. I shouldn't have asked."

"Lorna was a mite slow. It weren't all that rare in those days. Most families knew someone who was peculiar in one way or another, but oft time they were locked up somewhere—institutionalized. My pa"—she shook her head—"I heard him promise my ma he'd never do that. He said she'd be with us always. My father was a good man. But even he weren't enough. Not after ma . . ."

"So he put her in the state hospital?" Kieran asked.

Gran nodded and dabbed the tissue to her eyes. "He wouldn't talk about her after that. All he said was that they'd help her get better so she could come home."

"Did she?"

Gran's eyes closed. "I never saw her again. Years later I asked him about it, but then he insisted that she'd died with Mama. I think it was easier for him to say that. But I remembered. I'll never forget the name of that place."

"What place?"

"Chattahoochee."

The dark circles under her grandmother's eyes tugged at Kieran. She'd let this sad discussion go on too long just to satisfy her own curiosity. She reached over and touched the stone figure. "But now you have your mother's bird. I imagine it's like having a piece of her back, isn't it?"

Gran didn't even glance down. She laid her fingers over the carving and pushed it across the table to Kieran. "I wanted it for you. You were lost to me for years, much like this little bird. But now you're found. I want this to remind you that you're one of us—with all the Fullers and the McCauleys. You are a part of this family, no matter what your father did." She laid the stone in Kieran's palm, pushing her fingers around it. "But like a bird, you ain't tied to one place. You need to be ready to follow God wherever He calls you. Fly to him, child, and rest in the shadow of His wings. He's your true Father."

Kieran tightened her grip on the stone, tears springing to her eyes. "Are you sure? I found it for you."

Gran gave a little laugh. "I ain't sure of much these days, but this thing I know. You're a Lucas, a Fuller, and a McCauley. But most of all, you're God's."

• • •

The coals in the woodstove crumbled and sent a shower of sparks upward. The flickering light danced through the dark room. Zach rubbed his eyes, willing them to focus on the computer's glow for just a bit longer. He'd spent most of the day digging through park records and now at least half the night scouring the internet. There had to be *something* recorded about Rosie McCauley Fuller's death. The most he'd unearthed was a death certificate filed with the state of Tennessee, and the information on that was grossly unhelpful. Too many of the fields were blank. Cause of death: *unknown*.

These days, everything that happened in a national park seemed to trigger a mountain of paperwork. Work mishaps, wildlife interactions, missing persons, traffic accidents—it didn't seem to matter. If Marley came to him with a paper cut, he'd probably have to fill out an incident report. A full investigation would be conducted if someone died, and the cooperation between federal, state, and local law enforcement spawned its own ridiculous paper trail.

It was mind blowing to him that a woman could be shot to death at Great Smoky Mountains National Park and there was zero paperwork on it, even if it did happen back in 1942. Had she just fallen through the cracks, or had someone actively swept the records clean?

*Maybe it just never happened.* With such a glaring lack of information, it seemed plausible that Rosie McCauley Fuller died in some sort of accident, and an imaginative neighbor had created this false history that was keeping Zach up half the night.

Trouble was, Kieran's grandmother had the same story. Would the family perpetuate such a bizarre tale if there wasn't some seed of truth in it? Maybe—if they were hiding something. Perhaps the truth was even uglier, like Mr. Fuller had shot and killed his own wife.

Zach sighed, pushing away from the table. With the exception of Kieran's grandmother, everyone had taken the memory of the event to the grave.

Bruce might be having more luck with the local newspapers. Most kept collections of old issues. Samson had suggested it was a story that "everyone knew," so maybe it had been reported in the press, if not in park records.

Getting up, he crossed the kitchen and clicked on the lights. It hadn't been dark when he'd started this. He turned and caught a glimpse of the antique clock on the mantel. Two thirty in the morning? How was that even possible?

Wandering over to the fridge, he opened it and stared inside. How long were leftovers good, anyway? He grabbed an apple and headed outside to sit on the deck. The bugs were bad this time of year, but some cool night air might clear his head.

The night-light Kieran had left in the cottage created a gentle glow through its side window, almost like she was still there. Biting into the apple, the tart flavor held off the emptiness threatening to consume him.

The crooning of hundreds of lovesick tree frogs didn't prevent Samson's words from creeping back into Zach's mind. The thought that the park could be responsible for Kieran's great-grandmother's death had sent him reeling. If the tale proved to be true, would it change things between them? She couldn't hold him responsible for what some ranger did eighty-plus years ago, could she?

He'd been proud to wear the "flat hat," as the rangers referred to it. It represented a long and proud legacy of protecting the nation's history, culture, and natural beauty. But you couldn't work at Great Smoky without understanding the cost to the families whose land now lay within the boundaries of the national park. He'd never get used to talking to folks who cursed the park service one moment, then turned around and talked about how glad they were that places like Cades Cove had been protected. Eighty years had allowed the forest to reclaim its former ground and the wildlife to return, but it would take a lot longer to heal the human scars.

And he'd studied enough Native American history to know that the US government was notorious for not honoring their agreements.

*Lord, help me find the truth. And if I can be selfish about it, let it be a truth everyone can live with.*

His phone buzzed in his pocket, and Zach yanked it out. Kieran hadn't contacted him in days now, the pair of them falling into a strained silence he didn't understand.

Bruce's name appeared on the notification, and Zach blew out a long breath. *Not Kieran.*

He opened the message. Somehow Bruce had figured out how to both scan and attach an article to the email.

*Subject: Marysville Times, March 20, 1942*

GUNFIRE ERUPTS DURING MOONSHINE RAID, LOCAL WOMAN DEAD

TAX AGENTS AND PARK RANGERS WAGE WAR ON GREAT SMOKIES MOONSHINERS
WOMAN'S HUSBAND STAYS SILENT

*Responding to reports of illegal stills, federal "Revenooers" and park rangers converged on a home in Great Smoky Mountains National Park this Wednesday and were met with shotgun blasts that left one woman dead and one man gravely injured. The long-standing unwritten code of "no shooting and we'll let you run" broke down when these gutsy moonshiners decided to fight back, with a young woman caught in the crossfire. It is unknown who shot first, but the bloodshed that followed was regrettable.*

*The county sheriff isn't saying what went wrong this deadly night, but the shots that shattered the quiet of these mountains might usher in a new era of violence between locals and federal officials.*

# 24

Great Smoky Mountains National Park
1939

Rosie came from the goat shed, brushing bits of muddy straw from her trouser knees. The goat had been acting right puny of late, and she and Lorna had taken turns sitting with her.

Five years had passed since Will had dropped the critter off at her gate. He'd been trying to mend fences that day, but that was just afore her world tipped on its side and she somehow lost all sight of anyone else. Now every time she saw the fool animal, a sliver of guilt buried itself further into her soul. She'd hardly spoken to the man since.

*"I miss her, Rosie . . . I miss you too."*

Benton stepped down from the porch, little McCauley tucked under one arm like a piece of firewood. Girlish giggles spilled out across the yard. He lowered her to the ground, letting her totter across the clearing toward Rosie, arms outstretched.

All of Rosie's worries flew away as she knelt and let McCauley crash into her. She held the child close, as she'd done every day since Maudie first placed the squalling baby girl in her arms. Chest to chest, heart to heart. God's blessings came in mighty unusual ways. And with it God had somehow breathed life back into her.

Her husband grinned. "We're going to have trouble keeping up with her soon."

Rosie buried her face in McCauley's neck, pressing a row of kisses to her soft skin. "I'm afraid you might be right." She set her down, giving the girl a moment to balance herself before toddling toward her pa with a drooly grin.

They'd kept Lorna close to home during the last months of pregnancy and only had Maudie at the birth, so everyone in the holler naturally assumed Rosie was the mother. Even Lorna never seemed to question it. McCauley might have been "born on the wrong side of the blanket," as folks might say, but her birth had healed a world of hurts, pouring an oil of gladness into every gaping wound.

Benton swung McCauley into the air and then propped her against his shoulder. "Are you ready for your nap, Mac?"

"Don't call her that." He only did so to vex her. They'd discussed many names before fixing on McCauley—honoring both Rosie's kin and Lorna's role in the baby's birth. Merging the names McCauley and Fuller seemed beautiful in its own way.

Unfortunately, the best Lorna could manage with the name was "Mac." Now she had Benton saying it too.

He waited for Rosie to join them before turning toward the house. "So what's the word on Lorna's goat?"

"Can't tell iffen it's on the way out or just lonesome. They're herd animals. Ain't right to keep her alone like we been doing."

"Maybe we should get one or two more. Then, even if it doesn't make it, Lorna will have others to devote herself to."

Rosie turned to Benton, considering on her words. "Will Samson's got some new goat kids. Maybe we can barter one off him."

Benton's face darkened like it did every time anyone mentioned the Samson name. He had run into more signs of poaching and trapping in the area, and they both knew who was likely to blame. Rosie had long been suspicious the Samsons operated multiple stills up higher in the mountains as well, but she knowed better than to ask after it. Benton routinely checked around their woods but had yet to find one.

"I don't want any business with them. We could ask around in town."

His fingers ran lazy circles around McCauley's back as she laid a sleepy head on his shoulder.

"We'd pay twice as much there." Rosie climbed the steps. "Will raises good milkers, and he's fond of Lorna. He'd probably give one to her if she asked."

"No."

McCauley's head bounced up at the sharpness in her pa's tone. She laid a hand on his cheek, her petal lips turning down.

His expression softened at her touch, but his voice remained firm. "I know you have a blind spot when it comes to Will, but I'd rather pay cold, hard cash than be beholden to the Samsons. We can afford a new goat, and Lorna deserves the very best we can give her, considering."

"I ain't got no blind spot." Rosie reached for the baby, transferring the sleepy child to her own arms. "I'm trying to be sensible. But since you feel strongly about it, maybe you and Lorna could go into town later. Who knows—it might cheer Nanny up to have a little one around?"

He cracked a smile at that, reaching a hand to touch his daughter's head. "It certainly worked for us."

Rosie carried McCauley into the bedroom and laid her in the cradle Beau had built for Henry. She was big enough to rock the thing herself now, and they'd have to come up with a trundle or something soon. But for now she seemed content to curl up in the tiny space, pulling her thumb to her mouth and nestling into the quilt Maudie had stitched. The sight tore at Rosie's heart with its sweetness. She crept out, leaving her daughter to sleep.

Benton sat on the porch with his typewriter, working on another article. He'd been busily writing for years now, with pieces printed in *Audubon*, the *Auk*, the *Chat*, and a host of other scholarly bulletins. Every month she clipped out pages from the magazines and pasted them over the decades-old newsprint wallpapering the cabin. Rosie loved seeing their little bedroom covered in the neatly typed words and drawings of birds. She'd even added her ma's drawing of a chickadee to the growing menagerie. It looked right at home among the fancy magazine pictures.

Benton had laughed when he caught her gluing a tinted illustration of an Amazonian parrot to the wall near Mac's cradle just days afore she was born. "That drawing was done by one of Hayden's students. Actually, one of *my* students that Hayden stole out from under me."

She'd held the brush steady, careful not to drip glue on the floor. "I hope you don't mind. I thought the baby would like looking up at it."

"Not at all." He'd grinned. "I think he'd be honored. One minute you're at the top of your field, the next day your articles are lining a bird cage. Only the truly fortunate ones end up on a baby's wall."

It was moments like that she remembered how much he'd given up for her. And here she'd lectured him on the finer points of purchasing goats.

Walking out to the porch, she sidled up behind him and wrapped her arms around his shoulders.

He paused typing for a moment. "What's this?"

"My way of saying thank you."

"I'm not sure what I did to deserve that"—he turned and tugged her into his lap—"but did I earn a kiss too?"

"You deserve a lifetime of kisses. But how about just one for now?"

He leaned in and claimed her lips.

"Or maybe two."

• • •

Benton scrambled down the tree, careful to skip the third rung, which had come loose this past winter. It was good to see the owls returning to their snag after choosing a different location for their nest the past two years. He'd need to shore up the old blind so he could keep watch over the coming months. Maybe he'd even bring Mac up here to see them. Two years old was the perfect age to meet your first owl. Plus, it would be fun to show off his own progeny to Annie and Hoot. Wouldn't that be a turnaround?

In the distance, he spotted Lorna hurrying down the lane, veering into the trees toward Beau and Maudie's place. Benton groaned. He wanted to go into town to purchase a newspaper, and Lorna had said she'd come along. Just last night they'd huddled around the radio, listening to the news out of Europe. England had begun conscription efforts, and there were rumors the United States might follow suit. The thought of being forced to leave his family to go fight overseas had kept him tossing and turning half the night.

He'd best go after her. Benton dropped to the ground and brushed off the knees of his trousers. Hurrying after his sister-in-law, he unbuttoned his coat and let it swing free. The sun shone through the newly emerging leaves, the air flooded with the scent of promise. It was little wonder Lorna had struck off into the woods.

Keeping Lorna close to home had proven to be an exercise in futility. After a lifetime of rambling, she'd grown accustomed to her freedom. Once he and Rosie had their hands full with McCauley, she'd started slipping out again. Always headstrong, she was immune to both their pleas and their raised voices. He'd followed her a few times, watching as the woman sauntered about, lost in her own world—gathering stones in the creek, picking berries, and wandering aimlessly through the forest.

They'd probably never learn who had violated Lorna—a thought that sickened him. Likely as not, it had been a drifter passing through the park. The truth of what she'd endured weighed heavily on him. It had never occurred to him that some stranger might take advantage of the poor girl's naïveté. He should have known better.

Lorna evaded every attempt they'd made to question her about what had happened. Either she didn't understand, or she refused to face it. He couldn't really blame her.

He hurried along, hoping to catch Lorna before she disappeared into the hills again. Rather than her usual meandering path, today she seemed to have purpose to her stride. Where was she headed? She'd veered away from the Tiptons' and now paralleled the creek. A prickle crawled up his shoulders, and he slowed. They were skirting the edge of the Samsons' property. He'd assumed Horace's belt had long broken her of visiting their animals.

She paused along the creek bank, turning back to study the landscape.

He huddled behind a massive black walnut, willing himself to fade into the bark. She'd given them no reason to doubt her, so why did every hair on his arms rise as she continued on her path, ducking down a game trail with the assurance of having walked this way before.

Benton let her continue out of sight before he stood and followed after her. Lorna might be simple, but she was more aware and observant than people thought. If you watched her eyes, you could see the thoughts humming through her mind, thoughts she didn't know how to express. Her speech had improved, but she still managed little beyond two- and three-word sentences.

He stepped lightly, careful not to snap twigs. He'd have a tough time explaining why he was skulking around Samsons' property.

The forest opened out ahead of him, so Benton obscured himself behind some laurels, peeking out from among their broad leaves. A rundown shack lay at the far side of a grassy field, the front door hanging ajar on its remaining hinge. Two of Lorna's favorite corn-husk dolls were propped up in the window, as if keeping watch through the cracked pane of glass.

Benton's muscles uncoiled as he released a long breath. She'd found herself a playhouse. Hundreds of these old cabins remained scattered around the mountains, derelict reminders of the families who had departed. Since Mac had turned two, she rarely allowed Lorna a single moment of peace. It made perfect sense that she'd found a quiet place of her own to play. He only wished it wasn't so close to the Samsons' land.

He edged around the clearing, trying for an unobstructed view without stepping into the open. Lorna wouldn't appreciate him spoiling the secret of her hideaway's location. The trip into town could wait. The world's troubles weren't going away anytime soon.

Heavy treads behind him jerked Benton to awareness. As he turned, a strong hand gripped his arm and yanked him around, a fist meeting his face before he could catch a glimpse of his attacker. Pain burst through his eye socket just ahead of the ground rising up to meet him. His shoulder skidded into the dirt, followed by the rest of him. His glasses hung loose over one ear.

Rolling to his back, he dug his heels in to scoot away from whatever was coming at him next.

It was a boot slamming into the center of his chest. Benton curled inward, his body suddenly focused on the act of drawing breath.

Horace Samson's sharp voice roared in his ears. "That's what you get, slinking around like a rat to the trash heap."

This time the boot caught him under the chin and slammed his head backward into the ground. Pain seared as the world wobbled on its axis. If he didn't get his feet under him, he might not make it out of this alive. Benton squinted, forcing his eyes to focus, and managed to grab onto Samson's foot the next time it came close. Yanking hard, he pulled the larger man off balance.

Samson hit the earth like a felled tree, grunting with the expulsion of air.

Benton scrambled to his knees and then to his feet. The world swayed, but he kept his legs under him out of sheer determination. Samson might intend to kill him, but he didn't need to make it easy for the man. Not when he had a wife and daughter waiting at home.

As Samson lunged to his feet and plowed into Benton, the sound of Lorna's scream cut through the din. Even as they tumbled, Benton managed to ram a fist into Samson's face, using the momentum to relocate the man's nose somewhere to the center of his forehead.

"Behhhh—" Lorna's voice reached Benton's ears. "No! NO!"

*Lorna.* He crawled a few feet, Horace's blood sticky on his hands. *Get up. You've got to protect her.* He hooked one arm around a tree trunk and hoisted himself to his feet, casting about for Lorna with bleary eyes.

She was stumbling toward them from the cabin, tears streaming down her face. Her hair hung loose, her shirt askew. "Ben, no!"

"Stay back!" He swung around toward Horace, fire casting up from his belly. "You. It was you all along. I should have known."

As the man gained his feet, Benton surged forward and grabbed Samson by the collar now stained by the blood dripping from his nose. Benton landed two quick blows to the cur's face before Samson lifted a meaty forearm to block.

"I don't answer to you." Samson grabbed Benton's throat with one hand and shoved him back against the tree, smashing his head into the bark and pinning him there.

Lorna grabbed Horace's upper arm, shrieking like a wounded rabbit. The terror in her eyes sent a spear through Benton's gut. He couldn't let her see this. "Lorna, go—" The fingers against his windpipe cut off any other words.

Appearing out of nowhere, Will grabbed Lorna around the middle and pulled her back.

She fought against him, arms flailing like a crazed windmill, landing a few blows of her own.

Another bash against the tree caused Benton's legs to crumple, dropping him like one of Lorna's rag dolls in Samson's grip. He closed his eyes, barely aware of Lorna's screams as his skull made contact with the trunk again.

• • •

The hospital room's harsh light made Rosie's eyes burn. She wiped a tear with her free hand, keeping the other tightly wound around her husband's fingers. They were still covered in dirt and blood—his or someone else's, she didn't know. She stroked a finger across his cheek, avoiding the angry split along his cheekbone and the bandages covering a good portion of his head. Both eyes were ringed with bruises.

How could this have happened?

When Lorna had burst out of the trees, screeching to near wake the dead, Rosie thought her heart might stop. She'd known it was Benton even though she couldn't make sense of her sister's sobbing cries. Clutching McCauley to her side, she'd dashed after Lorna, not stopping until they'd found his broken body near the old Ogle homesite. She'd shoved the baby at her sister and dropped to her knees beside Benton, frantically checking for signs of life.

Beau arrived minutes later, drawn by Lorna's continued hollerin'. Betwixt the two of them, they hauled Benton down to the road and then off to the hospital hours away. It was all such a blur, she couldn't even remember how Beau had managed to get the Ford from the house. She hadn't been able to take her eyes off the rise and fall of her husband's chest. *You will keep on breathing. You have to.*

Her man was a gentle sort, never one to raise a fist. To see him bloodied and beaten made her heart shrivel in her chest. Whoever had done this, Benton had fought fist and skull to protect hisself—she could see it in his split knuckles and torn fingernails.

She stroked his cheek again.

One eyelid fluttered, the other too swollen to move. Benton groaned, shifting slightly in the narrow bed.

"Don't," she whispered. "Stay still."

His cracked lips parted. "Lor . . . Lorna? Is she?"

"Shhh. Lorna is safe. She's with Maudie. McCauley too."

His eye closed, air hissing through his open mouth. "Where . . . am . . ."

"The hospital in Knoxville. The doc says you're going to make it." Those words had been the first spot of joy she'd experienced in hours.

So much blood had soaked the ground beneath his head, she couldn't imagine Benton had any left in his veins.

"Hurts."

"I s'pect it does. But it means you're alive."

He shifted, a grimace etched into his face alongside the bruises and puffy cuts. "Rosie . . ."

More tears stung at her eyes, and she drew in a shaky breath. "Don't try to talk—just stay still." *And keep breathing.* That was all she asked.

The doctor returned a while later, but Benton was so groggy his eyes remained closed through most of the visit. The man pushed his hands into the pockets of his white coat. "He's lucky, though he won't feel like it for a while. He's looking at broken ribs, shoulder, and a cracked sternum. But the worst damage is to the head. There's a small fracture near his left eye socket and a good crack in the back of his skull."

Rosie sank into the chair, her thoughts scurrying for cover. "His skull? Will it heal?"

"In time, Mrs. Fuller. *Lots* of time." He ran a hand over his shirtfront. "It won't do any good to soften this. It's going to be a long road, and he might never be quite the man he was. Sometimes head injuries like this can change a person. Headaches, memory problems, mood changes."

"He's a scholar." She tightened her grip on the edge of the bed. "A man of science and words. Will that change?"

"We'll know more in a few weeks. For now he needs absolute quiet and dark. That's the best for healing."

"But he'll be well again?"

He adjusted his gold-rimmed glasses. "Yes, Mrs. Fuller. I believe he will. You wouldn't know it to look at him now"—he glanced back at Benton—"but I think he's a fighter."

# 25

## Nashville
## Present Day

Kieran set the stone bird on the dashboard of her parked car, closing her eyes to concentrate on what Zach was telling her over the phone. When she'd seen his name pop up on the screen, it had taken her several seconds to summon the courage to accept the call. Oddly, he hadn't said anything about her not texting him, just launched into a lengthy explanation of what he'd learned from an old newspaper article and the oral-history recording.

Was there a tiny edge to his voice?

Pressing the phone to her ear, she tried to focus on his words. "He said that?"

"Yes. As much as I hate to repeat it, he basically corroborated your grandmother's story almost word for word. The newspaper article I'm sending you is a little more vague. But then, they're supposed to search for facts. Samson can say whatever he wants. So I'm not sure which of them to believe."

Her heart stuttered. "I can't believe Gran was right. The park service killed my great-grandmother."

The line fell silent for a moment. "I didn't say that." Zach cleared his throat. "I think it will take some more digging, and we may never know the whole truth. I can't find anything official about it, and that does strike me as odd."

She ran a hand along the top edge of the steering wheel. "If they're responsible, I doubt they'd keep records about it." Kieran could almost feel Zach's discomfort over the miles. Whether it was because he preferred to be an unbiased historian or because the government wrote his paychecks, it was hard to tell. Maybe both.

"Well, I thought you should know. It's not going to help with your gran, but at least you know she's not . . . um . . ."

"Losing her mind?" Now she could totally picture him cringing. It was a sweet reminder of who he was. A person of integrity. Unlike her. "No, you're right. It's good to know the truth—or some portion of it, anyway."

She picked up the bird and tucked it into her pocket, glancing toward the diner. "Hey, I should get going. There's an apron with my name on it waiting for me."

"Right." Zach's voice lowered, as if full of meaning. "One more thing, Kieran. I know you didn't want to follow up on your great-aunt's story, but there was something on the oral history that got me thinking."

"Yeah?" She climbed out of the Volvo and locked the door behind her. The last thing she wanted was to hear more about her family ending up in the loony bin. She had her hands full with Gran's mental and emotional state. "What is it?"

"He said Lorna witnessed the shooting. And that she might have returned to the area years later."

Kieran stopped outside the diner. "Lorna got out of the mental hospital?"

"I know your great-grandfather refused to speak of his wife's death, but maybe your great-aunt did."

She slid her hand into her pocket, wrapping her fingers around the carving. "Gran said she went to Chattahoochee. I looked it up—it's in Florida."

"My sister lives pretty close to that area. Tallahassee."

A sliver of guilt pressed in on her. She'd told him she didn't want to pursue this, but her own curiosity had run ahead, anyway. "I made some inquiries. They have records, but nothing's online. I'd have to go talk to the archivist in person and search through the files myself."

Another long pause. "Good thing you have a friend who knows his way around archives."

"I couldn't ask you to do that. Especially after . . ."

"After ghosting me this week?"

She sat down on the edge of a brick planter in front of the restaurant. If only that was all she was guilty of. "I'm sorry about that. Since we found the cabin site, everything has just felt . . . different. I wasn't sure where we stood."

He sighed, the sound carrying through the call. "I care about you, Kieran. I don't want to just walk away. But if that's what you—"

"I don't." The words tumbled from her lips. "I don't want you to walk away. Please." Her throat tightened. Suddenly she was the little girl sitting in the back of a caseworker's car. She pressed fingers to the bridge of her nose and tried to settle her voice. "I miss you. I wish I could see you right now."

"I'd like that too." His tone softened. "I could come to Nashville this weekend if you want."

"Really?" She dug into her pocket again, frantic to find the bird. She'd need to find a safe spot for the thing, where no one would see it. "I'd like that. And you could meet Granny Mac."

"And if you're serious about wanting to visit the archives in Tallahassee, we could drive down and stay with my sister for a day or two. She'd love it. Pesters me all the time about coming to see her and the kids. We might be able to find out what happened to Lorna. After all, we work together so well."

"Oh, Zach." The idea of sneaking away to Florida's Gulf Coast with him sent her heart racing. How had they gone from not speaking to planning a road trip in just a few minutes? *Stop it. This isn't a romantic weekend getaway. It's a research trip.*

"No pressure." His voice sounded hesitant. "But I sure could use an afternoon at the beach."

"Me too." She laughed, hugging an arm to her chest. "When do we leave?"

• • •

Zach stood next to his truck and stretched, trying to work out the knot in his shoulder from sleeping on the sofa at Nick and Ash's apartment. The four of them had sat up talking and playing cards until well after midnight, which was probably a mistake since he and Kieran had a long drive ahead of them. But he loved road trips, and having Kieran in the passenger seat was an added bonus. His sister was ridiculously excited and had texted him dozens of times last night to ask for specifics regarding Kieran's tastes in food, drinks, and entertainment.

Kieran laid her bag in the back seat of Zach's truck. "I wish she wouldn't go to all this trouble. I don't want to be a bother. Ash only offered you a couch and a bowl of breakfast cereal. It sounds like Aubrey is cooking a five-course meal and leaving mints on my pillow."

"Aubrey's just an obsessive planner. I've never brought a girl to see her, so she wants everything to be perfect. Trust me, I prefer the sofa and cereal to being fussed over. But nothing brings my sister more joy than anticipating people's needs and desires."

"Granny Mac was the same way before her health started declining. You were really sweet with her, by the way. Thank you for letting her 'hug the stuffing out of you,' as she put it."

"I didn't mind. My grandma's a hugger too."

"So you're used to being gran-handled, then."

"Pretty much." Zach tossed his stuff next to Kieran's, pleased to see that she was a travel-light sort of girl. He'd suspected as much, seeing how well she did at his backyard shack, but one never knew for sure. "I was surprised you didn't tell your grandmother what we learned about her aunt."

Kieran ran a hand through her dark hair, freeing it from the Penn State hoodie she'd just pulled over her head. "I thought I'd wait and see what we learned in Florida. Just because some guy said it on a tape recording years ago doesn't make it true. If she'd been released, wouldn't my grandmother have been notified—or her father, at least?" She opened the passenger door before he could reach it and hopped into the front seat.

"It may have been after his death." He slid behind the wheel. "I wonder why she never looked into what happened to her aunt."

A dark look passed over Kieran's face. "It's surprisingly easy to lose track of people once they're in the system."

He headed down the road toward the interstate. "I guess you run into that in your line of work."

"In my . . ." She darted a glance toward him. "Right. Yeah, we see a lot of elders who seem to have little contact with their grown kids or other relatives. It's sad, really."

"My family's all pretty close, so I can't picture it happening with my folks. But my uncle's another story. His kids hardly talk to him since the divorce."

"That's terrible."

"I still call him sometimes, for building advice, but even our relationship is strained. I guess we all have a family member who makes bad life choices, but you don't just dump them." He tightened his grip on the wheel. "I'm not saying that's what happened with your aunt. I'm sure there was a good reason for your great-grandpa's change of heart."

"Gran said he'd promised his wife they would always take care of Lorna. Considering how young she was, it's surprising she remembers that so vividly, don't you think?"

"Sometimes things just stick. Don't you have childhood memories like that?"

The truck grew quiet, except for the rumbling of the tires against the pavement. He glanced at her. Every time he mentioned her past, she went silent on him.

"No." Kieran ran both hands over her face. "I don't really remember much, maybe because it wasn't worth remembering."

"Did you grow up in Nashville?"

"Pennsylvania, mostly. My father . . . my father's in prison." She fidgeted, sliding her hands up and down her thighs. "He went there after my mom died from an overdose. He was dealing."

His stomach lurched. "I'm so sorry. I can't imagine what that must have been like."

"You don't want to, trust me. But now you can see why I don't like talking about them." She shrugged one shoulder, turning her head and staring out the side window.

"Makes sense."

"And for Lorna, lost in the system? I get that too."

He reached a hand for hers—missed—and landed on her leg. He left his palm there, troubled by the trembling under his fingers.

"I grew up in foster care. Mostly they were decent homes, good people. But they weren't mine." She released a long breath. "I knew my own family was a mess, but I never realized the problems went back generations. Gran raised two sons—lost one to war, the other to drugs and prison. Her mother was killed tragically, her aunt locked up, her father distant and uncommunicative." She choked out a little laugh. "What's wrong with us? And how badly will I screw up our children?" She jerked. "*My* children. Sorry. I don't know what I'm saying."

Zach steered onto the next exit, pulling into a small city park. After shutting off the engine, he hopped out and came around to her side. *Please, Lord, give me words.* Opening her door, he reached out a hand to Kieran.

For a long moment, she sat without looking at him. When she placed her hand in his, he tugged her to her feet and into an embrace. They stood beside the truck for a long time, her head the perfect fit for the cleft of his shoulder. He thought of several comforting things to say but discarded each before they reached his tongue. Perhaps at this moment the hug was enough.

"I'm sorry. I shouldn't have dumped all that on you." Her breath warmed his neck.

He tightened his grip as much as he dared before placing a kiss on the top of her head. "I'm glad you did. Now I will stop saying stupid, insensitive things."

Her fingers moved across his sides, sending little charges along his spine. "You didn't. I should have told you before." She tipped her head up to gaze at him.

"Do you ever see your dad?"

A pained expression crossed her face. "A few times over the years, but not in . . ." She glanced upward, as if counting. "Not in a long time. I have no desire to see him."

He brushed away a lock of her hair that had fallen over her eyes, not wanting anything to obscure his view. Then again, too much of that and he'd be kissing her—probably not what she needed right now. "Thank you for trusting me with it. I'm guessing you don't share that often."

Her shoulders shook lightly with a silent laugh. "You'd be right about that. Can you just imagine—'Here's your biscuits and gravy, sir. How about a side of family drama?'"

"Ash knows, right? It would explain why she's so fiercely protective."

"Well, that's just Ash, I think. But yes, she and Nick are aware. Next to Gran, they're the closest thing I have to family."

"You realize, if your great-aunt was released, there's a chance she went on to have a family of her own. Maybe you have cousins you've never met."

She squinted up at him. "From the sounds of things, she might not have been capable of that sort of relationship."

"We won't know until we track her down. Shall we hit the road?"

Kieran took a last look out at the park. "Your sister might get worried if her baby brother doesn't arrive at the scheduled time."

He grimaced. "About that. My family has drama too. Ours comes out of sheer numbers. I hope it doesn't get overwhelming for you." Come to think of it, if she needed family, he had plenty to share. The idea of making her part of his clan was growing more and more appealing.

She wove her fingers through his as he reached for the passenger door with his opposite hand. "I think it sounds incredible. I can't wait to meet them."

• • •

Kieran walked up the flagstone path with Zach, appreciating the warm glow radiating from his sister's house. She'd never seen anything so welcoming. By the time they'd pulled into Tallahassee after nine hours of driving, they'd covered a lot of ground—literal and personal—and they were talked out. The only thing Kieran wanted was a hot shower and a soft bed.

A woman flung open the door, her honey-gold hair draped in waves over her slim shoulders. "Zachary, you made it! And this must be Kieran."

She grabbed Kieran's hands and tugged her inside. "Come meet the kids. They've been dying to see you. Oh dear, where'd they go?" Dropping her grip, she bolted off down the hall, leaving Kieran and Zach in the entry.

He leaned close. "And that's Aubrey."

Of course she was gorgeous. It must run in the family. Kieran ran a hand down her rumpled sweatshirt. Were those Cheetos crumbs on her sleeve?

Three little girls with matching curls and pink pajamas rushed in and threw themselves at Zach and Kieran, barking like a litter of overexcited puppies. A slightly older boy hung back, leaning against the wall and rolling his eyes. "They've been cocker spaniels all day."

Zach hauled the biggest of the girls up to his hip and squeezed her. "What kind of silly dog is that? We all know Labradors are the best."

The littlest one, perhaps about three years of age, wrapped herself around Kieran's leg and sat on her shoe. "I's a spaniel."

"Are you now? My favorite!" Kieran took a step, lifting the girl into the air.

The middle girl grabbed onto her other leg. "Me too! Me too!"

Aubrey reappeared, a flushed smile on her face. "Now you've done it. You and Zach will be hauling them around all night." She clapped her hands. "Let's show Uncle Zach and his friend where they're staying."

The girls loosened their grips and scampered off, their voices disappearing up the stairs.

Audrey turned to Kieran. "Where are your things?"

Kieran patted the bag slung over her shoulder. "Right here."

"Yeah, sis. Apparently not every woman needs three suitcases and a carry-on for a two-night stay." Zach chuckled.

She smacked his elbow. "I just like to be prepared for anything. The next time we have a natural disaster, you'll all be running to me for food, water, and medical supplies."

He leaned closer to Kieran. "And that's just what's in her purse. Wait until you see the pantry."

Their rapport sent a wave of warmth through Kieran. She'd spent her life longing for siblings, and as close as she and Ash had become, it wasn't quite the same. And to think, Zach had six of them.

The oldest daughter ran over to catch Kieran's hand. "You're staying in my room. I'm going to have a sleepover with Jenna and Maya. Uncle Zach is staying with Devon. *He* has bunk beds."

The warmth of the child's hand sent a thrill up Kieran's arm. "Thank you for letting me stay. I'm sorry to put you out of your bed."

"She ends up on their floor about half the time, anyway," Aubrey said. "We thought she'd like her own space as she got older, but I think she's afraid of missing out on all the fun. I'm sure they'll grow out of this togetherness phase eventually."

Zach headed for the door decorated with Harry Potter posters. "Lucky me—I got the quiet kid."

Kieran stepped into a pink bedroom and set her bag next to a stuffed elephant wearing a tutu. The twin-sized bed looked so soft, she had to stop herself from flopping onto it.

The herd of puppies pounded down the stairway as Zach filled the doorway. "Aubrey promised the kids ice cream before bed. Want some?"

"Count me in." She slid her arms around his middle, burying a yawn in his chest. "I don't know why I'm tired. I did nothing but sit there."

"Nine hours stuck with me will do that to anyone."

She turned her face upward. "That's not it, and you know it. I had fun today. I can't believe your sister and her family are letting me crash at their house."

"Aubrey is thrilled to have you here. And you saw the kids' reaction. You're one of the . . . one of the gang already."

He'd stopped short of saying "family." "We should get down there. I don't want to be rude."

"In a minute." He lowered his head to hers, pressing a kiss to her lips. "I've been wanting to do that since we arrived—before, even."

She raised up on her tiptoes and kissed him. The gentle touch of his mouth was even better than ice cream.

Zach kept his arm around her waist as they trotted down the stairs to the kitchen.

Aubrey cast them a huge smile as she dipped the scoop into a carton. "Jake was held up at work, so he might not get to see the two of you until morning. He puts in long hours at the station sometimes." She passed the bowl to her son, sitting at the far end of the table. "Now, I've got chocolate, chocolate chip cookie dough, or chocolate chip mint. You might see a trend there."

"Cookie dough sounds incredible." Kieran took the closest chair, but it didn't take long for Maya to clamber off her own seat and into Kieran's lap.

Zach sat down beside them and grabbed a napkin to wipe the little one's face and fingers. "Before you get Kieran sticky too."

Aubrey laid a heaping bowl in front of her. "I'm sorry. She's my little cuddlebug. Just pass her to Zach if you don't want her on your lap."

"She can stay." Kieran wrapped both arms around the toddler to keep her balanced. "I'm honored. Really."

As Aubrey scooped the next serving, she smiled at Kieran. "So tell us about your family. Do you have lots of nieces and nephews too?"

The way Zach clenched his spoon at his sister's question made Kieran smile. She touched his knee under the table to let him know she'd be fine. "I'm an only child, but I love being around kids. For me, it's a treat."

Devon rolled his eyes. "That's because you don't have little sisters."

Aubrey dried her hands on a dish towel. "I was surprised when Zach called. He never once brought Jordan by, and they were practically engaged."

Zach's face went as pale as the ice cream. "Aubrey!"

Kieran lowered her eyes and concentrated on digging out a chunk of cookie dough.

"I'm sorry. That was stupid of me." Aubrey backpedaled. "What I meant to say is, we don't see enough of Zach. I'm really glad the two of you are here." She patted her legs. "Okay, puppies, time for bed!"

The whimpers and yips only barely cut through the tension flooding off Zach even after Aubrey left the room. "Only my sister would drop a bomb like that."

"It's not a big deal. We've both dated other people, I'm sure."

The stiffness in his neck and shoulders suggested there might be more to the story. She reached over and rubbed his arm.

He stood, letting her hand drop free. "Tomorrow's going to be a busy day. We have an eight o'clock appointment at the records office. Maybe we should get to bed early too. Besides, I'm sharing with Devon, and I don't want him waiting up for me."

"All right." She gathered up the bowls and carried them to the sink. He must be really unsettled by his sister's comment. When was the last time she'd turned in before nine thirty? Probably the last time she'd slept in a room decorated with stuffed elephants.

"Aubrey has a big breakfast planned." He carried the cartons of ice cream to the freezer. "She'd better not embarrass me any further."

"I bet she has plenty of good dirt on you she could share."

He cast her an uncomfortable glance. "Exactly what I'm afraid of."

• • •

The chair squeaked as Zach sat down at a long table in the State Archive's research room. He opened a thick three-ring binder and ran his fingers down the list of years and names, trying hard not to think about last night's blunder. How could Aubrey bring up Jordan's name just when things were getting good with Kieran? He didn't need reminders of the man he used to be, and he certainly didn't want to air his dark secrets this early in their relationship.

But even as he'd prayed last night, God was already nudging him. A little truth-telling might be exactly what he needed to keep himself on course. After all, this was about the point in his romance with Jordan that everything went haywire, sending both their lives careening out of control.

Kieran sat across from him with another binder containing the organizational catalog for the records. "I can't believe they don't have all this online by now. It would be so much easier to search."

"That sort of thing takes time, money, and a staff." Or unpaid interns like Marley. He needed to remember to be nicer to her. It was a thankless job, really. Everyone wanted easy access to data, but no one bothered to thank the people who got it there.

She frowned, her nose wrinkling in a cute way. "It looks like there's a file of intake and discharge records, arranged by patient number. The next one is death certificates. Evidently the hospital has a large cemetery, and the stones are marked with numbers rather than names for patient privacy."

He tried not to imagine all the lives those files represented. "What good is privacy after you're dead? Then you become a part of history."

"Spoken like a historian." She flipped the page. "How do you determine patient numbers?"

"Was she committed in 1942, do you think? The same year her sister died? These seem to be chronological."

She stood and crossed to him. "Is that what life comes down to? Reduced to a handful of papers in a filing cabinet." Kieran pressed a hand to her stomach. "It makes me sick to think of it."

"No, absolutely not." He reached for the next binder. "These are just some of the fingerprints we leave behind."

"What do you mean?" Kieran stood facing him, one hand cupped under her elbow, the other hand fiddling with her long brown hair.

"Take Lorna, for example." He gestured to the catalog. "We haven't found her details yet, but we already know she had a sister who loved her. That love was passed along to Granny Mac, and it lives on in you. I can see it in your eyes whenever you smile." He touched her wrist. "That's Lorna's life. Not this."

"I'm glad to know my family passed along something positive." Her lips curved up, and she nodded toward the records room. "Well then, let's find the rest of her story."

"I think . . ." He scribbled some of the numbers from the binder. "We may have just done that." Hopping up, he took it to the request window. A few minutes later, the files were placed in his hands. He flipped one open and leafed through the papers.

Kieran crowded close, peering over his shoulder.

"Here's her intake form and several other documents." He handed it to her, the same thrill coursing through him as when he'd unearthed a pottery shard on one of his college digs.

She dropped into the chair, holding the eighty-year-old paper with trembling fingers. "Lorna McCauley, age thirty-two years. Date July 31, 1942. She wasn't very old, was she?"

Zach took the seat beside her and scooted close. "Does it give a reason for the committal?"

Kieran scanned the page. "Psychoneurosis, manic-depressive with depressive delusions, general paresis, and suicidal tendencies. Mental deficiency. Recurring mutism." She blew out a long breath. "It's a wonder she ever got out."

Zach skimmed the next page. "'Electroconvulsive therapy.' That's electric shock, right? Is that as bad as it sounds?"

"It was successful in some cases, but it was appalling by modern standards. No sedation or anything." She made a face. "Doctors still use it on occasion, but only in extreme situations and with better safety precautions."

He slid his finger down a list of dates and times. "It looks like she had quite a few treatments."

She leafed through several more pages. "This Dr. Morgan must have been in charge, since his name's on the ECT charts. Here are his notes."

Zach leaned closer, sliding his arm around the back of her chair. He squinted at the paper. "'Evidence of prior childbirth.' Is he serious?"

Kieran lifted her eyes from the paper. "Maybe one of the infant stones we saw?"

"They were all marked 'Fuller,' weren't they? She was a McCauley. Perhaps the baby lived and was adopted out. Or buried elsewhere."

"If the baby lived, I could have relatives I'm not aware of. Granny Mac might have had a cousin—she still might, for that matter."

"If Lorna and Rosie were sisters, then Lorna's baby would be Granny Mac's first cousin. That would make him or her your . . ." He opened his notebook and sketched out the possible family lineage. "Your first cousin twice removed? Or is it a second cousin once removed—I always get confused by that."

"You probably have more cousins than you can track."

The comment stopped him. "You don't have cousins either? What about on your mother's side?"

"Trust me, the courts went through all of that, or so I was told. My mother was an only child. My father had one brother who died in Iraq. Granny Mac—you've already seen her family tree. Her father never remarried. And my grandfather's siblings all died young." She shook her head.

He fiddled with his pen, trying to imagine what Kieran's childhood must have been like. "Do you want kids of your own?"

She glanced up from the paper, her brows lifting. "Most definitely. I want a big family someday."

Zach relaxed. *She's nothing like Jordan. Stop expecting her to be.*

He pulled the organizational binder closer and opened it to the list of doctors. "The baby must have been born before Granny Mac—otherwise she'd have known about it. Maybe we can find something on this Dr. Morgan."

"Listen to this." She continued reading. "'Patient suffering from self-derogatory ideas and delusional guilt leading to significant self-harm and suicidal tendencies.'"

"That sounds like a decent reason for your great-grandfather to have her hospitalized, no matter what he promised."

Tugging her ponytail over one shoulder, Kieran sat back in the wooden chair. "Poor Lorna. It sounds like whatever happened to Rosie was more than she could bear." She shook her head and flipped the page. Her breath came out in a quick gasp.

He leaned in, suddenly afraid she'd unearthed a gravestone number. "What? What is it?"

Kieran held up the paper. "A release date."

# 26

Great Smoky Mountains National Park
1939

THE ROOM WAS quiet and swathed in darkness. Rosie scooted to the edge of the mattress, reaching her toes for the slippers Benton had purchased for her last birthday. A lump stuck in her throat. If only he were home, then maybe she could sleep. She'd not gotten much shut-eye since she and Beau had carried him to the hospital two weeks ago, and while her days felt like she was walking through molasses, the nights were worse.

Rosie pulled a wrap around her shoulders and tiptoed to the kitchen in the darkness so as not to wake McCauley. Her little girl had been at loose ends since Benton was gone. She seemed to understand her mother's explanations, but her eyes always searched for him.

*We all want you home.*

The doctor had cautioned against it. Benton was sorely confused, and the sight tore at Rosie's heart. When he'd first woken up and asked after Lorna and Mac, she thought he'd remembered what had happened, but every short conversation since then made it clear that his mind was a jumbled mess. Evidently he'd not only been pounded into the ground, but a big part of who Benton was—or had once been—had leaked out the cracks in his skull.

Tears welled up afresh in Rosie's eyes. She made it as far as the table before sliding onto a chair and laying her face on the cool tabletop. *Lord, please. Please give him back to me.*

She'd only been able to make the long trip to Knoxville a couple of times, and it was killing her to have him so far away. He wouldn't be hisself until he got home and remembered who the Lord made him to be. He needed to walk the cabin's floor, hear his daughter's giggles, ramble the woods, and see his owls. There were no birds in that blasted hospital. How was he supposed to remember who he was if he couldn't hear birdsong?

Their early morning calls were already lilting through the predawn hours. Standing, she walked over and unlatched the door. The crisp morning air flooded over her, and she closed her eyes, taking in the sounds. Benton knew every one by heart. How many mornings had they lain in bed as he whispered the name of each bird in her ear?

That was what he needed. That'd make everything all right again.

"Papa?" The tiny call drew Rosie back inside. McCauley was sitting up, her little fists squirreling against her eyes. "Papa?"

"Shhh." Rosie picked her up. "It's too early to be up, little bird."

McCauley burrowed her face in her mother's neck, the tip of her nose rubbing against Rosie's collarbone. "I's wake."

"I see that. Come on, let's go sit by the stove." Carrying the toddler on her hip, Rosie walked out to the kitchen and added a handful of kindling to the banked ashes.

McCauley was dozing against her shoulder by the time Rosie settled into the rocker. The child's sweet breath warmed her cheek even as the fire warmed her toes. She tried to imagine Benton sleeping in the next room. *Why do we take such simple things for granted?*

The ladder creaked as Lorna clambered down from the loft. She pulled one of the chairs close and sat, yawning.

"It's early still," Rosie said. "Do you want some coffee?" She shifted the baby in her arms and reached a hand out to her sister.

Lorna scooted closer and laid her head on Rosie's lap. Staring at the fire, she heaved a heavy sigh.

Rosie ran her fingers through Lorna's hair, pulling the sandy-colored locks away from her face and tucking them behind her ears. If only she could somehow read her thoughts as easily.

Her sister hadn't said a word since they'd whisked Benton away, and she'd taken to hiding in the loft like she'd done afore he first walked into their lives. Maudie had stayed with her the first night, trying to wheedle out of her what had happened, but Lorna would only rock in place, digging long scratches into her skin with her nails. The purplish bruises on her arms were fading, but whatever she'd witnessed had left a mark on her spirit.

Rosie ran her hand along Lorna's back. "It'll all be better when he gets home. You'll see."

It had to be better.

Lorna sat up, her face splotchy. She held out a closed fist to Rosie and then uncurled her fingers. In her palm sat some of the torn shreds of quilt she'd tucked away in her trunk years before.

"Why do you still have those old things?" Rosie plucked one from her hand. It was warm to the touch, as if Lorna had been clutching it for hours. She remembered what Maudie had said about God having a beautiful quilt of store-boughten cloth ready for her.

Lorna nodded, then touched the center of her chest, patting it twice in their age-old signal for "love you."

The room fell silent except for the crackling of the firewood and the distant birdsong. She hadn't seen Lorna do that in ages. Rosie rubbed the scrap of fabric between her fingertips. If only she could piece together all the torn shards of her own life, it might make a quilt like no one had ever laid eyes on.

It could wait. It could all wait. Right now she just wanted to hold her family—those at home, anyway—as close as she could manage.

• • •

"Stop hovering. You've been fussing over me for six months now. Leave me be." Benton rounded on his wife, willing the pain to shrink down into a tiny clump small enough to be contained by his force of will. When the monster reared its head, no one was safe. The rain hammering on the roof of the screened-in porch had been enough to set it off today. What would it be tomorrow? "I don't want to eat. I want to work."

Rosie shrank back against the doorframe, as if she feared he might strike her this time. And truth be told, he'd come close. Too close.

"Please, go inside," he begged. Because if she didn't, he wasn't certain how long he could keep his heel on the beast's throat.

"The doc said you shouldn't be workin'—"

He jerked to his feet, but the sudden change in position sent the floor moving under his boots. He grabbed at the chair to steady himself. "Go, Rosie."

She retreated inside, shutting the door behind her. The distant sound of McCauley's crying blurred together with the drumming rain and the pounding in his skull.

The doctor treated him like a child. Benton spun the paper into the typewriter and glared at the blinding-white page. He might as well be staring at a field of iced-over snow. He'd promised a piece about meadowlarks to . . . to some journal. He pulled off the spectacles and pressed his fingers against both eyes, the throbbing sending his stomach lurching in sympathetic response.

"Healing takes time." The doctor had said it often enough to brand the words on his thoughts. It had been *six months*, and he still hadn't been able to string words together on the paper. Not any that made sense.

What if it never happened?

Beau should have left him there in the dirt.

Flashes of that day came looking for him when he least wanted them, a lightning bolt that sliced through the pitch black of his memories, bringing with it jarring pain and confusion. Rosie had begged him to remember what had happened, but a brick wall had gone up between them that day. She couldn't reach him—no one could. And he wasn't even sure he wanted them to.

*Lorna.* He remembered screaming her name—he could still feel it in his throat. A single moment of clarity that put everything else in the shadows. Whatever had happened, it had been for her.

Mac was still howling in the house, the sound provoking another wave of senseless rage in his chest. *She's a child, for goodness' sake. Your child.*

Benton lifted his head and gazed out at the rain. Maybe it could wash some sense into him. He eased himself up this time, not wanting to endure a second wave of vertigo. By the time he reached the forest's edge, his shirt was plastered to his skin and icy droplets traveled down his face and neck. He didn't have a destination in mind, and yet his feet carried him along familiar paths.

His ribs ached as he drew deep breaths, pushing his way up the ridge. A chill threaded its way through his frame, but it tangled with the pain and diluted everything he was feeling, giving his thoughts a rare moment of clarity.

*Lord, I'm hurting my family, and I don't even know why.* He doubled over with his hands braced on his knees, sucking in oxygen as fast as his lungs would allow. Whenever he closed his eyes at night, he heard Rosie whispering prayers over him—each one like a sip of cool spring water to his soul. So he'd taken to whispering too, whenever the pounding would allow. It was the only thing that brought any peace.

Sometime later he stood with his hands on the dripping ladder, a single foot braced on the lowest rung. He wasn't sure he had the strength, so he just laid his head against the wet tree and focused on breathing.

*"Just keep breathin."* Rosie's words sounded in his memory at the oddest of times. *"You promised me, Benton Fuller."*

And just like that another image drifted into his mind. Rosie, standing outside the Elkmont church looking so pretty with little flowers tucked in over her ears—kissing him before the wedding had even started. *"I never was good at waiting for dessert neither."*

"Nothing but dessert for the rest of your life." He murmured the long-forgotten words into the tree bark.

This wasn't what he'd planned for them. Nor were the three little stones in the muddy graveyard. But if he gave it enough time—with God's help—maybe they could find their way again.

"Benton?" A familiar touch. A hand slid around his waist. Rosie stepped in behind him, her gentle strength pressing in against his back.

"Is Mac . . ."

"She's sleeping. What are you doing out here?"

"I ca . . . can't climb the ladder." His teeth chattered.

"I know." She touched his outstretched arm, still gripping the rung, and drew it down to his side, wrapping her arms tight around him. "It's all right. The owls ain't nesting yet."

"They will." Another shiver coursed through him, but at least his head didn't hurt. "For life. They mate for life."

# 27

## Great Smoky Mountains National Park
## 1942

SIX-YEAR-OLD MCCAULEY RAN ahead, her bare feet pounding against the path. "I'll beat you to the top!"

Rosie nudged her husband. "Go ahead—I know you want to. She's expectin' it." Since Lorna was off helping Maudie with spring cleaning, Mac would be short a playmate today.

Benton bolted after his long-legged girl. Hoisting their daughter into the air, her yellow pinafore flapped above a pair of knobby, scabbed knees. He tossed her over his shoulder.

"Papa!" Mac shrieked, her voice piercing the woods like the scream of a red-tailed hawk. "You're cheatin'. Put me down." She kicked her dirty feet, probably landing a solid blow to the middle of his chest.

He spun around and placed her on the ground facing the wrong direction, then loped away.

Mac caught him in less than a dozen steps, surging past her father into the woods, giggling the whole time.

The sound were sweeter and more precious to Rosie than a Sunday singing. "You'll never catch her now. That child's got wings."

"She should. She spends her days running wild." He turned, holding his chest. "Listen to me. I'm wheezing like a locomotive. I'm getting too old for this."

She caught up and looped an arm through his. "You're a mite slower than when I first chased you through these woods, Benton Fuller, but you're no old man."

He pushed his glasses up his nose. "What about you? I've noticed a silver hair or two among the brown."

"My pa grayed early too—afore he was even thirty. He called it 'bloom for the grave.'" She made a face. "So give me a few more years and I'll have a whole head of silver."

"It will be beautiful." He cupped the side of her head, planting a kiss on top of her hair. "You'll always be beautiful. Even when you're an old granny hobbling down the path with a walking stick."

They reached the top of the ridge less than an hour later. Wisps of clouds draped over the forested hillsides in the distance, like so many white silk veils. Rosie wiped her damp forehead with the back of her wrist. "I'll never tire of that view."

"I'm not sure anyone ever could." He came to stand beside her.

Mac sat cross-legged, her arms gripped around her knees. She'd probably been waiting there a good spell now. "When you first came here, it was Ma's land, right?"

Rosie hid a smile. McCauley knew their story, but she still loved hearing Benton tell it. Storytelling was in the blood here in the mountains, and though her husband mightn't have been born here, he'd taken to it like a pig to mud.

"Before it became part of the national park, all the way from that ridge yonder"—he swung his pointer finger across the vista—"and across into North Carolina used to belong to folks like your ma. As far as you can see, pretty much. And they're still adding more to the park. So all these trees, mountains, and rivers are protected. Plus the animals and birds that call it home."

"But afore that, the ridge where I'm sitting was Ma's. And Paw Paw's."

"It's Rosie's Ridge." He cast Rosie a wink. "We should plant a sign. Like all those trail markers the park service keeps putting up."

Rosie folded her arms across her chest. "How about we spread our picnic blanket instead?" As Mac fixed the blanket, Rosie dug into the basket for the apples she'd packed, blinking away unexpected tears. The ridge would never belong to McCauley or anyone else. She'd only had eyes for herself and Lorna when she'd signed that paper so many years ago.

Mac would be all right, though. She was the kind of girl who fell down and then sprang to her feet and started a'running again. No tears, no muss. Strong, like her pa.

It had taken him nigh on a year to start journeying back from that injury to his head, and at times it still gripped him. But they'd plowed out a new path together. When he was battling the rage or sorrow, he'd disappear into the woods for a spell to grouse and pray until he could get it under control. The man's pride was a force to be reckoned with, and Rosie had learned to give him space. Thankfully, he always came home.

And now that men were marching off to fight in Europe, the doc had assured her that Benton wouldn't be called to go. It were a small blessing, but she thanked God for it anyway.

After gobbling her lunch, Mac scrambled down the far side of the ridge, looking for a bird that had flitted past them. Normally Benton joined her in such adventurings, but today he leaned back on his elbows and stared up at the sky.

Rosie watched their little girl pull away from them, a flash of yellow bouncing along the forest's edge like a meadowlark in the grass. "She's like you in so many ways."

He tipped his head to watch her. "I forget sometimes."

That she ain't his. Rosie heard the words even though Benton didn't voice them. "She's *ourn*. In any way that matters."

He turned to look at her. "I know who it was, Rosie."

She sat upright, spilling the box of gingersnaps she'd balanced on her knee.

Benton turned to the hillside below, lines forming beside his eyes.

His jaw was set, a tiny muscle twitchin' away in his temple. "And I'll see he pays for it."

"What are you talking about?"

"The man who fathered McCauley." He swallowed, his Adam's apple bouncing in his exposed throat. "The same man who beat me within an inch of my life. Samson."

"We don't know that." Her mouth was so dry she could hardly force the words out. Her husband had been so much better of late, but he still got muddled at times. Was this one of 'em? "We can't say for certain who interfered with Lorna. She's never said." She glanced at Mac in the distance, making certain she remained well out of earshot. They'd long been suspicious that Horace was responsible for Benton's injuries, being that it happened so close to their land. But Horace had never said nothing about it, and that weren't like him. "And it's more than six years past. Let's leave it there, Benton. Please."

"He lives a mere two miles from our place. Lorna won't be safe as long as Samson's around. What about Mac? You?"

"Stop it." She placed a hand on his arm. "You don't know. Horace ain't done nothing since you got home. He's a married man with a babe of his own. We hardly seen a hair on his head in four years. Not since he checked to see you was mending."

"Mending from the time he tried to kill me."

Something shriveled inside her. "Did you recollect something you ain't told me?"

"I see his face every time I close my eyes. I have for years now. It *must* have been him." He squeezed his hands into fists. "And you've seen how Lorna gets whenever she gets near their place. She's terrified."

"But why? Why would he try to kill you?"

"Maybe I stumbled on something—proof of misdeeds, perhaps. I'm not even sure why I'd be over there otherwise."

"Misdeeds could be Horace's middle name."

"Rosie." He grabbed her hand and squeezed. "I want to talk to the rangers. See if I can get the Samsons evicted."

Her jaw dropped. "What in tarnation are you gonna say? 'I think he might be dangerous'?"

Benton's mouth lifted into a wry smile. "No. I don't think they'd be impressed. But it wouldn't be hard to get evidence of their poaching. That should be enough."

"I kind of hate punishing Will for his brother's sins."

"He's done his share of the trapping. And he must have known his brother was behind my beating—he probably knows about Lorna too. And what's he done about it?"

A pit opened up in Rosie's stomach. "Nothing." Benton was right. If half of what her husband suspected was true, Will had cast aside any loyalty she might have owed him. "But maybe we can talk to them. Goin' to the government, it's just not the way of things hereabouts. You know that."

"Talk to them? That's worked so well in the past." The sarcasm in his tone didn't sound like the man she'd married.

She turned to watch Mac playing in the meadow below. Rosie had spent the better part of the past six years trying to hide from the truth of how McCauley came to be. She'd managed to convince herself that it had been some wandering stranger—probably one of those tourists lured in by the park or some down-and-outer on the run from the sheriff. That was what they got from turning their land over to federal ownership. Now anyone could wander up to their back yard and do God knows what.

But God *did* know. He watched 'em bury three baby boys, one after the next. He knowed what happened to Lorna. He was by Benton's side as he lay a'bleedin' in the grass. And yet where was the justice? Did God just sit back and watch as they suffered? *Lord, where are You?*

Benton blew out a long breath. "I can't see a way we can put Samson in jail for his crimes, but I can make it so he's not right here under our noses. You've got to see that's the right thing to do. He attacked Lorna. He attacked me. What if you're next? Or McCauley?" He touched her arm, weaving his fingers around her wrist. "And God forbid, what if he figures out that she's his flesh and blood?"

Her stomach churned. "All right. Do what you must."

• • •

The crate landed on the chief ranger's desk with a satisfying crash, thanks to the collection of steel traps hidden within. Benton might have started with some pleasantries, but after being forced to wait outside for an hour while the man took care of other duties, his patience had run thin.

Ranger Foss looked up. "And what's this, dare I ask?" He stood and opened the lid, glancing through the contents.

"Four jump traps and two long-spring traps. One with a mink still attached." Benton folded his arms across his chest. "You can return them to Horace Samson of Jakes Creek. He's leasing there while serving as foreman on your roads crew. I'm assuming this"—he jabbed the side of the box—"is a little side business of his and his brother's. One of several."

The ranger examined the mink carcass. "The man's not going to be pleased. He could have gotten good money for that."

The callous answer set Benton back on his heels. "It's poaching. I've reported him multiple times in the past, but no one seems to have the time to investigate. I thought I'd lend a hand."

The man's brows drew together. "I'm not sure I like your tone, Fuller. You've done some good work for us in the past, but that doesn't give you the right to march in here and tell me how to do my job. If the Samsons are poaching—"

"They are."

"—then we'll look into it."

Benton struggled to rein in his frustration. "What is it going to take for you to evict them? My wife and I are scraping by on my writing income and her honey sales while these fellas break every single rule you've set down for lessees. They hunt, trap, fell trees, distill moonshine, you name it—plus being employed on the road crew. There are countless honest men looking for jobs right now, yet you keep this lout on your payroll."

Foss lifted a thick folder. "This is how many letters I've gotten just this week from local men looking for work."

Benton's head was pounding. He needed to get out of here before he lost his temper, or he and Rosie would be the ones out on their ears.

"I can't fire a man on your say-so. But I'll send someone out to talk to him."

Heat erupted in Benton's chest. "And what is that going to accomplish?"

"I'm not here to mediate disputes between feuding neighbors. I've got enough work to do already."

"We're not feuding. This man has attacked my family." Benton laid both hands on the desk and leaned toward him. "Look, I've walked just about every acre of this park for you. I think that earns me some credit. Don't you?"

The man sighed and fixed Benton in his gaze. "If we find evidence of wrongdoing, you can be assured we'll act on it. We don't take poaching lightly, regardless of what you seem to think."

Benton shoved the box closer to him. "What do you call this?"

"You can go now."

His field of vision seemed to narrow to a pinhole. Benton pressed a hand to his forehead, forcing himself to weigh his words carefully even if it killed him. "I'm going. But I *will* see that man put off park property."

"Don't get yourself shot in the process. Let my staff take care of this."

"See that they do."

• • •

Rosie stirred the pot of beans, scraping the bottom to make sure they didn't burn. It was along about the shank of the day, but she hated to start without Benton at the table. Normally she'd figure him to be off birdwatching, dreaming up a new article on bluebirds or pygmy owls. But lately all he'd been able to think about was the Samsons. He'd taken to watching the road to see if the park rangers would keep their word to investigate. So far? Nothing.

A nut-sized clump of dread had settled into her gut when Benton went off to see the rangers, but now it had grown and solidified so it felt like a rock lived where her stomach should be.

If he succeeded in getting shed of the brothers, it might calm down, right?

She hadn't been able to shake the thought of Horace attacking her sister. The more she considered on it, the more she believed Benton was correct. The man's hatred of Lorna had spilled over on many occasions. The thought sickened her—not just the violence, but that Lorna weren't capable of voicing it, not even to those she loved.

She stirred the bean pot again. She'd kept the cornbread warming as long as she could, but it was so dry now they'd likely have to crumble it into the buttermilk and eat it with a spoon. Lorna and McCauley would enjoy that likely as not.

The sound of footsteps on the porch made her jump. She dropped the ladle and darted over to the ladder. "Lorna, Mac? He's home. Wash up."

The door swung open, and Benton strode inside. "I dropped the mail at Beau's on my way back." He took a deep breath. "That smells like heaven. I didn't know I was hungry."

"You're late. I've been holding it."

"I'm sorry."

She didn't ask where he'd been, just got the food to the table. Lorna clambered down the ladder, Mac following behind, as agile as a chipmunk. Within minutes everyone was at the table.

Benton laid his hand on top of Rosie's and bowed his head for the table blessing.

The warmth of his touch sent a shiver up her arm, not unlike that first time back in the tree blind so many years ago. How many broods had they watched Hoot and Annie raise? It probably wasn't even the same pair anymore.

She and Benton might only have been blessed with one living child, but they'd watched perhaps two dozen owlets take flight over the years. In a way, those were her brood as well.

". . . and, Lord, we ask Your protection over our family. And bless this food for the health of our bodies and our bodies unto Your service. These things we ask in Jesus's name." He squeezed Rosie's fingers.

"Amen!" Mac piped up.

Lorna already had a fork and a spoon in each hand. "Aaaaahhh-meh."

"Let's eat." He laughed, reaching for the serving spoon. Benton dished out the beans, but rather than returning the spoon to the cast-iron pot, he held it aloft, his eyes fixed on Lorna. "What's that you've got there?"

She snatched something from the edge of the table and hid it in her lap, but not before Rosie caught a glimpse of the faded fabric scraps. Lorna had taken to carrying them around in her pocket, using them as a handkerchief of sorts, and washing them out by hand. But she always kept them hidden from Benton for some reason.

Rosie passed him a piece of cornbread. "It's nothing. Just some old scraps of fabric."

He frowned. "Let me see."

Lorna shook her head, burying her hands in her lap. "Mine."

"I'm not going to take them."

Mac swiveled her head betwixt her father and her aunt. "It's pretty pieces of a blanket, Papa. I don't know where she got them, though."

Rosie added some honey atop her bread. "She's had them for many years."

"Then why haven't I seen them before?" He glanced at Rosie. "She doesn't hide things from me. At least, she never used to."

Rosie could read the question in his eyes, and she scrambled for a reply. He knowed they treated him differently since his injury—avoiding topics that would make him sad or angry. Mac, especially, had shown a talent for soothing her pa's stormier moods.

"Lorna?" He turned to her.

She shook her head again, more violently this time. "No. No, Ben. No."

"But why?"

"My Will—he give."

Air rushed from Rosie's lungs. Lorna had said the same when Will gave her Nanny years ago. *My* Will. The words were like cold fingers sliding across Rosie's skin.

Benton's hand found hers. "What does she mean?" He always could read her face.

"We can talk about it later."

"No." His voice rose, his grip rigid. "Now."

Lorna stood, her chair skittering back. She moved toward the ladder like she did whenever she were afeared.

But this time Benton jumped to intercept her. "Lorna, what is it? What are those from? Who gave them to you?"

"Does it matter?" Mac's voice pitched upward in fright.

"Will. Wiiiii-ll." Lorna wailed the name, tears spilling down her cheeks.

Rosie rushed over and grabbed her husband's arm. "Let her go. You're frightening her."

"Is he the one who did this?" He pointed to the scar on his face. "Is Will the one who—"

"No." Lorna shook her head so hard she nearly fell in the process, her tears flying. "No, Ben. Ho-Hors." She touched Benton's chest. "Ho-race hurt. Will give."

Benton took a long shuddering breath, his sister-in-law's hand still pressed against his chest. He clamped a hand over the top of it, likely so she wouldn't dash off. "And Horace—he hurt you too? He did things to you?"

"Benton . . ." Rosie cast a glance across the room to where McCauley sat frozen at the table, her eyes wide.

"Horace hurt you too. More than just the strap, yes?" He gripped Lorna's elbow.

Lorna gulped air, her eyes rolling upward. "Hurt. Bad man."

Rosie pulled Lorna into her arms.

Benton backed up two steps, turned on his heel, and snatched his coat from the hook. He headed for the door, stopping only long enough to yank the shotgun from its pegs.

• • •

Benton gulped deep breaths of night air as he stumbled through the night, the image of Horace Samson putting hands on his sister-in-law driving a spike through the last vestiges of his self-control.

He'd suspected. He'd feared. Now he knew.

*I'll kill him.*

The Winchester lay heavy in his slick palm. He was a lousy shot, but if he got close enough, it wouldn't matter. Benton pulled his coat flaps tight against the light rain, the cold droplets sliding down his face. He was done waiting for the sheriff or the park service to fix his problems. He needed to defend his family.

That man's blood ran in his daughter's veins. Benton stopped and pressed a trembling hand to his face, pushing away the horrific thought. *I'm her father. I'll always be her father.*

Would he have to explain this to her one day?

He crossed the creek, his footfalls sounding hollow on the wooden bridge. This was the spot he'd run into Rosie for the second time, her dark hair and winsome smile changing his life forever. He'd gone from dreams of prestige to a humble family man in the blink of an eye. But he couldn't—*wouldn't*—look back. The rage smoldering in his gut pushed him forward.

Light glowed from the Samson house ahead, drawing him in like a moth. He stood at the gate, suddenly not sure of what came next. Pound on the door? Yell from here and wait for the monster to show himself? Or brace the barrel on the fence and hope a shadow appeared in the window to guide his shot? He didn't want to think it through. He must act before the fire cooled.

Benton's hands shook. He couldn't seem to force himself to move to the door.

Motion at one of the windows drew his eye. He snapped the weapon up, pulling the stock against his shoulder and willing his arms to be still. He sighted down the long barrel, hoping the lessons had finally paid off.

A dark head bobbed into view, a woman's face illuminated by a candle she held close to her bosom.

Benton drew great drafts of air into his lungs as he lowered the gun. For a moment he'd forgotten Samson was married. His wife set the candle in the window and lifted a wrapped bundle, now illuminated by the flickering light. An infant, its mouth open in a loud-mouthed squall.

A tremor began somewhere deep in Benton's chest and worked its way outward. He stumbled back a step, then two. His ankle twisted as he turned, dashing down the road, the droplets pelting his face as he put as much distance as he could between himself and the horror of what he'd become.

He stopped at the edge of their yard, seeing the glow from his own cabin's window. *Lord, forgive me.*

Needing to gather himself before facing Rosie, he crossed the yard to the old goat shed. Lorna's little herd lifted their heads as he approached, pushing forward to greet him with necks outstretched. *God, thank You for stopping my hands.*

Leaning the gun against the split rail fence, Benton dropped to one knee and rubbed the animals' rough heads, winding his fingers between their horns to the perfect spot behind the ears that they loved to have caressed. "This shelter used to be mine, you know. And frankly, it's better than I deserve." He closed his eyes and lowered his head. Maybe he should spend the night out here with the stock. Or up on the rain-slicked platform in the trees. He certainly didn't deserve to be in the warm cabin with three of the most important women to have ever graced his life.

"Beh?" The familiar footsteps behind him brought a flood of tears to his eyes. "Ben? You mad?"

"Oh, honey." He looked over his shoulder at his sister-in-law. "No, Lorna. I'm not mad. Not at you, anyway."

She carried a wooden bucket looped over one arm. "S-sad?"

He continued stroking the goat and glanced up at the sky. The rain had slackened off, and a few stars were appearing in the openings forming among the thick blankets of clouds. "I guess 'sad' about covers it. I'm sad I couldn't keep you safe."

Lorna turned the bucket upside down next to him and sat, resting both palms on his arm. She lowered her eyes to the ground. "I sad."

He covered her hands with one of his own. "Why are you sad?" As if he didn't know.

"I sad . . ." She pressed her lips together for a moment, then pushed her chin forward. "I sad not keep *you* safe."

Her sweet soul put his to shame. If there was a deep hole somewhere, he'd like nothing better than to crawl into it right now. "I tell you what, Lorna. We'll keep watch over each other from now on. We'll keep all of us safe."

She smiled and stood, holding on to his fingers and turning to look toward the house. "Ro-sie, Mac, Ben, Lor-nah." She squeezed his hand. "Home."

In that moment, he saw the cabin with her eyes. The warm glow spread out over the yard, separating it from the dark trees beyond. Rosie was probably putting Mac to bed. Suddenly there was nowhere he'd rather be. He reached for the bucket. "Do you need help with that?"

She rolled her eyes and pointed at the house. "Go. Ro-sie worry."

He picked up the Winchester and loped toward the porch.

Rosie was on her feet before he made it through the door. "Benton—there you are. I—" Her eyes landed on the shotgun. "I . . ."

"Don't worry." He turned and placed it on the hooks above the door. He really should wipe it down after the long walk through the rain, but that could happen later. "I thought better of it. Or rather, God did. He intervened—opened my eyes."

Her head fell forward. "Thank the Lord. I was praying, you know."

"I figured you were." He crossed the floor and laid his hands on her shoulders. "I wasn't in my right mind. I'm sorry."

"If I hadn't had Lorna and Mac to worry after, I would have chased you down and dragged you back by your hair."

Benton chuckled. "I can imagine."

She pulled him down into one of the chairs, taking the seat beside him. "I've never been so right terrified, not even when I believed you was dying. The thought of you killing a man? It ain't like you, Benton."

"I got as far as their house before the Lord caught hold of me and gave me a firm shake. Like a father with a defiant child. I think if I hadn't listened, he'd have hauled out the switch next."

She shook her head, those dark eyes locking on his. "I don't think the Lord acts that way. We go headlong down our own sinful paths, but He's there to pick us back up when we turn to Him. Otherwise He'd have stopped Horace from doing what he done." Her eyes clouded, her chin lowering. "He'll answer for that. But not at your hand."

She ran her fingers across his knuckles. "You're a scientist and a writer, Benton. A fine husband and pa. I couldn't bear it if you was a murderer too. Don't let Horace turn you into one."

The memory hung a little too close, like the sweat still clinging to his skin. "But he's already changed me. I'm not the same man you married. You've got to see that."

"And I ain't the same woman who chased you up that ridge with a shotgun in *my* hands, neither. Back when all I cared about was the land under my feet." She dug in her pocket and pulled out the little stone bird she kept there. She placed it on the table in front of him. "I'm like one of your birds. If you was to cut down the tree where I built a nest, what would I do?"

"Peck my eyes out."

She blew out a loud huff of air, be it mirth or exasperation, he couldn't tell. "I'd fly off and build another somewheres else. But I couldn't see that back then. I pictured my life remaining exactly what it was until the end of time. Lorna and me, living here in this cabin my father built, forever."

"And so you have."

"No." Her voice softened, and she reached for his face. "I met you, Benton. And God used you to change me. It changed all of us."

The warmth from her touch remained on his cheek. "My whole life transformed."

"That's what I'm saying." She scooped the bird off the table and tucked it into his shirt pocket, just over his heart. "My life is with you. Wherever." She laid her hand against it.

He felt the hard stone press into his chest. "You're not making any sense."

"I don't need to be *here* no more. This bird's wings are made of stone, but mine ain't. I can fly away from here. And I think He's beckoning us now. Wanting us to leave this place. I can feel it."

"Rosie—"

"We mountain people live fierce, whether it be love, passion, loyalty, or hatred. I want you to have the first three but not lay claim to that last 'un. If it takes leaving here to keep that from happening, I'll be packing tonight."

"I won't let Horace drive us from our land."

"It ain't our land no more." She sprang from her chair and walked around the table to the far side. "We're living here by the government's say-so. Let's make our leavin' be on our own terms."

He shook his head. "I can't believe you're saying this. Rosie. I don't think it's right to run from our problems."

"You ain't hearing me." She leveled her gaze on him. "I'm not running. This land has been a shackle around my feet. God's been whispering His freedom to me my whole life. I just ain't had ears to hear it."

"What do you mean, 'His freedom'?"

"He's been saying I don't need this land—I need Him. And you. And our girls. Our family is who we are because of the promises we made to each other. You and me. Our promises to Lorna and to Mac. It's why Mac is *our* daughter regardless of how she came into this world. Because we promised her that the day she was born. But the land? It's naught but a page in our story." A smile grew across her face, bringing with it a freshness he hadn't seen there in years. "Benton, He's been calling me to let go. It's time to fly."

"But you love this place."

"I love you more."

He stood and came around the table to join her, pulling this crazy woman into his arms where she belonged. "You know, you could have just told me this the day I proposed the first time and saved us a whole lot of heartache."

"Maybe God had something here He wanted to show us first." She laid her head on his chest. "And we wouldn't have that perfect little girl sleeping up in the loft."

# 28

## Florida
## Present Day

KIERAN TIPPED BACK her head, letting the Gulf's air sweep over her. Seagulls screamed overhead. "This is perfection. Much better than musty archives."

Zach leaned against the boardwalk's railing. "Archives should never be musty. But it's tough to compete with ocean breezes."

Aubrey had recommended a five-star restaurant in town, but as soon as Kieran and Zach had extricated themselves from the house, they'd made a beeline for the beach. The hour-long drive out to Bald Point State Park had been worth every minute.

"I can see why my great-grandfather moved here after his wife died. For an ornithologist, Florida probably was the place to be." She gestured out toward the estuary.

"It must have been quite a change for him coming from the Smokies."

"Do you think he only stayed in Tennessee for her?"

Zach turned to stare at her. "What do you mean?"

"Well"—she shaded her eyes as she gazed out over the water—"it sounds like he came to the Smokies to study birds, but then he met and married my great-grandmother. And after she died, he left for Florida without looking back. It sort of makes you wonder if anyplace was 'home' for him."

He folded his arms, leaning on the rail. "If the lease was written to her, they had no standing in the park after her death. Or perhaps he was running from memories."

Kieran watched the waves lapping the white sand beach to their right. "I wonder what happened to Lorna after she was released? Did she try to find the family?"

"We have at least one story of her returning to the Smokies. But it's hard to say where she ended up. I didn't see any additional records for her at the state hospital."

Her throat tightened. "Since Lorna was released after her brother-in-law's death, she probably had no way of finding Granny Mac." More fractures on her family tree. "My family's bonds were a lot less solid than I'd imagined them to be."

He slid an arm around her shoulder. "You and your grandmother may not have a lifetime of holidays and cookie baking to tie you together, yet you've forged a heart connection that even dementia can't seem to sever."

Kieran leaned into his side as they walked. The wind picked up, and it felt good to have him for shelter. "It's been so wonderful having Granny Mac with me these past few years. I'd dreamed of a family for as long as I could remember. I hate to think what life will be like after she's gone."

"Family is what you make it." He tugged her closer so they formed a united block against the wind. "It isn't about bloodlines and legal relationships. I told you about how my uncle's choices have reshaped his family, probably forever. And you met Aubrey's Maya."

She looked up at him. "What about Maya?"

"They adopted her from foster care. But she's every bit as much family as the other kids. Family is a choice, a promise. It's about who God places in your life. You made the decision to take Granny Mac into your life. You chose each other." His head tipped closer.

The truth of his words trickled through her, pooling in the cracks that had formed around her heart. "That's why Gran's history means so much to me. I want to know the people who shaped her. I want to help her find those memories." Her heart surged. "And selfishly, I want to be a part of them. I know I won't have her much longer, but we can share this together." She pulled her purse close to her hip, thinking of the stone bird hidden in a nest of tissues, tying the generations together.

He brushed his lips against her ear. "Not to scare you off, but maybe—somewhere down the road—we could be family too. Then you'll have more siblings, cousins, nieces, and nephews than you can name. 'Cause I'm sort of a package deal."

Was he really suggesting what it sounded like? "I think that's a deal I could enjoy." She swallowed. "Someday."

He grinned before pulling her in for a kiss.

The warmth of his lips against hers sent a rush of longing through her. If he was going to start making half-baked proposals, there were a few things she needed to know. She pulled away but stayed in the circle of his arms. "Aubrey mentioned your last girlfriend. It sounded pretty serious."

A shadow crossed his face. "It's not something I like to talk about."

"Fair enough." She'd said the same to him several times. Releasing her grip on his arms, she stepped back. But it seemed a man looking to share his life with someone had to be ready to actually *share about* his life. He evidently hadn't reached that point. She turned and continued down the path, taking a long breath to clear her head.

"Kieran, wait." He followed.

"I don't want to pry."

"No." He gently snagged her elbow. "You've been honest with me. I need to do the same. But my history with Jordan isn't something I'm particularly proud of."

*Like I'm so proud of my drug-addicted parents.* "I get it."

"I don't think you do." He released her arm. "We met on an archaeological dig during grad school. The students would get pretty rowdy at night, lots of drinking and partying." He trained his eyes on his feet. "I'd been pretty sheltered, so it was a whole new scene for me."

She couldn't imagine him being a lot of fun at parties, but then, a lot of people went through a wild phase in college. By the time she'd reached Penn State, she'd had enough drama in her life.

"But Jordan?" He swallowed, his Adam's apple bobbing. "Nothing was too crazy for her. She did it all, and then some. A ton of fun, but—"

"Too much for you to handle?" Suddenly, she wasn't sure she wanted the details.

Shadows formed around his eyes. "Not for lack of trying, I'm ashamed to say."

Her throat tightened. "All right. So you had a relationship you regret. That's not unusual."

Zach looked skyward for a moment. "We'd only been together a few months when she got pregnant. It was all so fast. Everything just—"

"Wait." Kieran's thoughts jumbled, and she drew an involuntary breath. Zach—*her* Zach—was a father? "You have a child?"

He fell silent, turning to face the waves.

She stood staring at his back, willing him to speak. How could he drop this bomb and then go radio silent? "You talk about family like it's the most important thing in the world, and you don't even mention the fact that you already have a baby?" Something inside her had sprung a leak, emotions spilling out. "Where is this child? Are you part of her life?" Was Jordan still a part of his?

She scrambled to make sense of what she'd just heard. *No. No, I can't do this.* "You just said, 'Family is a choice, a promise. It's about who God places in your life.' What sort of choice did you make?"

"I didn't get the chance." The words bit back. He turned to face her, and the flash of anger on his face dissolved into something far more heart-wrenching. "She terminated the pregnancy. The day after I found out about it, she drove herself to the clinic."

The wind stilled, as if respecting the gravity of what he'd said. "Oh, Zach."

"I thought . . ." He cupped a hand over his mouth, as if fighting against what came next. Giving his head a quick shake, he continued. "I thought I needed time to process her news. I'm always a little slow on the uptake. But Jordan never waited for anything. Maybe I understood that deep down. I can't help thinking, if I'd said something right off—reacted better—she might not have acted so quickly. Maybe things would have been different." He closed his eyes. "She must have felt so alone."

She couldn't pull back the callous things she'd said moments before, nor would it scrub the pain from Zach's face. Kieran bit her lip, letting several minutes pass with nothing but the sound of the waves. She didn't even dare reach out to touch him. The fracture that had just formed between them wasn't so easily paved over. *Lord, please. I don't know what to do.*

Zach shook his head. "Say something, Kieran. I'm dying over here."

She couldn't force her voice to cooperate, but she reached out and wrapped her fingers around his upper arms, pulling him in.

He lowered his head atop hers. "I meant what I said earlier. Every word. Family is a choice. But sometimes . . . it's someone else's. If anyone understands that, I do."

"So do I." She pressed her ear against his ribs and focused on the rapid beat of his heart. "I'm sorry." Kieran squeezed harder, as if she could push away the hurt that had been burrowed in his soul for too long.

• • •

They were less than thirty minutes out of Nashville when Zach's phone buzzed. Even though Kieran was dozing beside him, he reached for the button on the steering wheel and clicked it through to the hands-free system.

"This is Andrea Perez from the Florida State Archives. I'm looking for Zach Jensen or Kieran Lucas?"

"I'm Zach, and Kieran's sitting right here too. We're in the car."

Kieran stirred, stretching her arms out in front of her.

"I was told you were looking into information on Dr. Morgan's patients at the state hospital. The lead archivist knows I've been working a similar project, so she sent me a note. I actually have a large box of correspondence from the doctor regarding many of his patients. I hope you don't mind, but Lisa gave me the patient's name—Lorna McCauley—and I may have something for you."

"Mind?" He glanced toward Kieran. "We're thrilled. What have you found?"

"I have a letter written to the hospital from a relative—a Mr. Benton Fuller. I believe he was a brother? I also have a carbon of the doctor's reply. He kept meticulous records. I wish all the doctors had been so fastidious."

Kieran grabbed Zach's arm and squeezed. "Could you send us copies?"

"Of course. I'll scan them right away."

Ten minutes later, the scans arrived in Kieran's email. She opened the first one on her phone, enlarging it as much as she could. She cleared her throat and read it aloud to Zach.

"'I am writing to enquire after a patient of yours, my sister-in-law, Lorna McCauley. When I entrusted her to your care, I did not intend for it to be a long-term stay. I hope you can update me on her status, because I am most concerned. She is my late wife's dear sister, and I made promises to see to her well-being. I am racked with guilt at being forced to hospitalize her. As you know, she made an attempt on her life—a situation that terrified both me and my young daughter. My prayer is that you can help her recover to a point where she won't be a danger to herself. I am confident she is not a danger to others, regardless of what it says on the intake form. If she has become increasingly agitated in the hospital, then I demand to have her returned to our care. Please advise. Sincerely, Benton Fuller.'"

"Here's the doctor's response." She frowned as she continued reading. "'The patient shows marginal progress, but I would strongly advise against any changes in her treatment protocol at this early date. These things take time, and I believe you should resolve yourself to a lengthy stay. There's no "magic pill" when it comes to treating this disorder, and the patient's lack of mental acuity complicates the situation. You should put away any feelings of remorse, Mr. Fuller, and concentrate on raising your daughter. Trust me, Miss McCauley is receiving the best of care.'"

"So it was the doctor's idea to keep her, not your great-grandfather's. That's something."

"There's more." Kieran twisted around in her seat so her body angled toward Zach. "This one's dated 1946. That's four years later. I guess he took the doctor's words to heart." She fell silent, reading to herself.

"Don't keep me in suspense. What does he say?"

Kieran cleared her throat. "After a cordial opening, he jumps right in. Listen to this. 'I'm distressed to hear of Lorna's recent incident with the orderly. I will not tolerate such abuses and am starting proceedings to have her remanded to my care. In regards to the other matter, what Lorna told you is true and not evidence of further delusion. My sister-in-law did, in fact, give birth to a baby girl in 1937 . . .'" Kieran's voice faltered as she stopped reading. "But that's . . ."

Zach reached for her hand. "The year your grandmother was born."

"Both sisters had a baby the same year?"

"Or . . ." Zach paused. "Benton and Rosie raised Lorna's child as their own." Zach ran his thumb along Kieran's knuckles, stopping to consider what this meant for the family. "So what now? Do you tell Granny Mac?"

"She's already struggling with truth and reality. I think this would just muddy the waters." Kieran sighed. "In Gran's heart, Rosie was—is—her mother. I don't see how it would help to tell her otherwise. Especially since we don't have proof."

"That's the trouble with research. Sometimes you end up opening boxes that you wish you'd left closed."

"He said he was petitioning for Lorna's release." She lifted the phone and slid a finger across the screen, likely reading through the message again. "But that's the same year he died. She didn't leave Chattahoochee for another two years."

• • •

Kieran leaned into the mound of pillows she'd piled on her bed, a closed book sitting forgotten beside her. When she and Zach had first started dating, it had been thrilling to exchange texts, emails, and late-night calls. Now, it just wasn't enough. Only a few days had passed since he'd headed back to the park, and she already missed the touch of his hand, the strength of his shoulder. Oh yeah, and the kisses. There was no way she was forgetting those.

Her bedroom was quiet except for the murmur of the television out in the family room where Nick and Ash were watching the game. Kieran rolled the stone bird between her fingers, moving it from one hand to the other.

Zach's story kept rattling around in her head. The pain in his voice had nearly dropped her to her knees. Jordan's decision—and the role he may have played in it—had left a giant hole in his heart. It was little wonder he obsessed about rules and doing the right thing.

She balanced the figure on her leg, studying its tiny eyes. The things this bird must have seen, passing through so many hands and lives.

There was so much more to Granny Mac's puzzle than she knew when she'd first started down the road to recover the heirloom. Those tiny graves. Rosie's death. Lorna driven to the edge of herself. And Kieran's great-grandfather forced to break a promise. The figure was no lucky charm, that much was certain. Her thumb slid over the stone, resting perfectly in the indentation between the head and wing. The carver might have given it shape, but it seemed entirely plausible that a long line of women had worried it smooth.

"I'm not sure why Gran thought I needed you, but it's incredible to think that you're a connection that runs all the way through my crazy, broken family."

*"Family is a choice."* Zach's words filtered through her mind. She'd scoffed a bit when he'd first said it—this man with his ideal upbringing. But his confession had settled into her soul. He'd experienced the best God could offer in families. He'd probably have stretched out that offer to Jordan if he'd had the opportunity.

He'd be a married man now. A father. The thought niggled at her.

She tried to picture herself in Jordan's shoes, but it was too much to grasp. She'd spent her whole life longing for family, so when she met Granny Mac, she'd grabbed on to that relationship with both hands. A baby, even an unplanned one, would have been the same.

And Zach . . . Warmth washed over her. She'd take Zach in a heartbeat, baby or no.

The bird stared at her, as if saying, "You made choices too."

Kieran shoved it under the pillow and reached for the book. She didn't need a rock judging her. She was pretty good at doing that herself. Unfortunately, her eyes refused to focus on the page.

She could almost feel the small, folding shovel in her hands and the stone figure dropping loose from the muddy soil.

Zach had explained the law and why it was important to leave a historical site undisturbed, yet she'd disregarded his wishes and done her own thing. The bird was the sole witness to her lies and deceptions.

*I did it for Gran.*

But in the long run, did it matter?

On the drive home, she and Zach had talked more about faith, and the ideas still stirred deep inside her. How come God seemed so real—so alive—in him, Granny Mac, and her best friends, but He still seemed so out of reach to her? She curled her fingers, placing them against her chest.

*Granny Mac says I'm part of Your family, Lord. I'm not entirely sure what that means, but I know that I want it.*

# 29

Great Smoky Mountains National Park
March 1942

ROSIE LEANED AGAINST Benton's shoulder as he pressed the field glasses to his eyes. The light was fading quickly, but the two owls were sitting on branches just outside their tree cavity, preening. The male puffed up, shook his feathers, and then carefully picked through each one with his short beak. "The eggs must have hatched by now, don't you think?"

"Mm. Probably. They started a little late this year, though, so it's hard to say. I hope they have a good clutch."

Rosie stretched before turning to check on the cabin below. The lights had come on, evidence that the girls were moving about in the kitchen. Hopefully, they'd finished redding up after supper and Lorna was making sure Mac got ready for bed. It had been a while since Rosie had joined Benton on the birding platform, but it felt wonderful, like they was courting again—even if he had eyes for no one but the owls. Laughter bubbled in her chest, but she swallowed it down. It made sense that after nine years of marriage, she might have to work a little harder to get the man's attention. Though it still didn't take much, mind you, and for that she was thankful.

Over the past few days, they'd talked more about the future and where the Lord might take them. Benton said he would write some letters and see if there were any universities that might be interested in his skills. At one point in her life, she'd have found the idea terrifying, but now it was as if God had lit a fire under her. She loved the Smokies and the little cabin in the woods that her Pa had built so many years ago. But the prodding from the Lord was clear. The land had been home to the Cherokee, to her grandparents, and now to the park. But had it ever really belonged to any of them? God put the earth into motion, lifted the mountains, designed the trees and the rocks and even the owls. If he said it was time for the Fullers to get gone, who was she to argue?

A yellow light bobbed in the distance along the creek.

Rosie straightened, fixing her eyes on the odd glow. It seemed late for tourists to be out walking the trails, but she never could comprehend what some of them was thinking. The park seemed to draw all sorts. She nudged her husband.

He lowered the binoculars. "What is it? Am I ignoring you?"

"Yes, but that's not it." She pointed a finger. "What's that yonder? That light?"

He squinted and adjusted his glasses. Lifting the binoculars, he trained it on the lamplight. "Someone's working on something down by the creek. But not far from our cabin."

"A camper, you reckon?"

"A bit rocky for pitching a tent. But maybe." His brow wrinkled below the brim of his hat. "I think I see two men, but they're in silhouette."

"I s'pose they ain't hurting nothing." She turned back to the owls, squinting to see them in the growing darkness. One of them had flown, but the female sat just shy of the cavity, gazing around with her big yellow eyes. Even Annie seemed to be watching the activity in the nearby creek bottom. Perhaps she was concerned they'd scare off all the varmints she liked best for supper.

Benton tensed, the muscles in his upper legs cording as he straightened to see better. His attention on the odd scene sent an unsettled feeling circling around her heart. "What is it?"

He lowered the glasses and handed them to her. "Take a look."

She squinted through the eyepieces, turning the dial to focus the view. A barrel-shaped object sat atop the smoldering campfire, light glinting off its metallic surface. Her throat tightened. "A still?"

"Looks that way."

She lowered the binoculars. "I told them to *never* put one of those on our land. He swore they wouldn't."

"Who swore?"

"Will. Years ago, afore you came. They wanted to put an operation on the branch just upstream of us."

Benton pushed up to his knees. "That's it. I'm going for the sheriff. This is exactly what we needed."

She grabbed his arm, her fingers closing around his bicep. "Be careful."

He placed his hand over the top of hers and leaned in for a quick kiss. "I will. First, I'll get a closer look and make sure it's them." He scooted down the ladder.

Rosie headed back to the cabin, murmuring prayers of protection for her husband. She'd nearly lost Benton once to the Samson brothers, and now he was walking right into the lions' den. Thankfully, Benton's years of birdwatching had trained him to stalk silently through the woods, and he'd gotten to where he knowed this ridge and the holler better than anyone.

Rosie sang a shaky verse of "Nearer, My God, to Thee" to calm her heart as she walked home. Benton was in the Lord's hands. Only God knew the number of his days.

Swinging the door open, the fragrance of fried pies washed over her, still hanging in the air from supper. She'd saved a dried apple pie under a cloth for her and Benton to split this evening. Rosie ran brisk palms over her upper arms and glanced up to check that the Winchester hung in its place above the door.

Lorna came in from the other room, humming softly under her breath. "Owl?"

"Yes, we saw both of 'em. Fluffy and fierce, as always." She could see the question in her sister's eyes, so she tried to keep her voice bright. "Benton is off checking something up the creek bed a ways. He'll be home soon."

She nodded. "Mac sleep." With that, she also clambered up the ladder to bed. Morning came early, especially with goats that needed milking.

Rosie shuffled into the bedroom and pulled a cozy sweater off the hook. The evening was warm, but a chill had gripped her as soon as she spied the moonshine still, and it weren't fixing to let up anytime soon. She squeezed her arms around her sides, feeling for the stone bird snug in its pocket. She'd sit on the porch and wait for Benton to return. Nothing like the rocking chair to keep pace with her prayers.

• • •

Benton led the caravan of vehicles along the dark country lane, most of them traveling without headlamps to avoid announcing their arrival to the moonshiners.

"I hope you know what you're doing." Ranger Foss sat beside him, one hand gripping the dashboard as they bounced along the rutted road. "Calling in federal agents could be a feuding offense 'round these parts."

"This man has been a problem since the first time he pointed a rifle at me nearly ten years ago." *Horace Samson had hurt his family one too many times. It wasn't going to happen again.*

"When we get out there, I want you to hole up in that cabin of yours and not come out. Moonshiners don't usually shoot at agents so long as they hear them coming. But if they label you as a turncoat, the bullets might start flying. For the sake of my men and your three little gals, I don't want this to get heated. You hear?"

"I just want to see Horace Samson hauled to jail and then for the superintendent to send him packing. Will this be enough to accomplish those ends?" Then maybe he could convince Rosie that God wasn't calling them to leave.

"If we catch 'em? I'd say so." The ranger grabbed the edge of the seat as the car bounced over a rock and through a mudhole. "Slow down."

Benton eased off the accelerator. It had taken hours to arrange this little party, and every minute that ticked past was one more the Samsons could use to clean up and go home. Rolling up beside the house, he cut the engine and stepped out. The ranger followed, settling his flat hat over his balding dome. Within a few minutes, several more vehicles pulled up behind them. Two federal agents from the Alcohol Tax Unit, a county deputy, and two additional park rangers poured out of the cars, each armed with a pistol or a rifle.

He pointed the way up the path and stood in the yard as they doused their lights and headed upstream.

"Benton?" Rosie's voice trembled behind him from the vicinity of the porch.

What was she doing outside? He turned and headed her direction. "Shhh. They're getting in position."

She stood in the open doorway, her arms clutched around her midsection. "What's going to happen?"

He climbed the steps to join her. "The rangers want us to stay indoors until they're done. They plan to arrest the Samson boys and see no one gets hurt."

Rosie reached for his hand, tugged him across the threshold, and latched the door after him. "Tell me you'll stay out of it."

"I think it's a little late for that." He took off his glasses, wiping them on his sleeve. "I'm up to my eyeballs in this."

"If they don't catch 'em and Horace gets wind you was the one to fetch the G-men—"

"Let's not borrow trouble."

The loft ladder squeaked. He turned in time to see Lorna climbing down, the hem of her nightgown flapping with each step. "Did we wake you?"

"Cars?" His sister-in-law tucked a wrap around her shoulders and frowned.

"It's nothing for you to worry about." Rosie fetched the kettle. "Just some folks doing things they shouldn't."

Lorna's brows drew down, her mouth puckering. She slapped a hand against her leg twice. "Tell. Me."

"It's the Samsons." Benton moved to the window, wishing he could see out into the darkness. "They put up a moonshine still on the creek upstream. The agents are going to take care of it."

Lorna's face blanched. "Wi?" She launched herself toward the door.

Benton intercepted her, colliding so hard they both grunted with the impact. "What are you doing? You can't go out there."

Lorna thumped her fists against Benton's chest. "Go. Will—"

"No." A flash of heat scored through him. "There's no way I'm letting you out there. I promised to keep you safe. All of you."

Rosie's eyes widened as she came up behind Lorna and tugged on her arm. "Lorna, sit down. What in tarnation's gotten into you? You're going to wake Mac."

Stumbling, Lorna landed hard in one of the chairs. "No, no, no . . ." She wailed, tipping her face into her hands.

Her cries drilled into him. Could they be heard outside? Benton took a knee in front of her. "Quiet down. It's going to be all right. The agents will arrest them and take them out of here. They won't ever bother you again. You'll be safe." Fingers of pain crept up his neck, always the first sign of the blistering headache to come. Within an hour it would have him flat on his back. *Please, not now.* He gripped the back of his head, bending forward.

Rosie came up behind him, her hands cool against his skin. "Headache?"

"Just starting." He groaned. "Why now?"

"I'll get a powder."

Lorna shoved past him, springing for the door and yanking it open. In a flash she was down the steps and out into the darkness.

Rosie's shriek blistered through Benton's skull, but he couldn't wait for the pain to ease. Lunging to his feet, he went after Lorna before the screen door had fully closed. Stopping on the porch, he stared into the darkness, unsure of which path she'd taken. Lorna was never quiet in her movements, but the pounding in his head drowned out any clues. Had she run for the trees? The goat shed? Or was she pummeling straight toward disaster?

Benton bolted for the creek. If Lorna was determined to put herself in the middle of a shootout, he needed to catch her first. He'd vowed to keep her safe, even if it meant protecting her from herself.

He didn't slow his pace until he nearly plunged into the ring of men gathered on the bank, guns drawn.

The firelight's dancing glow did little to obscure the sneer on Horace's face. He turned from the gathered lawmen and sneered at Benton. "I knowed you was behind this." He braced his rifle against his ribs and spit at the ground. "I should've put you in the ground when I had the chance."

"Horace." Will held a shotgun loose in one hand, his eyes dark. "Hush up. This here's gone too far."

Ranger Foss intercepted Benton, throwing an arm across his chest. "I thought I told you to stay put."

"My sister—"

"We all know this small still here ain't worth anyone's time." Horace's shout cut through the crowd. "So maybe if these here revenooers would agree to stand aside, we could settle this like neighbors should?"

"Put down your weapon," the lead agent called out. "We don't want bloodshed."

Horace dropped a hand from his gun and pointed it toward Benton. "He's the one got you feds involved. You gonna protect him?"

Benton eased sideways, moving closer to the agents and scanning the area for Lorna. "You're not talking your way out of this. Should I fill the deputy in on some of your other crimes?"

Two of the rangers were easing to the far side, cornering the Samson brothers against the rocky slope that bordered the creek.

Benton curled his fingers against his temple, willing the pain back to the pit where it belonged. Faced with the man who'd unleashed this monster in his brain, every ounce of Benton's self-restraint cut and ran. He shoved past the ranger, straight toward the barrel of Samson's repeating rifle. "What's say we discuss my sister-in-law? You ever tell your brother how you not only took your belt to her when she trespassed on your land, but you actually had the gall to *violate her*? Is that what it takes to make you feel like a man?"

Horace's brows shot up for a moment before his lips drew back from his tobacco-stained teeth. "I never—" His voice pitched to a roar. "I *never once* laid a hand on that moron. How dare you—"

Will dropped his weapon and surged forward. "Don't you call her that." He yanked his brother's arm with his good hand, pulling him off balance to face him. "Don't you do it. You's got no right—"

Benton took that opportunity to launch himself forward, reaching for Horace's barrel and twisting it to the side. "She told me, Samson."

"Put it down! Put it down!" Every pistol was already drawn, and the circle closed as the agents moved in.

Horace wrenched loose from his brother's grip and sent Benton spilling to the earth in one swift motion. "It weren't me."

As his shoulder collided with the ground, Benton caught a quick glimpse of the agents' determined faces. But between them all, a lone figure burst through the line, flying at him faster than an eagle. *Rosie—no.*

Jamming the barrel against Benton's chest, Horace leaned closer and lowered his voice to a hiss. "I tell you, Fuller—it *weren't* me. I done all I could to keep 'em apart."

She'd nearly reached Horace's side as the bullets began to fly.

• • •

*This here's my fault.*

Rosie had never run so fast in all her days, but seeing Horace pin Benton to the ground with that rifle had kicked off a hornet's nest in her belly, and the next thing she knew, she was near flying.

By some miracle, the agents' shots missed their mark in those first few seconds, giving her time to lay hands on the barrel of Horace's gun and wrest it away from her man's heart. She'd tussled with Horace afore, back when she was nigh on fifteen years old. Iffen he didn't remember the gut punch she gave him back then, he'd remember soon.

"Rosie, get back!" Will's grip crushed into the soft flesh of her arm, yanking her free from his brother's gun.

Rosie's heart pounded as Horace turned the rifle back to its target. He wouldn't murder her husband right afore her eyes—not with federal agents glaring down their pistol sights. "Horace, no! Leave him be!"

In that horrifying moment, Benton's gaze fixed on her as if they was the only two people out here in the night. Maybe the only two anywhere.

She latched on to that crazy thought even as Will jerked her back against him, her shoulder blade colliding with his chest.

The shot that rang out was different than the high-pitched pops coming from the pistols. This one was the deeper report of shotgun.

Rosie shut her eyes out of self-preservation, the horror of witnessing her husband's death more than she could fathom.

Only the blast hadn't come from in front of her, but from somewhere else. Will's grip loosed as he fell forward. She tumbled free, the momentum carrying her across Benton until her forehead collided with the ground.

Benton's arms must have encircled her as he rolled, pulling her underneath him and covering her body with his own. When she opened her eyes, all she could see was the brown wool of his vest pressing down on her. She flung her hands up, grasping his heaving sides. *He's alive. Lord be praised.*

Horace's muffled voice sounded distant and garbled, like she was hearing him from the bottom of a well. "Will, what have you done? Hold still, you idiot."

The sound blurred into pounding feet and shouting voices as Rosie breathed in the scent of her husband's shirt mingled with dirt and the reek of gunpowder. Benton held her in place, the warmth of his blessed weight pressing her into the cold ground, his heart pounding against her own ribs. He braced his arms, rising slightly to look at her. "Rosie . . ." A stitch formed between his eyes. "You're . . . you're bleeding."

"It must be . . . Will's." But with her next breath, she realized Benton was right. A dull pain lodged in her side, and a wave of nausea swept over her.

He lifted his hand from where it had gripped her side, his fingers covered in her blood.

She stared up at it, somehow not comprehending what her eyes were telling her. So much blood. Could she feel it spilling out of her, soaking the ground where she lay?

In the next few seconds, the fear that had plagued her for the past hours drained away, every muscle uncoiling and melting like she was slipping into a hot washtub after a long day in the garden. Or like God had come alongside and taken her hand.

Rosie turned her head, laying her cheek against the mountain dirt, staring toward the house in the distance. *Freedom. Free of this place.*

Lorna stood frozen, her nightgown flapping in the breeze. She gripped the Winchester in both hands, her eyes as wide as Rosie had ever seen them. For a long moment, their gazes locked, carrying Rosie back to the first time she'd held her sister the day she was born. Those same round eyes had stared up into hers even as their mother had slipped away. *"I'll watch out for you, little sister. Forever and always."*

Lorna dropped the gun at her feet as she mouthed silent words. *I sorry. I sorry. I sorry.* She thumped a hand to her chest twice before turning and running for the house.

No matter how hard Rosie had tried, there had been no sheltering her sister from life's sorrows. Who would see Lorna through this one? And McCauley?

A small whisper sounded in her heart. *Who loves them more—you or Me? Trust Me to take care of them.*

"I trust You, Lord," she whispered. "I do."

Benton leaned over, dropping his forehead to Rosie's cheek. "Rosie, don't leave me. You belong here."

"I . . . I don't." She'd been telling him that for some time now. God had made her a creature with wings. She'd been holding on to the branch and stretching her wings, but now she had to loosen her grip. "It's . . . time to fly."

"No." He shook his head with more violence than a man with a splitting headache ought to be able to muster. "We're leaving together."

"Take Mac. Lorna . . . promise me."

"Anything, Rosie. Just stay here with me."

Rosie closed her eyes. The man always had a plumb hard time listening to what he weren't wanting to hear. The Lord would have to work on him. But He had time. "Lorna didn't mean to . . . Forgive her."

He lifted his head, staring toward the house.

"Protect her. Promise me."

"Shhh." He squeezed her hands. "I promised long ago."

She curled her fingers round his, pushing the last bit of her strength into her grip. One last squeeze. The time had come to let go of the branch.

# 30

Great Smoky Mountains National Park
Present Day

*"I DON'T MAKE the rules. I just have to abide by them."*

Zach pushed through the glass doors and headed for his office, thinking back to that first day Kieran had come to visit him at the Collections Preservation Center. She must have thought him arrogant and overbearing as he'd expounded on the laws protecting historical sites in national parks, even quoting the ARPA regulations.

Ever since their trip to Florida, he couldn't stop wondering about Granny Mac's treasured heirloom buried at the family's old homesite. If that bird figure had really been hidden, it seemed entirely plausible it would still be there. No trail ran through the site, so it had been largely undisturbed.

Everything he'd told Kieran was correct. Unfortunately for him, she had then proceeded to burrow her way into his life, just like Benton Fuller had planted his wife's keepsake in the mountain mud. Maybe that was why he'd spent the last two nights sleeping in the cottage, burying his face in the pillow that still smelled like Kieran's shampoo.

Or perhaps he'd just turned into a pathetic fool.

Zach managed to sneak past Marley and slip into his office unseen. She'd notice him eventually, but it was nice to have a few minutes of peace before starting the day.

Spending time with Kieran as they'd pieced together her family's story had created cracks in the veneer of rules he'd long used to protect himself. God gave His children rules out of love, but somehow Zach had managed to reshape it into a suit of armor. If he just did everything by the book—plus a few extra layers he'd added for insurance—he'd never get hurt again. Letting Kieran into his safe little world had given him the first breath of joy he'd had in years.

Since he'd gotten home, he'd spent time combing through the laws and procedures that protected the historical sites in the park. At times the National Park Service had initiated digs to search for artifacts, usually before the construction of a road or building. But recovering items for families? It was unconventional, but he might be able to make an argument for it based on the Cherokee heritage and the limited scope of the recovery effort.

Zach opened a new document on his computer and started typing out a list of reasons the park might wish to undertake such a project. Sitting back, he stared at the page.

The process would take ages to gain approval, and the family wouldn't be allowed to keep the memento, but possibly they could hold it in their hands at least once. Then a nice display site could be found somewhere, maybe at Sugarlands or Oconaluftee. Or if it was confirmed to be of Native American origin, possibly at the museum down at Cherokee, North Carolina. He added that to the document.

The most important reason was one he couldn't put into the report—Granny Mac deserved a chance to see it again.

His phone vibrated, and Zach glanced at the clock. His shift hadn't officially started yet. Kieran must have overslept, because she usually sent her good-morning text before he even left the house. He loved the fact that she respected his work hours.

As he slid the phone from his pocket, he pictured her sitting cross-legged on her bed, sleep-mussed, like she'd been that morning at Aubrey's. Far too intriguing of an image. A surge of emotion welled up inside him. Who was he kidding? He was in love with this woman, no question. He clicked on the message.

*Granny Mac is in the hospital.*

He fumbled the device, nearly dropping it, before getting his thumbs into place to reply. *How bad?*

*Ministroke. TIA, doc said. I'm scared.*

Zach groaned, tugging at his green uniform tie. If only he could be there. *I'm so sorry. Are you at the hospital? Should I come?* He glanced around the quiet office. He'd already expended most of his leave time. Would his supervisor count a girlfriend's sick grandmother as emergency leave?

*Ash is here. I'll be all right. Just pray.*

*Done.* His fingers hovered over the keys. There needed to be more. He set the phone on the desk and rubbed his palms on his pant legs. Taking a deep breath, he reached for it again. *I love you. Wish I could be there.*

She answered with a single heart.

He stared at it for a long time, even as the clock ticked past the hour.

Kieran had already endured so much in her life, and Granny Mac was the last living link to her family. He would do almost anything to protect her from one more loss.

His laptop kicked into screensaver mode. *If Granny Mac passes away without ever seeing that stone bird, it would be a crime.*

Zach rolled his chair back and headed for John's office. He'd lay out the case in person. There were enough reasons to justify an archaeological dig, small as it was. He should have made the appeal the first day Kieran had come to him with the simple request. The delay had been a mistake. If Granny Mac died without holding her mother's carving, that was on him.

He stopped just outside the manager's office, staring at the ergonomic silver handle, ADA approved. The government did everything by the book, just like him. Maybe that was why he fit in so well with the National Park Service. Filling out forms, managing red tape, quoting the regulations. Putting history up into acid-free boxes with computer-generated labels in climate-controlled shelving and cabinets. Bruce's oral-history tapes were already filed away in the facility's high-tech freezer.

The chill in the air didn't stop the glaze of perspiration gathering on his palms. Even if he put in for a special exemption, it would take time. Lots of it. Time Granny Mac might not have.

John's door opened, and the man filled the doorway. "Zach, hey. What's going on?"

"We need to talk."

Ten minutes later, after he'd spilled all of Kieran's story for his boss, Zach scooted forward in his seat. "John, we've got to do this. It's the right choice."

John pulled out a yellow legal pad and took down some notes. "You make a compelling argument. I can talk to Tracy and the superintendent, see what they say." He clicked the end of the black ball point pen several times. "It has to clear the district office too. We've got procedures. I can fast-track it, but I can't make any promises."

Zach stood, pacing to the window. "We might not have time. This means a lot to the family, but it has to happen before McCauley Fuller passes away. Otherwise, what's the point?"

"And this young woman you told me about—Kieran. She's your . . ."

"My friend."

"Girlfriend?" The implication hung heavy in the air.

"I don't see how that affects anything."

John tapped the pad with the tip of the pen, his brow furrowing. "Zach, you know I think highly of you. You were my top pick for the curator position even though your government experience was limited. I pulled strings to get you here."

"I understand. And I appreciate that. You'll never know how much."

"I like to take care of my people, and I feel strongly about the rights of the families who lived here before we arrived. We've made it our mission in recent years to reach out to this community."

Zach tensed, sensing a huge "but" coming his way.

"I'll do what I can. I think it's a good idea."

"You will? You do?"

"Absolutely. I'll make some calls. But, Zach"—he stood—"you've got to be realistic. It's never going to happen in the time frame you've requested. We're looking at several months minimum. Chances are it's going to be much, much longer. And I wouldn't say anything to the family. We don't want to get their hopes up."

Zach managed to nod, a lump forming in his throat. "Thank you, sir. Can I make one more request? I need another day off."

"Sure. Just mark it on your time sheet. Going to the hospital?"

"Yes, sir. I think I should."

"Good man."

Zach headed for his desk. There were a few things he needed to grab on his way out. Meeting with John had been encouraging, confirming the "rightness" of this decision. And yet sitting there listening to the man talk, Zach had felt every minute that passed. Each tick of the clock reverberated through his heart. Now he realized what needed to happen—and when.

Was he going to the hospital? Yes, absolutely.

But he wasn't going empty-handed.

• • •

Instead of the lemony scent of Gran's normal room, this one carried the essence of wilting roses. A massive bouquet sat over by the neighboring bed.

Shifting in the chair, Kieran gripped the cup of tepid coffee Ash had forced on her. Flowers. She hadn't even thought of such a thing. She opened her phone and typed "hospital flower delivery" into the search engine. Her eyes blurred as the options scrolled past. Roses, carnations, daisies, teddy bears. She couldn't afford them anyway.

"Lord, please let her be all right," Kieran murmured. "I don't want to be alone in this world." She still fumbled her way through prayers, but somehow this lifeline seemed as important as the heart monitor beeping nearby.

She glanced back at Zach's last text. *I love you. Wish I could be there.* Pressing the device to her chest, she tried to imagine him saying those words.

"Kieran?" Gran's eyelids fluttered.

The phone slipped from Kieran's fingers onto the chair, but she didn't bother to go after it. Instead, she jumped to her feet. "I'm here, Gran."

Granny Mac lifted a hand, turning it slightly to stare down at the IV taped to the back. "What happened?"

"You gave us a little scare." Kieran reached for the mauve-colored pitcher on the rolling table. "Are you thirsty?"

"Yes. Tea."

*Figures.* "How about a sip of water to start?"

Her grandmother accepted the straw Kieran raised to her lips. Resting her head against the pillows, she sighed. "Thought I died." She closed her eyes. "I saw my mother."

Kieran set down the cup and reached into her pocket for Gran's stone bird. "Sounds like a nice dream. But I'm thankful you're still here with me."

"She said she's waiting."

The words burrowed deep. Kieran leaned in. "You tell her to wait a little longer. I'm not ready to let you go yet."

"Loosen your grip. You hold everything too tight."

She touched the back of Gran's hand, the fragile skin soft and loose, like silk sheets a size too big. "You're my family. I need you." She pressed the bird into Gran's palm.

Gran turned her hand to enfold Kieran's, the tiny stone held between them. "You'll make your own family. And I'll . . . I'll watch over you."

• • •

Brightly hued autumn leaves fell across the trail, the light casting a golden glow on the path as Zach's boots crunched along. Usually the sight brought a surge of joy, but right now his heart pounded so hard, he could barely breathe.

"Slow down." Miguel panted behind him. "Dude. Slow down."

Finding his best friend raiding his fridge had actually made Zach stop and think about what he was doing—at least for a few minutes. But it hadn't changed his mind.

Miguel had insisted on tagging along, but the closer they got, the more Zach regretted giving in. There was a fine line between moral support and being an accomplice.

Stepping off the main trail, Zach picked his way through the trees, clambering over logs and shoving through brush. *Lord, forgive me for this, but I don't know what else to do. You love Granny Mac even more than Kieran does, so I'm sure You understand—right?*

Miguel remained a few paces behind him. "This isn't like you. You do things by the book. You're practically obsessed with it."

"I'm not obsessed. I was arrogant about it, putting rules before people. I was more concerned about protecting myself than doing something to help a friend. If I'd applied right away, it might not have come to this." And if he hadn't delayed taking responsibility for his actions when he was younger, things might have ended differently with Jordan too. Indecision had a cost.

*Family is a choice.* And the time had come for him to make his.

"Does this girl really mean so much to you?"

"She does." He waited for Miguel to catch up. "But I'm doing it for her grandmother. And for all the people who called this place home."

"You could lose your job."

"I know." Putting the wheels in motion with John meant the park was now aware of the artifact, and there would be no hiding what he'd done. But he couldn't wait for the administration to act, especially when they did so at a governmental pace. He wanted to set this figure in Granny Mac's hand, and every minute that passed, the opportunity would be slipping through his fingers.

He shoved past a scruffy ash tree, sending a cascade of leaves fluttering down. The chimney stood sentinel in the distance, framed against the autumn-tinged hillside. *Rosie's Ridge.* The time had come to recover Rosie's treasured keepsake. Somehow he thought the woman would understand.

"So where is this thing exactly?" Miguel stopped to catch his breath. "And how deep are we talking? I feel like we're off to bury a body."

"By the chimney." He knew Miguel was trying to lighten the mood, but Zach wasn't having it. If he was going to break the law, he wanted to feel the gravity of his choices—every single crack to his personal code. "This way."

As they approached, he shrugged off his pack and unzipped the main pocket. He'd grabbed a good collection of folding spades, trowels, and picks. They would work slowly and methodically, marking everything. It did little to assuage his guilt, but there was still a proper way to do this. He wasn't some two-bit pot hunter.

Coming around the far side of the chimney, Zach dropped to a crouch, his heart wedging in his throat. He reached out to touch the mound of soil loosened around the edges of the flagstone and studied the boot prints where someone had pressed it back into place.

"Tell me that's not what it looks like." Miguel took a knee.

"Someone beat us here." And Zach knew exactly who it had been.

• • •

Kieran let the hospital door click shut behind her and stopped to relish the fresh night air. Nick was coming to pick her up, but she needed a few minutes to gather her thoughts before she faced anyone. She'd never seen Gran look so small, the big hospital bed dwarfing her withered frame. When had she lost the weight? She'd seen her nearly every day, except for the few she was in Florida.

Maybe she'd been so concerned about the dementia that she'd overlooked other aspects of Gran's health. Ever since the doctor had adjusted her medications last month, Gran seemed to be having more lucid moments. But what if those adjustments had led her here?

This stroke might have been worse if the nursing staff at Sycamore Terrace hadn't spotted the signs right away and called for an ambulance. Kieran trotted down the ramp leading to the sidewalk, trying to shake off the terror that had consumed her since the early morning phone call. She still wore the sweats and ratty T-shirt she'd slept in.

Dr. Reynolds's no-nonsense blond ponytail had matched her bedside manner, her voice a sensible mixture of sympathetic and truthful. It was the truthful part that had shattered Kieran into a million pieces. Gran was likely to have another stroke, and the next one could kill her. Suddenly dementia seemed like small potatoes.

Kieran stopped to wait at the curb. Nick's truck wasn't there yet, and that was a good thing. She needed to find a way to swallow this bit of news before she could repeat it to someone else.

She was no stranger to loss. Not only had she lost her mother, but she'd been to countless funerals for clients. She'd comforted families, helped with final details, closed up the apartments that she'd helped seniors move into. Death was a part of life, and really it was just one breath away for everyone. But not Gran.

Kieran closed her fingers around the pocket bird, rubbing her thumbnail along the grooves marking its stone wings. If Gran passed away, she wasn't sure she could ever face its little eyes again. It had been wrong to take it in the first place.

Zach's final text still tugged at her. He loved her. He trusted her. He'd counseled her about families and choices, always coming back to doing the right thing. He was the voice of honesty.

A car door shut some distance away, breaking Kieran from her thoughts. She glanced around, suddenly realizing she was standing in a dark parking lot by herself. Nick had said to wait inside, but when did she ever listen? Not to him. Not to Zach. Only to her own stupid desires.

The figure coming toward her took on a familiar, blessed shape—Zach.

She shouldn't be surprised he'd driven to Nashville after receiving her texts this morning. Her throat squeezed. "You didn't have to come."

"I know." His face was grim. "How's your gran?"

She stepped forward to meet him, wrapping her arms around his waist and kissing his cheek. "You are the most incredible man. I can't believe you drove all this way to check on us. She's doing a little better, but the doctors are concerned that she could have another stroke. They're keeping her for a few days while they run more tests."

He kept one arm stiff around her and used the other to push off his cap and straighten his hair. "You've got to be exhausted. Can I buy you dinner or something?" His voice was low, as if weariness pulled at the words.

"Are you kidding me? You just drove three hours. I'll buy dinner—or cook for you. Ash and Nick will be happy you're here."

Zach sighed. "I'll get a hotel room for tonight. I don't want to take up their couch again. But we need to talk—so dinner first? Just us?"

The word "talk" settled somewhere down in her chest. "What's wrong?"

"I don't want to do this here. Let's go somewhere. Please." He dropped his arm and retreated a step.

A sudden weakness spilled over her. *Do what?* The tension was pouring off him in waves. "Nick is coming to pick me up."

"Text him."

"I can't—he's already on his way. Just tell me."

He tipped his head back, his face suddenly filled with the lamp's glare. Dark shadows ringed his eyes. "Kieran . . ."

*He's breaking up with me. Now? Here?* All the talk of family, choices. The confession of what had happened with Jordan. It had spooked him. She should have seen it coming. And then his clumsy declaration of love via text—she hadn't even answered it. Just sent a dumb emoji heart. The words built up in her chest like an overinflated balloon. *I love you, Zach Jensen. I love you. Don't quit on me now. Not today of all days.*

"The bird, Kieran. Do you have it?" He lowered his chin and met her gaze. "Did you go to the homesite and dig it up?"

Her breath caught. She stepped back, nearly snagging her heel on the curb. "I . . . I . . ." A scream started somewhere in the depths of her being, wanting nothing more than to crawl out her throat. "I did. I had to, Zach. My gran—"

"You had to?" He brought both hands up behind his head, lacing his fingers together, as if to keep his brain from exploding. "When? When did you do it?"

"The . . . the morning after we found the site."

"So you've had it all this time and never said a word." His voice faltered. "During our Florida trip?"

The pain in his face cut into her. "Yes."

"I told you it was illegal. That you could get fined—go to jail, even. Did none of that matter to you?"

"It mattered, but—"

"Kieran, you broke a federal law. What am I supposed to do? Look the other way? This is my job. And you lied to me this whole time."

A hole might as well have opened in the pavement under her feet. "You're turning me in."

"Where's the artifact?"

"Zach, I—"

"Where is it?" He crushed the ball cap in his hands, his volume kicking up a notch. "Do you have it on you?"

Another door slammed nearby, but Kieran didn't dare look away from Zach. She put her hand in her pocket, pulling the figure into her fingers and rolling it in her grip. "I do."

Nick appeared in the fringe of light surrounding them, his voice wary. "Kieran, is there a problem?"

Zach shot him a brief glance before returning his attention to Kieran. "Has your gran had a chance to see it, hold it?"

"Yes. I showed it to her." Kieran lifted a hand toward Nick to make sure he stayed put.

"Then give it to me."

Her mouth went dry. "Gran wanted me to have it." She squeezed the bird in her palm. "It belongs in my family. Not to the park."

"It has to go back."

Nick pushed up his sleeves. "Let's take this out of the parking lot, shall we? Can we go somewhere a little more private and talk about this sensibly before things get out of hand?"

"I tried that." Zach set his jaw. "Kieran, the artifact."

"It's not an artifact." Her emotions bubbled over. "We're not talking about the Holy Grail. It's a rock that my great-grandfather buried eighty-odd years ago. I dug up a rock, Zach. Not a graveyard. This is the last piece of them I may ever have."

His hands dropped to his sides. "Then we're done, Kieran. You've made your choice." Hunching his shoulders, he turned and walked toward his truck.

*Your choice.* The words pierced straight through her. Her knuckles ached from where she clutched the stone. Is that what she was doing?

*Loosen your grip. You hold everything too tight.*

Kieran pulled her hand from her pocket and opened it slowly, gazing down at the carved bird. What had it meant to Rosie? A connection to her home and her people? Or a symbol of flying free and trusting God to take care of her? She lifted her eyes, watching as Zach walked away from her.

Kieran started forward, only to have Nick grab her elbow. "I think you should let him cool off."

She wrenched free and raced after Zach. "Wait!"

He turned enough to meet her eyes, keeping his body angled toward the truck.

The stone lay warm and heavy in her grasp. She caught his hand and placed it in his palm. "I'm sorry."

Zach closed his fingers over it, his eyes searching her face. Lowering his head, he gave her a short nod and turned back toward the truck. "I hope it was worth it." Climbing in, he started the engine and drove out of the parking lot.

Standing under the flickering streetlight, Kieran's eyes blurred with tears as she watched his truck turn toward the highway.

# 31

Nashville
Present Day

Chilled from her early morning walk, Kieran pulled a heavy sweater out of the closet. She'd taken to exercising more often this winter, since it had a way of clearing her brain of all the messes she'd made. For months now she'd been expecting the tap on her door or a formal piece of US mail. How long would she have to wait before she'd be forced to face up to what she'd done? Zach had made it clear that he had little choice but to turn her in.

*You broke a federal law.*

His words had sent a wave of panic through her that she'd still not quite shaken off. She and Nick had sat down at the computer and done the research. She could face thousands of dollars of fines, plus jail time. With her gran in such precarious health, jail would be torture. *Lord, please help the judge understand.*

Nick and Ash wanted her to call a lawyer right away, but she just couldn't bring herself to do it. The thought of paying legal fees on top of the fines was too overwhelming. And a second convict in the family? Her stomach turned. She'd done her best to rely on the Lord's strength rather than her own, but evidently God knew she needed more practice.

She didn't have a shift at the diner today, and a new novel waited on her bed. Plopping down, she pulled it into her lap and tried to focus on the pages.

When her phone buzzed, Kieran tossed the book aside and opened her email. It was from Andrea Perez at the Florida State Archives.

*Kieran, I hope you don't mind, but I couldn't resist doing a little more digging in regards to your great-aunt. I put out a request for information to some of my genealogy circles and came up with a fantastic hit. I'll attach the letter below. I hope it finds you well.*

Kieran opened the file.

*Dear Andrea,*

*You'll never know how tickled I was to receive your email. I did know Lorna McCauley—in fact I considered her a dear, dear friend. As you know, I worked at the Black Mountain Orphanage (now Black Mountain Home for Children, Youth, and Families) in North Carolina for many years. Our director met Lorna in 1949, a year after she was discharged from FSH. Evidently the sweet gal had come north seeking her family who had lived in the Tennessee section of the Smokies. She had been unable to locate them and fallen on hard times. The director extended an invitation to join us at the home.*

*Lorna was slow in speech, but she was also lovely, gentle, and kind. She was prone to bouts of sadness sometimes—possibly why she was at FSH?—but she never took it out on another soul. She loved the children, and they adored her in return. It was good for them to meet someone like Lorna and understand how our good Lord makes people in all sorts of ways, and yet each of us has a purpose and an honored place in His family.*

*She worked as a janitor in our building for over thirty years until she passed away in 1979. I guess she was around seventy years of age? She wasn't certain of her birthday, so we'd declared it to be St. Valentine's Day, and the children would shower her with cards and sweets on her special day. Some women never get to have children, but Lorna had hundreds.*

*I found some old photos in my album, so I'm scanning and attaching them to this email. I hope they bring some peace to her family. I'm tickled to be a part of bringing them back together. One of the pictures shows the time my husband and I took Lorna on a trip to visit her old home up in the Smokies. She placed flowers on her sister's and parents' graves. That was difficult but also quite healing, I believe.*

*Please forward this to her family—from ours—with much love.*

*Georgia Allen. Black Mountain, North Carolina*

Kieran had never even known Lorna, but the letter from Mrs. Allen brought tears to her eyes. One more limb of her family tree restored. She scrolled through the grainy photographs, Lorna's smile a sweet reflection of Granny Mac's. *Mother and daughter?*

She downloaded the images and sent them to the printer. If Gran was feeling strong enough, it might be time to reacquaint her with her aunt Lorna. She wouldn't tell her every detail, but she could at least share Lorna's happy ending. *We need more of those, after all.*

Before clicking off her phone, she skimmed through her texts. Zach's last message was buried now since months had gone by without a word from him. Still, her finger gravitated toward his name, clicking it open.

*I love you. Wish I could be there.*

Tears blurred her vision. Things had gone downhill so abruptly, it felt like they'd stumbled off a cliff. It had taken a few weeks for her to realize that she'd set the end in motion the moment she'd picked up the shovel. She'd gripped on to that dream of returning Gran's bird with the tenacity of a bulldog, unable to let go.

She'd borrowed a book off Granny Mac's shelf last week, and a quote from Corrie ten Boom had been circling through Kieran's memory ever since. *Hold everything in your hands lightly; otherwise it hurts when God pries your fingers open.*

Zach would not be able to forgive her. Once he'd learned she wasn't trustworthy, he'd had no choice but to end their relationship. It didn't matter if she had reasons. She could have been defusing a bomb that would destroy the world as they knew it—it wouldn't have made a difference.

He believed in the rules.

*Wish I could be there.*

She wished it too.

The phone vibrated in her hand, startling her into dropping it. After a quick laugh, she scooped it up and read a caller's name she didn't recognize. She lifted it to her ear.

"Hey, Kieran. You don't know me, but I got your number from my friend's phone."

*Likely story.* "Which friend?"

"Zach Jensen. I'm Miguel Delgado. We met at Zach's cabin a while back. Um, I sort of walked in and—"

"I remember." She straightened, her heart skipping along at a faster clip. That wasn't the sort of thing a girl forgot.

"He wouldn't want me talking to you, but I thought you should know. He's going to court soon, and—"

"Court?" She fisted her hand into the blankets. "Why is he going to court?"

The man's voice fell silent for a long moment. "I thought you knew."

The dreaded knock at the door had never come. She pressed a hand to her cheek. "He took responsibility for it, didn't he?" Kieran sucked in a quick breath. "Of all the inane, idiotic . . ." *Heroic.* ". . . self-sacrificing nonsense to pull—I never asked him to do that. Oh no, did he get arrested? Fired?" Heat flooded over her, chased after by cold.

"Um, yeah. Pretty much. I thought maybe you could be a character reference or something."

"When does he appear? Does he have a lawyer?"

She scribbled down the information on a torn envelope she'd been using as a bookmark and thanked Miguel for calling. Rushing into the kitchen, she poured a glass of water with trembling hands and chugged it down before turning back to her phone.

The last few weeks of indecision came down to this moment. Now she knew exactly what she had to do.

• • •

Zach shifted on the hard wooden bench. The US District Court building in Knoxville was not designed for comfort. He leaned forward, bracing his hands on his knees and taking deep breaths. Miguel sat on one side, John on the other, but it didn't make him feel any better.

The judge adjusted his glasses. "Miss Lucas, I want to clarify one point before continuing. Am I correct in understanding that Zachary Jensen of the National Park Service made you aware of the Archaeological Resources Protection Act when you met with him prior to the incident? And Mr. Jensen explained how this law affected the status of the artifact you wished to recover?

"Yes, your honor."

"So in spite of this knowledge, you took it upon yourself to dig up and remove a historical artifact from federal property."

"Yes, your honor." Kieran's black dress made her look more confident than her quavering voice suggested. The attorney Zach had originally hired for himself sat at the table beside her. At least he was fully versed in the case, having heard it from both sides now.

Zach studied the rest of the room. Nick and Ash were in the front row, and a smattering of park service folks had attended as well. Even Marley was here.

The judge leaned forward. "You, in fact, stole this piece of property."

Kieran's voice grew softer. "Yes, your honor."

He sat back, staring at the papers in front of him. "We take these cultural property crimes very seriously because when you steal from public lands, you're stealing from everyone. If you loot a historical site, you're not only vandalizing and damaging the location. You are separating an item from its historical context, and it proceeds to become little more than a trinket. Such an action can have historical and scientific ramifications."

Zach gripped the edge of the bench. The judge was treating Kieran like she'd desecrated a burial mound. He had to take into account her situation, her history. Didn't he?

John placed a hand on his shoulder. "Take it easy," he whispered.

Judge Watkins cleared his throat. "Before sentencing, I'd like to give you the opportunity to make a statement. You may do so in writing, or if you prefer, you can read your statement aloud."

Minutes later, after being seated in the box beside the judge, she lifted her head to scan the room. Her eyes fixed on Zach for a moment before she redirected her attention to the paper in front of her. With a careful, even voice, she explained the situation she faced with her grandmother, inserting a brief description of her working life, including her return to the newly reopened SeniorCo.

At that point, her statement turned personal. "It's true that Mr. Jensen took the time to explain the laws to me. I wish I could say that I was ignorant of the situation, but it would be a lie. In fact, when we undertook the search for my great-grandparents' homesite, I did so with every intention of finding the artifact." She blinked hard, as if fighting tears. "He was unaware of this. I deceived him. And for that, I'm truly sorry."

Zach lowered his head, her emotion gutting him.

"After we located the cabin, I returned the next day and dug up the stone bird. It had belonged to my great-grandmother and to her mother before her. My great-grandfather was the one to bury it before leaving the land to the park's possession."

She took a shaking breath. "This doesn't excuse my actions, Your

Honor, but my intent was to return the stone to my grandmother who is suffering from dementia. I thought—" She choked on the words at that point. "I thought it would provide a touchpoint that might keep her with me a while longer." Kieran hesitated.

"May I interrupt, Miss Lucas?" The judge's voice was soft.

She glanced up, reaching a finger to brush tears from her lashes. "Of course."

"Did it?"

"I'm sorry?"

"Did it help? My mother had Alzheimer's."

Kieran's mouth opened slightly, then closed. "I'm sorry. Honestly, I'm not sure." Her chin wobbled. "I . . . I think it helped her to know that I understood the tragedy her family had endured." She glanced toward Zach for a moment. "*My* family." She pushed the letter away, her voice taking on a more natural cadence. "I grew up in foster care. I didn't put that in here, because it felt like an excuse somehow. But I only reconnected with my family a few years ago. Gran wanted me to feel a part of the long line of women who had held on to that bird before me—all the way back to her Cherokee great-great-grandmother."

The judge nodded.

"As Zach helped me learn more about my ancestors, I came to understand that I didn't need an object to feel connected to them. I didn't need the cabin they'd lost or answers about my great-grandmother's death." She took a shaky breath. "I just needed to choose. I chose to rejoin my family, Your Honor. After all the failures and tragedies that befell my parents and my kin in the Smokies, they're still a part of me. They're my people. I'm part of a long line of very proud, very flawed individuals."

She lifted her gaze to meet the judge's eyes. "I didn't need the bird. I needed to open myself up to accept help from others instead of trying to fix everything myself. God's been working on me about that, teaching me to trust Him and others. I've learned I needed time with Granny Mac, listening to her stories. And days with Zach Jensen, talking about the Smokies, faith, and family. And everyone else who helped me glue my family tree back together.

"Digging up the artifact was a horrific lapse in judgment. I don't know why my great-grandfather buried it. Maybe to break the chain of misery that had plagued his family—losing three babies and his wife. Losing their land." Kieran shook her head. "But mistakes still followed him, as they always do. Evidently they follow me as well.

"So I don't ask for leniency. I learned a powerful lesson, and for that I'm deeply grateful. My one request would be for my grandmother. She won't understand if I suddenly disappear from her life. So if I must go to prison, I'd . . . I'd like to arrange to still see her—somehow."

The judge nodded, gesturing for her to step down. "I will take some time to consider. We'll have a short recess."

After the judge went out, the courtroom dissolved into soft conversations. Zach stood up and moved into the aisle.

Miguel latched onto his elbow. "Are you sure about this?"

"Yeah." He eased his way past a few people and made his way forward. Nodding to Ash and Nick, he waited behind the railing. When Kieran finally looked up from her conversation with the lawyer, he summoned his most convincing smile.

She echoed it, a deep sadness still clinging to her eyes. Without saying a word, she reached out to him.

He took her hands. Placing one of his on top, he tried to rub some warmth into her skin.

"I can't believe what you almost did. For a man who follows all the rules, would you really have perjured yourself?"

"It wouldn't have been a complete lie. After I heard about Granny Mac's stroke, I went to the site with every intention of digging the thing up myself."

Her head jerked up. "You did?"

"Imagine my surprise."

Kieran's brow crumpled. "You'll never know how sorry I am that I took advantage of your trust. I really blew it."

He kept his hands locked around hers. "I did too, so I'm not sure I'm in a position to throw any stones."

"Can you forgive me? I know I don't deserve it—not after everything you did for me."

"I forgave you long ago." He leaned forward and pressed a kiss to her cheek. "I only hope you can forgive me as well."

"For what?"

"For how I treated you that night in the parking lot. All I can say is, I was struggling with my own stuff right then. It had brought back everything I'd buried with Jordan. Even though I felt awful for the mistakes I'd made, I also blamed her for what she did—for cutting me out and not giving me a chance to make things right. I thought if I were more careful, I could keep myself from stumbling again." He shook his head. "And there I was, back on my knees in the dirt."

"I'm sorry I pushed you to that."

He'd wanted to tell her this for so long, but suddenly it was difficult to find the words. "It took some time for God to show me I needed to stop blaming others for my own failings. No matter how hard I try, I'll still mess up. That's why He offers grace." Zach squeezed her fingers. "And I needed to extend that to you as well."

She ducked her head, as if fighting tears. "I don't deserve that, but I'll take it."

"Did you mean what you said about God helping you?"

A shy smile graced her lips. "You were a big part of that."

"It sounds like we have a lot of catching up to do."

The room hushed as the judge returned. Zach released her hand.

Ashleigh scooted closer to her husband and patted the bench next to her.

Zach joined them, pleased to be welcomed back into their good graces.

The judge made a few brief remarks before turning to Kieran. "Miss Lucas, I must confess to being strongly moved by your case. Nothing like this has ever come across my desk before." He lowered the black-framed readers in order to fix his eyes on her. "The Archaeological Resources Protection Act of 1979 was designed to protect archaeological resources and sites on federal and tribal lands, and your actions in Great Smoky Mountains National Park clearly fall under the scope of its authority. I appreciate that you have taken responsibility for your decisions and chose to plead guilty in this case. That does simplify the situation."

He shuffled the papers in front of him. "In terms of sentencing, regulations state that for a Class A misdemeanor violation, a first-time offender be fined not more than $100,000 or imprisoned not more than two years, or both."

Zach's knee bounced as he willed the judge to show mercy. The attorney had gone over these points with him in fine detail both before and after Kieran had come forward. She'd been concerned about potential complications, such as if he'd counseled Kieran to excavate the item on her own or if Kieran had sought to employ him to procure the artifact for her, in which case they'd both be standing before the judge on additional counts.

The judge took his glasses off. "It seems to me that your infraction in this case was fairly minor, and I do want to take that into account. According to records, the damage was limited to a small patch of soil and the artifact was returned in the same condition in which it was removed.

"Miss Lucas, your statement was moving, but it doesn't change the facts. If you felt the artifact should be excavated, there were proper channels for such a request. However, none of those would have led to it being remanded to your possession, regardless of the item's origin. I believe that is the actual reason you did what you did."

The tension in Kieran's shoulders seemed to deepen, as if she was bracing herself.

"That said, I see no reason to impose a maximum sentence in this case simply in order to make a statement, as the prosecutor has so eloquently recommended. Therefore, I sentence you, Kieran Lucas, to pay fines and restitution in the amount of $5,000. In lieu of jail time, I am sentencing you to four months probation, including a required condition that you complete one hundred hours of community service. I'm recommending it be conducted under the oversight of the National Park Service, ideally in the area of historic preservation, as that seems appropriate in this case. If any of these conditions are violated, probation may be revoked and you will serve out the remainder of your time in federal custody. Do you understand?"

"I do, Your Honor."

By the time court was adjourned, Zach felt like he'd run a marathon. He stood with Nick and Ash, waiting as Kieran thanked the attorney and made her way over to them.

Nick had one hand on his wife's shoulder, keeping her from surging forward until the appropriate moment. When she slipped out of his grasp, he turned to Zach. "Those two are like sisters. You might want to get used to it."

"I grew up with several of them, so I'm fully versed." He held out a hand to Nick. "I'm thankful she has the two of you. She's told me many times that you are the closest thing she has to family."

Nick shook the outstretched hand. "We think of her as part of ours as well. Ash has already started calling her Auntie Kieran."

"Auntie? Are you guys—"

"Early next summer, God willing." His lips lifted slightly. "Long time coming."

"Congratulations." Zach glanced over at the two women embracing like they'd been separated for weeks, rather than hours. Kieran must be thrilled for her friend. The way she'd jumped right in with Aubrey's kids made it evident that she'd always be the fun aunt, regardless of whether she had a legal right to the title.

He couldn't resist reaching his arms out to Kieran when she approached, even though before today they hadn't spoken in months.

It had almost killed him.

He pulled her into an embrace. "Good work. I'm so happy for you."

She rested her cheek on his lapel and wrapped her arms clear around to the center of his back, squeezing hard. "You can't know how glad I am to hear you say that. I thought I'd never hear from you again."

Zach lowered his chin to the top of her head, wondering at how easily she fit into his arms even after all this time. Would they be able to recover the closeness they'd had before? "One hundred hours of community service in historical preservation? I've got at least that much work stacked up. I'm not letting you near any shovels, but I've got tons of dusty old boxes for you to sort."

She laughed and released her grip. "And here I thought dust wasn't allowed in your pristine, climate-controlled facility?"

"You should see some of the mildewed donations that get dropped off every time someone moves or goes through their grandparents' attic. Bring tissues—and a sweater."

"I will." Her eyes shone.

Maybe they had a chance after all. Besides, he owed her a hike to Laurel Falls. And a hundred other hidden spots.

# 32

Great Smoky Mountains National Park
Present Day

"Eeeeeee-hah!" Granny Mac's voice rang through the quiet forest as she clung to the railing on the side of the four-seater ATV. "You're gonna kill an old lady with this thing. Slow down there, tiger." She batted one hand at Zach's arm as he guided the vehicle down the trail.

Kieran leaned forward in the rear seat so she could keep an eye on her grandmother. "This is the slowest it goes, Gran."

"We could walk faster," Zach offered. "But it'd be a bit of a hike."

Gran settled her pocket book primly on her knees, as if she were headed off to church, not hitching a ride into the woods. "My pa had a 1930 Model A Ford. Can you believe that?" She frowned. "This isn't the road, is it?"

Zach eased them over a clump of roots. "It's a walking trail now. I had to get a special-use permit."

Kieran shifted a little further, checking that Gran was stable in the seat. Her stroke had been eight months ago now, and while she'd regained most of her strength and mobility, the doctor still warned she was at a high risk for another. When Zach had first brought up the idea of Gran attending the Decoration Day event, Kieran had shrugged it off. It seemed unrealistic to take her so far from home.

But during the past two weeks, Gran had so many lucid periods and such a spring in her step that Kieran started to seriously consider it. As quickly as Gran was losing old memories, she deserved a few new ones. It was a risk, but then, so was living.

It might take another lifetime, but Kieran was finally learning to loosen her grip—first in her knitting, then her dreams of a perfect family, and finally on Granny Mac. As Gran kept reminding her, God couldn't fill her hands if she kept them closed fast.

Staying in Zach's cottage made the trip easier, and since he'd set it up with all sorts of wonderful senior-friendly features, she might have trouble convincing Gran to go home.

*This is crazy. Are we crazy to be doing this?*

"Look at all the trees. Have you ever seen anything so lovely in all your living days?" Gran tipped her head back, placing one hand on the top of her yellow sun hat. "I don't recollect there being this many trees."

"It's probably grown up a lot since you lived here."

"So have I. My Pa always said I was knee high to a firefly back then."

Zach eased the ATV to a stop and gestured at the mountainside that had come into view. "The ridge."

Gran's intake of breath sent a rush through Kieran. "Rosie's Ridge. My gracious. I never thought I'd see it again."

Once they finally parked the ATV, it only took a slow ten-minute walk to get Gran to the old cabin site.

When the river rock chimney appeared ahead of them, Gran stopped cold, her hands hovering in front of her. "Ohhh . . . I'm home, Mama. I'm home." The brambly shrub by the chimney was covered with late-season roses, and the scattered pink petals perfumed the air with their soft clove fragrance.

They walked closer, letting Gran choose her steps. She pointed out where the porch had been, gesturing with her hands to draw pictures in their minds of the small structure with a main room, a loft overhead, and a small lean-to bedroom, where her parents had slept.

"I used to race down that ladder every morning, eager to get outside and visit the goats and the chickens." She turned around, her eyes hazy as she faced what had been the yard. "The goat shed was down there, and the bee gums over that way." She pointed, a smile pulling at her lips, softening the lines that resided there. Her gaze roamed the small clearing. "It's all grown up so much. Hardly looks like we was ever here."

Zach helped her take a few more steps. "The forest is taking over. But that chimney has withstood the test of time."

Kieran snapped several pictures of Gran as she explored the cabin and the yard. Today was going even better than she'd dared hope. She could almost see some of that six-year-old girl in her eighty-six-year-old grandmother. It was as if coming home had given her both a window into her past and a boost of energy. She'd be tired tonight, but whatever came, this was worth it.

"Whenever you're ready, Gran, we'll head up the hill."

Granny Mac met her eyes and smiled. "I was born ready."

Zach chuckled, careful to guide her over the uneven ground. "We'll take it slow. It's a bit of a walk yet."

Kieran waited a moment, catching a shot of the two of them heading up the trail.

Turning, she looked back at the chimney that stood as a testament to their past. She could still feel the sensation of the dirt between her fingers the day she'd dug up the stone bird. It was crazy to think how vital it had seemed to recover this link to her family—to touch something that had lain forgotten in the dirt for eighty years. But it had never been the bird she needed. It was the people. They were the ones who had given her wings.

She was glad the carving would find a new home at the Museum of the Cherokee Indian—a place of honor that should make her distant ancestor proud.

She hurried after Zach and Gran, not wanting to miss the next surprise. A group of people stood in the family cemetery, holding quiet conversations. It seemed so unlike the lonely graveyard they'd first stumbled upon last year with its handful of simple memorials paying homage to lives that had gone before. The graves had been cleaned, downed limbs removed, and stones straightened. Flowers rested against several of the markers.

Kieran had been stunned when Zach informed her that the park service regularly maintained the cemeteries within park boundaries, especially in preparation for Decoration Day. It was one simple way to honor the families who had called this land home.

Seeing the folks waiting for Granny Mac sent Kieran's heart racing. Would Gran welcome the attention, or would it only confuse her?

A middle-aged woman with red hair and a wide smile approached them, arms outstretched. "Is this McCauley?"

Granny Mac's eyes narrowed. "Do I know you?"

"No, you don't. But I wanted to meet you." She waved an older man and two young boys forward to join her. She settled her hands on the youngest's shoulders. "My name is Brandie Tipton Ownby. My great-grandparents were Beau and Maudie Tipton. They was neighbors to your kin—just over the hill yonder. And they was good friends, from the stories I heard."

Gran took her offered hand, gripping her fingers tight and stepping forward. "My pa talked about Beau and Maudie often. Said they were the first to really accept him into the community. Maudie was a granny woman—she saw me born."

Brandie smiled. "Well, we've got three generations of Tiptons here to welcome you home. This here is my grandson Beau—named after his great-great-grandpap. And my husband, Roy Ownby. His kin was from round these parts too. And this—" She turned to the older man. "This is my father, Don Tipton."

Granny Mac accepted hugs and handshakes all around, tears clinging to her lower lids. "You came just for this?"

"You bet, Mac. You're our people."

Another group joined them, kids running about underfoot and adults reaching out to shake hands.

"Nice to meet you, Ms. Mac." A heavyset gentleman hefted a toddler to his shoulders. "I'm Mark Oliver, and this is my wife, Janie. My grandmother was Tildy Walker. She remembered your ma fondly. She was right sorry about what happened. I heard the tale."

Several other people introduced themselves, each one with a story and a welcoming hug. Granny Mac's smile started glazing over, so Kieran walked her to a quieter part of the cemetery to give her a chance to catch her breath. One of the groups had set up a cluster of camping chairs, and Kieran helped Gran settle into one.

Gran shook her head. "So many. And they all had kinfolk here?"

"Here or nearby. Evidently the historical society has been good at helping people stay connected." Maybe that was something that had been missing in Gran's life ever since her father swept her out of the Smokies at the tender age of six. She'd lost "her people."

"So kind of them to come," she murmured, her chin trembling. "So kind."

Kieran pulled a water bottle from her pack and helped her grandmother take a few sips. "We can head home if this is getting to be too much."

"Oh, no, no. This is . . . wonderful. It *is* home." She squeezed Kieran's knee as she blinked away tears. She turned toward the stone markers. "They brought flowers."

"We did too. Zach has them in his bag." Kieran ran her hand down Gran's arm. "But there's no rush."

Granny Mac slid forward in the canvas seat, struggling to get her feet under her. "I've waited eighty years. Get me outta this thing."

Kieran laughed and helped her wriggle out of the rickety chair.

Walking slowly, they approached the gravestones with the reverence such a moment deserved. The years had worn away some of the inscriptions, but many remained, including Granny Mac's grandparents. The three tiny memorials to Granny Mac's brothers still tugged at Kieran's heart.

The final stone had the most detailed inscription, flowers already heaped at its base.

"Mama." Gran's voice quavered, sounding every bit like the little girl she'd been. "There wasn't a stone when we left. Pa must have paid someone to put it in later." She closed her eyes for a long moment. "The soil was heaped up in a little hill over the top. I remember the black earth." A shuddering breath escaped her lips as she opened her eyes and read the engraved words aloud. "Rosie McCauley Fuller. Beloved wife, sister, and mother. Rooted on earth. Now flies free." She laid a hand against her chest. "I don't think Papa ever got over losing her."

Zach dug the largest bouquet from the bag and held it out to Granny Mac.

She turned to Kieran. "You do it, honey. She'd have liked to meet you. You look just like her."

Kieran took the flowers and carried them to the headstone, laying them gently against the marker. "Here you are, Grandma Rosie. I wish I could have known you, but I kind of feel like I do."

A woman split off from the rest of the group and came toward them. "Some of us are getting ready to sing a few songs and say a prayer, if you'd like to join us."

Granny Mac beamed. "I'd like that very much."

The lady dropped her gaze for a moment, her dark lashes standing out against her pale skin. "I should introduce myself, but I'm not sure you'll want to know me."

Gran reached for her arm. "Are you another of Maudie's kin?"

"No, I'm not, though I've heard of her." She adjusted a silver bangle on her wrist before pushing her long dark hair over her shoulder. "My name is Monika Smith. My grandfather was Will Samson."

Kieran stopped short. Samson was a name that had come up many times, but rarely in a positive light. They'd shared some of their research with Gran, but not every detail. It never seemed the right time to burden her with the more tragic aspects of her history, especially since she already battled nightmares of her past. They'd told her just enough to ease her mind, but no more. "Maybe we should talk later," Kieran interjected. "I think my gran is getting tired. Perhaps we'll just go join the singing and then take her back to the car."

Monika nodded. "I thought you might feel that way."

Gran clutched at the woman's wrist. "No. I want to hear. I have such trouble putting things together anymore. The memories blow away like fall leaves. Tell me about Will."

*Please, Lord, be gentle.* Kieran wanted to beg the woman to wait, but whatever Gran learned today—and whatever she faced tomorrow—God would see them through it.

"My grandpa was a sweet man and great storyteller, but he carried a load of guilt with him to the grave. He was there when your mama died, and he showed me the scars. He told me he was nicked by the same bullet that killed your mama." She cast a worried glance between Gran and Kieran. "I took care of him in his final days." She reached for Gran's hand. "He called himself the worst of sinners, but he wouldn't tell me why. I remember him saying, 'I deserved worse than I got. Lorna was only trying to protect her sister when she pulled that trigger. It was my fault.' Miss Mac, he never stopped praying for your family, hoping they would forgive him for what he'd done."

Gran reached out to cup the young woman's face. "I don't believe my ma would have held a grudge against a neighbor. It weren't like her. She would have offered forgiveness, and so do I. We all sin, child, but we have a Savior who washes us clean." She squeezed the woman's arm. "It sounds like he was lucky to have you."

"Thank you, ma'am." Monika reached down and gave Granny Mac a quick hug. After nodding to Kieran and Zach, she walked over to where Brandie was strumming a mountain dulcimer while her husband tuned up a mandolin.

"So it was Lorna all along." Gran sighed. "That must've hung heavy on her all those years."

Kieran put her arm around her grandmother's waist. "Why would your father tell you it was the government who killed Grandma Rosie, do you think? Was it easier than the truth?"

Gran looked back toward her mother's stone. "He vowed to protect Lorna. And I guess he did, in his way." She reached out a shaky arm and snagged Zach's hand. "I suppose that means your park service is off the hook. At least for that part of it."

He helped find chairs for the three of them over where the group was gathering to sing. Brandie led them off with several hymns. After those were done, she turned to Granny Mac. "Do you have any requests? Maybe a favorite of your ma's or pa's?"

Gran's head had started bobbing in weariness at this point, but she perked up when Kieran leaned close and repeated the question for her.

"Ma always loved 'I'll Fly Away.' You know that one?"

Brandie strummed the dulcimer, its bright tones ringing through the small clearing. Smiles broke out all around as everyone joined in the spirited song.

Zach took that moment to press something into Kieran's palm.

She opened her fingers and gasped, the little stone bird peeping out at her. "Zach, why do you have this here? It's supposed to be in a museum."

He leaned close. "It's a replica. There's an artist in Cherokee who helps us re-create pieces for display. I know it's not the same as having the original, but I thought you might like one of your own to hang on to. Or give it to your gran if you like."

Tears filled Kieran's eyes for the umpteenth time today. She rolled it between her fingers, appreciating the fine craftsmanship. "Thank you." The tiny eyes looked up at her. "This little figure taught me a lot."

"How's that?"

She paused for a moment, lost in the lyrics of the song. "Gran passed along something her mother had said to her: 'If a bird wants to fly free, first it has to release the branch.'" She kept her palm open. "I'm learning to let go of 'my way' and open myself to what God has for me. It's usually so much better."

The bird bumped against the gold engagement ring Zach had placed on her finger last week.

She'd gone looking for a family and ended up with two.

He slid an arm behind her back. "So what do you think of your kin now that you've put the pieces together?"

"I'm glad to have people I can claim as my own." She pulled him close. "Especially you."

# Acknowledgments

FOR SOME CRAZY reason, I thought writing would eventually get easier. Don't believe it. Taking a story from idea to completed manuscript is as tough as it sounds, and *When Stone Wings Fly* would never have been finished without the help of these generous individuals.

- Tipper Pressley and her wonderful website, The Blind Pig and the Acorn. In addition to her blog and videos celebrating Appalachian culture, she also served as a beta reader for *When Stone Wings Fly*. If you enjoyed Rosie's Smoky Mountains dialect, please thank Tipper. (If you found errors, blame me!) She also pointed me to the *Dictionary of Smoky Mountain English*, by Michael B. Montgomery and Joseph S. Hall, which was an invaluable resource.
- Bob Miller, former public affairs officer at Great Smoky Mountains National Park, who served as my guru on the NPS, park geography, history, and basically everything else.
- Literary agent Rachel Kent, my trusted guide to the publishing world. Without her I'd be off wandering in the fire swamp somewhere.
- The incredible team at Kregel Publications, particularly Janyre Tromp, Catherine DeVries, Steve Barclift, Sarah De Mey, Dori Harrell, and Katherine Chappel, for championing this novel from the beginning.

- Heidi Gaul, Christina Suzann Nelson, and Marilyn Rhoads—thank you for the critiques, the laughter, and the prayers.
- My patient and understanding family, without whom none of this would be possible. It's a good thing you like fast food!

# About the Author

BEFORE BECOMING A novelist and public speaker, Karen Barnett worked as a park ranger and naturalist at Mount Rainier National Park and Oregon's Silver Falls State Park. When not writing, Karen enjoys photography, hiking, public speaking, and decorating crazy birthday cakes. With two kids in college, she and her husband are adapting to the empty-nest life at their home in Oregon.

Karen loves chatting with readers, so be sure to connect with her at KarenBarnettBooks.com.